Jessica Blair grew up in Middlesbrough, trained as a teacher and now lives in Ampleforth. She became a full-time writer in 1977 and has written more than 50 books under various pseudonyms including *The Red Shawl, A Distant Harbour, Storm Bay, The Restless Spirit, The Other Side of the River, The Seaweed Gatherers, Portrait of Charlotte, The Locket, The Long Way Home, The Restless Heart, Time & Tide, Echoes of the Past, Secrets of the Sea, Yesterday's Dreams, Reach for Tomorrow, Dangerous Shores, Wings of Sorrow* and *Stay With Me* all published by Piatkus.

For more information about the author visit: www.jessicablair.co.uk

KU-350-551

Also by Jessica Blair

The Red Shawl
A Distant Harbour
Storm Bay
The Restless Spirit
The Other Side of the River
The Seaweed Gatherers
Portrait of Charlotte
The Locket
The Long Way Home
The Restless Heart
Time & Tide
Echoes of the Past
Secrets of the Sea
Yesterday's Dreams
Reach for Tomorrow
Dangerous Shores
Wings of Sorrow
Stay With Me

Sealed Secrets

Jessica Blair

piatkus

PIATKUS

First published in Great Britain in 2010 by Piatkus
This paperback edition published in 2011 by Piatkus

A CIP catalogue record for this book
is available from the British Library.

ISBN 978-0-7499-3986-1

Typeset in Bembo by
Action Publishing Technology Ltd, Gloucester
Printed and bound in Great Britain by
CPI Mackays, Chatham ME5 8TD

Piatkus
An imprint of
Little, Brown Book Group
100 Victoria Embankment
London EC4Y 0DY

An Hachette UK Company
www.hachette.co.uk

www.piatkus.co.uk

For
Joan
who took me along a road of joy

and
Anne, Geraldine, Judith and Duncan
who filled our road with wonder

and
Jill
who banished the dark that threatened my road

With grateful thanks and love

Bill

Acknowledgements

There are no words to express my gratitude for the support of my family throughout the writing of this novel. My daughter Judith read the manuscript and gave advice as it was written. Her twin, Geraldine, read the completed manuscript, picked up errors and offered advice for improvement. My eldest daughter, Anne, and my son, Duncan, showed continual interest and gave support and encouragement throughout.

I am grateful for the encouragement from my editor at Piatkus, Donna Condon, and for the support of all the staff who work with her. A pleasant team makes a happy author.

I cannot praise enough the work of Lynn Curtis who has edited all Jessica Blair books. She was there at the birth and without her there may have been no Jessica Blair. For her advice and continued interest and the friendship that developed I will be ever grateful.

The interest of friends is always encouraging. I cannot mention them all but I must say 'Thanks, Jill'.

1

'Father, I *am* going!' insisted Betsy. 'I've arranged for Aunt Chris to look in on you so ...'

'It's not safe for you to cross the moors alone,' broke in her father Samuel sharply, concern clouding his eyes. His lips tightened. 'I'll come with you tomorrow. I'll get my things ready.' He started to struggle out of his favourite chair placed before the fire.

Betsy restrained him gently. 'You'll do no such thing. You were most unwell yesterday and it has left you weak.'

'Then let the miners wait for their jewellery and jet.'

'We can't, Father. They'll be expecting their orders, and if we don't deliver on time we could lose out. The future looks good for us there with talk of expanding the mines.'

He gave a little nod. 'I know, but you are more important to me than any orders.'

Betsy smiled and kissed him on the cheek. 'I'll be all right. I know the way – we did it together this time last year,' she reassured him.

The bond between Samuel Palmer and his

twenty-year-old daughter had strengthened since his wife had died in 1848. Although only ten years old then, Betsy had been a pillar of strength in the days following her mother's death. With her encouragement, and spurred by her growing interest in his jeweller's trade, Samuel concentrated on the business that immediately after the tragedy he had begun to let slip. Now the enterprise was so successful that, while keeping the shop in Church Street on the East Side of the River Esk in Whitby, he and Betsy had moved six months ago to a new house in Well Close Square, on the expanding and more salubrious West Side.

Last year had been a good one for their business and 1858 was developing nicely so far. Samuel felt he was finally seeing the fruits of his endeavours. His own interest in jewellery had been inherited from his mother who came from a well-to-do Whitby family but had incurred the wrath of her parents when she had married for love; or 'married beneath her' as they put it, cutting her off without a penny and not disguising their disgust whenever her name was mentioned. But her love for a fisherman blossomed into a happy marriage that had produced Samuel, though to her regret no other children.

Although Samuel initially followed the family trade, he gave it up at eighteen when his father was drowned after his ship foundered in a storm. The boy then turned to his other talent, inherited from his mother, a deep interest in and knowledge of jewellery. He saw the potential to establish a jeweller's business locally, catering to Whitby society. Tragically his mother died of a heart attack two years later, unable to survive the loss of her beloved husband. Life for Samuel was not easy at first but he persevered, in memory of his parents and to succeed and provide well for his wife and daughter. It pleased him, too, to be seen to prosper in the town where his estranged maternal grandparents still lived.

The evidence of Samuel's achievement was there for all to see in the shop in Church Street and now the new house on the West Side. His one regret was that his dear wife Jenny had not lived to share the height of his success. Never a day passed without him thinking of all the solid support she had offered him, and the gift of children: their daughter Betsy, and Thomas, their son, two years older than his sister. He was ever grateful to her, too, for persuading him to let Thomas pursue his desire to go to sea: 'Let him go, Samuel, and he'll do well. Restrain him and he'll never be happy,' his wife had advised. Her wisdom had paid off; Thomas was a devoted son, frequently sailing out of east coast ports but always returning home whenever he could.

Jenny's influence had also helped turn Betsy into a loving and charming daughter. Sam's main ambition, once he had seen his daughter's interest in jewellery, was to leave her in a better position financially than he had been when he'd started out. He wanted to leave her a thriving business, and hoped and prayed that her marriage, whenever it happened, would be as happy as his had been, and that whoever her husband was, he would understand and appreciate her love of the jewellery trade.

3

Now Sam shrugged his shoulders, sighed and gave Betsy a small smile. 'Gone are the days when my daughter obeyed her father without question.' He held out his hand to her lovingly and she took it and held it. 'You are old enough to go away unaccompanied,' he said wistfully, regretting the passage of time. 'And you know the business as well as I. It will be yours one day, after all. Just take care crossing the moors.'

'I will, Father. Now I must get ready for tomorrow.'

He was about to give her more instructions but held back; he knew she was well able to make all the arrangements herself – a trap would be ready at the coaching inn for her and she would collect the jewellery and jet from the shop. He nodded his acceptance and his heart lurched momentarily when he saw the light in Betsy's pale blue eyes beneath thin arched eyebrows ... oh, so like her mother. The smile that was never far from her full lips revealed perfect white teeth. The gentle curve of her chin hid a determination that he had been thankful for on a number of occasions when business deals seemed to be turning against them. Her brown hair, which shone like copper whenever the light chose to play upon it, was parted in the centre and drawn smoothly away from her face into a bun at the nape of her neck.

Betsy paused at the door, turned, blew her father a kiss and was gone. She went upstairs to her room, chose her bonnet and cape, and in a few minutes was leaving Well Close Square to head down Skinner Street and Flowergate to the Angel Inn, hoping that the May weather would continue like this, clear and mild; it would make her journey across the North York Moors much more pleasant.

As she approached the inn, the rotund, red-faced landlord greeted her with a jovial smile. 'Good day, Miss Betsy. I suppose you are here to check all will be ready for you tomorrow. Usual time, miss?'

'Yes, seven o'clock, if you please.'

'Charlie is checking the trap as we speak.'

'Thank you, Mr Glazeby, I'll see you tomorrow then.' She hurried away from the building and crossed the river to the shop in Church Street.

'Good morning, Miss Palmer.'

'Good morning, Toby.' Betsy returned their assistant's greeting brightly, wishing the sallow-faced young man of twenty-six did not look as if he carried all the cares of the world on his shoulders. He may look glum but she knew that there was a dry sense of humour lurking behind his dour expression, and the sharp brain too of a man who had learned the jewellery trade quickly from Samuel, had accepted the responsibility of running the shop efficiently but had no desire to take on any greater commitments than that. 'You've put the jewellery together for me?' she asked.

'It is all ready as you ordered, packed and secured.'

'Good. And the orders for jet?'

'There are two workshops still to deliver, but I received their assurances that the items required to fulfil your orders for the Rosedale miners will be in my hands today.'

'Good. Then I'll pick them up at the usual time in the morning.'

5

'Very well, miss.'

Betsy started to turn away but looked back at him. 'Is Maggie any happier now she's had a month living over the shop?'

'Oh, yes, miss. I suppose it was understandable – living above ground level was a bit strange for her at first, but she sees the advantages now. Where we were before, in Hobson's Yard, was very cramped and some of the neighbours were not really our choice. Here we have much more privacy and, as I pointed out to Maggie, we're much safer with all the bolts and locks on the shop. We were very grateful for the opportunity and I ...'

Betsy waved his thanks away and interrupted him – she knew that when Toby got into full flow he took some stopping even though he still looked glum about whatever he was saying.

When Betsy rose at five-thirty the following morning and parted the curtains a little to view the weather prospects, she frowned. A sea roake hung over Whitby. She hoped it would not spread into an inland fog, hanging shroud-like over the moors; but whatever it did, she would have to cope.

She carried out her toilette and dressed quickly, wanting to see that her father was comfortable and provided for before she left. She said goodbye to Samuel, assuring him briskly that she would be all right. With a heavy cape around her shoulders and her bonnet tied tightly under her chin, she stepped out into the mist that restricted visibility to within a few yards. Nevertheless she was not a minute late arriving at the shop, an hour and a half before the usual opening time of eight o'clock.

'Did the last two orders arrive, Toby?' she queried as soon as he unlocked the door.

'They did, miss. Everything is packed away in the usual two boxes.'

'Good, then let us go.'

'Your father, miss?' His voice reflected bewilderment to see her alone.

'He's off colour, not fit to travel. You can carry one box for me to the Angel. Now, let us be on our way.'

Betsy picked up one of the boxes her father had had specially made to hold jewellery for transportation. Toby picked up the other. Once outside, he locked the shop door again and they set off for the Angel. Toby was a little flustered by the knowledge that she was travelling alone but deemed it proper not to question his employer.

Betsy found the horse and trap ready for her with Charlie in attendance. As Toby was stowing the boxes securely in the trap, Mr Glazeby bustled out of the inn.

'Everything in order, miss?' he enquired.

'As usual,' she returned with a smile of appreciation.

The landlord glanced around the yard. 'Your father, miss? I did not see him come into the inn.'

'He's not with me – he's not feeling too well,' she explained.

'I'm sorry to hear that, miss,' said Mr Glazeby, frowning with concern. 'Nothing serious, I hope?' And then added quickly, 'Of course it can't be, otherwise you would not be going.' But his eyes still held a look of misgiving.

'He has picked up somewhat from a mild indisposition but is not fit to travel.'

'So you're going alone, miss?' Unease crept into the inn-keeper's tone.

'I must, Mr Glazeby. There are orders to be filled. Missing them could cost us money.'

'But you should not be going alone, especially in this sea roake, miss.'

Betsy smiled. 'It'll not persist inland.'

'You can never be certain, and it can be foggy on the moors ...'

'I'll be all right, I know the way. I don't anticipate any problems.' Then as if to put an end to this exchange, she climbed up on to the driver's seat and reached for the reins, signalling for Charlie to move aside as she set the trap rumbling out of the yard.

Mr Glazeby gave a slight shake of his head. 'A stubborn lass, but I admire her spirit, Toby.'

'Aye,' he agreed, and added, 'I couldn't have better employers. I do hope she has a safe journey.'

They watched the trap turn out of the yard and pass from view.

Betsy did not hurry the horse out of Whitby, steadily following the track along the Esk Valley instead. Even in the fog she had the comfort of passing through the villages of Sleights, Egton, Glaisdale and Lealholm. At the last she was thankful to halt the horse outside a cottage on the outskirts of this tiny village tucked under Lealholm Moor.

The door opened and a stout, motherly woman, drawn by the creak of the trap and the jingle of its harness, peered out then flung the door wide.

'Eh, lass, I niver expected to see thee today. Come away in. Where's your father?' She looked beyond Betsy, expecting to see Sam Palmer.

'Not well, Mrs Dobson. I persuaded him to stay at home.'

'You're on your own?' she asked as she fussed the girl into the cottage. Without waiting for an answer she called out, 'Bob, get in here!' then glanced at Betsy. 'He's mending the back door. I told him to leave it until the weather cleared but he would make a start.'

As she finished speaking a short, robust man, face weathered by wind and sun, bustled in. 'Martha, what is thee yelling ...' His question faded away. 'Betsy Palmer! What's the likes of you doing out in this fog? I'll give your father a piece of my mind ... where is he?'

Betsy smiled at his concern. 'I won't melt, Mr Dobson. And Father's not well. Only a little off colour but I insisted he stay at home.'

'And that's where you should be, lass.'

'Orders to deliver,' she replied as Mrs Dobson took her cape and bonnet.

Bob grunted his understanding but expressed no approval of her being out alone in this fog. 'Want me to see to the horse?'

'Please,' replied Betsy. This was the usual question and answer whenever she and her father stopped here, which they always did on their way to and from Rosedale. The relationship had been established by Betsy's father early last year when he had jumped at the Dobsons' offer of a resting place at their home.

'Sit thisen down. Soon have you a bowl of warming soup,' said Martha.

An hour later, warm and refreshed, the horse rested and fed, Betsy thanked her friends for their hospitality and said goodbye, though the fog still had not dispersed as anticipated.

'Maybe it will when I get on the tops,' Betsy called out as she set the horse on its way at a gentle pace. The climb from the village was hard enough without straining the animal unduly; it would need all its energy to negotiate the undulating track across the moors. The hoped-for clearing of the fog did not materialise, even when she reached the heights. Clammy tendrils swirled around her and Betsy felt a shiver run down her spine. She glanced anxiously from one side of the track to the other. Only mist visible! She frowned and tightened her lips, annoyed with herself for succumbing, even momentarily, to feelings of unease. This was nonsense. It made no difference if she was alone. Her reassuring thoughts faltered. But what if ...? Exasperation with herself heightened then and she shook the reins irritably. The horse responded but only with a slight quickening of pace. It was as if it too was reluctant to press on through the shroud of fog that had settled over them. Progress was painfully slow. Betsy tried hard to convince herself that she was still on the right track even though any familiar landmarks, and they were few and far between in this desolate landscape even on the best of days, were obscured.

She tugged her cape tighter around her shoulders, trying to cocoon herself in its comfort, but could not allay her mounting unease. How she wished she was safely at her destination!

The track dipped and turned. The trap juddered, tipped to the right and came to a jolting halt that almost threw Betsy from her seat. Quickly gathering herself, her immediate concern was for the horse. She was relieved to see it still standing. She called to it in a quiet, soothing tone and continued to do so as she eased herself carefully to the ground. A study of the situation showed her that the vehicle had strayed too near the edge of the track which had given way, allowing one wheel to drop into a ditch and break. The horse had managed to keep its foothold but a shaft of the trap had also broken. Despair filled her. She was marooned on a desolate moor. It was hardly likely there'd be other travellers. All her brave words in Whitby counted for nothing now.

Betsy sank against the side of the trap and tears started to flow. How long she remained like that she did not know but gradually the sobs began to ease. It was only when she straightened up and began to take a grip on herself that she realised the fog was dispersing. She gave a despairing laugh at the irony of her circumstances. Why had it waited until now to lift? If only it had done so sooner, she would not be in this quandary. Despair flooded through her again but then she dismissed it. She had to do something. It was no good just standing here feeling sorry for herself.

11

The horse could yet be her saviour, but it was growing restless. 'Soon have you out of that harness,' said Betsy decisively. 'Then you can carry me to Rosedale.' But the task was too much for her; she could not loosen some of the buckles. Her head sank against the animal's side and she started to weep again.

After a moment's despair she inclined her head, listening, straining to decide if she had really heard the sound of hooves. Yes, the unmistakable rhythm was audible. She swung round. There was as yet no sign of a rider. He must be in the dip in the track and out of view, but now there was no mistaking the sound of a horse's approach. Her whole body was tense with the prospect of receiving help. Then she realised the familiar sound might just as easily herald danger for an unprotected female. She looked round for something with which to defend herself and grasped a spoke, broken from the wheel.

The horseman rose out of the dip, body rising and falling with the motion of his mount. Betsy saw he sat his horse well, a big man clad against the weather in a dark brown cape. His brown checked trousers were folded into ankle-length black leather boots and a small bowler hat was clamped to his head. Immediately he saw what lay ahead he slowed his mount and, seeing the spoke in Betsy's hand, put his horse into a slow walk.

'Good day,' he called out to her in a friendly tone.

Betsy did not reply, continuing to regard him warily. She judged him to be in his late-twenties, handsome enough, with a firm jaw and eyes that were sharp and used to assessing whatever he

12

encountered. Still a few yards away, he pulled his horse to a halt.

'You look to be in trouble,' he called. 'Want some help?'

Betsy found his tone affable and judged his concern to be genuine; besides, he wore a bowler hat – out here the sign of a position of authority. Reconsidering her behaviour later, it amused her that it was that bowler hat which had persuaded her that the offer of help was genuine.

'I'd be obliged,' she called out.

'And I'd be obliged if you'd get rid of that spoke! I don't fancy a thwack round the head with it.'

'Oh . . . yes . . . sorry.' Betsy blushed with embarrassment and dropped the piece of wood.

'Understandable,' he said as he swung down from his horse. He stood beside it, his hand resting on the saddle. 'My name is Jim Fenwick.'

Betsy waited for him to go on but he stood in silence as if waiting for her to say something.

In those few moments she was struck by the way he held himself, giving an impression of strength and competence. This was a man who would be willing to deal with any situation that arose and probably end up master of it. But she felt a sudden spurt of irritation, too, that he was just standing there without coming to her assistance. She gave a little shake of her shoulders and momentarily tightened her lips before she spoke. 'Mr Fenwick, if you are to help me, pray don't just stand there.'

He smiled as he walked forward. 'I could do nothing else – I was paralysed by your beauty, Miss Palmer.'

13

Betsy was struck by the warmth of his smile but there was still an edge to her voice. 'This is no time for flattery, Mr ...' Her voice filled with astonishment, then matching the look in her eyes. 'You know my name?'

'When I saw a woman as beautiful as you in Rosedale, I asked questions.'

'Rosedale?'

'Yes. I work for the mining company – supervising the transfer and shipment of the ore. I am not always in the dale but I have seen you there. You come with your father who is a jeweller in Whitby. He brings items to sell to the miners.' He saw curiosity in her eyes. A little embarrassed by the way she looked at him, he went on quickly with his explanation. 'Yes, I freely admit it, I enquired about you. I'm on my way there now, as I take it you are? Or rather were, until you had what looks like an unfortunate accident. Better see what I can do. I'm surprised to find you alone, though.'

'My father is not well and my brother is with his ship at present, somewhere between Newcastle and London.'

He moved away but was aware that she still watched him.

'My horse seems unharmed. I was trying to free it so that I could ride into Rosedale and seek help.'

'You ride?'

'Yes.'

'Then there is the solution.'

He set about releasing the horse from the shafts, careful that the splintered wood did not inflict any injury on the animal. He talked soothingly to it as he went about the task and Betsy was struck by the gentleness of his tone. He had a way with animals. 'Hold these a moment,' he said as he extended the reins to her. 'Your luggage?'

'The two identical boxes and the small valise.'

He nodded, took a knife from his pocket, cut a length of leather from the trap, threaded it through the handles of the two boxes and slung them behind the saddle of his own horse so that they were evenly balanced. 'You ride my horse, I'll ride yours,' he instructed.

'But you'll have no saddle,' she said with concern.

He laughed. 'I've ridden bareback before, but I'll use your rug if you don't mind?'

'Of course not,' she replied quickly.

'Then let me help you up. Sorry it's not suitable for side-saddle.'

Betsy blushed. 'I'll be all right,' she said firmly, and held out her arm for support. She felt his strong reassuring grip haul her into the saddle with ease. She quickly adjusted her dress and settled herself in position.

'Comfortable, Miss Palmer?'

'Yes, thank you.' She steadied the horse which, sensing a gentle yet confident touch, co-operated immediately.

Jim nodded his approval. He put the rug over the back of the livery horse, picked up the valise and hauled himself on to the animal. Taking up a position to Betsy's right, he allowed her to set a steady pace.

'Do you frequent Whitby often, Mr Fenwick?'

she asked after a few minutes, breaking the uneasy silence that had threatened to settle between them.

'I have been doing so during the last six months, but I don't see it continuing.'

'You don't like the town?'

'I find it a fascinating place, Miss Palmer, but it looks as though my work will soon direct me elsewhere.'

'Away from Rosedale?'

'No.' He gave a little shake of his head.

Betsy embarrassed herself by feeling relieved to hear this. What had sparked that sensation? She did not know this man and yet ... Her thoughts were interrupted as he went on, 'I have been looking into the possibilities of shipping ore by sea from Whitby. There would be no difficulty as far as the port is concerned but the conveyance from Rosedale to Whitby would be more difficult than the present system of taking the ore to Pickering for rail transportation.'

'So there's no solution?'

'Far from it, Miss Palmer. The solution, to my mind, is to build a light railway from Rosedale.'

Betsy raised her eyebrows in surprise. 'But wouldn't that be very difficult?'

'Certainly, but we're used to doing things the hard way in this trade.'

'And that will be your recommendation?'

'Yes.'

'And if your suggestion is taken up, will that be the last of it as far as you're concerned?'

He smiled. 'Not at all, Miss Palmer. I would be engaged upon planning the route and to some

16

extent supervising its construction, though experts in railway construction would be engaged also.'

'So you are likely to be in Rosedale for some time?'

'Some considerable time,' he confirmed.

Silence settled for a few minutes while once again Betsy felt a stirring of relief to learn that Mr Fenwick would not be moving from Rosedale any time in the near future.

The fog had completely dispersed by now and warm sunshine lit the high moors that rolled away as far as the eye could see.

'This will be a glorious sight later in the year, when the heather is in full bloom. It's like riding through a vast purple sea,' Jim commented.

'You like the country?' Betsy asked, believing she knew the answer from the tone of his voice.

'Love it, though I do feel a yearning at times to be beside the sea.' He pursed his lips thoughtfully, eased the valise in his grip and asked, 'Where do you stay in Rosedale?'

'With Mrs Dodsworth.'

'Hasn't she a house in the village close to the church?'

'Yes, do you know her?'

'Not personally, but I have seen her over the counter when buying some of her cakes and pies in Gill's General Store. Comes from an old Rosedale family, I believe.'

'Yes, good farming stock. She lost her husband four years ago after he was gored by a bull.'

'I didn't know that. Tragic,' he said sympathetically.

'We didn't know her at the time, but when my father saw a market selling jewellery to the miners he came to Rosedale looking for lodgings and they reached an agreement.'

'I don't think you come every week?'

'No, it's every other week, unless we have special orders.'

'So your father found convenient lodgings with Mrs Dodsworth?'

'Yes. The arrangement suited her. After her husband died she sought to be financially independent of a son who had a wife and four children to provide for, so she approached Mr Gill and offered to supply him with all manner of baked goods. He liked the idea and gave her a counter in his shop in return for a percentage of her profits. It gave her an income and then, seeing she could get a little extra by letting us have a couple of rooms when we required them, she came to the agreement with Father also. We were extremely lucky to find such good accommodation. She spoils us.'

'She looks that type of person – motherly.'

They fell silent but neither of them felt uncomfortable with it. Only a short while ago fear had gripped Betsy when she'd heard this man's approach through the fog. Now she was comfortable with him and even glad of his company.

The track dropped away from the heights and, with the fog completely cleared, the dale below was revealed. Amidst its undeniable beauty were the buildings and workings associated with mining for iron, close by and across the valley. Rows of brick-built cottages had been erected along the hillside to house the families of the men who would wrest wealth from this ground, and more were being built.

The village that took its name from the dale nestled in the narrowest part of the valley, hemmed in by its steep sides. In spite of the mining throughout the dale this place maintained the essence of a farming village, a small but close-knit community. Its people had accepted industrial development and the newcomers it brought with it, thankful that the mining companies had built little in the village itself. Nevertheless, the influx of so many new people had had its effects. The men and their families had to be catered for: food supplies expanded, and schooling, religious and recreational facilities provided. New money had come into the dale, and with it those who would line their own pockets at the expense of the miners.

As the track flattened and widened, Jim brought his horse alongside Betsy's.

'Well, here we are, without any further misadventure,' he said with a smile.

'Thank goodness for that,' she breathed with some relief. 'And thank you for your help.'

'I'm glad I came along when I did.'

'Thank goodness you did!'

They reached the first houses. The village was busily involved in its daily routine: housewives heading for the shop, stablemen taking horses to the blacksmith's, a dray rumbling towards the Crown Inn, children playing chase or clinging to their mothers' skirts while they gossiped with friends.

Jim guided the way to Mrs Dodsworth's where he slipped from his horse and was quickly beside Betsy's mount. After helping her to the ground, he secured the two horses to the railings in front of the house.

'I'll take them to the stables after we have you settled, Miss Palmer, then I'll see about having your trap recovered and brought in for repair,' he offered.

She knew from the firmness of his tone that he would not brook any polite protests. 'Thank you, Mr Fenwick,' she replied gratefully. 'Mrs Dodsworth's son is a joiner. He has his shop just around the corner.'

'Couldn't be better! Right, let us get these boxes inside.' He handed her the valise, retrieved the two boxes and followed her up the short path to the front door.

Before they reached it a plump woman bustled out. Black hair frosted with white was taken tightly back into a bun at the nape of her neck. The severity of this style was countered by a round open face with rosy cheeks, and the light of welcome in her eyes and smile. Her black dress strained across an ample bosom and flared from the waist to the tops of her boots.

'Betsy ... welcome!' She held out her arms and hugged the girl.

'Mrs Dodsworth.' Betsy returned the embrace. Stepping back, she became aware that her landlady was surveying her with puzzlement. 'Father's not with me. He is not well,' she explained.

Before Betsy could expand on this Mrs

Dodsworth broke in, 'Nothing serious, I hope?'

'No,' Betsy was quick to reassure her. 'And with Cook and a maid in the house, and my aunt to call in, I decided it would be all right for me to come alone.'

But Mrs Dodsworth sensed there was something more to the presence of the young man standing quietly by. She raised an eyebrow in his direction.

'Mrs Dodsworth, this is Mr Fenwick. He rescued me,' Betsy told her.

'Rescued?' Mrs Dodsworth's voice rose in alarm.

'My trap went into a ditch – broke a shaft and wheel. Mr Fenwick happened along shortly after and saved the day. And here I am, unharmed.'

Relief showed in Mrs Dodsworth's expression as she looked at Jim. 'Thank you for looking after Betsy.'

'It was no trouble, ma'am. A pleasure, in fact. Now, I will take the horses round to the stable and then go and see the joiner. Your son, Miss Palmer tells me?'

'Aye. Richard – Dick – he'll see you right,' she confirmed.

'Good. We should have the trap brought in and repaired as quickly as possible. Miss Palmer must be back in Whitby on schedule otherwise her father will worry.'

'Very thoughtful of you, Mr Fenwick. Come and take tea with us after you've stabled the horses and seen Dick.'

'That is very kind, Mrs Dodsworth. But first I'll put these by the door.' He started forward with the two boxes then led the horses away.

'Come along in, lass.' Mrs Dodsworth picked up the boxes and led the way into the house. 'Your usual room is ready,' she called over her shoulder.

'Thank you.'

The stairs led straight up from the front door. To the left was the living room, and to the right another room from which there was access to the kitchen. Mrs Dodsworth mounted the steep stairs and led the way to the small bedroom that was made up for Betsy.

'There you are, lass,' she said, putting the boxes down on the floor. 'There's fresh water in the ewer and clean towels on the stand. You freshen up and then come down for your tea. Mr Fenwick seems a nice young man.' She was keen to study Betsy's reaction to this.

'He was most polite and helpful,' she agreed. 'I don't know what I would have done without his help. I was trying to unfasten the harness to free the horse but it was too tight. He soon had it done, though.'

'I have seen him around the village.'

'He said he'd been in the shop. He's a supervisor, dealing with the shipment of ore out of Rosedale.'

Mrs Dodsworth nodded approvingly. 'Responsible job. Now I can't stand here gossiping ... I'll away and get the tea set. Come down as soon as you're ready.'

When Betsy came into the kitchen, the table in the centre of the room bore evidence of Mrs Dodsworth's skills as a cook. Bread and butter and home-made jam, fruit scones and plain ones, a chocolate cake and a jam sponge . . . the sight made Betsy's mouth water.

'Sit yourself down, lass. I shouldn't think Mr Fenwick will be long now.'

Betsy pulled out one of the chairs. As she sat down she wished her father was here; she knew he enjoyed and appreciated Mrs Dodsworth's hospitality as much as she did. This was a cosy house with a happy atmosphere, the home of someone content with her lot and who made the best of what life had dealt her. Betsy knew that, at times, life had not been easy for Mrs Dodsworth, but she was in good form today and kept up a flow of chatter as she busied herself around the kitchen, which was neat and tidy with little out of place. The flagged floor was spotless and the black range shone with frequent polishing. The floral curtains seemed to bring a touch of summer into the room. Betsy knew the adjoining scullery, with its stone sink, copper boiler and mangle, would be just as orderly and attractive.

A knock on the front door sent Mrs Dodsworth hurrying to open it. A few moments later she was ushering Mr Fenwick into the kitchen.

'Sit yourself down.' She indicated a chair opposite Betsy.

'This is most kind of you, Mrs Dodsworth. I didn't anticipate such a fine spread, if I may say so,' he said, shrugging himself out of his coat.

'It's my pleasure, Mr Fenwick. And only right after you helped Betsy.' She was hanging the kettle on the reckon as she added, 'Did you see Dick?'

'Aye. He's away to collect the trap now.'

'Good. He'll do a proper job.'

Jim glanced at Betsy. 'It will be ready for you the day after tomorrow. I told him that's when you want to leave.'

'You did right, Mr Fenwick. I want to be back with Father as soon as possible so I'll do all my trading tomorrow and be ready to leave early the next day.'

Mrs Dodsworth mashed the tea and brought the pot to the table.

'I have a meeting tomorrow, to make my report,' continued Jim Fenwick. 'I am sure that will result in a trip to Whitby, to negate any concerns about shipping Rosedale ore through the port for now. Then I'll probably be heading for Teesside and County Durham for a short while. With your permission, Miss Palmer, I will accompany you to Whitby and make sure you don't meet another calamity.'

'That is most considerate of you, Mr Fenwick, but there is no need for me to hold you up.'

'You'll not be doing that, Miss Palmer, and it would give me reassurance to know you were safely home.'

'I think it would be a good idea to have someone with you, Betsy. It will certainly ease my mind to know you are not crossing the moors alone again,' put in Mrs Dodsworth as she poured tea into the cups.

Betsy hesitated for a moment. 'Very well, then. I am most grateful for your offer, Mr Fenwick. And I will be pleased of the company.'

'It will be my pleasure, Miss Palmer,' said Jim, his eyes meeting hers.

She thought she detected something a little more than casual interest in his glance and felt a surge of elation at the way her father's illness and the broken trap had brought Mr Fenwick into her life. Would this be a new direction for her? Was she bound for a future beyond the jeweller's shop that she knew her father hoped she would take over?

Her agreeable fantasies were pulled up short when Mrs Dodsworth told them to help themselves to whatever they liked.

Why was she thinking like a love-sick schoolgirl? Betsy chided herself. She knew almost nothing about this man. She judged him to be thoughtful and kind, a practical sort who could sum up a situation and act upon it speedily. And he was fine-looking, it was true. Beyond that, apart from knowing his official position, she knew nothing about him. Would she have learned any more in two days' time?

2

Theodore Addison sat back in his dining chair at the head of the table. His home, Bell House, stood sedately in its own grounds in Adderstone Crescent, Jesmond, Newcastle upon Tyne. He experienced a deep sense of satisfaction, revelling in the thought of the announcement he was about to make. He dabbed his lips with his napkin as he surveyed his family seated around the table.

Emily, his wife of thirty years, sat at the opposite end. He had married her when she was twenty and he twenty-five. Their love had survived ten turbulent years while he was struggling to make his way in the mercantile world then expanding in Newcastle and along the River Tyne. Emily had supported him in his endeavours and he had succeeded on the back of determination and hard work. Now the Addisons were accepted as one of the leading families in Newcastle. Theodore was grateful to his wife who, in his eyes, was just as beautiful now as she had been the first time he saw her. Her brown eyes sparkled and her face showed little of the passage of time, though there was the odd streak of silver in her copper-brown hair. No matter what time of day it was, she was always immaculately turned out. Her slim figure showed little sign of her having borne two children, Robert, now twenty-three, and Zelda who was twenty. They sat on either side of the table, Robert finishing off his apple pie and cream, Zelda her syllabub.

Theodore eyed them with pride. They had been born when his mercantile company was well established and the future set fair. Mary Prior, the governess Emily had employed when Zelda was three, had turned them into well-educated and mannerly young people. When the time came for Robert to go to St Peter's School in York, the governess took charge of Zelda's education until she was eighteen. Even now Mary, from her own home provided by Theodore a short distance away, was still a confidante to her.

Both children had inherited good looks from their mother. Robert had come out of St Peter's a handsome young man full of confidence in his own ability, which could only benefit the firm that one day would be his. Robert knew what the future held for him and resolved not to jeopardise the chance his father had given him. He also appreciated the freedom his parents allowed him and, within the bounds he set himself, lived and played hard without any detriment to his work with his father. He was well liked in the social circles in which he moved and never at a loss for a female partner, whatever the occasion. Though neither parent ever questioned these flirtations, they both hoped that one day he would find the right girl to remain by his side for life.

His sister, too, was never at a loss for a partner at the balls she enjoyed so much, and her effervescent personality ensured her name was always one of the first on any invitation list. Emily was guarded about steering her daughter to settle down, but subtle queries always brought the same reply: 'Mother, I want to enjoy life before I do that. Don't worry, my future will be safe. After all, I have a good example to live up to in you and Father.' And Emily knew there was nothing she could say to refute this!

Seeing everyone had finished dessert, Theodore called to the two maids who were standing by: 'We'll take coffee in the lounge.'

They bobbed a curtsey and left the dining room. As soon as the door closed Emily started to rise to her feet.

'A moment, my dear,' called Theodore.

She sank back, looking askance at her husband.

He blew out his florid cheeks and cleared his throat. Robert and Zelda exchanged glances. They knew from their father's actions that something serious was coming.

'I bought Elston Hall today,' he announced proudly.

For a moment everyone was stunned by this unexpected statement.

Emily took it the most calmly; she was long used to Theodore's 'surprises', though it had been some time since she'd had one on this scale. 'Why?' she asked. There was no condemnation in her voice, merely curiosity.

'I thought it was time we had a country house.'

'So we'll leave here, Father?' enquired Zelda.

'No, no.' He gave a little shake of his head as he went on, 'We'll still need a town house so we'll keep this one.'

'So *that*'s what you were going to do when you left the office this afternoon?' commented Robert.

'Yes, I was going to finalise the purchase. But I said nothing about my intention because I wanted it to be a surprise for you all.'

'It is certainly that,' commented Emily, but behind his wife's expression he read excitement at the prospect of living in the country while remaining within easy reach of Newcastle and Bell House. She glanced at Zelda and could tell all sorts of ideas were already running through her daughter's mind.

'Has it stables, Papa?'

'It has.'

'I'll be able to have my own horse then instead of hiring one in ...'

'You will.'

Zelda let out a whoop of excitement.

'Have you bought the whole estate?' asked Robert.

'Yes.'

'So we'll have to think about management ...'

'You are racing ahead, son, but that's not a bad thing. Let us leave all that until after we've seen the property. I have ordered a carriage to be here for ten o'clock tomorrow. Is that all right for you, Emily?'

She started but replied, 'Of course.'

'You looked preoccupied. Is there something wrong? Don't you approve?'

'Of course I do,' she replied enthusiastically. 'I was just thinking that our neighbours will be the Booths of Cantonville Hall.'

'Not so, my dear,' announced Theodore. 'The Hall was sold last week.'

His family looked surprised.

'Who ...?' started Emily.

'A ship–owner from Hull named George Jordan.'

'You know him?'

'Not really, but I've heard of him. He built up a thriving business along the Humber and is now looking to expand on the Tyne. He could be useful to us.' With this last remark, Theodore cast a glance towards his son.

'Is he married?' asked Emily.

'Yes. He and Paula, his wife, have two children, Adele and Mark, about the same age as our two.'

Robert raised an eyebrow. 'Adele?' he mused.

Zelda gave a little smile. 'And Mark ... well, we'll have to make their acquaintance.'

'I don't think that will be any trouble to you two,' commented Theodore knowingly.

'All in good time,' cautioned Emily. 'I don't suppose they've moved in yet and it will be a while before we get Elston Hall to our liking.'

'Then we'll have to throw a party, Mama!' cried Zelda, an excited light in her eyes.

Her mother laughed. 'Just like you to anticipate all the pleasures before we are even settled.' She eyed her husband. 'I wonder what Grace and Morgan will say? Your sister will no doubt approve.'

'Aye, she always supported my views and ambitions, even when we were young.' His lips tightened when he went on, 'My brother-in-law could have been in the same position as we are now. He was part of the business, but wanted the freedom of being on his own and proving himself.'

'I know, Theodore, and you were extremely generous to him – setting him up alone, without any conditions.'

'It was only in a small way. It was what he wanted. I felt I should help.'

'We must visit and tell them our news.' Emily rose from her chair. 'Let us go and have coffee.' She paused then added, 'And we can plan tomorrow's visit to Elston.'

'Can we all go, Mama?' asked Zelda.

'Of course. You'll want to know what it's like, and you'll have your rooms to choose.' She glanced at Theodore. 'What are we going to do with this house? You indicated you want to keep it.'

'It will be useful for Robert and me if business requires us to stay close to work, and I have no doubt it will be an asset to you and Zelda when you come into Newcastle, shopping or visiting friends.'

'Do you intend to keep the same staff on?'

'Yes. It will be more convenient to do so.'

'What about staff for Elston?'

'When the previous owner left, he instructed the agent to keep all the staff employed looking after the house until it sold. The agent has given me a list of their names and positions.'

'So we keep the same staff?'

'I don't see why not, if they are satisfactory. The previous owner must have thought they were. You can assess the worth of the indoor staff for yourself.' He handed his wife a list. 'I'll do the same for the outdoor employees.'

She scanned the paper. 'I see you have pencilled in wages?'

'That is what they have been paid. A guide for you, my dear.'

With her quick eye she had already done some reckoning. 'Can we afford this?'

Theodore's laugh was indulgent. 'Ever the cautious one, Emily. I appreciate that. Yes, we can afford it. And if after a month, you think anyone is worthy of a rise, we'll consider it. We need to establish good relations there from the start.' He glanced at Zelda and Robert then. 'There's no need for me to say this, I suppose, but I will. Both of you please bear in mind that I intend Elston Hall to be a happy home for us all.'

Only Theodore appeared calm as the carriage turned through the open gates on to the drive leading to Elston Hall. Familiar with the house, he drew his excitement from his family's reactions on first seeing the Hall. In a quarter of a mile the wood through which they were driving gave way to open parkland, stretching for a mile ahead of them towards the mansion situated on the brow of a low hill.

Everyone gasped at the sight. As they rode on, each of them made their own assessment of the building. The stone-faced Georgian house stood two storeys high with the six sash windows on the upper storey matching those on the ground floor, and facing on to a terrace that stretched the full width of the house. At the east end was a servant's wing.

'It looks cosy,' commented Emily, half to herself though Theodore caught the words.

'Does that mean you wish it was bigger?' he asked with concern.

'Oh, no,' she emphasised. 'It looks just right from the outside, and if I judge correctly from my first impression it will be the same inside. Any bigger and it would be too forbidding.'

'What do you two think?' he asked his children.

'I think it's the finest house I've ever seen,' Zelda told him enthusiastically.

'Imposing yet welcoming,' said Robert. 'I'm sure it will be the same when I go inside.'

Theodore breathed out silently in relief. A good start, and from his prior knowledge of it he was sure the house would continue to impress his family.

Before the carriage had rolled to a halt beside the four steps that led up to the balustraded terrace, the glazed double doors of the front entrance were thrown open and a middle-aged man and woman appeared. He was quickly down the steps and opening the carriage door. She followed without visible haste but was there in readiness before Emily had alighted. The man bowed and the woman bobbed a curtsey.

'Welcome to Elston Hall, ma'am,' she said.

'Thank you,' said Emily. 'You'll be Mrs Woodley, the housekeeper?'

'I am, ma'am.'

'And you'll be Mr Shields, head butler?' Emily added, turning a friendly eye on him.

'At your service, ma'am. And yours, sir,' he added, turning to Theodore who had stepped out of the carriage after his wife.

'Thank you for your greetings,' he said. 'This is our son Robert and daughter Zelda.'

With the welcomes over, Mrs Woodley and Mr Shields led them into the house where in the entrance hall, not exceptionally big but well proportioned, they found the staff drawn up waiting in two lines.

Emily cast a quick glance over the scene and knew immediately that in Mrs Woodley she had a good organiser who was most particular about the appearance of her staff. The housekeeper introduced each servant in order of seniority, imparting their name and role in the household. Turning to the second row, Mr Shields took over and beckoned to a man who stood a little apart from the rest.

'Sir,' said Mr Shields, addressing Theodore, 'I must introduce Mr Hood. He is in charge of all the estate workers and has been working under orders from a firm of estate managers in Newcastle. With your permission, I will let him introduce you to his team.'

'Very well,' replied Theodore, who liked the look of this tall upright man whose rugged face bore the signs of outdoor living. His sharp eyes told

34

Theodore that he was used to observing and would miss nothing. He had an air of competence which Theodore liked. After the introductions were over, the new master said a few words expressing his hopes that all the servants at Elston Hall would remain happy under his ownership.

Mrs Woodley dismissed them after that and then turned to Emily. 'I expect you are all anxious to see the house. I've ordered coffee to be ready when we are finished.'

'An excellent suggestion, Mrs Woodley. Then you and I must have a talk. You have your staff splendidly turned out, I see. I think you and I will get on very well.'

'I'm sure we shall, and thank you, ma'am.'

'You go ahead with Mrs Woodley, I'll join you in a few minutes. I want a word with Hood first.' Theodore called to the estate manager who had remained standing by the servants' door, 'Hood – a moment of your time.'

'Sir?' he answered.

'Let us stroll on the terrace for a moment, Hood – Julian, isn't it?'

He nodded.

'I was impressed by your attitude when we first met while I was considering buying Elston,' Theodore went on.

'Thank you, sir. I hoped you would buy it.'

'Well, here we are. I've pondered what you told me then about the estate and I've made certain other enquiries.'

No doubt about me, thought Julian Hood.

'I expect you are surmising those enquiries were

about you,' said Theodore with a small smile. 'Well, I was impressed by what I learned and I see no reason to continue using the Newcastle firm of estate managers. I think you are more than capable of running this estate efficiently enough for me, so I intend to dispense with their services immediately.'

Julian, taken unawares by this proposition, was almost lost for words. 'Thank you ... I am most grateful for your confidence in me, sir,' he said finally.

'I will be frank with you: I know nothing of farming or estate management, but I am good with figures and interpreting results and returns on investments.'

'Sir, it is natural that working on the land as I do, I have ideas about what should best be done with it. My hands were tied rather by the last owner's arrangements. I had thought of moving on, but when I heard that Elston was to be sold, I decided to stay until I met the new owner and learned his wishes for running and developing the estate.'

'I hope I have satisfied you and that you will remain with us?'

'May I ask how far my responsibilities would extend?'

'I will want you to run this estate efficiently and to make money from it. And remember, although I know nothing of such things, I learn quickly. Any major changes or advances I will require you to discuss with me – after all, I will be financing whatever you decide upon so you must justify that decision to me. But that applies only to any major developments. The day-to-day running of the estate is in your hands and what you do will be entirely up to you. If you are satisfied with that arrangement you may take over immediately, with the promise of a rise in wages because of the added responsibility I am placing upon you. Initially it will be only a small rise, but I will review it after six months.'

'I thank you for your trust and confidence in me, sir. I will not let you down.'

The determination in Julian Hood's voice, the way he set his shoulders and the gleam in his eyes, were more than enough for Theodore who now felt sure he had done the right thing.

'Good.' He nodded approvingly. 'With my business to run in Newcastle, expect me here when you see me. Over and above that, we will arrange meetings whenever necessary. Now, I must rejoin my family.'

He was about to go upstairs when Emily appeared with Mrs Woodley from a passage that he knew led to the dining room. They were followed by Zelda and Robert, conversing animatedly. 'Do you like it so far?' he asked hopefully.

'Delightful!' his wife told him. 'Though the rooms are devoid of furniture, I can picture the two drawing rooms and dining room filled with our own things.'

'And I'm looking forward to helping Mother choose a few new ones,' said Zelda in a tone that signified her approval of what she had seen so far. That continued when they went upstairs where Zelda was not slow to specify the room she would like in case Robert had his eyes on it.

'You have that one, Zelda. I'd rather have the one at the end of the corridor. It's a corner room so I get views in two directions.'

'I think mine's cosier.'

'So long as you are both satisfied,' commented Emily, then turned to her husband. 'We have four to choose from. The other three will be guest rooms.'

The choice was duly made and they all returned downstairs.

'Have they seen my study, Mrs Woodley?' Theodore asked then.

'No, sir. I thought you would like to show it to your family.'

'Quite right, Mrs Woodley!'

'Now you've seen it all, I'll go and check that coffee is ready. It will be served in the dining room in a few minutes.'

The study was large with three walls lined with bookshelves from floor to ceiling. Two large windows and a glass door faced on to the terrace, flooding the room with light.

'You'll enjoy using this room, Father,' commented Robert.

'It's large enough to accommodate a desk for you too. That could be useful if we both need to work from here, or either of us for that matter,' said Theodore. 'Apart from that there is sufficient space for books for us all to share.'

Emily came to stand beside him and slid her arm under his. 'This is wonderful,' she said. 'I'm sure we can all be happy here.'

They left Elston Hall well contented, each busily planning in their own mind how they would make a new life in this fine but friendly house.

'We have more furniture than we want in the Newcastle house so some of it can come to Elston, but we will need more ...' Emily mused.

'My dear, I give you carte blanche as far as that is concerned,' said Theodore. 'Except I must insist on choosing my own desk.'

Emily smiled. 'I didn't expect to be able to do that for you.' She looked at Robert. 'You had better choose your own, too.' She turned to Zelda then. 'You and I will make full use of your father's generous offer.'

'Starting tomorrow,' the girl agreed.

About the same time as they were being driven into Newcastle, a trap with a horse set comfortably between its new shafts was about to leave Rosedale for Whitby.

'I'm sorry your visit has been curtailed, Betsy.'

'So am I, Mrs Dodsworth, but I should like to get back to Father. I've done the essential thing – delivering the orders we were given last visit. Maybe next time, if Father is well, we'll manage some casual sales.'

'I hope you find him recovered. Give him my good wishes.'

'I will. And please give your son my thanks again for doing such a good and quick repair, and also for harnessing the horse this morning.'

'I will.' Mrs Dodsworth looked around. 'Where is that Mr Fenwick?' she added with a sharp note to her voice. 'I hope he isn't one to forget or not bother, after promising to see you safely back to Whitby.'

'I hope so too.' But there was more than hope of having an escort in her mind for, since he had made his offer, Betsy had been looking forward to having Jim Fenwick's company. Now he was ten minutes late and she was beginning to feel disappointed.

There was no sign of Jim Fenwick among the people of the village either, and Mrs Dodsworth's son had reported that, when he had collected Betsy's horse, Mr Fenwick's was not in the stable. Betsy's lips tightened. Where was he? Maybe he had been called away on another job. If so, he could have sent word – that at least would have been some consolation.

'Mrs Dodsworth, I really can't wait any longer. I'd better be off,' she said decisively.

'All right, lass. I'm sorry you're not going to have an escort, though. I'll be worried for you.'

'Don't be, Mrs Dodsworth. I'll be all right. It's a fine day.'

'Take care, mind. That Mr Fenwick will get my tongue round his ears when I see him!'

Betsy laughed. 'Don't be harsh on him. He might have a perfectly good reason.'

'Whenever you see him ... if you do ... don't be beguiled by a slippery tongue.'

'Goodbye, Mrs Dodsworth. I hope my father will be with me when I return in two weeks.' Betsy flicked the reins and guided the horse towards the track that climbed from the village to the moorland heights. She settled herself more comfortably on the seat, allowing the horse to set its own climbing pace.

Her mood was sombre. She had liked Jim Fenwick, found him attractive, and the promise of sharing further time with him had more than occupied her thoughts in Rosedale. But now ... Betsy sighed and chided herself for entertaining foolish romantic notions. She pushed them aside and considered her visit. It had been successful – all orders had been delivered and paid for, and she had had disappointment expressed by some of the miners when she had told them she had decided not to set up the usual stall for casual buyers because she wanted to hurry back to her father.

She was halfway up the hill when the rattle of hooves on the stony track behind her interrupted her thoughts. Could it be ...? Her thoughts began to race but she reined them in, not wanting her disappointment to be greater than need be. She glanced back but the horse behind had not rounded the last bend. She pressed on but then, as the sound drew closer, pulled her trap to a halt to let the rider pass unhindered.

She turned in her seat. Jim Fenwick! Relief and joy filled her mind. Relief that he was there; joy at seeing him again. She smiled brilliantly as he pulled his horse to a halt beside hers.

'Mr Fenwick!'

He doffed his hat. 'Miss Palmer. My sincere apologies. I was unfortunately delayed and could not get word to you.'

'Think nothing of it, Mr Fenwick.'

'But I do. I don't like not keeping my word. I promised to escort you to Whitby.'

'And here you are now, so all is well.'

'You are very understanding.'

'I appreciate your coming after me when I had left. Now, shall we be on our way?'

'Of course.'

Betsy set off smartly and he rode alongside the trap, holding back any attempts at conversation, waiting for her to speak first. After a few minutes she made a few casual comments but soon the exigencies of the track demanded he fall behind. Half a mile on, he saw the opportunity to come alongside her again.

'Miss Palmer, I cannot talk to you from horseback. If we are to travel together, why should I not be seated beside you? I can tie my horse to the trap.'

Betsy pulled to a halt. 'Why not, Mr Fenwick?' she answered brightly. 'It would indeed make more sense.'

Without another word Jim slid from the saddle and quickly tethered his horse behind the trap. In another moment he was seated beside her.

Betsy glanced at him. 'Comfortable, Mr Fenwick?' she asked with a twinkle in her eye.

'Indeed I am. Rather more so than in the saddle, Miss Palmer.'

'Next thing then – I think such formality is uncalled for between rescued and rescuer.' She held out her hand to him. 'Good day, Jim.'

'Ah, you remembered, Betsy,' he said, taking her hand.

She smiled. 'As did you.'

She flicked the reins and the horse responded, moving into a steady trot.

'It would seem this meeting was destined,' commented Jim.

'Do you believe in fate then?'

'Sometimes I believe it affects our lives, but who really knows?'

'So you think a father's illness and a broken trap have influenced the course of our whole lives?'

'Only the future can tell us that.'

For a moment Betsy's expression conveyed the seriousness with which she considered his words but then a trill of laughter escaped from her. 'Indeed. But we are having a very serious conversation for such a glorious day as this, are we not?' She turned her head momentarily and, after meeting his eyes with a quick glance, looked upwards to survey the blue sky. He watched her with his heart racing. He saw his own joy reflected in her eyes and was thankful that the concern he had seen in her face at the mention of her father's illness had vanished now. A troubled mind did not suit her. Jim felt as if he wanted to protect her from any danger or problem she encountered, and with that realisation came confusion. He had been on friendly terms with other girls but none had affected him like Betsy, and he had only known her a few days.

Wanting to abide by her every wish, he answered, 'Maybe you are right.'

Betsy felt a twinge of disappointment. Had she stopped him from saying more? Had she stifled . . .

She pulled her own thoughts up short. This was no way for her to be thinking. She had known Jim but a very short time; knew nothing about him, really.

She immediately put their conversation on a more mundane level. 'When we reach Lealholm, I must call on Mrs Dobson. She's always looked after my father and me on our way to and from Rosedale. She'll be wondering how I fared on my own.'

'Then we must put her mind at rest.'

'And she makes a good cup of tea, with all the right accompaniments.'

He smiled. 'I won't say no to that.'

Before the trap had even stopped Mrs Dobson was out of the cottage and extending a welcome. 'I'm that relieved to see you, Betsy!'

'And I'm glad to see you,' she replied, then caught Mrs Dobson's glance at Jim. 'This is Jim Fenwick. Jim, Mrs Dobson.'

He doffed his hat. 'I'm pleased to meet you. I've heard a lot about you on my way here.'

'All good, I hope,' said Mrs Dobson, raising an eyebrow.

'From what I have heard of your brew and what goes with it, nothing bad could ever be said about you.'

Mrs Dobson's lips twitched at his praise. She glanced at Betsy. 'He's got a flattering tongue on him. Beware, young lady!' Quickly, before she received any answer, she said, 'Come along in and we'll see if what you've heard is true.' As they were speaking, her husband appeared. After greetings and introductions were made, he said, 'Away in with you, I'll see to your horses.'

An hour later, their story told, they made their goodbyes.

'Mrs Dobson, your refreshments surpassed everything I had heard about them,' said Jim, about to climb on to the trap.

'You're welcome to call in any time you're this way,' she replied warmly.

'I'll make a point of it.'

Their hostess, with her husband beside her, looked up at Betsy, already seated in the trap. 'We hope you find your father recovered, and look forward to seeing him soon.'

'Thank you. I'll tell him.' Betsy shook the reins and the trap rolled away from the cottage.

'I hired the trap and horse from the Angel,' she explained. 'I'd better take them straight round.'

'I'll be able to get a room there for the night and stable my horse. And I can help you with your boxes.'

'That is most kind, Jim. You don't have to. I can ...'

'I want to, Betsy. And I would like to meet your father.'

When they reached the house in Well Close Square, she could tell Jim was nervous. As she opened the door she whispered, 'He won't bite.' Then called out, 'Father, I'm home.'

A door at the end of the passage opened and her father came to greet her with a broad welcoming smile on his face. 'Betsy!' He held out his arms to his daughter but dropped them when he saw a stranger standing in the doorway behind her.

'Father, you are up and looking so much better,' she cried joyfully, rushing to hug him.

Sam laughed. 'It was only a bout of sickness. Your aunt's ministrations proved successful.'

'I'm so glad. Father, I want you to meet Mr James Fenwick.'

'Good day to you, sir,' said Jim.

Samuel took his proffered hand. 'And to you,' he said, pleased that the young man's grip was firm.

'We've much to tell you, Father,' Betsy put in. 'Mr Fenwick came to my rescue on the way to Rosedale . . .'

Her father looked concerned. 'What happened?'

'Let us get rid of our outdoor clothes and sit down first,' said Betsy. She glanced at her companion. 'Put the two boxes down there, Jim,' she added, pointing to a spot near the foot of the stairs. As soon as she had used his Christian name, she realised she had let her guard down and noticed that her father had not missed the familiarity either. She quickly diverted his attention. 'We could do with a cup of tea.'

'Of course, of course,' he blustered. 'I'll tell Mrs Wilson and Lucy.' As he headed for the kitchen, Sam called over his shoulder, 'They followed your instructions well.'

'Our cook and maid,' Betsy said by way of explanation to Jim.

They shed their outdoor clothes and she primed her hair in the hall mirror before leading the way into a pleasant drawing room that reflected good taste and comfort.

'This is pleasant,' commented Jim.

Before any more could be said, Betsy's father hurried in.

'Now, tell me what happened,' he pressed them, indicating with a gesture for Jim to sit down.

Betsy related her story, the only interruption coming when Lucy brought in the tea and Betsy thanked her for seeing to her father in her absence.

'I only followed your orders, miss, and those of your aunt,' said the girl quietly, embarrassed by the praise.

'You and Cook were here, Lucy, and that was a comfort to me.'

The maid bobbed a curtsey and hurried from the room.

Betsy resumed her story.

'I must thank you, Mr Fenwick, for coming to my daughter's aid,' said Samuel when she had finished.

'Jim, please, sir. And I only did what anyone would have done.'

Samuel nodded his acknowledgement of the use of Jim's Christian name. 'I'm not sure everyone would have done what you did – a girl alone, in a precarious state, on the moor – who knows what could have happened to her? So I am very grateful to you for what you did and also for escorting Betsy back here to Whitby. I hope it has not inconvenienced you?'

'Not at all, Mr Palmer. I needed to come to Whitby before going on to Teesside.' Jim noted Mr Palmer look askance at this and went on, 'I supervise the shipment of ore from the Rosedale mines. As you probably know, we move it by horse and wagon to the railway at Pickering for onward shipment to furnaces along the Tees and further north. I have been looking into the possibility of moving it by ship from Whitby, but consider that the track between Rosedale and here might well be more hazardous than the one to Pickering. I wish to make further checks in Whitby before I move on to explore the possibility of building a light railway from Rosedale to the extension proposed by the North Yorkshire and Cleveland Railway that would run to Kildale.'

'A big project, Jim.'

'But I think not impossible. You see if we were to ...' He pulled himself up short, looking embarrassed. 'Here am I, gabbing away, and you'll be wanting to spend some time with your daughter, to hear how she got on with her sales and receive messages from your Rosedale friends.' As he was speaking he rose from his chair. 'I must away and leave you in peace. Thank you for your hospitality, Mr Palmer.'

'It is I who must thank you, for looking after Betsy. You are welcome to call here whenever you are in Whitby.'

'That is kind of you, sir. I don't think I'll be in the town again for at least three weeks.' Jim shook hands with Samuel first then turned to Betsy and said, 'Thank you for your company.'

She thought she detected more than polite acknowledgement in his eyes. 'Thank you for your help,' she answered demurely.

Father and daughter escorted him to the front door and made their goodbyes.

When they returned to the drawing room Samuel said, 'A pleasant young man who seems to have a very responsible job.' He saw that his daughter had read a note of approval in his voice so added quickly, 'But don't get carried away by first impressions, Betsy.'

3

For three weeks after Theodore Addison became the owner of Elston Hall the place was swarming with traders and craftsmen. Emily had soon made up her mind what she wanted doing to turn it into the attractive, homely residence she desired. Theodore showed interest in her proposed alterations but did not interfere, apart from giving guidance on which contractors should be employed and instructing Julian Hood to make sure the work was done to his satisfaction.

At the end of the third week the Addisons moved in. On arrival they found the staff assembled to greet them again and that Mrs Woodley, together with the cook, had organised a special meal for the occasion. Appreciating the thought, Theodore came to the servants' dining room and presented them with two bottles of his best wine to have with their own meal.

'That was a wonderful evening,' sighed Emily when she sat down in front of her dressing table later that night.

'Indeed it was,' agreed Theodore, coming up behind her and running his hands over her shoul-

50

ders before bending to kiss her on the top of her head.

She reached up and took his hands, at the same time turning on her seat to draw him down beside her. Her eyes not only showed her love for him but also expressed her appreciation of their move to Elston Hall, which he had made possible. She kissed him on the lips and he held her close. 'I know we are going to have a wonderful life here,' she whispered.

'It can be nothing else with you at my side,' he replied.

She smiled longingly at him.

Later, as they lay in each other's arms, Emily said, 'Theo, I didn't tell you but I asked Hood to try and keep in touch with what is happening at Cantonville Hall.'

'Did he?'

'Yes. And the latest information is that the Jordans moved in two days ago. It seems they were having alterations and renovations done too.'

'Then I think we should invite them to visit. We should get to know our neighbours.'

'I'll send an invitation.'

'Three weeks today, if that is suitable.'

'Ma'am, a boy has just delivered this. He said it was from his mistress at Elston Hall.' The maid held out a silver tray on which lay a folded and sealed sheet of paper.

'Thank you, Alice. Is he waiting for an answer?' asked Paula Jordan.

'No, ma'am.'

She nodded and Alice left the room. Before breaking the seal, Paula looked at the handwriting on the letter and pursed her lips approvingly. The script was neat and well executed. The writer had clearly been taught properly. She unfolded the sheet of paper and read the words.

'George,' she said, glancing at her husband sitting at the opposite end of the dining room table, 'we have an invitation.' Their two children, Adele and Mark, looked up from their plates in anticipation. 'The owners of Elston Hall have invited all four of us to dine with them three weeks yesterday.'

'That's very civil of them,' her husband replied. 'I think they too have recently moved in ... from Newcastle, I'm told. Merchant in Newcastle ... he could be useful.'

'Don't let business matters get in the way of friendship with our neighbours, George,' Paula warned him gently.

'Of course not.' He smiled. 'Good relationships in the neighbourhood are essential. Besides, Hull will always remain the centre of our business, though there are many chances to be exploited in Newcastle ...'

Realising from the glint in her father's eyes that he was getting carried away by his pet subject, Adele spoke up. 'Have they any family?'

'Yes,' replied her mother. 'A son and daughter of about your age.'

'I hope they haven't got their noses stuck in the air,' commented Mark.

'You'll find out in three weeks, if you don't

come across them before. I must get my acceptance off today,' his mother told him.

'No doubt Mrs Addison will note that you follow etiquette by replying within twenty-four hours, just as she has done by giving us three weeks' notice,' observed Adele.

'Well, it helps to set a certain standard between us. Now it's up to both families to find out how far our friendship will go.'

Three weeks later, the Addisons awaited the arrival of their guests a little nervously. First meetings on a social level always created apprehension, but the Addisons each hid the trepidation they felt.

Similar feelings were being experienced in the carriage that drove towards Elston Hall.

'The grounds are well kept,' commented George for something to say when the chatter in the coach had faded into an uneasy silence.

They swept up the gravelled carriage drive. The coachman steadied the horses and drew them to a halt. Almost immediately a footman was down the steps to open the vehicle's door. The Addisons emerged on to the stone terrace and came down the steps to greet their guests.

'Welcome to our home,' said Theodore with a warm smile that enveloped all the new arrivals.

'It was kind of you to extend the invitation, and we are delighted to meet you,' George returned the compliment.

The tone was set and the two families quickly exchanged introductions and greetings.

Robert's initial doubts were drowned instantly

in a sea of admiration. The young woman who stood before him was more beautiful than he had dared to imagine. The babble of voices around them was no distraction. He caught her name and savoured it together with the vision of a terrestrial angel with the gentlest of voices. This was a young woman who obviously considered her appearance carefully. Her evening dress of white net, decor-ated with yellow beading and worn over white satin, looked even more attractive when she slipped off her three-quarter-length grey felt cloak. The dress plunged from her shoulders into a low neck-line.

Adele smiled as she unfolded the evening wrap she was carrying and swung it round her exposed shoulders. Robert held his arm out to lend her support as they walked up the steps. She smiled and mouthed her thanks.

Alongside them Zelda was escorted by Mark who, from the moment of their introduction, had felt delighted to sense in her an outgoing personal-ity, one that was not stifled by too many parental restrictions. Zelda was clearly allowed to be the vivacious young woman she naturally was. He guessed she had tolerant, forward-looking parents and was thankful his own were the same. Both of them being cast in the same mould should make for an easier relationship. The move from Hull, which he had not been looking forward to, now took on a more promising aspect.

They had reached the stone terrace and moved towards the entrance to the house.

'My other daughter will be sorry she is missing

this occasion,' offered Paula, peeling off her gloves.

'I did not know you had another,' commented Emily.

'There is no reason why you should. Victoria is seventeen. She has been with my sister Anne for some time. Anne's husband Stephen died a year ago; they had no children so Victoria went to be with her aunt. At present, the mourning period being over, Anne has taken her on a tour of the Continent.'

'I'm sorry to hear about your brother-in-law,' Emily commiserated.

'Yes, it was sad. I'm afraid he had a heart attack due to overwork.'

Emily ushered her guest into the house. They were followed by Theodore and George. Amidst their own exchanges, Theodore had caught the last remark between their wives. 'Overwork?' he enquired sympathetically.

'Stephen was a financier in London. He was called in to sort out the affairs of a large concern that shall remain nameless. He unearthed some illicit dealings involving some of his friends. The unenviable position in which this placed him took its toll.'

'I'm very sorry to hear it.'

The servants had come forward to take all the outdoor clothes and Emily led the way into the drawing room. Drinks were served and the parents seated themselves on two sofas arranged at an angle in order to make for easier conversation. The younger generation drifted towards a window seat. Adele and Mark were soon learning what life in

55

Newcastle and the surrounding area had to offer them.

'What brought you north from Hull?' Theodore enquired of their parents.

'I haven't burnt my boats,' George informed him. 'I still have my business there – shipping, as you probably know. I'm looking to develop a similar business on the Tyne. We kept our house in Hull, so I'll be here or there as work demands. Some day Mark will take over from me.'

'Robert will inherit too,' said Theodore. 'He is already interested in the business – in fact, he's quite an asset. So our situations are similar except I'm a merchant, not a ship owner.'

'George, what did I tell you before we left home this evening?' There was a touch of admonishment in Paula's tone. 'No business talk.'

'Just putting things in perspective, my dear,' he replied, and quickly added as he glanced back at Theodore, 'We might well be able to do business together.'

'Why not?' said Theodore, pleased with their new neighbours. 'You'll be wanting premises in Newcastle, no doubt? Maybe I can help with that.'

'I'd be most grateful if you could.'

'What about the day after tomorrow? The young men can accompany us.'

'If that's the case,' put in Emily, 'you and I, Paula, may as well go too. You'll want to know the best shops.'

'Indeed,' she agreed, seizing the chance.

'And no doubt the two young ladies will not

want to be left out so we'll take two carriages. The young ones can travel together.'

The ease with which the older members of the party had settled down together was also evident amongst the younger generation. Their unforced conversation continued throughout the meal and the rest of the evening, until the Jordans declared it was time for them to go. With outdoor clothes on, their carriage awaiting, they made their good-byes.

'It is good to know that we have such friendly neighbours,' declared Paula, taking Emily's hands in hers. 'This far north was unknown territory to us but we have been blessed.'

'It is gracious of you to say so,' replied Emily. 'I felt upon your arrival as if I had known you all my life.'

'Theo, my grateful thanks for a most pleasant evening and I look forward to the day after tomorrow. I feel it will be the start of a profitable working relationship,' said George.

'I'm sure it will, as well as a new friendship.' Theo's feelings about the future were reflected in his firm grip which was returned by George as if a pact were being sealed.

'Thank you for your delightful company this evening, Zelda,' said Mark. 'I look forward to sharing more time with you.'

'You'll have to if you want me to improve your dancing, though I suspect it's not as bad as you led me to believe,' she returned with a teasing twinkle in her eyes. 'We'll see at the next ball.'

'I look forward to that too.'

As he escorted Adele to the carriage, Robert said, 'I have enjoyed meeting you and eagerly anticipate the day after tomorrow.'

She replied with a smile.

The Addisons waved goodbye as the carriage pulled away. They watched it for a few moments before turning back into the house, each satisfied with what had turned out to be a most pleasant evening and one which seemed to augur well for the future.

'I'm sorry, sir, Mr Palmer and Miss Palmer are not at home.'

Jim's eager anticipation upon arriving at the house in Well Close Square dissolved into disappointment. 'Have they gone to Rosedale?' he asked hopefully.

Lucy shook her head. 'Oh, no, sir, they are both at the shop in Church Street.'

'Oh!' He brightened. 'Thank you. I'll try and catch them there.' He turned away and was soon heading down Skinner Street to make for the bridge. He crossed the river but, reaching Church Street, realised he did not know where the shop was situated, though he reckoned it wouldn't take much finding. He was proved right; in a few minutes he spotted the words 'Palmer, Jeweller' above the two-windowed shop. He did not hesitate, his hopes buoyed by the thought that he would soon see Betsy again. But those hopes were dashed when he did not see either her or her father. Instead there was a glum, long-faced young man behind the counter. He did not look up immediately from the pocket watch he was repairing but said tersely, 'I'll be with you in a minute.'

Jim, itching to make his query, remained silent, interested to see the man's long fingers handling the delicate mechanism as if caressing a willing female. He smiled to himself at the impression that had been created even though this young man looked the most unlikely of lovers. But, Jim reminded himself, still waters run deep.

The man closed the back of the watch with care, gave a sigh of contented satisfaction as he straightened, looked Jim in the eye and said, 'I'm sorry to have kept you waiting, sir, but now I am entirely at your service, what can I do for you?'

'I was told Mr Palmer and his daughter would be here, but I see they aren't and I did want to visit them before returning to Rosedale.'

'Well, sir, they are here but not here,' said Toby with a twinkle in his eye. 'That is, they are not in this room but they are here in the office – at the back, sir. Who shall I say wishes to see them?'

'Jim Fenwick.'

'Very good, sir!' He went to a door behind the counter and disappeared, to return almost immediately, saying, 'Come this way, sir.' He lifted the hinged section of the counter to allow Jim admission and indicated the door. 'Go through, sir.'

As Jim entered the office, Samuel Palmer rose from behind his desk.

'Good day, Mr Palmer,' said Jim, reaching across to take Sam's proffered hand.

'Good day to you, Mr Fenwick,' returned Sam politely.

Jim turned to Betsy who was seated at one end of the desk, a ledger laid in front of her. Deeming it wisest to use her surname in front of her father, he said, 'And to you, Miss Palmer.' He bowed with a respectful inclination of his head.

'I hope you are well, Mr Fenwick,' she greeted him.

'Indeed. I am on my way to Rosedale but could not be in Whitby without enquiring after your father's health.' He glanced at Sam. 'I trust you are completely recovered from the indisposition you were experiencing the last time I saw you, sir?'

'I am indeed fully recovered, thank you, and most grateful for your solicitude. Do sit down.' He indicated a chair.

'Thank you, sir,' Jim said. 'I won't intrude on you for more than a few moments. I am pleased that you are well, and your daughter too.' He was aware of Betsy's eyes fixed on him. Though she looked away as soon as he glanced at her, he was sure he had caught an expression of interest in her eyes.

'Have you been in Rosedale since I last saw you, just over three weeks ago?' he asked.

'No,' replied Sam. 'Betsy and I were just planning another visit, leaving here the day after tomorrow.'

'Then perhaps you will allow me to accompany you?'

'Will that not delay you?'

'No, sir. A day or so either way will make no difference to me.'

'Then we will be pleased of your company.'

Betsy's thoughts raced. Events were turning out

better than she could have hoped!

'I'll look forward to that,' said Jim.

'Will you be in Rosedale long, Mr Fenwick?' Betsy enquired. 'Or will your work demand that you are soon away again?'

'It is more than likely I will be there some time now, if the situation develops as the mine owners and railway authorities hope.'

'Extracting more ore and developing that railway line you mentioned when we last saw you?' queried Betsy.

'Yes.'

'Then they were no idle rumours?'

'Far from it,' replied Jim. 'There always was substance to them. Now I can confirm them, though the news won't be made official yet, so please keep what I tell you to yourselves until it is public knowledge. A rail link from Rosedale to the line currently being extended from Stokesley to Kildale is distinctly possible.'

'Then a line from Rosedale, linking up as you describe, would give access beyond Stokesley,' mused Sam.

'An easy way to the Teesside furnaces and those in County Durham.'

'So a boom time could be coming to Rosedale, if you get permission to build your track?'

'Yes. I can tell you in confidence that permission has already been sought and there is every possibility that an Act to enable the railway's construction will be passed before very long.'

Betsy was beginning to wonder why Jim, whom they hardly knew, was telling them all this.

'More miners are wanted, plus men to construct the railway and others to work on it ... there could be boom years coming, Mr Palmer. There'll be money in the dale, and men do like to spend their money.'

'I take your point, Mr Fenwick. Palmer's of Whitby could very well help those men to spend their wages.'

'Exactly, Mr Palmer! I thought you ought to know now so that you can buy in at better prices, before the boom.'

'And sell at ...'

'Quite so, Mr Palmer.'

Betsy's mind was racing with the possibilities of making a bigger profit by being able to buy cheaply before this news broke. Mr Fenwick was doing them a very good turn by giving them such advance information. Why he should do this except ... was *she* the reason? She started at the thought and saw that Jim was rising to his feet.

'I must be on my way, sir. I have things to see to here.'

'It was kind of you to call,' replied Samuel, making no further reference to the information Jim had given them; he sensed the young man would not want attention drawing to it. 'We look forward to seeing you the day after tomorrow. We start early, leaving the Angel at seven.'

'I'll be there, sir. In fact, I'll get a room there for the next two nights.'

They shook hands.

'Betsy, will you see Mr Fenwick out?'

With her hand on the doorknob, Betsy hesitated. She turned to face Jim.

'I am grateful for your kind enquiry after my father's health.' Her hesitation was barely noticeable before she added, 'Our gratitude for your news.' She knew he would read the inference though he showed no sign of having done so.

'I look forward to seeing you again the day after tomorrow, Miss Palmer.'

'And maybe we will see you in Rosedale also. I know my father would appreciate talking to you. We will be staying with Mrs Dodsworth as usual.'

Their eyes met and each of them knew with certainty that more lay behind that casual invitation than there appeared on the surface.

'I will remember that, Miss Palmer.' Betsy opened the door for him. Jim stepped outside and turned back to her. 'Goodbye for the present. I guarantee, no broken wheels this time.' His eyes filled with merriment for a brief moment before he turned and strode away. She watched him go, her mind and heart filled with joy that he had called on her – for that, she told herself, was the real reason for his visit.

When she returned to the office her father said, 'What do you think to that news? I'd say it was genuine. There'd be no reason for Mr Fenwick to tell us if it were not. He seems a most forthright and upstanding young man.'

'Oh, I'm sure it is correct,' agreed Betsy, maybe a little more eagerly than she had intended.

Her father caught her mood and said, with a twinkle in his eye, 'I wonder why he chose to tell us?'

Betsy could not hide the reddening of her cheeks.

They both knew they would have agreed on the reason if either of them had cared to voice it.

'It has given us a real advantage. An influx of workers to Rosedale could mean more business for us,' she pointed out.

'And we should take advantage of it,' said her father thoughtfully. 'We should buy in all the good jet work we can before the news breaks. With a bigger market for jewellery and jet, prices will rise. I'll start buying tomorrow.'

The following evening when Sam came home to Well Close Square, Betsy heard him enter the house and came straight into the hall to greet him. 'You look tired, Father,' she said with concern as she took his coat and handed it to Lucy.

'Just a bit,' he said, trying to reassure her with a smile. 'It's hard tracking down and choosing items suitable for our requirements. It takes time and concentration and some people aren't easy to deal with ...' He gave a little shrug of his shoulders and said, 'Still, here I am.'

Betsy took his arm and led him to the stairs. 'Up you go. Once you've washed and changed I'll be in the drawing room where I'll have a drop of whisky awaiting you.'

He smiled and kissed her on the cheek. 'You're a good lass.'

She watched him climb the stairs, his steps a little heavier than usual.

When he returned to the drawing room, Sam saw the glass of whisky ready on a small table beside his favourite chair and Betsy seated close by, reading while she awaited him.

'Feels better with the grime of the day washed away,' he remarked as he crossed the room.

'Now relax and enjoy your drink while you tell me how you fared,' she said, closing her book and laying it on one side.

He sank back in his wing-chair with a contented sigh, picked up his glass and took a sip. 'That's good.'

Betsy was relieved to see his eyes looked brighter. 'Well, did you get it all done?' she asked.

'Not near all. I called on Mr Withersgill first. You remember he said he might have some jewellery to sell? I thought it might be a good time to look at it.'

'And was it?' she asked, recalling the visit to their shop by a man who had made a fortune in the Lancashire cotton trade before retiring to Whitby. Six months ago he had lost his wife and decided the memories her jewellery invoked were too painful for him to keep it.

'It certainly was,' replied her father. 'There was a lot of it and it took time to assess its worth, in the light of what he was asking.' He paused, sipped his whisky and then added, 'I tell you what, Betsy, we got a bargain but he was happy with our final deal. It was obvious he was intent on selling, did not want to get anyone else involved, but he put no pressure on me to buy.'

'Good. Then I look forward to seeing it. When do you get it?'

'I could have brought it with me but chose not to. I wanted to hand over cash for it, and that will have to be tomorrow because he is going away for a month the day after.'

'Just as well you called on him today then.'

'Yes.'

Disappointment was already filling Betsy's mind. 'If you are seeing him tomorrow, what about our visit to Rosedale? We'll have to postpone it?'

'I would in any case if we are to take full advantage of Mr Fenwick's information. I still have over half the jet workshops to visit. But it crossed my mind that it would be better if I completed those visits in a slightly more leisurely way than today. So why don't you go to Rosedale as planned? It is not as if you will be travelling alone again. I know you will have a reliable and honourable escort.'

Betsy's heart raced faster and faster with every word of her father's proposal but she hid her excitement, merely saying, 'Are you sure?'

'Of course! It will be greatly to our benefit if I can complete the purchasing here. I propose that I join you at Rosedale in a week's time. How does that sound?'

'If that is what you want, Father,' she replied diplomatically.

'I think it the best solution,' Samuel said seriously, then added with a faint smile touching his lips, 'I don't think you will mind having Mr Fenwick for an escort.'

Betsy made no comment but her blushes made their own revelation.

The following morning, accompanied by her father carrying her valise and Toby carrying the two boxes from the shop, Betsy arrived at the Angel just before seven. The usual trap was

66

attended by Charlie who also kept his eye on a horse that Betsy recognised as Jim's. Charlie immediately took charge of the luggage and stowed it in the trap. While all this was going on, Jim Fenwick emerged from the inn.

'Good day, Miss Palmer. I trust you are well and looking forward to our drive across the moors this fine day. And you too, Mr Palmer,' he added, turning to Sam.

'Oh, I'm not coming, Mr Fenwick.'

Surprise and concern crossed Jim's face but before he could express them Sam said, 'Betsy will explain. There's no need for me to hold you both up.'

Jim nodded. 'Very good, sir. Let me assure you, I will see your daughter safely to her destination.'

'I'm sure you will, Mr Fenwick, I'm sure you will.' Sam then made his goodbyes to Betsy, assuring her that he would be all right on his own. He watched the trap, handled by his daughter, turn out of the Angel's yard with Jim riding a few feet behind. Then he turned to his assistant. 'Let us away, Toby. There's a lot to do today and the rest of the week before I too head for Rosedale.'

'Yes, sir,' said Toby, falling into step with his employer.

Betsy allowed the horse to set its own pace as it took the strain of pulling the trap up the long incline out of Whitby. Having checked that she had the trap in hand, Jim allowed his own horse to drop behind, but once they had reached the heights beyond the town, where the track levelled out, he drew alongside her.

'An easier ride from here on.'

She agreed but added, 'Except for a few ups and downs.'

He nodded. 'A bit like life.'

Was this an opportunity for her to get to know him better? She took the chance 'You've experienced those?'

'Aye, who hasn't?' He paused and Betsy thought she was going to get no more but then he said, 'Can I come on board?'

She made room beside her and, with a sparkle in her eyes, said, 'You're welcome.'

Jim swung to the ground, tied his horse on a long rein at the back of the trap then ran alongside to climb up beside Betsy.

'You were saying?' she prompted.

'I was born in Hull, the youngest of seven. Ten years between me and my nearest sister Rebecca. Father was a bad 'un, always had been, especially when he was drunk. Used to beat us cruelly, so my sisters and brothers left home just as soon as they could. When I was two he took Ma, Rebecca and me to Newcastle. Rebecca walked out three years later. Ma died after another three years.'

'And you were left alone with what sounds like a monster?' commented a horrified Betsy.

'I was eight, coming up to nine, with no mother to try to protect me. So I scarpered too.'

'Alone? What did you do then?'

'Roughed it. Sleeping where I could; pinching food. Then after about a month I was found by a good man and his wife, Mr and Mrs Rimington, who had no children of their own. They took pity on me, took me into their home and gave me back my life. I was a lost child, frightened of what might happen to me next, but their kindness and goodness reassured me that life was not always as I had experienced it.

'They educated me and at seventeen I got work with the railway. Even though I say it myself, I'd a sharp mind – though from whom I got it I don't know, unless it was from my mother, a trait in her that had been repressed by my father's cruelty. Well, there it was; I had my opportunity and was determined to make the most of it. I was doing well, had shown ability, could take responsibility and was not afraid of hard work, whether physical or mental. Then, in the 1853 cholera epidemic in Newcastle, my benefactors died. They left me everything they had. Although modest enough, it gave me comfort and a base on which to build. I soon found I could not bear to stay in Newcastle where memories of those good people were too much for me, so I went to York and the railway there. My ability came to the notice of some far-sighted and influential people. They saw potential in the Rosedale mines and sent me to look into possible developments there.'

'Oh, Jim, ups and downs all your life! And here am I who can complain only of losing my mother,' said Betsy with heartfelt sympathy for him.

'But that can be the biggest loss of all,' he said wistfully. 'I'm glad you have been spared others.'

'Who knows what lies ahead?'

'True, but we shouldn't anticipate such losses, we should think only of what we stand to gain. My latest such advantage was being sent to Rosedale. If it hadn't been for the events that precipitated that, even the bad ones, I wouldn't have met you.'

As he was speaking Jim reached out and took her hand. She answered the look of entreaty in his eyes and their lips met in a caress that expressed all their hopes that love could develop between them.

4

The Jordans' carriage was on time as it pulled to a halt in front of Elston Hall beside the Addisons' empty carriage, attended by their coachman. George alighted and had started up the steps when the Addisons appeared.

'Good morning,' he called.

His bright tone was reciprocated by their friends as they came to join him and extend a welcome to the others.

'We have a fine morning,' commented Paula.

'And long may it continue,' returned Emily. 'You and George could ride with us, if you don't mind the young ones using your carriage?'

'Not at all,' agreed George.

The easy association that had been established between the younger generation on first meeting continued as they climbed into the vehicle together. In a matter of a few minutes, with the older people also settled in comfortably, the two carriages moved off.

'I'm looking forward to this visit,' said Paula eagerly.

'You've not been into Newcastle before?' said Emily, somewhat surprised.

'I haven't had time since we arrived. I've been too busy seeing to the house.'

'But you must have been, George?' asked Theodore.

He smiled. 'No.'

'What?' Theodore did not hide his surprise. 'But I thought you were looking to expand your business here? So surely you would look at the prospects first?'

'I instructed my three captains to look at possibilities for expansion whenever they visited the Tyne. Their independent reports were all very positive so I decided to act on their observations without any further investigation of my own. Then I decided to buy Cantonville Hall, and from that base explore the possibilities in more detail.' He hesitated slightly then added, 'I see you think that an unusual way to go about things.'

'Well, to have bought a property such as Cantonville Hall, I'd have thought you'd want to make sure of your business base first.'

'Ah, but that base remains in Hull. Anything in Newcastle is merely an addition, albeit hopefully a profitable one. As regards Cantonville, I would have bought it in any case. I wanted a property somewhere other than our home in the East Riding. It had to be in the country and within reasonable distance of Hull. Linking that with my idea of expanding the business to the Tyne, I looked for somewhere in the Tyne Valley and found Cantonville Hall. It fitted in perfectly with what I had in mind and gained Paula's approval when she first saw it. So here we are. And now, thanks to you, I am on my way to see what Newcastle and the Tyne can offer me.'

'I'm sure we will find somewhere to suit you. There are several likely properties along The Quay which suffered in the great fire of nearly four years ago. They've been restored but still remain unoccupied.'

'We heard about that,' said Paula. 'It must have been terrible. Fire is the one thing I fear.'

'It started in a worsted manufactory in Gateshead on the south side of the river,' Emily explained.

'Unfortunately that was in the early hours of the morning, so it had got well hold before it was discovered,' added Theodore. 'Then it spread to an adjoining bonded warehouse containing highly inflammable materials. When that lot went up, I tell you, it was unbelievable. It was like day over Gateshead, and not far off over Newcastle.'

'The explosion scattered burning timbers over roofs, so the blaze spread further,' added Emily.

'And ships in the quays nearby were only saved by prompt action in slipping them from their moorings,' put in Theodore.

'So how was it that property along Newcastle's Quay suffered? There was a river between them after all.'

'Close to the warehouse where the fire started in Gateshead was another bonded warehouse, also filled with highly combustible materials,' explained Theodore. 'The second explosion was enormous.'

'And that destroyed buildings all along The Quay?' asked George, adding when Theodore nodded, 'Unbelievable!'

'The whole area shook and the blast was felt many, many miles away. It was terrifying.' Emily's voice faltered. She was visibly moved by the recollection.

'There were many people killed or injured, but the loss of life could have been much higher – people had crowded on to the High Level Bridge to watch the fire in Gateshead,' said Theodore to relieve his wife of the necessity of continuing. 'It was a stupid thing to do, you'd think people would have had more sense. That second explosion could have destroyed the bridge and taken all those folk with it. As it was, the bridge held. I tell you what, though, it was soon empty! It was that explosion that flung burning debris across the river. Thank goodness the blaze was contained at The Quay and some adjacent buildings. Otherwise, if it had really got hold, Newcastle could have lost the elegant new developments created by Richard Grainger in the thirties. You'll be seeing them soon.' He took this opportunity to change the subject slightly. 'We'll leave the carriages near the station and conduct our day from there.'

'Are you going straight to The Quay?' asked Emily, pleased to have all talk of explosions, fires and death dismissed from the conversation.

'I think that's best,' her husband replied. 'Then we'll take luncheon at my club, the Frobisher ... named after the Elizabethan explorer,' he explained, glancing at George. 'That will give me the opportunity to introduce you to some useful contacts.'

'Admirable,' he replied. 'I'm most grateful for what you are doing.'

74

'Think nothing of it.' Theodore turned to the ladies next. 'Will that fit in with your day?'

'Once we leave the carriage, we'll be independent of you so timing won't matter. Don't worry about us – we'll enjoy ourselves in our own way,' Emily told him.

'Are we wise in letting them loose in the shops?' teased Theodore, casting a look of enquiry at George.

'No doubt our bank balances will be lighter when we next meet.' He sent a despairing glance heavenwards.

'And make that meeting back at Cantonville,' said Paula. 'I've organised an easy supper with Cook, for whatever time we return.'

'Splendid!' cried her husband. 'This has all the makings of a good outing, and we are most grateful to both of you for devoting a day to our introduction to Newcastle.'

'May I face the way we are going?' Adele's request, shyly presented, was met with instant concern by Robert.

'Of course.' He was on his feet, steadying himself against the sway of the carriage as it started forward. 'I'm sorry, I did not think to ask if you had a preference. Please, have my seat.' He held out his hand, ready to support her. 'Does it trouble you to have your back to the way we are going?'

She took his hand gratefully as she moved across the carriage and sat down opposite him and next to Zelda. 'It does sometimes. Silly, isn't it?'

'Not at all,' he replied sympathetically.

'I prefer to ride my own horse rather than be in a carriage, but that's not always possible.'

'You ride then?'

'Oh, yes,' she answered in a tone that implied it could not be otherwise. 'Living in the Yorkshire Wolds, what else would you expect?'

'Of course,' replied a chastened Robert, 'I didn't think.' Then he added quickly, 'Will you have a stable here?'

'Yes. I couldn't live without a horse.'

'Father's renovating one of the old stables,' put in Mark. 'They had fallen into disuse.'

'As soon as they are ready, I'll be looking for a mount. Well, we both will,' said Adele. 'I presume you both ride even though you lived in Newcastle?' She spoke as if she would be horrified to hear that they didn't then added, 'Of course you do! Otherwise you'd be lost, moving into the country.'

'We do,' confirmed Zelda. 'Have done since an early age.'

'Good,' said Adele with enthusiasm, 'then you can both help us choose our new horses when the time comes. You must know the best dealers, or at least where we might look.'

'We will be delighted to do so,' said Zelda, knowing she was speaking for her brother as well, for she had a strong suspicion that, even at this early stage in their association, Robert was particularly interested in Adele.

'You'll miss your friends in Yorkshire?' he said.

'Naturally,' agreed Mark. 'But we look forward to making new ones here. I think we have already been lucky in finding two who live so close to us.' As he concluded his remark he shot Zelda a glance and her answering smile, brief though it was, told him she was of like mind.

'We'll miss them,' Adele agreed, 'but we are not cutting ourselves off completely. There will be times when we will be going back to stay in Yorkshire. And some of our friends will come and stay with us here.'

Robert wondered who those friends were and if any of them was special to Adele.

'Does your interest in horses extend to race meetings?' he asked.

'Oh, yes,' confirmed Mark enthusiastically. 'We never miss Beverley races or York. What about you?'

'We have racing on the Town Moor, the main meeting being held in June when the big event is the Northumberland Plate. There are always huge crowds for that,' Robert explained. 'There's racing in Hexham and Durham too. We have been to those and to other meetings on the Town Moor, but we never miss the Northumberland Plate. You must come with us next month.'

'Now, Mark, we really have something to look forward to,' said Adele, her eyes bright with anticipation.

This was the first piece of news they broke to their parents when they alighted from their carriages in Newcastle. It was greeted with enthusiasm by George who immediately suggested that the two families should mark it as a day to be shared.

'And now we are in your hands for today,' he concluded, looking expectantly at Theodore.

'We'll walk to The Quay – you'll see something of the town on the way. Paula, Adele, I'll leave you in the hands of my wife and daughter.'

'And we shall have a very good day,' said Emily with a smile that embraced Paula and their daughters.

With that the two groups parted.

'That fellow Grainger you mentioned has certainly done a good job,' commented George as they headed for The Quay. 'His vision has produced such elegant buildings which are laid out to full advantage.'

'I think so,' agreed Theodore. 'Of course, he had his critics and those who disagreed with the general consensus, there are always such people, but they were in a minority.'

The town was alive with people going about their daily business. Two-horse conveyances were held to a steady pace by their coachmen while those in charge of one-horse carriages and traps moved a little more quickly, some trying to make up time before an appointment. Men on horseback had an easier passage down the main thorough-fares. Couples in elegant morning dress strolled along the pavements, passing the time of day with acquaintances. Clerks in flat caps, or wearing peaked hats carrying their firm's insignia and proclaiming their trade, hurried about their masters' business. Ladies paused to look in shop windows where all manner of goods were on display, in most cases attractively arranged to catch the eye of potential buyers. Awnings had been let down to shade the windows and offer cover to pedestrians. A mail coach rumbled past and goods were being unloaded from wagons in several locations.

George felt the beating pulse of prosperity at the heart of this town. He was getting a good feeling about the prospects for extending his shipping business to Newcastle, helped by all the useful information Theodore gave him as they walked to The Quay.

They reached the road that ran alongside the river. It was lined to the landward side by buildings housing the offices of shipping companies, merchants, chandlers, and an area of warehouses and stores of every size. Horse-drawn carts and wagons rumbled by about the business of transporting cargoes to and from their ships tied up along the full length of The Quay. These were predominantly sailing ships with their masts trellising the sky, but there were several vessels whose smokestacks proclaimed the coming of steam.

Theodore could sense the excitement and enthusiasm in George and his son as they absorbed the vitality of this whole scene that spoke of buoyant trading, a port alive and enthusiastic about its present and its future.

George realised he had been fortunate in gaining Theodore Addison as his neighbour. Here was a man who could help him get established on Tyneside; who could open doors for him sooner than he might have done on his own behalf.

Theodore was a man respected all along The Quay, not only by his fellow merchants and ship owners but by the stevedores and sailors – a sign that, even though he had stepped out of his former sphere thanks to his own drive and ambition, he had never forgotten his roots.

'Well?' he asked as they walked along The Quay.

'From what I'm seeing, I'm keen to establish myself here as soon as possible.' George glanced at his son as he spoke.

Mark saw the query in his father's eyes and was more than grateful that his approval had been sought for he knew that one day the firm would be his. 'I think the ideas we discussed at home in Hull can easily be fulfilled here, Father,' he answered enthusiastically.

'Good.' George smiled, pleased to have his son's backing. 'Theodore, we need new premises and then I will send word to Hull to dispatch one of our ships, the *Adventurer*, to be based permanently here.'

'I'm pleased you are going to establish a subsidiary of your Hull business here; it will be good for Newcastle. Before we go to my club, I'll introduce you to some shipping agents and port officials with offices along here. We may come across some property owners, but that is more likely to happen at my club.'

By the time they were leaving The Quay, Theodore had introduced George to several useful contacts, all of whom were very encouraging about the prospects for a new business in the port.

As they approached the Frobisher Club, a few

paces behind their sons and just out of earshot, George spoke. 'I am most grateful to you for what you have done for me today. I should say "us" because Mark is becoming more and more involved in the business nowadays and I noted he was very enthusiastic today, and very content in Robert's company.'

Theodore dismissed these thanks with a wave of his hand. 'Think nothing of it. My pleasure. I too am pleased that our sons seem to be getting on so well.'

'And I'm glad to see you involve Robert in your business ... it should make for a good relationship between our firms, two generations in accord.'

They entered the club where George was immediately impressed by its opulence, and by the deference shown to Theodore and Robert by the two stewards on duty.

'My usual table, please, Hugh.'

'Yes, sir. It will be set for four. Half an hour, sir?'

'Capital,' confirmed Theodore. He placed orders for drinks and led the way into a large room scattered with easy chairs, sofas and small tables. Paintings of Newcastle adorned the walls, the most important one looking along Grey Street towards the monument erected to Earl Grey in 1838. He paused, surveying the room quickly before taking his guests over to four comfortable chairs that, grouped together, gave them a good view of the room.

Their drinks arrived. While they enjoyed them, Theodore and Robert pointed out gentlemen, relaxing with their newspapers or engaging in quiet

81

conversation, who might be useful to George's wish to establish himself and his business in Newcastle.

As the gentlemen headed out of Newcastle two hours later in their carriage, the conversation between the four of them was full of enthusiasm for what had been achieved and the contacts that had been made on George's and Mark's behalf.

Reaching Cantonville Hall they knew, from the parcels littering the lobby, that the ladies had already arrived.

'Left them there on purpose to let us get used to the idea,' laughed George. 'But who cares if they've had a good time and are happy?

'Looks as if you four have enjoyed yourselves,' he commented as they all entered the drawing room.

'Indeed we have,' replied Paula. 'It was a nice change from the shops in Hull. I've ordered a new table for the dining room. Adele was very enthusiastic about it, too, and said she knew you would definitely approve.'

'Yes, you will, Father,' added his daughter enthusiastically. 'And I got a lovely evening dress.'

'What about you, Zelda?' asked Theodore.

'A day dress for me,' she replied with equal delight.

'Good.' He eyed his wife enquiringly.

'A pearl necklace.'

'The one you had your eye on?'

'Yes. I finally couldn't resist it.'

'It's exquisite,' approved Paula. 'Well, what sort of a day have you had?'

'Splendid,' her husband replied. 'I've got my eye on some premises.'

'And we've made several contacts who are eager for us to come to Newcastle,' added Mark enthusiastically.

'Good.' Paula turned to Emily but her words embraced all the Addisons. 'We are so grateful to you. You have made all of us feel at home so quickly that any doubts we had about moving here have vanished completely.'

'Thank you for coming, Mrs Jordan,' said Robert, but capturing his quick sideways glance Adele knew his thanks were all for her.

Jim let the horse dictate the speed at which they negotiated the steep slope down into Rosedale.

'It's a beautiful place,' commented Betsy wistfully. 'More mining and a railway will spoil it.'

'But don't forget, it brings work to a lot of people. That will help many poor families, and the village and dale should benefit too,' Jim pointed out.

'Have you no soul?'

He glanced at her enquiringly as he said, 'I would hope so but life has to be sustained. What would happen to the people currently deriving a living from the workings if our transport arrangements were not improved? They might lose everything if the ore grew too difficult to move. You and your father, living so comfortably in Whitby, are already making money from the men who work in this dale. Expansion here could bring you even more.'

83

'I know, but ...' Betsy let her voice trail away.

He gave an understanding smile and patted her hand. 'Don't let it worry you. If it hadn't been for the mines and the possibility of a railway, we wouldn't be sitting here side by side now.'

'I know.'

The villagers were going about their daily lives, mingling with miners relieved from work until it was time to start their shift further along the dale. Recognising Betsy and Jim, people greeted them in passing.

Jim drove straight to Mrs Dodsworth's cottage. She greeted them brightly but looked concerned when she asked, 'Where's your father, Betsy? Not ill again, I hope?'

'No, he's perfectly well but work has kept him in Whitby. He'll join me a week today. I hope that is all right with you, Mrs Dodsworth?'

'Of course it is, love. Now get your things inside, lass. The kettle's on the boil. You'll stay for a cup of tea, Mr Fenwick?'

'It's Jim, Mrs Dodsworth. And, yes, I'd love to.' He winked at her as he added, 'And a slice of your sponge cake?'

Her smile told him she was pleased he had asked. 'It's as good as that?'

'Better,' he flattered.

Less than ten minutes later, with Betsy's luggage in her room, they were sitting at the table feeling contented with their day.

'How long are you here for this time, Jim?' Mrs Dodsworth asked.

'I won't know until I see the bosses tomorrow.'

'I hope you're not going to be away from the dale,' put in Betsy.

Mrs Dodsworth smiled to herself. Were her suspicions about these two correct? If so, she judged there could be no better match.

Jim showed up at Mrs Dodsworth's early in the evening of the following day.

'Have you had a good day, Betsy?' he enquired.

'I got all the orders delivered, so people would know I was here, and at the same time spread the word that I would be in the village hall tomorrow. What about your day?'

'It went well. I'll be here all this week.' He felt a surge of pleasure when he saw her eyes brighten at the news.

'That's good,' put in Mrs Dodsworth. 'You'll be here for the Gypsy Party on Friday. A great day,' she added, seeing their querying looks. 'We need a fine day because there's a cricket match between Rosedale and Wrelton, followed by a high tea and then dancing on the village green.'

'And no doubt the beer will be flowing?' said Jim.

'Aye, and more besides,' said Mrs Dodsworth knowingly. 'Last year when it was getting dark a lot of folk gathered at the big house at the end of the village to continue the dance in the parlour there and enjoy prolonging the gypsy revelry.'

'We shall look forward to it,' said Jim, casting a glance at Betsy that invited her to agree.

'We certainly shall,' confirmed Betsy, knowing from Jim's relieved smile how he had interpreted her words.

85

Throughout the succeeding days the coming celebration was never far from Betsy's tongue when she was with Mrs Dodsworth.

'Thee's excited about it, lass,' commented her landlady the day before it was to take place. 'I hope you won't be disappointed.'

'I won't, so long as Jim is there.' This admission was out before Betsy realised it. She blushed, revealing the depth of her feelings towards Jim Fenwick.

He was as good as his word and arrived at the cottage at the stated time to find Betsy awaiting him. Mrs Dodsworth discreetly disappeared to the kitchen.

'You look wonderful,' said Jim, admiring Betsy's day dress of light blue batiste decorated with lines of narrow lavender piping, coming close at the waist from the high neckline and shoulders. From the tight bodice the dress fell in folds to a hem that almost brushed the floor. The three-quarter-length bell-shaped sleeves were decorated with bows and revealed an under sleeve ending in a tight cuff.

Delighted at his compliment, she did a little twirl and said, 'You don't look so bad yourself.'

Jim wore a black frock coat over a striped waist-coat, cut low to reveal his white shirt with a yellow cravat tied neatly at the neck. Dark grey trousers came tight to the top of his highly polished black shoes. He acknowledged her praise with a smile and slight bow.

'Then we are ready for off,' he said.

As if she had known just the moment, Mrs Dodsworth appeared then from the kitchen. 'You make a right handsome couple,' she commented. 'Enjoy yourselves. I may come across you in the crowd.'

They hadn't far to walk to the village green where they found crowds of people reclining on the grass, sitting on chairs, standing or strolling about. Children raced round seeking places to play or jealously guarding those areas on which they had made a claim, or pestered their mothers and fathers for an ice cream from the cart where the owner, thankful it was a warm sunny day, was doing a brisk trade. The buzz of conversation was in the air but it was hushed so as not to intrude on the sound of bat on ball, or the calls of the batsmen making decisions about whether to run or not, or the appeals of the fielders desperate to see an opponent departing for the makeshift pavilion – an area designated by benches.

'Someone's done well to scythe the wicket as close as that,' commented Jim, admiring the skill that had gone into its preparation.

'Do you play cricket?' Betsy asked.

'I have done, but only occasionally. Moving around, as I have been, I've not had the chance to play regularly.'

They strolled around the green, watching some of the play unfold, but were more interested in each other.

'You seem to be well known around here,' commented Betsy after he had accepted greetings or exchanged banter with villagers, miners and railway men up from Pickering for the day.

'My job means I have to mix. It cuts across

everyone engaged in getting ironstone to the furnaces of Teesside and Durham as quickly and cheaply as possible.'

'And that's why you're looking into expanding the railway?'

'Aye, but it means we'll have to ...' Jim broke off and said with a laugh, 'We're here to enjoy ourselves, not talk about my job!'

She grinned. 'Sorry.'

'Oh, don't be. It's flattering that you are interested.'

'My interest shall be resumed another time.'

'I hope so. Come on, let's get some home-made lemonade from Mrs Rafferty's stall over there.' He automatically took Betsy's hand as he led the way around the field. She did not object but matched her pace to his. After purchasing two glasses they moved to one side of the stall to allow other customers access. They watched the cricket and exchanged their own comments among those thrown by the spectators at the cricketers out in the middle, endeavouring to put in a match-winning innings or bowling performance that would still all the shouts of derision.

Betsy cast her eyes over the colourful dresses of the women, many brought out for this special day; few ladies had left their best wear at home. For the men it was different because those who were due on the next shift at the mines were dressed in their working clothes: collarless shirts buttoned down the front and with sleeves rolled up to the elbows, thick trousers tucked at their calves into socks, their feet in stout leather working boots and flat caps on their heads. In contrast, those not due at the workings wore dark brown or grey tweed suits, trousers tapering to the tops of their black shoes. Some wore waistcoats, patterned or plain, and most had white shirts worn with a bow-tie. When they were not at work they chose to wear brown felt, low-crowned hats.

The village pub, The Crown, was crowded. Its customers spilled out with beer glasses in hand to watch the cricket a while then return for a refill, minds more on the contents of their glasses than the sport — unless eyeing the girls who constantly strolled past was their preferred game. Flirtatious shouts made the girls blush, laugh, or offer bold remarks in return.

The Rosedale Brass Band and the Blue Ribbon Band provided music in turn, each managing also to find time to partake of the gargantuan tea that was spread across several tables around the field, with all the mouth-watering sandwiches and cakes provided voluntarily by the village people and some from outlying farms.

When the word went round that Rosedale wanted ten to win with their last batsmen at the wicket, the crowd swelled around the boundary. Rosedale and Wrelton followers shouted with equal enthusiasm for their respective players, but as the bowler set off on his run a deathly hush settled over all — to explode in a cacophony of sound as the ball was played or missed. The tension heightened with each ball, each run, until it reached fever pitch when only two runs more were needed to ensure victory. Four balls that the batsman missed; four balls that failed to hit the stumps. Then bat struck ball and the batsmen bounded down the wicket: one ... two ... The sound exploded; whoops of triumph or dejected moans. Everyone agreed that it had been a fitting end to what was proving to be a grand celebratory day. That day continued with further music and the consumption of more beer, tea and food as people mingled, exchanging news and light-hearted banter.

After a rest from playing, the Rosedale Brass Band started the dancing off and soon the green was a swirl of colour. With laughter on their lips from the joy of being together, Jim and Betsy moved smoothly into step to match the other dancers and soon were lost in happy intimacy.

When Jim ventured to kiss her at Mrs Dodsworth's door, Betsy's heart soared. She felt a great desire to beg him not to leave. Her head was light as she went quietly to her bedroom. It was only as she undressed that she realised he had made no suggestion that they should meet tomorrow. The reason why was revealed when she came into the kitchen the next morning.

'Just right, lass. The tea's mashed and the bacon's sizzling. Sit thisen down.' Mrs Dodsworth continued breezily, 'There's a letter for you on the table. I found it under the door when I came down this morning.'

Curious, Betsy picked up the envelope as she sat down. Who could be writing to her? She slit the envelope open with a knife and withdrew a sheet of paper. Her eyes sped over the words.

Dear Betsy,

I told you I was to be in Rosedale all this week but my instructions were changed early yesterday before the celebrations started. I must be away before sunrise on my way to Middlesbrough from where I will be going to Sunderland and Newcastle. I will be away at least two weeks, maybe more. I did not tell you this yesterday for fear of spoiling our day together. May I say it was a day I enjoyed very much, and I hope you will permit me to see you when I return?

Yours affectionately,
Jim

Betsy's heart sank. Her joy had been boosted by the knowledge that she would have Jim's company here for a whole week. Now there was a blank space of time awaiting her. Her eyes started to dampen with disappointment.

Mrs Dodsworth, bending over the pan of bacon, sensed something was wrong. She straightened up and turned to face Betsy. 'What is it, lass?'

'Jim is going away. In fact, he'll have gone already. He'll be away for two weeks – maybe longer.'

'But he'll be coming back?' Mrs Dodsworth tried to comfort her.

'Yes. But is this what it will always be like – him coming and going?' Tears were threatening.

'Ah, lass, don't take on. We all have disappointments to face.'

Betsy tightened her lips; she knew Mrs Dodsworth

was right but that did not ease her disenchantment or answer the question that had recently occurred to her — what would happen when Jim's job for the Rosedale Mining Company was finished?

5

During the weeks leading up to the race meeting on the Town Moor, the new friendship between the Addisons and the Jordans prospered.

George became a member of the Frobisher Club on Theodore's recommendation to the committee. He became a popular associate, and on the back of that purchased a vacant building on The Quay from one of the other members who was looking to raise capital to invest in his business. He and Mark worked hard to get everything established before the arrival of the *Adventurer*. In that they were helped by Theodore and Robert who, through their recommendations of who best to deal with, greatly assisted in the settling-in period.

The two families gathered on The Quay to greet the arrival of the Hull vessel. Word had got round about her arrival and George was gratified by the number of Newcastle people from all stations of life who turned out to greet her; a new ship to be based in the town deserved a proper welcome.

With the completion of the stables at Cantonville Hall, Adele kept Robert to his promise to introduce her to a horse dealer based in the Tyne Valley near Hexham. He needed no persuasion to do her this service and, two days later, having made the appointment, he drove her to the stables, accompanied by Mark and Zelda who were not to be left out. They were joined there by Mr and Mrs Jordan; after all, there would be purchases to be approved.

Ten animals were paraded for them. Adele felt no hesitation. She immediately fell in love with a chestnut mare whose empathy with her was displayed by its gentle nuzzle against her shoulder when Adele came close. Mark took a little longer to make his choice but eventually fell in with Zelda's suggestion. The arrival of two new horses in the renovated stables of Cantonville Hall set the seal on the Jordans' new residency on Tyneside.

They also gave the four young people an excuse to spend more time together. As a foursome they could present the impression of acting as each other's chaperones; there was no other way if they were to ride. But Robert was not going to let his relationship with Adele be anything but open, so following the etiquette of the day he sought permission from Mr Jordan 'to call on his daughter'. His request met with approval from both her parents. Not one to lag behind, Mark sought similar approval for his friendship with Zelda and duly received approval from her parents. The two families had been brought even closer together and a stable future that could augur well for both firms was anticipated by both Theodore and George.

'There is a special dinner held in the Assembly

Rooms on the evening prior to the racing – I've booked tickets for us all,' Theodore announced a week before the meeting. 'It will give you the opportunity of meeting my sister Grace and her husband, Morgan Granton. They live in Newcastle but have been in London on business since you arrived. I know they will be here for the races, they never miss them.'

'We look forward to meeting them,' said George, and added, 'What does your brother-in-law do?'

'He has an export-import business. Small in its way, but that is how he likes it. A competent staff enables him to be away from Newcastle whenever he chooses.'

George and Paula took to Grace immediately, seeing in her the generous, amiable nature of her brother, but they were not so struck by her husband. He was friendly enough – at times a little too boisterous, at others somewhat withdrawn – but with an underlying nervousness that made George wonder if all was perhaps not well in his business. Morgan got on well with the younger folk, though George suspected this was a forced bonhomie, as if he were trying to obliterate something from a troubled mind. George realised it was not his place to comment or question so kept his feelings to himself, except later in the privacy of their bedroom when he mentioned them to Paula, and found her assessment corresponded with his.

'I can't say I liked him,' she concluded. 'Though I don't want to say it, there was something not quite genuine about him. I just couldn't put my finger on what it was exactly.'

They were all together each day of the meeting, enjoying every aspect of it. The Jordans, although they had attended colourful race meetings in Yorkshire, each with its own individual atmosphere, admitted they had never experienced anything like the last Saturday in June, the day of the Northumberland Plate. The crowd was bigger and brighter and buzzed louder with enjoyment as people were determined to make the most of their outing and retain special memories of this particular day for a whole year.

The crowd moved in waves of colour, ebbing and flowing, turning and twisting, stopping to talk or to make purchases from those crying their wares: 'Biscuits from my basket!' 'Ballads for sale!' 'Chestnuts! Chestnuts! Get the best 'ere!' The general discord competed with the sweet and mellow tones of Northumberland bagpipes.

'May I say, you outshine any of the ladies here,' said Robert quietly in Adele's ear, having cast an admiring gaze over her light blue gabardine dress worn over a medium-sized crinoline, bell-shaped from her waist to her ankles. Her three-quarter-length beautifully fitted red coat had a high neck and tight sleeves that allowed trimmings of white lace to peep out at her wrists. A small red velvet hat, perched cheekily on her head, revealed hair cut short to her neck.

'Thank you,' she replied graciously. 'This is fun,' she added, eyes sparkling with delight to see the activity all around her. She had insisted on walking through the crowd to the special enclosure for those wanting more space and privacy. 'Sweetmeats!' She headed for a stall set out with all manner of colourful, tempting sweets. Her eyes moved swiftly from one to the other and then, to the delight of the buxom woman behind the stall, Adele chose her recommendation and added two more of her own choosing. Zelda had already made her selection. With purchases made, they all set off in a bright mood; they paused to listen to the betting and, once they had joined their parents, discussed the entries for each race and made their choices. Some lost; others had seen their bets prosper. Excitement was high by the time of the Northumberland Plate.

'Come on, Uncle Morgan,' cried Robert jocularly. 'You can make up your losses on this race.'

'Of course I can,' replied his uncle, feigning a positive ring in his voice. 'Gypsy Queen for certain.'

'You think so?' said Robert. 'What about Flyer? With a name like that, it must win.'

'No,' said Adele firmly. 'Proud King it must be.'

They approached the man who had taken their bets throughout the afternoon. 'Here to line my pockets again?' he teased them with a broad, friendly smile.

'To line ours,' returned Morgan, with nervous laughter.

'You don't sound so sure, sir?'

Morgan set his face determinedly. 'Oh, I'm sure. Gypsy Queen.'

'Nice horse, sir. Good jockey up,' replied the man as he took the bet.

Morgan turned to Robert and Adele. 'There, I told you! Gypsy Queen it is.'

Adele shook her head. 'No. It must be Proud King.'

'Flyer for me,' said Robert, deliberately keeping to his selection so that there would be competition between them, though he did not reveal that was the reason behind the choice.

Hooves pounded the turf; jockeys pressed their mounts harder. The crowd, caught up in the excitement of the race, was vocal in urging its favourites on. Adele and Robert saw their horses in the lead when they reached the last furlong. Adele's voice rose in excitement, there was laughter in her eyes, she shook her arms as if that would spur her jockey on to greater effort. It seemed as if he must have known what she wanted: at the winning post her horse had its nose just in front of Robert's.

She cheered loudly. Her joy was infectious and he could do no other than laugh with her. Laughter was still on their lips and in their eyes as they turned to tease Uncle Morgan, but they held back when they saw the cloud of dark disappointment on his face. This was not the moment to be frivolous with him.

The whole party basked in the joy of those who had won. It seemed the ladies had a keener eye for a winner as Zelda had chosen the same horse as Adele and the mothers had approved their daughters' choice. Only Morgan was glum, though he did not do a bad job of disguising his displeasure once he had got over his initial disappointment.

Not far away Jim Fenwick hurried away from the position he had taken up near the winning post, collected his winnings, retrieved his horse and left Newcastle to ride south.

When Betsy and her father arrived in Rosedale near the end of June, she lost no time in enquiring if Mrs Dodsworth had seen Jim.

'No, lass, I haven't.'

'But he said he would be back in two weeks and he's been gone three,' she exclaimed in disappointment.

'I expect he'll arrive any day.' Mrs Dodsworth tried to look on the bright side.

'Maybe.' But Betsy's tone carried a desultory note.

Her father tried to lift her spirits during the next three days, grasping at the fact that their sales had been better than expected and pointing out that, if rumours were proved true about new developments in the dale, their future looked bright indeed.

The days had slipped into the first week of July when a voice interrupted Betsy's concentration as she arranged a jet necklace for display in the village hall. 'I'll take that, for my best girl.'

'Jim!' She looked up, eyes ablaze with delight. He held out his arms and she fell into them, feeling a thrill run through her as he hugged her tight. She looked up at him with an eagerness that could not be disguised. Thankful that they were the only ones in the hall, he kissed her and she let all the disappointment of the last days and weeks drain away.

'Where have you been?' she asked. 'I expected to see you during my last visit.'

'Work kept me away longer than I expected,' he replied, but offered no further explanation.

'Ah, well, you're back now,' she said contentedly.

'Aye, but I may not see as much of you here as I'd hoped. Approval's been given to make the rail link into Rosedale. That's going to be a big job: having to lay the line up the hillside from Ingleby and installing all the necessary haulage gear. And while I'm overseeing that, there will be continued shipments of ore through Pickering to see to as well. I'm going to be very busy with little time to escape, but I'll try.'

She pouted but he stopped her from protesting further.

'The bosses are always right and we mere mortals must jump to their command.'

Their conversation was interrupted by the sound of footsteps approaching the hall.

'Hello, Jim,' cried Sam, enthusiastically shaking his hand. 'Now at last I might see a smile on my daughter's face.'

'If I can help with that, I will.' Jim smiled at him.

'You can start right now.' Sam glanced at his daughter. 'Off with you, lass, I'll manage here for an hour.'

Betsy grabbed her shawl and swung it round her shoulders, eager for the hour's freedom. 'Come on, we'll walk and talk,' she said to Jim, starting for the door.

Jim picked up the necklace, whispering to Sam as he did so, 'Pay you when we get back.'

He nodded knowingly and smiled.

Jim slipped the necklace into his pocket and hurried after Betsy.

Strange how things work out, Sam thought as he watched them leave; Betsy had taken a special liking to that necklace when he had bought it from one of the workshops in Whitby.

Pleased to have him back with her, Betsy slipped her arm under Jim's. 'Which way?' she asked.

'Lastingham track,' he said. 'I could do with looking the first part over.'

'Hey, you're with me. No work for just one hour.' She gave him no chance to reply but started to impart all the news from Whitby.

They walked for half an hour and then started to retrace their steps. After a quarter of an hour they stopped, hearing a horse approaching from behind, and moved to one side of the track. The rider was a young man who was handling his mount well. He brought it to a halt in front of them and held it steady.

'Hello, Jim.'

'Good day, Alex,' said Jim, and seeing the man glance at Betsy, introduced them.

'Pleased to meet you, miss. I have seen you in the dale occasionally when I've been home.'

'Alex comes from Rosedale but works on the railway in Pickering. That's how we met,' explained Jim.

Betsy acknowledged Alex with a smile.

'Better be on my way,' he said, but added, looking at Jim, 'we were far away when I last saw you. You were collecting your winnings at the end of the Northumberland Plate last Saturday!' He caught Jim's expression then but interpreted it wrongly. 'Ah, unofficial time off, I see. It's all right, Jim, mum's the word.' With that he set his horse off in the direction of the village.

'What did he mean by that?' demanded Betsy, her face dark with indignation. 'You pretended you were at work but were at the races in Newcastle?'

'Betsy, I . . .' Jim fumbled for words.

'You deceived me, Jim Fenwick. Deceived me!'

'I . . .'

'Don't look for excuses,' she stormed, fire in her eyes. 'You told me you would soon be back, but you had no intention of it at all! Instead you were gallivanting off to Newcastle, enjoying yourself. What other delights did you experience while you were away?' She started away from him but he grabbed her by the arm and pulled her back to face him.

'The answer to that is none, though I'll not deny that I went to the races.'

'How do I know you are telling me the truth? How could I *ever* know in the future? Well, that doesn't matter because there'll be no future for us!' Tears came to Betsy's eyes but she fought them. She was not going to weaken in front of him. She tried to pull away but he held her tight with one hand while he fished in his pocket with the other and pulled out the necklace.

102

'A token for your forgiveness?' he said.

'Keep it,' she snapped, 'it would always be a reminder of your deceit. Give it to one of your other girls. No doubt there are plenty I don't know about!' She tore herself free from his grip and strode back towards the village.

Jim let her go then followed thoughtfully, making no attempt to catch her up. He went straight to the hall.

'I've called to pay for the necklace, Mr Palmer,' he said pleasantly.

'Betsy not with you?' Sam asked with a little surprise.

'She wanted something from Mrs Dodsworth's,' said Jim. Not wanting to answer any more questions, he handed over the money and said, 'I must be away. Can't be late for my next appointment.' He hurried from the hall, leaving the shrewd Sam surmising that something had gone wrong on the walk though he knew he would not enquire; Betsy would tell him if she wanted him to know. This was one of those times when he dearly wished he still had a wife and Betsy a mother.

They continued to visit Rosedale. With the influx of workers connected with the laying of the new line, preparing to extend mining operation as well as building more houses, they saw their profits soar. But they only caught glimpses of Jim Fenwick from then on and Betsy showed no desire to make any further contact with him.

As the year wore on the Jordan family became more and more established in Newcastle society.

103

George attracted business by his open and likeable personality as well as his efficiency in dealing with customers. With prospects looking good, he ordered the building of a new ship at one of the yards along the Tyne. To ease his present commitments he hired another vessel so he was able to accommodate Theodore's shipments and obligingly fitted in Morgan's cargoes for London too, small though they were.

Whenever time permitted, Robert arranged to go riding with Adele, always openly accompanied by Zelda and Mark – at least until they were away from the usual tracks, where by unspoken arrangement they would separate before coming together at a prearranged rendezvous and time so that they could return as a foursome. And it was as a foursome that they attended fairs, the theatre, readings and lectures, and on occasion accompanied their parents to soirées, dinners and balls.

'Are you happy about Robert and Zelda spending so much time with Adele and Mark?' Emily asked cautiously one night as she and Theodore were preparing for bed.

'Yes,' he replied, 'though I suspect you are looking beyond a mere friendship?'

'I suppose I am.'

'Well, *I* think both couples are well matched.'

'So do I, and if all works out as we hope it will certainly save us a great deal of hard work, searching for other parties we think suitable.'

He came to her, placed his hands on her waist and looked lovingly into her eyes. 'It worked well for us.'

'We must have had very discerning parents.'

He smiled. 'We must. But let our children make their own choices.'

'I think they already have.'

Theodore saw Robert working with more enthusiasm. Recognising his son's desire to take on more responsibility as a sign that he was looking to the future, he allowed him to do so. Some of those responsibilities led to his dealing with Mark who now held a similar position in his father's operations in Newcastle. It pleased both fathers that their sons got on so well, not only at work but socially too.

'We'll have to be thinking about where we are going to spend Christmas,' said Paula one evening at dinner, 'though it will depend on your commitments, George.'

'They can be arranged depending on where you want to be, here or in Hull,' he replied.

No immediate reply came from anyone so Paula added an observation. 'People make more of New Year here than Christmas, and you are used to our Christmases in Hull.'

'I'll miss our usual Christmas celebrations if we stay here,' said Mark tentatively.

'We could have the same celebrations here and invite the Addisons,' suggested Paula.

'Educate them about a Yorkshire Christmas?' Mark's attitude brightened at the thought of being in the company of Zelda for the celebrations.

'What about you, Adele?' asked her mother.

She had been considering the idea. She would miss celebrating with her friends in Hull, especially Philip Bowen, son of the owner of a large estate near Redbourne in North Lincolnshire, who had been particularly attentive last Christmas. As a result, Adele had not at first been particularly keen on moving to Newcastle and the Tyne Valley, though the move had been better than expected; Robert Addison had given her a new perspective on the area. The two men were on her mind now. Christmas in the company of Robert promised something different, but Philip still drew her and Hull was steeped in the traditions she had known since childhood. Would she feel her youth was at an end if they stayed for Christmas at Cantonville Hall?

'You are being very thoughtful about it.' Paula's words asked for her decision.

'Oh, I don't know.' Adele grimaced then added quickly, 'I'll do whatever you and Papa want to do.'

Paula glanced at George. 'There you are. It's your decision.'

Expecting this, he had been weighing things up. He guessed what was running through Adele's mind: Philip or Robert? He liked them both but saw greater advantage if Robert became a family member – a merchant as opposed to a landowner. A future union between ship owner and merchant would seem to promise more.

'We'll stay here,' he said firmly, without elaborating on the reason behind his decision.

'That's settled then. We'll invite them all to

spend Christmas Day with us,' said Paula. 'I'll send an invitation at the appropriate time.'

Adele had felt her heart sink a little at her father's announcement. Philip was a fine dancer, better than Robert, and she loved dancing ... but it was no good dwelling on thoughts of Christmas in Hull. Her father had made his decision. She would make light of the situation and enjoy herself.

But she couldn't wait until the invitation had been formally made to the Addisons. A day after the discussion about Christmas, when she and Robert had left their horses and had parted from Mark and Zelda to stroll by the tree-lined river, she said, 'I have news, but you must keep it to yourself until the proper invitation is received.' She stopped, teasingly, holding back the information.

'Come on,' he prompted. 'What is it?' He liked her in this mood; behind her teasing he always saw a bubbling enjoyment of life.

'Ah, now, what do I get if I tell you?' Her eyes flashed an invitation.

'Do you want payment in advance?'

She hesitated over her reply, looking thoughtful.

'Does it need that much consideration?' he said.

'Well, a girl must be careful what she says,' she pondered, glancing coyly at him. She nodded slowly. 'I think payment in advance would be acceptable.'

He kissed her on the cheek. 'Now I will have your news.'

'Well,' she started, only to pause and purse her lips before she said, 'we are going to stay here for Christmas.'

For one brief moment the significance of her words did not register with him and then, when the full meaning struck, his face lit up in a broad smile and there was laughter in his eyes. 'Tell me more. I've been wondering what you would be doing at Christmas. I thought you might be going back to Yorkshire though I hoped not.' He took her hand and they strolled on.

'Mother brought up the question at dinner last night and the decision was made. Don't say anything until after the formal invitation, but she is asking you to spend Christmas Day with us. We thought you made more of New Year up here whereas we make more of Christmas in Yorkshire. So you might like to share a Yorkshire Christmas with us.'

'Splendid!' he said with great enthusiasm. 'At the right moment I will suggest we introduce you to a Tyneside New Year. We usually attend the New Year's Eve Ball in the Assembly Rooms.'

'I'll look forward to that,' said Adele, casting aside any doubt that lingered; maybe Christmas at Cantonville wouldn't be so bad now there was the added attraction of New Year with the Addisons.

When she received the invitation from Paula, Emily's family immediately approved her decision to accept it.

After letting a few moments pass Robert said, 'If we are going to the Jordans' for Christmas, should we not ask them for New Year?'

'Oh, yes, do let's,' put in Zelda.

Theodore, sitting back in his chair, caught

Emily's quick glance and slight nod of approval. She knew what he was going to suggest.

'I think it might be a good idea for the Jordans to stay with us in the town house. We will be closer to the celebrations in Newcastle and not have to contend with snow if the weather is against us. And you young ones will be handy for attending the New Year's Eve Ball in the Assembly Rooms. There is a special celebration at the Frobisher Club for members and their wives – I will suggest Mr and Mrs Jordan accompany us there before we join you at the Ball.'

'You've had this in mind all the time?' said Robert.

'Your mother and I have, but could not suggest it until we knew if the Jordans were going to Yorkshire. Now, with this invitation, we can.'

Emily sent her own invitation along with her reply, and by return received Paula's acceptance. The Jordans would spend New Year with the Addisons at their town house in Newcastle.

Some days later Theodore called Robert into his office.

'I have to go to Edinburgh for a few days, leaving by train the day after tomorrow. There is the prospect of more business from a firm there.' He noted his son's enquiring look. 'I don't want to say any more at this stage in case it is something we don't want to be part of.'

'Sounds illegal,' he joked.

His father saw that his observation was delivered lightly and replied jocularly, 'Could be.' Then he added quickly, 'Seriously, I suggest we both stay in the town house tomorrow night; it will easier for me to catch the train and I suggest you remain there in town until I return. I think you should be close to the office as you will be in sole charge while I'm away.'

'Yes, sir. Does Mother know of this arrangement?'

'Yes. She'll be seeing to the packing of some clothes for you.'

'Anything else I should know?' Robert was already looking forward to shouldering the new responsibility that was being offered to him.

'We are expecting the Mason consignment to arrive tomorrow, and the Copland goods should be coming in for onward shipment. Check with Mark when they will be doing that.'

'Very well, Father.'

'And, of course, deal with any new business that comes our way.'

Two days later father and son left the town house at seven in the morning in a hired cab.

'I must go to the office, Robert. I left some papers there that I might need.'

'Don't miss your train.'

'I won't. I know this cabbie – I've instructed him. He'll get me there on time.'

Reaching the office Theodore hurried to his desk and in a matter of moments emerged, stuffing some papers into his brief-bag.

Robert bade his father goodbye, saw the cab away and returned to his own desk. He sat down with a glow of satisfaction; he was in charge, the success of the firm rested in his hands. This was what it would be like later in life when his father resigned to enjoy a well-earned retirement, leaving him to run the business. He knew he had something to live up to, to emulate his father's success, but did not lack for confidence, something he was sure he had inherited from his father and which had been strengthened by his education. Besides that there was his determination to be a success for Adele's sake; so that he could provide for her in the way he wanted and show that his love for her was boundless.

He broke his reverie. There were things to be done. He pushed himself from his chair. He would check the two consignments his father had mentioned. Knowing the relevant files would be on Theodore's desk, he went to get them. As he picked them up he noticed some keys on the floor. He recalled his father's haste; he must have dropped them in his rush, probably when he was pushing the papers into his brief-bag, and hadn't noticed. Robert was about to put them on the desk but then paused and looked hard at them. What secrets did they hide? Because secrets there must be if they fitted the drawer in his father's desk that was always kept locked.

Robert was curious. Keys in hand, he started to bend down towards the drawer. Then he straightened up, frowning. He had no right to pry; no right to distrust his own father. But distrust wasn't the motive, was it? He was merely curious, or at least that was what he was telling himself. Then he tried to convince himself: if it concerned the firm he had a right to know, and what if something related to the contents of that drawer arose while his father was away . . .

Without further thought Robert bent, thrust the key into the lock and pulled the drawer open. He saw two small note-books. If there had been anything else there it must have been the papers he had seen his father stuffing into his brief-bag. He closed the drawer and took the two note-books to his own desk where he sat down and opened the first one a little tentatively.

A list of figures in his father's writing, each dated in an accompanying column, met his gaze; sums of money without any other explanation. He flicked through the pages. There was no consistency about the entries except that they reflected the passing of the months but with no regular payments within each month. Realising he had missed the first page, he turned to it quickly. Maybe it would offer a clue. All he saw was the word 'Deposits', with not a mention of where they had been made. He picked up the second book; its first page told him it contained 'Withdrawals'. It was set out in the same way as the other but again showed no consistency, and when he tried to compare the entries and dates in the two books there was no relationship that he could see except that in some months there had been both deposits and withdrawals for the same amounts, though there was nothing else to relate them.

Robert was puzzled. He sat there staring at the books. What did they mean? What had his father been doing? He was beginning to think they could only relate to cash transactions paid directly to Theodore, but if so why hadn't they gone into the firm's accounts? He pushed himself from his chair and went thoughtfully to the chief clerk's office.

'Watson, I believe I'm right in saying that all cash transactions would be entered in our accounts monthly, along with any other method of payment?'

'Oh, yes, sir.'

'And the same with any cash payments?'

'Yes, sir.' He hesitated a moment. 'I do put a small c against cash transactions, sir,' he added a little nervously. 'It is purely for my own convenience whenever I'm striking a balance. I hope that is all right, sir?'

'Of course it is, Watson.' The clerk wouldn't have posed this question if his father hadn't condoned the method. 'In fact your system might help me. May I take the appropriate ledgers with me?'

'Of course, sir.' Relieved that young Mr Addison was not questioning his practice, Watson agreed quickly.

Robert returned to his office, laid the ledgers out and began to compare the cash entries in them with those in the two note-books. Nothing tallied. He sank back in his chair, trying to still his racing thoughts.

What had his father been doing? It seemed he must have been receiving and spending cash that was not appearing in the firm's books. Why? Where had the cash come from? The most likely answer to that was from cash payments which his father had not passed on to Watson. The withdrawal entries might only be a record of his father's disposal of the money and not to any one account. But where was the money, if indeed it still existed and had not been spent? Or was his father using cash for illegal, inappropriate or illicit activities?

Robert bit his lip. What exactly had he unearthed? What was his father engaged in? His mind was awhirl but of one thing he felt certain: his father was appropriating what was rightly the firm's money. Now he realised he was presented with a dilemma – did he confront his father, and if he did, what would he uncover next? What disgrace might follow? How many lives would be affected? Certainly his whole family's. Friends would turn away from a disgraced man. The Jordans. Oh, no . . .! Adele! How would he be able to face her when his own father's shameful secret became public? He need not disclose what he suspected, of course, but could he live with the knowledge that people who had backed his father, people who had put money into the firm, were not getting their just returns? On the other hand, could he unmask his own father as a thief?

It was a problem he must live with until he was sure he had made the right decision.

6

Robert stared thoughtfully out of the window of his office at the ships lining The Quay. The port was thriving and with it the firm of Addison & Son. Business was prospering while Theodore was away. Normally Robert would have been looking forward to making a report about their progress when his father returned, but as yet he had no idea when that might be. After a week Theodore's absence was beginning to trouble him. This was the longest his father had ever been away from home – what was he doing, and had it anything to do with those two note-books that were now safely locked away again in the drawer of his father's desk?

They had haunted Robert since he had examined them. How he wished he hadn't let curiosity get the better of him; there was something to be said for blissful ignorance. No matter how he'd tried to thrust them to the back of his mind and then into oblivion, he could not. How he wished he had someone to consult who could help him from his dilemma, but he could not voice what he had discovered to anyone. And what course of action should he follow on his father's return?

That decision faced him mid-afternoon two days later when, to the accompaniment of a stiff wind lashing Newcastle with rain, his father burst into the office, beating water off his frock coat.

'Father!' Robert jumped up from his chair and came around his desk. 'You're soaked. Let me help you out of your coat.'

'Horrible out there.' Theodore grimaced as he dropped his brief-bag on the floor, swept his top hat from his head and allowed his son to help him.

'I hope your journey hasn't been too bad,' said Robert, taking the soaked garment and hanging it on the coat-stand in a corner near the door.

'It wasn't, apart from the rain.'

'And Edinburgh – I trust all went well there?' said Robert, his heart beating a little faster at the query.

'It did, but I didn't get the business I expected, though there is hope for the future.'

His father offered no more information but remained vague and offered no opening for Robert to put any further questions to him. He was on the point of casually probing but thought better of it.

Instead, he turned to his desk, opened a drawer and took out the two keys. 'I found these on the floor just after you had gone. I think you must have dropped them in your rush.'

'Oh! Thank you. I hadn't realised.' His father took the keys and slipped them into his pocket without further comment. Then he dropped into a chair opposite his son as Robert sat down again.

'How is your mother?'

'She is well ... looking forward to your return.

As you know, I was staying in town but I went out to see her on a couple of occasions.'

'And your sister?'

Robert smiled. 'In good spirits, as usual.'

'The Jordans?'

'I've only seen Mark, and that's chiefly been on business matters, but he assured me the family are well. The *Adventurer* should be arriving with a cargo of Spanish wine tomorrow – you remember we had samples from her previous voyage and decided to take a shipment? I passed those on to potential customers and now have sufficient orders to dispose of the whole cargo.'

'Good! Well done.'

'And I have a cargo of glass and pottery in the warehouse that Mark will ship out to Holland as soon as the *Adventurer* is ready to sail again.'

'Excellent. You two seem to work well together.'

'He's easy to get on with.'

Their talk continued, bringing Theo up to date. Everything was so normal that Robert began to wonder if his imagination had run riot. Yet still his father's failure to elaborate on his visit to Edinburgh left nagging doubts. Robert wondered if his mother knew about it. If it was business it seemed hardly likely she would, but it was possible she was in her husband's confidence. Robert could hardly ask her, it wouldn't be right, and besides he might unearth something that would be better left buried. Fear and doubt began to cloud his mind.

Robert himself was not aware that his attitude to Adele was affected by his worries, but she herself sensed that his flirtation with her had lost some of its former sparkle and began to wonder if his feelings towards her were cooling. He appeared still to enjoy their time together but at times she suspected he used the excuse of work to avoid her company. This led her to examine her own feelings for him. She had felt an instant liking for him on their first meeting, and as the weeks and months passed by, his charm, politeness, concern and warmth had drawn her to him more and more so that she was always looking forward to their next meeting. But now, having to face what might be described as a hiatus in their relationship, a feeling of despondency sometimes took her over, especially alone in the solitude of her room. One night tears came to her eyes as she realised a real spark of love for Robert Addison had been kindled in her. But was that love futile? If so then their Christmas and New Year celebrations were certainly not going to live up to her expectations.

Two days later her mother received a letter which made Adele wonder if, at this precise moment, fate was toying with her.

Paula read the letter at the breakfast table.

Dear Mrs Jordan,
I hope you will not think it forward of me to write to you with a request. Philip and I will be journeying north to Berwick-on-Tweed to spend Christmas and New Year with my brother. We are travelling in our own coach in order to visit friends on the way and see something of the countryside. On the 16th we

will be passing very close to you. Would it be convenient if we called on you mid-morning of that day after our overnight stay in Durham to renew our acquaintance for a short while?

I remain yours in friendship,
Philomena Bowen

Paula glanced around the table to convey its contents and said, 'I will reply immediately and say we will be delighted to see them.'

Adele tensed as her mother read out the letter. Philip coming here! Was her heart really racing because she would be seeing him again, or was it because she was being forced into making the comparison between Philip and Robert, which she knew was inevitable no matter how hard she tried to resist it?

When she woke on the sixteenth she felt an excited fluttering in her heart. As mid-morning approached, her stomach tightened in anticipation of seeing Philip again.

'Adele, you've been in and out of this room so many times it is making me nervous,' said Paula. 'Do sit still.'

Adele tightened her lips and did as she was told, sitting on a high-backed chair by the window from which she could see the drive. She anxiously clasped and reclasped her fingers, staring out of the window and wondering how she might be affected by seeing Philip again.

Several long minutes passed and then she jumped to her feet, shouting, 'They're here!' and turned to rush for the door.

'Adele!' Her mother's stern voice brought her up short. 'Please conduct yourself with the decorum befitting a young lady of your age and upbringing.'

She looked sheepish as she muttered, with a penitent dip of her head, 'Sorry, Mama.'

'Very well, then let us go together to meet them.'

Adele followed her mother sedately from the room after Paula had rung the bell to warn the two maids they were wanted in the hall.

Paula and Adele stepped out on to the terrace and stood at the top of the steps, watching a carriage drawn by four horses steadily approaching.

Almost before the coachman had pulled the horses to a halt, an under-groomsman sitting beside him jumped to the ground, moved briskly to the carriage door, opened it and positioned two folding steps ready for the passengers to alight, standing by ready to assist if required.

A tall young man stepped down from the coach and turned to assist the older lady he accompanied. She paused briefly at the top of the steps to adjust and straighten her dark pink dress worn over bell-shaped hoops that accentuated her wasp waist. Over the dress she wore a light brown, three-quarter-length jacket with attached cape and wide sleeves. A small pink bonnet was held in place by a scarlet ribbon tied under her chin.

The young man beside her wore the new style thigh-length sack coat which fitted loosely to reveal a dark blue patterned waistcoat beneath, worn over a white linen shirt with a yellow cravat tied neatly at the throat. His sand-coloured trousers came tight at the ankle to low-heeled brown shoes, matching his soft-crowned hat. He carried a light cane and held himself erect.

Adele's heart fluttered at the immediate impact Philip made as he matched his pace to his mother's, but held himself slightly behind so that she should present herself first. For some reason at that moment, Adele did not quite know why, she recalled how elegant he always looked in the saddle on the occasions she had visited Redbourne. She started, drawn out of her reverie by her mother moving down the steps to greet their guests.

'Mrs Bowen, welcome to our new home.'

'It is most kind of you to receive us for a few hours,' she replied. They kissed and then Mrs Bowen turned to Adele. 'Miss Jordan, I am pleased to meet you again.'

Adele made a small curtsey. 'And I you, Mrs Bowen.'

At the same time Philip, who had doffed his hat, was accepting Paula's greeting. As she rejoined Mrs Bowen to escort her to the house, Mrs Bowen said, 'Philip insisted we must call on you.'

'He did right,' Paula approved.

Adele, who was in the midst of greeting Philip with a sparkling smile, caught those words and commented quietly, for only him to hear, 'I would have been most disappointed if he hadn't.'

Philip smiled, took the hand she had proffered in welcome and raised it towards his lips as he said, 'It is my pleasure to see you again, Miss Jordan. I hope you have been enjoying good health and that you are settled and enjoying Tyneside?'

'So many questions in one sentence. But first, Mr Bowen, I recall that when you were at Redbourne we were on Christian name terms. I think that should continue here at Cantonville.'

'That pleases me, Mi—Adele. So, your answers to my questions?'

They followed their mothers at a leisurely pace.

'I have been in good health and still am. I am quite settled on Tyneside, having made up my mind to be so. It was no good doing otherwise. I like many aspects of life here but I do miss much of East Yorkshire, Hull, and ...' she added after a pause '... North Lincolnshire.'

'I am pleased to hear all those things, particularly the latter.'

Adele made no comment to this but said, 'How have you managed to find time to escort your mother to Berwick?'

'Ah, life has changed somewhat at Redbourne. You may recall that when we first met I was, at Father's insistence, working on the land so that I would know what it was like to do so. Now, having purchased more farms, he has appointed an agent and brought me alongside him in the capacity of landowner. He believes I should learn every aspect of land management and be able to put it to the best use when the time comes for me to take sole ownership.'

'I congratulate you. What about your three brothers? How do they feel about it?'

'They have always accepted that, as I am the eldest, I will inherit. But Father has made it clear that he has provided amply for them, on condition they carve out successful careers in whatever field they choose.'

'And you are happy with that?'

'Oh, yes. Redbourne is where my heart is and ...' he cast Adele a glance upon which all manner of connotations could be hung '... I hope whoever I marry will come to share my love for it.'

She diverted him from this delicate subject. 'Are any other members of your family joining you in Berwick?'

'Oh, yes. My uncle insisted that we all come, but my father, brothers, and all three sisters are going to travel by train. Mother wanted to visit friends and needed an escort, so here we are in most pleasant surroundings. And, of course, delightful company.'

Adele acknowledged his compliment with an inclination of her head.

The rest of the visit passed off pleasantly. Mrs Bowen was impressed with Cantonville Hall and the exquisite luncheon but, more than anything, she enjoyed her chat with Paula. Adele was pleased that the weather was fine for it meant she and Philip could escape the house and stroll in the garden which she knew would interest him. She remembered how kindly and attentively he had always behaved to her. He still did so and she liked that because it showed he enjoyed the relationship they shared and still thought well of her.

After their goodbyes, she and her mother watched the coach drive away. As they turned back into the house, Paula said, 'A most polite and attentive young man and not at all bad-looking. In fact, I would say verging on the handsome.'

Adele did not comment but that night as she lay in bed her mother's words came back to her. Had she been dropping a hint to her daughter because she had noticed that Robert's visits had not been as frequent lately and that he had been less attentive than usual? Such thoughts inevitably engendered comparisons. Adele could not deny that she had allowed deep feelings for Robert into her heart but his recent attitude had caused her concern. Yet at other times he was still the Robert who had touched her heart, the man she admired, someone who could set her pulses racing in anticipation of their next meeting. Which was the true Robert? Which one would influence the future? There was only one Robert with whom she could share her life. But now Philip had presented himself again and being with him had brought doubt into her mind about her future life remaining in Tyneside.

In Newcastle Robert sat staring at some papers on his desk but not really seeing them. His thoughts had turned again to those two note-books and the suspicions they had raised in his mind. His lips tightened in exasperation. How he wished his father had not dropped those keys, and he himself had not been tempted by curiosity and the lure of the locked drawer.

There were times, especially when he was with Adele, when these thoughts nearly faded away, but they had an insidious habit of leaving their mark on him. People interpreted this in different ways.

Adele saw it as a slight cooling in their relationship even though most of the time he was his old outgoing self. She hoped the Christmas and New Year celebrations would restore his spirits. His father wondered if the extra responsibility he'd thrust on his son had been too much – he would wait until January to reassess the situation, he'd decided. The festivities might help lighten Robert's attitude to his work. His mother worried that he might be ill, but she had no concrete evidence for this and thought she was probably fretting unnecessarily. His sister hardly noticed the change in him except on the odd occasion when he snapped at her, and then she thought something must have troubled him at work and dismissed the possibility of its being anything more serious.

The door to Robert's office opened and his father strode inside in his usual vigorous manner. 'Now, my boy, have you those figures for me?'

Figures? Robert started. Did his father know he had seen the two books? He tensed as if to defend himself against the tirade to follow and then realised he had reached the wrong conclusion. Earlier that day Theodore had requested a summary of the recent wine trade figures from him.

'Just about ready, Father,' he answered, relieved.

'Just about? Mr Felton will be here in ten minutes and you know full well I want to look them over before he comes.'

'Yes, Father.' Robert scrabbled at his papers. 'I've one more page to check and then I'll bring them to you.'

'See that you do.' His father made as if to leave then looked back. 'What's got into you?' It was a question that did not expect a reply, but it made Robert think. If his nagging worries about those note-books were leaving their mark in ways he hadn't realised, he had better pull himself together and forget them completely.

He picked up a pencil and concentrated on the figures his father wanted now, then he would be away to a ship at its moorings a hundred yards down The Quay, to check its manifest with the ship's captain and clear it for sailing.

Maybe if he threw himself more vigorously into his work and into his frequent outings with Adele, the troubling suspicions could be cast aside and he would return to his old untroubled state.

The four young friends had reached their usual place for going their separate ways.

'See you in an hour,' called Mark.

Robert raised his hand in acknowledgement and held his horse steady as Mark and Zelda rode away. Watching them go, he gave a little chuckle.

'What is it?' asked Adele lightly.

'I just wondered what our parents would think if they knew our chaperones had left us?'

Adele laughed as she gave her opinion. 'My mother would be horrified!'

Robert grinned. 'So would mine. Ah, well, what the eye doesn't see, the heart doesn't grieve over. Shall we ride?'

They put their horses into a walking pace.

'I like your new riding habit,' he commented.

'Thank you,' replied Adele, pleased that he had noticed it was new. 'A Christmas present from Mother and Father.'

'But it's not Christmas yet!'

'It's not far off and I couldn't wait to let you see it. It's a new style that the dressmaker said is all the rage in London.'

The navy blue tailored jacket with a high V-neckline was cut tight across her breasts, came into a slim-fitting waist, and had long, tight-fitting sleeves. The matching skirt, which reached the top of her low-heeled black boots, was full but easily manageable. A white necktie accentuated Adele's rosy complexion. She wore black leather gloves to match her low top hat and carried a short riding whip she would never use.

'It suits you. In fact, it is as adorable as you are,' he complimented her.

The flirtatious twinkle in Robert's eyes set her heart racing. This was the young man who had first attracted her. It was as if he had never changed. Maybe his feelings towards her hadn't been cooling. Maybe something outside their relationship had been troubling him and now that was in the past. She hoped so! And that Christmas and the New Year would help to maintain this buoyant mood in him.

'So I'm only as nice as my clothes?' She pouted as if she was hurt.

'Even if you wore the same clothes every day, they would become more and more beautiful in my eyes,' he declared gallantly.

'Hah! You would soon get tired of seeing the same dress.'

'Never!'

'And I would get tired of wearing it, and you may not like the change in me then.'

'Oh, I would, because I like the person who would be wearing the dress.'

'You flirt with me, Mr Addison,' she teased.

'Indeed I do, Miss Jordan,' he replied in the same formal tone, then added, his eyes sharpening with challenge, 'And you like me to.'

'And long may I go on liking it, no matter how our circumstances change.' She did not wait to hear his reply for she suddenly wondered if she had been too forward. Her horse responded immediately to a tap of her heels and was into gallop. 'Race you!' she shouted over her shoulder.

Taken unawares by her action, Robert sent his horse after hers, joyfully speculating about her vision of the future.

They galloped for a mile without Robert catching her. He only did so when the track became unsuitable for a gallop and they had to slow to a walking pace. A little further on they left the trail and took a path that they knew led to the riverbank. They pulled their mounts to a halt and sat quietly in their saddles, staring across the swirling waters of the Tyne, she wondering if he would make any reference to her last observation, he considering whether he should do so. In those moments Adele found herself speculating as to how Philip would have responded, and immediately chided herself for thinking about him now. Meanwhile her words, 'circumstances change', came to Robert's mind and he seemed to see again two note-books. They had changed his circumstances because he had let them; he had not been strong enough to reject them, no matter what they signified. He cursed himself for allowing such thoughts to intrude once again.

'We'll have snow before the day is out,' he said to break the lengthening silence.

Adele was taken aback by the blandness of his remark. 'You think so?' she asked coolly.

'Those clouds gathering in the west look ominous.'

She gave a little shrug of her shoulders, regretting the passing of their earlier rapport. 'You know the signs up here better than I do.'

'Before the day is finished there will be snow.' He took in her pained expression. 'You don't like snow?' he asked.

She saw a chance to lighten the atmosphere. 'Oh, yes. It is so pretty and can be such fun.'

'Yes, it can.' Enthusiasm crept back into his voice. 'We'll make the most of it over Christmas and New Year.'

She read, in the appropriate emphasis of certain words, that he was referring especially to themselves.

'We will,' she agreed, with a light in her eyes that showed him she had read his meaning. She would make sure it was a special time for them both. Hopefully, whatever had troubled Robert was at an end now. And they had the whole of the holiday to look forward to.

Robert's next question was designed to be light-hearted. 'So now you've had your Christmas present, do you expect any more?'

'Oh, I'll get one from Mark, and I think I can expect one by post from Victoria and one from my aunt, now they are back in this country.'

'Is that all?' he asked.

She looked thoughtful. 'Well, there is a certain gentleman, not too far away, who just might try to sway a poor girl's feelings towards him,' she said coyly.

'Ah, you've been flirting with him to that end?'

'Well, I supposed it was worth a try.'

'You think so?' Without waiting for her reply he asked, 'When are we coming to you?'

'I think Mama is writing to your mother with the final details. Probably right now.'

'I look forward to hearing them so I shall know when I will be with the girl with the most elegant riding habit.'

'Oh, you have seen one better than mine?' She assumed an expression of mock-disappointment.

'We'll see. There are a few days before Christmas yet,' he teased, putting his horse into a walk.

She watched him for a few moments. Oh, yes, Robert Addison had found a place in her heart. But, she wondered, if her heart were ever tested, would it be strong enough to hold him?

7

Sam called a halt to the visits to Rosedale when the early-November weather turned for the worse.

Whenever Betsy had been in Rosedale lately she had only seen Jim from a distance. She knew from Mrs Dodsworth that he would be extremely busy with developments at the mine and with the new railway. He had made no attempt to contact her. Not that she expected him to after the way she had dismissed him, but nevertheless there were times when she still wished he would. This made her wonder if she had been too harsh on him; too quick in her judgement. But what was done was done, and could only be undone if he came to her ready to admit his deceit and beg her forgiveness.

Going about her usual life in Whitby, Betsy found herself wondering where Jim might be. Was he in Rosedale? And if so, would he leave before conditions became too harsh for the men to work and the dale was cut off? Where would he go then? If he came to Whitby maybe she could consider her judgement of him again and re-establish a relationship that had made its mark on her, try as she might to forget it.

There was some accounting work at the shop for her to do, but her father and Toby could see to most of the rest. She began to make plans for Christmas, but with only her father, the cook and Lucy to consider, there was not a lot to plan. Nevertheless, she let her preparations blank out any thought of Jim and where he might be spending Christmas.

But she received a surprise that shattered her expectations of a sedate festive season.

Sitting in the drawing room, embroidering a tablecloth she wanted to have ready for the Christmas table, she heard the doorbell ring. A few moments later the quick footsteps of the maid crossed the hall, then Betsy was aware of some exchanges of conversation but could not make out the words. Expecting Lucy to appear at any moment, she sat with her needle poised in the middle of a stitch.

Startled by the sudden opening of the drawing room door, she pricked her finger.

'Surprise, surprise!'

'Tom!' The pain forgotten, she sprang to her feet, dropping her needlework in the excitement of seeing her brother and giving him a welcoming hug. 'What are you doing here?'

'The ship has just put in and the Captain gave me permission to pay you a quick visit before we leave this evening for London.'

Disappointment replaced her initial excitement. 'Oh, but I hoped ...'

'I know. I'm sorry it's not longer but I do have news you'll probably like more. When we return

132

to Middlesbrough, the ship will be laid up for repairs and the crew laid off until the second week of January. So I'll be home for Christmas and the New Year!'

'Tom, how wonderful!' She hugged him again in her excitement.

'Is Father here?'

'No, he's at the shop, but I'll send Lucy to tell him you are here for a short while.' As she was speaking Betsy went to the bell-pull and within minutes the maid was on her way to Church Street.

Once he had received the news, Sam Palmer left Toby in charge and lost no time in reaching Well Close Square.

'You look well, Tom,' he said after their initial greeting.

'Sea air suits me.'

'Your mother always said that, when you were but a bairn. Seems she was right.'

Betsy sensed his regret that their mother was not there now to admire this strong, well-built young man with the far-seeing eyes of a sailor, used to seeking out distant horizons. That resolute attitude was also reflected in his voice but did not wholly disguise his naturally gentle and considerate nature.

'How long are you going to be with us?' Sam enquired.

'We sail on the evening tide,' replied Tom apologetically.

Sam looked glum but, resigned to their parting, shrugged his shoulders. 'Can't be helped. That's a sailor's life.' He brightened up then. 'But it's good to have you here.' He glanced at his daughter. 'Is the kettle on?'

She smiled and raised her eyebrows at Tom. 'He's still living in the past when I used to see to the tea. He can't get used to having a maid to do it.' She looked at her father and said confidently, 'Lucy knows Tom is here. She'll have seen to it.'

He nodded. 'Where are you bound, Tom?'

'London, from the Tyne, with a cargo of iron goods. We might be doing quite a few of those. London's expanding fast.'

'So we might see you more often?'

'I can't be sure, Father. The Captain knows better than I. He's a good sort – gave me special leave because he knew you lived locally.'

'Well, thank him for me. Who is your Captain, by the way?'

'William Payne. He's just taken over the ship.'

'Not *the* Will Payne with whom I used to haunt the docks here in Whitby?'

'The same.'

'Well, I nivver! It's a small world. I lost track of what happened to him after the family left Whitby. Seems he's done well – Captain, eh?'

'He interviewed every man on the crew when he took over, and when he saw my name and enquired where I came from, he asked at once if I knew Sam Palmer.'

'And was flabbergasted to learn you were my son?'

'Aye, but pleased too. I reckon that's why he gave me this shore leave, brief though it is.'

'It was kind of him. I'll come and thank him myself.'

'Good,' his son told him. 'I know the Cap'n'll be pleased to see you.'

'Tom has a bit more news I know will please you, Father,' put in Betsy as she poured the tea which the maid had just brought, along with a plate of scones and home-made jam.

'This looks delicious,' said Tom enthusiastically. 'A bit different from ship's tack!'

'Come on, lad, what's this news Betsy's talking about?' Sam broke in.

'That I'll be home for Christmas and the New Year!'

His father beamed. 'Wonderful! That just about sets the seal on your visit today and will make the festive season so much jollier for us, especially your sister.' He looked at Betsy. 'It'll help take your mind off Jim Fenwick.'

'Who's he?' asked Tom.

'No one,' she interposed as her father started to explain, but it did not stop him clarifying his comment – much to her embarrassment. 'She thought a lot of him even though their friendship was short.'

'I did not!' she protested firmly.

Sam gave a little shake of his head and said, 'You think we parents don't notice the feelings of our grown-up children. But if we love 'em, we do.'

'Well, then, can we let the matter drop?' demanded Betsy sharply. 'Jim Fenwick no longer exists as far as I am concerned.'

'If you say so,' said Sam, accepting an end to this line of talk, but his knowing glance at Tom told him that Jim Fenwick was not so easily eradicated from Betsy's mind.

Caught between the two of them, Tom wondered who was right. Naturally diplomatic, he enquired about the jewellery trade and after Toby and his wife Maggie. As their conversation ranged across all manner of Whitby subjects, bringing Tom up to date, his permitted time ashore flew past and the three of them were forced to hurry back to the quay. They bade a quick farewell to him and returned his wave from the deck before he disappeared below.

As Tom stepped on board, Captain Payne strode down the gangway. The friendly handshake exchanged between him and Sam spoke volumes about the time they'd shared in their boyhood years. 'Will, this is my daughter Betsy,' Sam introduced her.

He saluted her. 'You've a fine lass, Sam, and a fine son. Tom will go far.'

'Pleased to hear it. He tells me you're likely to be coming into Whitby fairly frequently, so call in and see me, won't you? I live in Well Close Square. We've a lot of time to make up.'

'Aye, we have that. You'll definitely see me now I have this command.' He nodded at the ship. 'The *Fair Weather* has just been acquired by a new Tyneside firm, Jordan's, that has its head-quarters in Hull. The cargo we carry has come through a firm of Newcastle merchants, Addison's. Seems they have shipping agreements. If this one works well, and I don't see why it won't, it could lead to more lucrative and exotic voyages. I suspect both firms see the benefits that working closely together will secure them. From what I have seen, both of them are managed by ambitious and talented men. If they expand, there could well be an opening for Tom. Has he told you I've promoted him to First Mate?'

'He never said a word,' said Sam, surprised and disappointed that his son had not mentioned this.

'Why on earth didn't he tell us?' put in Betsy peevishly.

'He's a very modest young man.' Captain Payne hoped his observation would satisfy them. 'Well, must be away.' He shook hands with Sam again, touched his peaked cap to Betsy and strode quickly up the gangway which was promptly hauled aboard by two sailors.

Meanwhile Tom had come back on deck in his capacity as First Mate, and as the *Fair Weather* slipped away from the quay Sam and Betsy shouted their congratulations and he saluted them.

'Even more to celebrate at Christmas!' Betsy shouted excitedly. She waved and waved as she watched the ship taken towards the twin piers at the harbour mouth and the open sea beyond.

'Aye, there will, lass,' agreed Sam as they turned away from the quayside to walk home. 'We'll make it something extra-special.'

Work on the steep Ingleby Incline, which would link Rosedale to the main railway line at Battersby, was behind schedule. Jim Fenwick felt the weight of responsibility press down on him as he struggled to achieve his target before the worst of the winter weather arrived, bringing everything to a standstill and isolating the dale. Locals, from long experience, predicted that more snow would fall within three days.

Jim was here, there and everywhere, constantly cajoling the men to work faster. Thoughts of Betsy persisted in his mind but he was unaware that they were affecting his judgement and concentration.

'Come on, get those wagons up!' he yelled at the men, urging them on to greater effort.

Murmurs of dissent circulated round this particular gang. Under the men's breath, curses were directed at their supervisor.

'What's wrong with the sod these last few weeks?'

'Never satisfied!'

'This cable's too tight!'

'Boss, this 'ere cable ...'

'Doesn't concern you!' snapped Jim. His lips tightened. 'Just get on with it. We need to have this part of the job finished before the snow comes. Get those wagons up – give 'em a push! Help the winder.'

The cable tightened in the winding gear but the wagons barely moved.

'Get your backs into it!' yelled Jim. He wanted this job completed and then he'd be off to Whitby.

He stepped to one side of the track, looked up at the winding shed, cupped his hands round his mouth and yelled, 'What's wrong up there? Get more ...' His words were cut off by the sharp cracking sound that resounded over the hillside.

The six men at the wagons raised their heads, bodies taut with fear.

'Cable's snapped!'

The blood-curdling shout of warning brought expressions of horror to their faces.

'Jump!'

No one needed to be told twice. Six men flung themselves out of the way of the wagons that were rolling back down the incline with ever-increasing speed. Six bodies hit the dirt and rubble beside the track, oblivious to their torn clothes and grazed hands and knees. Then a single scream rent the air, cutting through the terrifying sound of the iron wagons gaining momentum.

Jim, eyes wide with horror, saw a man struck by a wagon. Then the heavy vehicles were past, moving faster and faster, until the track could no longer hold them. They left the rails and over-turned, tearing up sleepers and earth until finally they came to a halt amidst a scene of destruction: twisted metal, broken timber and ripped earth.

'My God!' Jim's whispered words were charged with disbelief as he stared about, dumbfounded by the destruction. Then cries and shouts brought him back to reality and the enormity of this calamity. Men were hurt, maybe dying; long days of work gone for naught. He ran to men struggling to their feet, aware now of cuts, grazes and scarred faces. Only one man did not move.

Jim dropped to his knees beside him. 'Jack! Jack!' he called, grasping at the man's shoulders. Fearing for Jack's life, Jim's own heart was pounding. He was responsible. He had taken no notice when the men had called his attention to the cable.

'Jack!' There was a groan and a flickering of the

man's eyelids. Jim felt relief sweep over him. He became aware of others around him, all talking at once. He must take charge. 'Lay still, Jack, we'll get you seen to.'

Jim looked up and saw the sea of anxious faces gathered around him. He pushed himself to his feet and immediately started giving orders.

Soon calm descended on the sea of chaos. A stretcher appeared. Jack was eased on to it and a sombre party of volunteers carried him carefully up the hill and then to the nearest building. Someone who had witnessed the incident from the top of the incline had already rushed to the village where, thankfully, he had found the doctor visiting a patient. Without delay the doctor responded to their call. After examining Jack, he diagnosed a broken arm as well as extensive lacerations, some of them deep.

'Is he going to be all right?' pressed Jim, his face taut with concern.

'If the arm mends correctly, and there is no reason why it shouldn't, he should be able to resume work.'

'What about all those other wounds?'

'I can treat them myself. Several will need stitching, but they'll mend given time. He's a lucky man. I think a wagon must have caught his out-flung arm as he jumped. If he had been hit full on ...' The doctor left the consequences to the imagination.

Though Jim was relieved at the news that Jack should return to good health, he knew that, as the person in charge, the ultimate responsibility for

140

what had happened rested with him. With snow imminent, he realised that evidence would be gathered quickly and he would then be called before his employers.

Two days later the company's representatives called Jim before them in Rosedale Village Hall.

'Mr Fenwick, yesterday we gathered evidence concerning the accident. Now we wish to hear your version,' said one grave-faced gentleman with grey, mutton-chop whiskers whom Jim knew was Sir Francis Weldon, a major shareholder. Leaning forward on the long table that had been provided for the occasion, he concentrated his penetrating gaze on Jim.

He licked his lips and glanced along the line of four men whom he recognised as those who had interviewed him for his job. He gave his own version of events, precisely and clearly, holding nothing back. When he had finished silence descended on the room. Jim felt uneasy.

Sir Francis glanced at the others. 'Has anybody any questions?' he asked gruffly. He grunted when no one responded and stared expressionlessly at Jim. 'Wait outside, please.'

With racing heart and mind, he left the room. A snarly wind blew down from the moors, its chill matching his thoughts. Ten uneasy minutes passed before he was called back.

He felt that the atmosphere was charged with doom as he stood in front of the sombre gathering.

The chairman cleared his throat. 'James Fenwick, your own version of what happened, along with that of witnesses, points to gross negligence on your part. You were in charge and possessed the specialist knowledge to assess the strength of the cable and the capability of the workforce. In order to get the task accomplished more quickly, you put the men in a position of danger. We can only thank God that no one was killed or seriously hurt. Fortunate for you, as well. If there had been loss of life or severe maiming, you would have been instantly dismissed.

'We do commend you for your frankness in summarising the incident and for not holding anything back. And we admire you for not trying to apportion blame elsewhere.

'When we employed you, we recognised your suitability for the role we had in mind. We have to concede that, until now, you have filled that role admirably. From what you have told us, we conclude that your mind was not fully concentrated on the job on that particular day. We hope and believe that from now on your mind will always be fully focused on the task in hand. We conclude that we do not wish to dispense with someone of your undoubted ability, who has come to know what we are attempting to achieve here and has worked hard to that end. I must also say that all those we interviewed have spoken highly of you. Therefore, James Fenwick, consider yourself severely reprimanded on this occasion, but you will remain in our employ in the same capacity.'

Jim breathed a deep sigh of relief and murmured his thanks.

'Very well,' said the chairman. 'Things have to be put right here. As you are no doubt aware, we have started to clear the incline. How far we will get before it snows I don't know, but I think it will be here very soon. You can get back to supervising things there, but as soon as snow comes you personally are off that particular job. We want you in York, seeing to the purchasing of rolling stock to replace that which was lost. You can also spend some time recruiting an enhanced workforce, to start as soon as weather conditions are suitable. Take lodgings in York. You can report to me at my office there.'

Two days later, dark clouds driven from the north-east by a gentle wind began to shed their snow across Scotland and the North of England. The inhabitants knew the signs, and that before long the high ground would be heavy with snow and the valleys lost in a white world. Railway workers and miners left to escape the isolation and to await their return to Rosedale, which would more than likely be well into the New Year.

Under orders, Jim was one of those who made their way to Pickering and thence York and the other towns from which they had come to earn their living in Rosedale. The flat country would see less snow and life would be more bearable there.

Jim was tolerant of his situation; there was no sense in being otherwise. It was not what he had wanted but under direct instructions from Sir Francis he could do no other than come to York. He knew he'd been lucky to escape instant dismissal, but that did not ease the thought that it would be well into the New Year before he would have a chance of getting to Whitby, and even then it might be difficult with so much ground to make up after the accident. He faced a long, lonely winter.

Gloom filled his mind when he reached York. He found lodgings of a reasonable standard and the following day walked the snow-covered streets to the wagon works. Since the railway works had been established there some seventeen years ago, the industry was thriving and there were rumours that the manufacture of railway wagons was to be further expanded. Jim made an appointment to see Sir Francis but was told it could not be held until the second week of January. This did nothing to lighten his mood. Until that time he would inspect the type of wagons on offer and decide which would be most suitable for the work in Rosedale; then he would have to await Sir Francis's approval. He saw little use in recruiting new workers at this time of the year. That would have to wait until the New Year too.

Time would weigh heavy on his hands, he knew. Maybe, just maybe, he could ... But that idea was scuttled when he heard that there had been more heavy snowfalls on the North York Moors and Whitby was cut off. He cursed his bad luck in having his trip to the Northumberland Cup announced in front of Betsy. Her peremptory reaction still stung him

As he walked the streets of York on Christmas Eve with revellers all around him, people hurrying home to loved ones, a cheery fire and Christmas fare, he felt the gloom deepen in his mind. Lonely and at a loss, he drifted through the streets, caught up in the last-minute rush but not a part of it. To escape he trudged from inn to inn, but even there had to fight to find a corner where he could hide himself away from all the noise and chatter. What alternative had he – a comfortless room in a lodging house? Here he sat alone but at least there were people nearby, even if he was shunning their company in order to immerse himself in his own misery. With hands cradled round a tankard, he stared at the ale, watching the froth gradually disappear.

Jim liked a tankard of ale but was not used to an afternoon and evening spent drinking. His steps were heavy as he eventually lumbered into The Highwayman. Its dark panelling and dingy lighting fitted his mood. After obtaining his tankard of ale, and taking no notice of anyone else, he lurched towards a corner table and flopped down at it heavily, spilling some of his beer as he did so. In his mind it was no longer Christmastime but high summer again, and he was about to meet Betsy, taking along a jet necklace that he knew she was going to love ...

'You look as though you need some company.' The voice was soft and caressing. It made him aware of someone close beside him. Hope surged. Betsy! She was here! No, she couldn't be. He hadn't gone to Whitby. He stared almost unseeingly at the person beside him. 'I'm not in Whitby,' he slurred.

The laughter that met these words was light, amused by his observation, not derisive. 'No, love, you're in York.'

'York? Ah, yes. But I want to be . . .'

When he paused, as if trying to clear his mind, she finished for him: 'In Whitby?'

He nodded. 'Yes, Whitby.'

'Well, from what I'm told, you won't be able to get there.'

'Oh, you know that too?'

'Yes, and I also know that in your state you aren't fit to be walking the streets of York on your own at night, so it's just as well you've found me. What's your name?'

'Jim.' He was about to go on but she stopped him.

'That's good enough for me. You can call me Lily − Lil, if you like.'

He stared at her and immediately thought, Pretty little thing. He reached out and touched her face. 'Are you real?'

'As real as I'll ever be.' Her pause then was charged with invitation. 'And you *can* find out.' She took his hand and started to get up. He did not move but glanced questioningly at her, his mind telling him this wasn't Betsy.

Then she tempted him. 'It's Christmas Eve. You shouldn't spend it alone. I'm alone, and I shouldn't be.'

He nodded in agreement.

Holding his hand, she led him from The Highwayman.

With arms wrapped round each other, they wove their way through the snow, slurring their words, giggling at each other's remarks, avoiding drunks who staggered into their path or any sober passer-by who eyed them with disdain. Jim was unaware how

146

far they went but it was far enough for the cold air to drive away some of the fog that had clouded his reason, though he was a long way from being sober.

'Here we are.' Lily stopped in front of a terraced house with five steps leading up to the front door. She took her arm from around his waist, smiled and kissed him on the lips. 'Now have to find my key,' she slurred. She opened her bag and started to rummage inside.

'Here, let me help.' He plunged his hand into the bag.

She pulled it away and slapped his wrist. 'Naughty! A gentleman shouldn't rummage in a lady's bag.' She stared at him for a brief moment as she continued to feel for the key, then, with a loud cry, held it up. 'Here it is!' The words burst from her lips and then dissolved into laughter which made her hand unsteady as she fought to insert the key in the lock.

Jim stood swaying at the bottom of the steps, watching her through bleary eyes.

'Done it!' She turned to him triumphantly. 'Come on, I've unlocked the door.'

He did not move but stood looking up at her, swaying on his feet.

'Come on, Jim.' This time the invitation was made in a sultry voice and Lily's eyes smouldered with promise.

Jim, uncertain, stared at her. The blurred figure came into focus for a moment — it wasn't Betsy. Without a word, Jim turned away, hunched his shoulders and trudged home to his lonely bed.

★

'Betsy, what's wrong?' Tom pressed her as they left the house in Well Close Square during the afternoon of Christmas Eve. After they had persuaded their father to have a rest so he wouldn't be too tired for the Midnight Service, Tom had suggested a walk on the West Cliff. They would enjoy the light snowfall, the view of the wintry sea and reminisce about their childhood past-times of snowballs, snowmen, sledging and skating.

'There's nothing wrong,' she replied.

'I know my sister,' he countered. 'Oh, you were your usual self when I arrived, excited at having me home for Christmas and the New Year, but that excitement has tempered a little.'

'Naturally,' she said dryly. 'You've been home nearly three days.'

'Ah, but there's more to it than that. I've seen you lost in thought, turning in on yourself. That's not like my sister. She was always bright and cheerful. It's not Father, is it?'

'No.'

'Are you not well?'

'I'm all right. It's nothing.'

Betsy had been swept away by excitement when Tom, arms full of presents, had made his breezy return. She had been determined that this should be a memorable holiday, for who knew when he would be home again at this time of the year? It was only in the privacy of her room that Jim Fenwick haunted her thoughts. Or so she'd imagined. Much to her chagrin, though, some of her preoccupation must have shown, even though she had tried to hide it.

'Come on, Betsy,' Tom urged again. 'Let me help if I can. I'm a good listener. Maybe it would do you good to talk about whatever is bothering you.'

'Really, Tom, it's nothing. It's all my own silly fault.'

'When I saw you last, Father mentioned a certain Jim Fenwick. Does this concern him?'

Betsy did not answer but her reddening face told him that it did.

'Let me help?' Tom said gently.

Maybe confiding in her brother would help.

As they walked, enjoying the sharp air and being with each other, she told him all about meeting Jim Fenwick, the development of their relationship and how it had ended.

'You sent him packing because he attended the Northumberland Cup?' Tom queried in surprise.

'It wasn't that he was at the races. It was because he deceived me, Tom. Deceived me!'

'All right,' he said with a calming gesture of his hand. 'But you were pretty harsh on him, weren't you? If it hadn't been for that chance meeting, you would never have known.'

She gave a little shrug of her shoulders, accepting his observation, and said, 'But I *do* know and that's the difference.'

'Maybe he had a reason he couldn't disclose to you?'

'Oh, come on, Tom. You're just looking to excuse him because he's a man.'

'I wouldn't do that if I thought he had deliberately hurt my sister, but we don't know that.'

'But . . .'

'No buts,' he cut in. 'I suspect you are regretting what you did?' His question pressed for an answer but it also revealed he had read her mood accurately.

She gave a little shake of her head and then accepted what he had said. 'I suppose it's no good trying to hide things from you, Tom?'

'No good at all. I always could read you like a book.'

Betsy tightened her lips; she knew it was no use denying it any longer.

'You must apologise for your attitude when you next see him, and take it from there.'

'But when will that be? With the snow lying deep across the moors and Whitby cut off, goodness knows when he will get back to Rosedale! If indeed he left before the snow. If he did, I wonder where Jim is now, at this very moment, and how he is spending Christmas Eve?'

8

'Mama, will we ever be ready for the Addisons by tomorrow?' Adele asked as she draped holly around the pictures in the drawing room on Christmas Eve.

'Of course we will.' Paula smiled to herself at her daughter's excitement, recalling the time she was that age and just as thrilled to be having guests at Christmas – or one in particular.

Decorating the drawing room, dining room and hall had been going on since early morning when two of the maids had been delegated to start. Wreaths of greenery draped with red and yellow ribbon had been hung on all the doors, and a special one was ready for the front door, to be hung by George and Mark when they came home from the office where everything would be closed down early until the day after Boxing Day. They would also be there to greet the arrival of the Christmas tree which two of the estate workers had cut down and bedded in a large pot, ready to be brought inside. Paula knew it would have been examined for its suitability for a place in the drawing room by their butler Andrew, whom they had brought with them from Hull.

Adele had completed her section of the drawing room when she heard the front door open. 'They're here!' she cried, and rushed into the hall.

Paula hurried after her, calling to one of the maids to inform Andrew that Mr Jordan was home. Coming into the hall, she found her husband and son slapping snow from their clothes.

'Snowing again,' commented George.

'Is it deep, Papa?' cried Adele with concern.

'Not too bad.'

'The Addisons will get here tomorrow, won't they?'

'I think they'll make every effort to do so,' he replied in a comforting tone.

But her brother had to tease. 'All the more for us to eat if they don't.'

'All you think about is your stomach!' snapped Adele, drawn to his bait.

'Christmas tree!' announced Paula, drawing a line under any dispute.

A few moments later two manservants, supervised by the eagle-eyed Andrew, came into the hall carrying the tree. They took it into the drawing room and placed it in the spot which the butler and his mistress had chosen.

Everyone stood back and surveyed it.

'Splendid! Splendid!' approved George with undisguised admiration.

'I like Prince Albert for bringing this idea to England,' cried Adele, clapping her hands together noiselessly. 'Now for the decorations!'

★

On Christmas Day at three o'clock, the designated time of arrival, the Addisons' carriage drew up in front of Cantonville Hall. The footman, who had positioned himself conveniently beside a front-facing window, was quickly at the door.

Emily hurried in, followed by Theodore, Zelda and Robert, all suitably clad against the inclement weather, but all with laughter on their lips as if the journey through the snow, short though it was, had been an adventure.

The concern the Jordan family were feeling when they hastened from the drawing room was instantly dismissed as they took in their friends' infectious gaiety.

Greetings were exchanged; coats, hats, bonnets and gloves taken and quickly disposed of by the two maids. They then returned to take charge of the parcels so carefully wrapped by the guests. The Jordans' thanks merged into more general chatter as the new arrivals were escorted into the drawing room. The parcels were placed under the tree, with those already there, then the maids handed round the glasses of hot punch being dispensed by one of the footmen.

Adele raised her glass to Robert whom she had managed to manoeuvre to one side without any undue difficulty. 'Welcome to Christmas at Cantonville.'

He gave a slight nod of acknowledgement as he raised his glass to hers. His eyes were fixed upon her as he said quietly, 'To the most beautiful girl I have ever seen.'

'You flirt with me, is that a good sign?' she replied demurely.

'It could be, depending on how you choose to take it?' he replied, with a questioning arch of his eyebrows.

'We shall have to see.'

'Once again your dress is exquisite, perfectly matching your beauty.'

'Oh, dear, once again it is my dress that dazzles you rather than me.' She pretended disappointment but there was a teasing light in her eyes.

'Yes, your dress does dazzle me ...' He eyed it with approval, taking in the tight, square-necked bodice above an overskirt supported on the small hoops of a crinoline above a full, flounced silk underskirt. The two shades of green of the dress were set off by the delicate lace edging the cuffs of the fitted sleeves. Adele carried a hand-painted fan and raised it coquettishly to her lips, watching him above it as he added, 'Though it would not dazzle but for the girl who wears it.'

She did not get a chance to reply, casting him a demure glance instead as she turned to see Zelda and Mark approaching them.

'A beautiful tree,' commented Zelda. 'Is it from the estate?'

'Yes.'

'Did you decorate it?'

'Yes, with Mama and two of the maids.'

'Someone has an artistic eye,' said Robert, admiring the arrangement of holly, ivy, colourful glass ornaments and coloured candles.

'Mama,' replied Mark. 'You'll see it in her embroidery.'

As the afternoon progressed, glasses were

continually replenished. The festive spirit had well and truly engulfed the Jordans and Addisons. Nothing made this more obvious than when they exchanged their Christmas gifts and parcels. Thanks and exclamations of surprise and appreciation passed back and forth accompanied by kisses. Then Andrew came in to announce, 'Dinner is served.'

The men automatically acted as escorts to the ladies; Theodore offered his arm to their hostess and led the way to the dining room; George escorted Emily, to be followed by Robert and Adele, Mark and Zelda.

The double doors had been opened. An oblong mahogany table, draped with a white and red cloth, stood in the centre of the room, adorned with highly polished glass and silver cutlery. A silver stand, filled with a tempting array of fruit, stood in the middle. The pale-coloured walls reflected the light from several sconces, supplementing that from the three oil lamps hanging above the table.

Place-names, carefully written by Paula, were already in position, indicating the seating arrangement, with their hosts to either end. Three maids and a footman stood to one side of the door, adjacent to the service corridor; Andrew and the housekeeper, Mrs Chandler, stood to the other. As soon as the two families were seated, Mrs Chandler left the room to supervise the service from the kitchen. Andrew made a signal to his staff when the baize-covered service door opened and two large tureens of steaming green pea soup were brought in and placed on mats arranged on the mahogany sideboard. The three maids served it quickly, without appearing to rush, and soon appreciative comments were being made by those at the table.

Conversation flowed generally between neighbours and across the table. The soup was followed by roast turkey and ham with vegetables from the kitchen garden, accompanied by appropriate sauces. Special piquant-flavoured sliced apples cooked in butter brought exclamations of delight. The meat was rounded off by a Christmas pudding, served with flames dancing around it as it was brought into the dining room.

The wine had flowed freely throughout the meal and the chatter had mounted. In the midst of it, Emily put a question. 'Paula, the last time I saw you, you told me you were expecting visitors. Did you enjoy seeing them again?'

'Oh, yes, indeed. It was good to catch up on all the news from North Lincolnshire and East Yorkshire. I derived great pleasure from seeing Mrs Bowen again, and I'm sure Adele enjoyed seeing Philip. They used to be such friends.'

Adele looked down at her hands in her lap. Sensing Robert's eyes turn to her, she felt her face reddening.

He leaned towards her and whispered, 'Philip?' as if to say, Why didn't you mention him?

She looked up to find his gaze fixed on her. Could she detect a hint of jealousy there? She felt flattered by his reaction and turned it to her advantage. 'I thought if I did, you would be jealous.'

'I would have been,' he admitted, 'even though I do not know what your relationship with this Philip is. But then, I would be jealous of anyone who had your attention.'

'I have known him for nearly three years. We met at a mutual friend's party and I was invited to his home near Redbourne in North Lincolnshire, a large estate which, he told me the other day, he now runs in conjunction with his father.'

'You and he ...?' Robert let the words fail on a query she could not mistake.

'We get on well. He is kind and considerate ...'

She had to stop mid-sentence when her mother called out, 'Shall we leave the gentlemen to their port and cigars?'

The men rose from their chairs when the ladies did likewise and remained standing until the door closed behind them, having heard Paula say, 'Don't be long, George.'

The port was poured and cigars were lit, except by Mark.

'You don't smoke?' asked Theo, somewhat surprised.

The young man shook his head. 'Never felt inclined, sir.'

Theo shrugged his shoulders. 'Each to his own taste, I suppose.' The implication being that he thought it unmanly not to smoke, and that it was unusual for anyone not to do so in the gentlemen's clubs of Newcastle. It was there, in the smoking rooms over a glass of port and a cigar, that many of the most advantageous business deals in the city were made.

When they rejoined the ladies they found Paula engrossed in showing Emily some embroidery, and the two young ladies exchanging opinions about *Barchester Towers* which they were both reading after making an agreement to do so one day when they were riding by the banks of the Tyne.

'A game of cards?' Mark suggested when he and Robert joined their sisters.

'All right,' Adele agreed, and was quickly out of her chair to get the card table into a position around which the four of them could sit. In a flash Robert was beside her, helping. Mark found the cards and asked Zelda what she wanted to play.

'One and Thirty,' she cried without hesitation.

'Ah, ever the gambler!' he observed. 'We have a box of farthings we keep for card games. I'll get it.'

In a few minutes the game was underway.

The other gentlemen had joined their wives.

'We could have a sing-song round the piano when they've had enough of cards,' George suggested.

'A good idea,' agreed Theodore jocularly. 'I'm in fine voice!' He gave a little trill, to show them, and followed that with, 'An excellent dinner, Paula, excellent. I think we should . . .'

'I know what you are going to say, Theo,' broke in Emily. 'And I have already thanked the cook and the housekeeper on everyone's behalf. I got Paula to take me through to the kitchen.'

'Well done, my dear.'

'It was most considerate of you to thank them personally,' said Paula. 'They will appreciate it.'

High spirits continued when they were grouped

around the piano. Their voices soared in unison as Adele and Zelda took turns to play, laughter was in the air, and in the relaxed atmosphere the young men sneaked their opportunity to get their arms round the girls' waists – and the girls took any chance they could to encourage it, knowing that their parents, under the influence of more wine than usual, were less attentive than they might have been.

With voices flagging, they changed to party games especially Blind Man's Buff and Charades which heightened the general hilarity until eventually they all sank back in chairs to imbibe some restorative coffee.

The Addisons' coach was finally brought to the front door by their coachman who had been well looked after in the Jordans' kitchen.

'There's been no more snow since we arrived,' said Emily thankfully as they stepped out on to the terrace.

'A beautiful night,' commented George, gazing heavenwards at the star-filled sky in which a winter moon hung wreathed with a magical, ethereal light.

'It has been a perfect Christmas Day. Thank you all so much,' said Theo.

'Mr Addison!' called Adele. She stepped forward and drew her hand from behind her back to hold a piece of mistletoe over his head. As she kissed him she said, 'A Happy Christmas.'

'Oh, my!' he exclaimed. And then: 'And a Happy Christmas to you, my dear young lady. How delightful.'

The sprig of mistletoe was swiftly passed from

hand to hand and put to good use. When Robert managed to claim it, he came over to Adele while everyone else was making their final goodbyes. They were standing halfway down the steps. He held it over her head and kissed her on the lips. 'Happy Christmas, my love,' he whispered.

She grabbed the sprig from him, held it up and kissed him back. 'And to you.'

'So, is that a sign I have no rival?'

There was laughter in her eyes and a smile on her lips when she said, 'Who knows?'

'Robert, come on, we're waiting!' shouted Zelda from the coach.

'Tell me?' he said quietly, trying to gain a promise from her.

'Some day I will,' she said, and teased him with a smouldering look in which he could read any answer he wanted. 'Go now, and sleep tight.'

As the coach pulled away, the horses' breath clouding on the sharp air, everyone shouted their farewells. Robert, with his eyes fixed on Adele, wondered if he would ever have the answer he sought tomorrow.

9

The air was sharp, the day bright, when the Jordans' carriage took all the family into Newcastle in the early afternoon of New Year's Eve. When it drew to a halt they were in front of Bell House, the Addisons' town residence, where they were to stay for three nights, and attend the New Year's Eve Ball in the Assembly Rooms. Servants were quickly out to look after them and see to their luggage while the two families exchanged greetings.

Once inside they were shown to their rooms and left to settle in, with the information that tea would be served in the drawing room in fifteen minutes. When they came down they found that Theodore's sister Grace had arrived with her husband Morgan.

'Now we have a full house for three nights,' announced Theodore rather proudly as the tea was being handed round, 'and we look forward to having you all as our guests at the Ball.'

Amidst the general chatter, Robert was most solicitous to Adele.

'Are you trying to charm me into giving you that answer?' she challenged him.

161

'I'm merely being attentive to a guest in my parents' house,' he replied.

'Ah.' She bit her lip thoughtfully. 'Then I think I'll keep a certain young man waiting until the New Year.' Her eyes sparkled as she added, 'Now I must be sociable and have a word with your aunt,' and slipped away from him.

He watched her cross the room, admiration in his eyes but also a touch of jealousy – she still had not answered his question about Philip.

He glanced around him. Everyone seemed to be glowing with good humour, the New Year spirit seeping into everyone, but then his gaze fell on his father and Uncle Morgan who appeared to be deep in a serious conversation. Surely not discussing business on New Year's Eve? But, knowing his father, it could be; he was never one to miss an opportunity, and who knew what new investment Uncle Morgan might have found? But almost as soon as Robert's eyes had settled on them, the two men parted. Emily rang a table bell to bring a hush to the room.

'Can I have everyone's attention, please? I am altering our usual times of dining, bringing them forward an hour. There will be a light tea at four o'clock, and dinner will be at seven.' She paused and looked across the room at her husband. 'Theo.'

'Carriages will be ready at half-past nine,' he continued. 'George, your coachman will have been briefed by mine. I hope that is all right.' George nodded his approval which Theo acknowledged with a raised hand. 'Good. That is all. Now, everyone, enjoy yourselves.'

162

In the aftermath of his announcement their exchanges were charged with excitement.

'It is so exhilarating to be going to the Ball,' Adele commented to Robert.

'And, right now, I am reserving the first dance with you, as well as the one just before midnight,' he returned.

'Very well,' she answered with a smile and an inclination of her head.

'I've still not had your answer about Philip but I demand he does not enter your thoughts this New Year's Eve, nor . . .'

'Ask me no more, Robert,' she cut in and turned away to Zelda, leaving him wondering and slightly perturbed.

The tone of the evening had been set. The dinner Emily had arranged was a triumph.

Praises were loud and everyone took the opportunity of the earlier dining hour to relax afterwards, but excited anticipation of the coming event prevailed among the younger members of the party.

Adele and Zelda made a stately descent of the stairs together when they knew the gentlemen were waiting in the hall. Conversation stopped, leaving the men staring at them in silent admiration.

Adele's small crinoline supported a dress of pink gauze with two large red bows decorating the skirt above four rows of frills. The V-shaped waist ran from a shoulder neckline trimmed with lace that was also continued on the short sleeves.

Zelda's dress also had a low neckline, its black

lace bold against the delicate blue of the silk taffeta that carried bands of ruching from the narrow waist to the hem of the skirt. Both had their hair drawn tightly back from a centre parting but had allowed it to fall in ringlets on their shoulders. Each carried a woollen shawl complementing the colour of her dress.

The men were loud in their praise which was extended also to the older ladies who now made their own entrance.

'You don't look too bad yourselves,' returned Emily, approving the black tail coats and satin waistcoats, some white, some black. All wore white shirts and bow ties, black trousers, highly polished black shoes, and carried a black crush hat. These admiring exchanges set them out of the house in high good humour.

That excitement heightened further as the three carriages joined the queue approaching the Assembly Rooms. Once they had reached the elegant façade of the building, with its colonnade of six pillars and two attractive side wings, the Addison party was helped to the ground and escorted into the building by footmen. After attendants had taken their outdoor clothes, Theodore and Morgan explained to their friends that there were card rooms available should anyone fancy a game and also a saloon. The room for private assemblies would be used this evening as a tea and refreshment area while on the lower storey was another assembly room as large as the great ballroom they were about to enter.

When they did so the Jordans were almost overwhelmed by its huge proportions and elegance. Seven brilliant glass chandeliers lent enchantment to a scene of whirling colour as people danced to the music of the orchestra in the gallery above. The joy of people determined to enjoy themselves, saying goodbye to the old year and ready to welcome the new, permeated every corner of this magnificent room. A polka came to an end and the dancers clapped; partners bowed to each other, the gentlemen escorted their ladies to chairs and remained in conversation or else made their thanks and went to greet another friend. After a few moments of preparation the music started again for a quadrille.

'You made a promise,' said Robert to Adele.

'I did,' she replied, and took his hand. They moved on to the floor along with the rest of their party. From that moment on they danced and danced, laughed and laughed, and changed partners constantly throughout the next hour.

After a while Robert took Adele for some refreshments. When they re-entered the ballroom, she hesitated. A group of young people, laughing amongst themselves, had just entered the room ... Philip Bowen among them!

Robert offered his hand to her but she did not take it. Puzzled, he glanced queryingly at her.

'Your aunt is alone.' She inclined her head in the direction of Grace. 'I think she deserves another dance with you. You should circulate more. I'll sit here and gather myself.'

He knew it would be boorish not to comply. 'Very well, but don't stray.' As she sat down he bowed to her and made his way over to his aunt who smiled graciously at his invitation to her to dance. Adele watched them for a moment then, as soon as they were lost on the crowded floor, stood up so that she could see more clearly the group of new arrivals.

Her mind whirled. What was Philip doing here? He was supposed to be in Berwick. She felt her heart lurch. Even as the dancers whirled past she could see he cut a fine, tall figure in his well-fitting evening clothes. Knowing how gracefully he danced, she felt a sudden urge to be in his arms, guided with ease through all the difficult steps. She could not avoid meeting him which meant that he and Robert would soon come face to face. After that mention of Philip's visit to Cantonville Hall and Robert's jealous reaction, she felt disturbed by the prospect.

She saw Philip glance in her direction and an expression of surprise cross his face. He spoke briefly to the other members of his party then started across the dance floor in her direction. She could do nothing but wait; she could not evade him all night.

'Adele, what a delight to see you here!' he said with that friendly smile she knew so well. 'It crowns my evening.'

'What are you doing here? I thought you were in Berwick?'

'I was. We had a splendid Christmas and, as you know, intended to be with my uncle and aunt over New Year. But Uncle was taken ill ... not seriously, thank goodness, but sufficiently incapacitated for him to be unable to enjoy New Year. He did not wish to spoil the general enjoyment and insisted that all we young ones should enjoy seeing in the New Year at the Ball in Newcastle. We came down the day before yesterday and will return in a couple of days' time.'

Still a little bewildered, she asked, 'Where are you staying?'

Philip smiled. 'One of my cousins works in a bank in Newcastle. He has a house here so we are able to use that.' He left the slightest of pauses then said, 'You should not be a wallflower. Let us dance.' He held out his hand to her but at that moment the music finished. A disappointed expression crossed Philip's face but disappeared when the orchestra struck up almost immediately with a waltz. 'Your favourite,' he said.

As Adele took his hand she glanced round for Robert, experiencing some relief when she saw he was still at the far side of the room and could do no more than dance with his aunt again.

Philip and Adele glided away, in unison with each other and with the music. Adele enjoyed the intimacy of the waltz, something that various authorities had frowned upon and criticised when the dance was introduced to Britain not so long ago. She had always enjoyed dancing with Philip and now found herself comparing his dancing with Robert's. Philip was much lighter on his feet and had an unerring ability to guide her without appearing to. Although Robert was a good dancer and held himself correctly, she felt less confident with him than she did with Philip.

She realised all at once that Robert and his aunt were close to them on the floor. Her eyes met his and she saw curiosity, hostility, jealousy, in his gaze. Although she had enjoyed piquing him by her references to Philip, Robert's reaction now revealed something in him that ran a lot deeper than she had imagined.

Alarm bells rang in Adele's mind. Robert had touched her heart but might a future with him be blighted by his jealousy? She knew that would never be the case with Philip. Life with him would have a steadiness and security that would suit many young women ... but would it suit her? Or would she be left craving for the adventure and excitement she knew she would have with Robert?

The dance finished with a final spin that made Adele throw back her head in laughter, eyes sparkling with unbridled pleasure. Philip laughed with her, his own eyes shining brightly with admiration for the girl who had slid from his hold.

'Happy memories of days past,' said Philip. 'Thank you for reviving them,' he added as he bowed and held out his hand to escort her back to her seat.

Adele's sidelong glance around the room had shown her Robert advancing across the floor towards them. She could see anger in his expression, though when he arrived she realised he was fighting not to show it.

'Adele,' he greeted her coolly.

'Robert, I hope you enjoyed that dance with your aunt?' Before he had time to reply she continued, 'This is my old friend Philip from Redbourne.

I think I have mentioned him before.'

'You have,' he said curtly, and turned to Philip, giving a slight inclination of his head in reluctant greeting. 'Sir.'

Philip smiled and returned the formal greeting, 'Sir,' but spoken with a note of friendliness and jocularity. 'We are being rather formal for New Year's Eve ... Philip, please.' He held out his hand.

For one brief moment Robert intended to refuse it but caught Adele's sideways look. He took Philip's hand and felt the strong grip of a determined man.

'You must come and meet my brothers and sisters and cousins. They'll be pleased to meet you, Robert, and to see you again, Adele.'

At that moment the orchestra, because of the enthusiasm with which the last dance had been greeted, started to play another waltz.

Robert seized his chance. 'May we join you after this waltz? Adele promised it to me.'

'Of course,' replied Philip. 'You must allow her to keep her promise.'

Robert and Adele glided away. 'How dare you?' she snapped. 'I had made no such promise. I couldn't know another waltz would be played now.'

Robert ignored her scolding. 'What's he doing here?'

'Don't take that tone with me! Philip has every right to be here.'

'I think you knew he was coming, saw him arrive and suggested I dance with my aunt to get me out of the way.'

His words stung her. 'So you believe that of me, do you?'

'Well, what else does it look like? You told me he was going to Berwick, yet here he is. He can't have travelled from there to attend the Ball.' Robert's temper was on the boil. His steps became faster and faster but Adele matched them. She would not be outdone.

'You're implying that he and I planned this when he called at Cantonville Hall with his mother?'

'Seems like it to me.'

'Then you have let your fancy run away with you. Did we arrange for his brothers, sisters and cousins to come too?' Her voice was filled with reproach and anger. 'How ridiculous you are being.' She went on to tell him exactly what had happened in Berwick with a righteous indignation that could not help but convince even Robert. 'Now, those are the facts, Robert Addison. Believe them or not, at your peril. Accept what I say or spoil New Year's Eve for yourself and for me. And let me tell you something else: you had better get rid of that jealous streak of yours. I knew it was there after you heard of Philip's earlier visit, but this evening it has appeared in all its ugliness.' She could see he was about to say something but countered it with, 'Now let's finish this dance and then go and meet my friends in a civilised fashion.'

Robert's lips tightened as he fought down the urge to retaliate. He realised that if he didn't behave graciously it could mean the end of his relationship with Adele. He did not want that, but this evening had raised certain questions in his mind about a possible bond between her and Philip.

A few minutes later they were joining Philip and his relations who were in such a happy mood that it raised the spirits of everyone else. Mark and Zelda were happy to join them. In that atmosphere Robert was compelled to keep his own annoyance under control.

Never a dance was missed, with everyone changing partners as dance followed dance. Robert's mood eventually lightened, something Adele was pleased to see, and it seemed their altercation had been forgotten. The last dance before midnight was announced — a waltz. Robert excused himself from one of Philip's cousins and headed for Adele who was talking to Philip. He felt a surge of jealousy. Was the upstart trying to knuckle in?

When he reached them, and before he could say anything, Philip said, 'Your dance, I believe, Robert.'

He bowed his acknowledgement, took Adele's hand and moved on to the dance floor which was filling up. Steps flowed to the music; dresses whirled in colourful display; the minutes moved towards midnight. Neither of them referred to their clash of earlier in the evening.

The music stopped and immediately everyone was rushing round to find the friends with whom they wanted to welcome in the New Year. Philip's cousins, Robert and Zelda quickly marshalled the Jordans, the Bowens and the Addisons into a circle among the others being formed, filling the room. Adele looked askance at her partner.

'"Auld Lang Syne",' he said.

'I know it,' she replied.

'It's a custom that's becoming popular in Scotland and spreading into Northern England. We form a circle of friends with each one crossing arms and linking hands with the person to either side.'

On the stroke of midnight the orchestra struck up and hundreds of voices sent the song to the heavens, amidst much joyous laughter and some tears from those who remembered friends who were not there.

The last note faded, the last word was sung, to be replaced by calls of 'Happy New Year' and the exchange of kisses.

Robert swept Adele into his arms. Their lips met. A kiss of repentance ... one beseeching forgiveness? she wondered. Then they were pushed apart as kisses and well wishes were claimed and exchanged all around them. With people determined to forget the past and look to the future the air resounded with good fellowship as friends and strangers continued to exchange good wishes. In the mêlée Robert, who had become separated from their group, was swept away across the crowded floor. He struggled against the press of people, trying to find Adele who had been lost to his sight. Then he saw her and Philip embrace and kiss. A New Year gesture ... or was there more to it? He felt a desire to intervene but could not escape the press of those around him.

He was near the edge of the dance floor when he saw his father at the top of the flight of stairs leading to the room below. He started towards him but then, with people all around him, pulled up short, immobile in the crush. His father was in what appeared to be a deep and earnest conversation with a smartly dressed young woman. She had her back to Robert. How he wished she would turn ... even half a turn might do. As if she had read his thoughts she did so. His lips tightened in annoyance. He did not recognise her but one thing was revealed: she was plainly beautiful.

Robert gasped. Who was she? How did his father know her? What lay behind the earnestness of their conversation? Then an even bigger question drove the others into the background. What could be in the envelope his father had just passed to the young woman? The smile that crossed her face then was radiant. She kissed the fingers of her right hand and touched his cheek, a fleeting action Robert would have missed if his eyes had not been focused on them so intently. His father smiled back, patted her arm and walked away. She watched him for a moment before she took the steps downstairs.

Robert was tempted to follow her but knew he would soon be missed. He could not afford to let that happen. Questions might be raised that he would find awkward to answer.

The band struck up again. People started leaving the floor, freeing it for those who wanted to dance. Robert, deep in thought, made his way over to join his family and friends who were gathering together, some to go for refreshments, others to dance. A few moments after he had joined them, his father arrived, seemingly without a care in the world. But Robert reckoned there was something troubling him nevertheless and before long found himself wondering if there was a connection between the two note-books in his father's desk and the envelope he had passed to that beautiful woman?

'You're looking serious, Robert. If you're going to look that sour for the rest of the night, I'll dance every dance with Philip.' Adele's statement jolted him, as she'd meant it to do.

'Sorry,' he spluttered. 'I was miles away.'

'And in a serious place, quite unsuited to New Year's Day.'

Robert smiled weakly. 'True.' He took her hand. 'And I'm sorry about earlier.'

'I accept your apology,' she said, somewhat stiffly, and then added more forgivingly, 'Let's dance together and start the New Year aright.'

No one in the ballroom seemed to tire. The dancing went on and on. As much as he wanted to, Robert realised he could not monopolise Adele and found that troubling streak of jealousy rising in him every time he saw her dancing with Philip.

Eventually the last waltz was announced. Robert looked for Adele and spotted her at the other side of the room with Philip. The floor was filling, forcing him to walk round the edge of the dancing area. He hurried but was hindered by people rushing to dance. He kept glancing in the direction of Adele who appeared to be in deep conversation with Philip. He saw her shake her head. Philip spread his hands, looked around then back to

Adele with an expression that seemed to say, Where is he? Robert quickened his steps, weaving and skipping round people who were oblivious to his haste.

'My dance, I believe, Adele,' he panted.

She inclined her head graciously. 'You are right. I was just telling Philip this dance was promised.'

As they glided away Robert indulged himself in a little feeling of triumph, but did not see the look of apology that Adele directed at Philip over his shoulder.

When they had all dismounted from the carriages at Bell House, Theodore called out, 'Everyone ... wait a moment. We have got to have a first footer. A dark-haired man should be the first to enter the house on New Year's Day, to bring good luck to the house and its people. George has the darkest hair. He should let the New Year in to Bell House for us.'

Everyone gave a cheer of approval.

'Normally,' Theo went on, 'this would happen on the stroke of midnight. He would leave the house by the back door, walk round the house and enter by the front. But, as we are already outside, it will be perfectly all right for George to walk round the house from here and then go in at the front door.'

'But aren't there certain items I should take into the house?' asked George.

'Yes,' replied Theo. 'Silver for wealth, bread for sustenance, salt for seasoning, coal for warmth – which can't be lit unless there is also kindling and a match.'

'Where on earth am I going to get all those at this hour of the morning?' pleaded George.

'Here in a bag, by the front door!' cried Theodore. 'I got them ready before we left for the Ball.' He picked up the bag and handed it to George. 'Now, off you go. Once round the house.'

Pleased to be chosen as the first footer for Bell House, George set off, leaving the others bantering happily and commenting on the calmness of the night as their breath vaporised on the cold air and was whitened by the moonlight.

George received a big cheer when he returned. Theo unlocked the front door and pushed it open without stepping inside. He stood back. 'After you, George.'

With a broad smile he entered the house, stopped in the middle of the hall and turned to greet the others. 'Happy New Year to you all,' he proclaimed loudly, 'and may this house bring you happiness, good health and luck throughout this year!'

Everyone cheered and once more passed their own personal wishes and kisses to each other.

Robert whispered to Adele, 'May you find everything you want this year.'

She made no significant response.

Later, as he lay in the silence of his room, Robert wondered if showing his jealousy had marred any possibility of his being included in those final words he had whispered to her.

Adele was also awake, thinking of two men. Since meeting Robert she had become close to him, sharing enjoyable and happy times. She had found herself always looking forward to being in his company, but this evening had been alarmed by his show of jealousy. Was it an insidious streak that could grow or had it been merely a childish display of petulance that could be conquered? She had seen neither trait in Philip. She recalled him always being the perfect gentleman, a man she was sure could be trusted, in whatever company.

Even in her dreams the two of them haunted her, competing ceaselessly for her attention and, ultimately, her love.

10

'Tom, we have enjoyed having you with us. Take care, son. Have a good voyage. We look forward to seeing you again.' The handshake exchanged between father and son then was firm. They were standing on the quay beside the *Fair Weather*.

'It has been a splendid Christmas and New Year with you, Father. Thank you.' Tom turned to his sister then. 'And with you, Betsy.' He hugged her and sensed she was holding back tears at parting from him. 'Take care,' he whispered as their father turned to greet Captain Payne, coming down the gangway towards them. 'And heed what I said.'

She pressed his shoulder in response then leaned back to look into his eyes. 'You take care too.' She kissed him on the cheek. 'I hope we'll see you again soon.'

'That will depend on Captain Payne's orders.'

They both turned towards the gangway where Captain Payne and Sam were exchanging pleasantries.

'Good day, sir,' said Tom.

Captain Payne nodded. 'I hope you had a good Christmas?'

'I did, sir.'

'We are sorry to be losing him,' put in Sam.

'I understand, but you'll be seeing him again before long. The *Fair Weather* will be making more voyages between the Tyne and the Thames for a while, and there are prospects of linking the iron trade on Teesside with Western Europe. We won't come back with our holds empty; there'll be cargo to be dropped here on the return voyage, so you'll be seeing Tom again soon.' He glanced at his crew member. 'There are rumours that Jordan's might add to their fleet. It's not going to happen overnight but, when it does, there could be a chance of promotion there for you. You'll have my recommendation.'

'Thank you, sir. I'll get aboard and supervise the stowing away.' Tom indicated the three heavily laden wagons rumbling towards them along the quay. 'Are we sailing on the next tide, sir?'

'Aye,' the Captain replied.

Tom made a last goodbye to his father and Betsy. Once on deck, he immediately marshalled the crew to take the goods aboard.

Sam and Betsy stood on the quay, waiting to see him sail. As she watched the *Fair Weather* slip towards the sea, Betsy recalled her brother's parting words which had been referring to Jim Fenwick.

At that moment Jim was giving his report to Sir Francis Weldon on the recruitment of new men to work in Rosedale.

'You've done well, Fenwick.' Sir Francis leaned back in his chair, still tinkering with the pen he had picked up from his desk top. 'I thought you might have difficulties.'

'So did I at first, sir. The prospect of living in a remote dale does not agree with many, especially at this time of year when the area is cut off. But I painted a better picture of life in the place throughout the summer and that persuaded those desperate for work to sign on.'

'What are the arrangements for notifying them when the dale is accessible?'

'Once I had the required number plus another half dozen, because there will always be drop-outs, I assembled them all together, appointed a foreman for the group and told him to report to your junior clerk every morning from next Monday, to verify the situation. He will then be responsible for letting everyone know when to head for the dale.'

'Good, that seems satisfactory. Except for one thing.'

'What is that, sir?' asked a puzzled Jim. He'd thought he had covered everything.

'I think we should transport the men as a group to Rosedale, then we'll know if we have them all. There'll be no turning back on the way. Will you organise that tomorrow?'

'Yes, sir.' Jim was relieved it was something he had not overlooked. He had expected the men to make their own way to Rosedale but saw the sense in Sir Francis's scheme, one that had needed authority from the top to implement.

'Be sure you do it tomorrow because I want you to move on to another job in a couple of days' time.'

Jim was crestfallen. It seemed that his chances of

ever seeing Betsy again were being constantly thwarted. 'Yes, sir,' he answered lamely.

'I want you to look into the prospects of opening up trade between the Yorkshire coalfields in the West Riding and the docks at Hull.'

'But isn't that trade already in existence, sir?'

'It is, Fenwick, it is, but the docks in Hull are owned by a single company and the NER dominates rail services in the area. Now,' Sir Francis leaned forward with one arm on the desk, the other pointing his pen at Jim in determined fashion, 'I reckon those monopolies are not good for trade in this area and should be broken. I have supporters within Hull Corporation who see my proposals as advantageous to the town. Once you have set up transport for the new workers at Rosedale, I want you to go to Hull and then throughout the West Riding, looking for the possibilities in initiating such a scheme. I need a thorough report as soon as possible. In order to do that, I am offering you the incentive of a ten percent wage rise and all expenses paid.'

The initial disappointment that this would take him away from Rosedale and from seeing Betsy, once the snow had cleared from the North York Moors, was somewhat salved by this offer, even though after his lenient reception after the Ingleby disaster, Jim felt he was in no position to refuse. Besides, it did offer him improved prospects for the future. 'Thank you for your trust in my ability, sir. I will have my report for you as soon as humanly possible. Will you want me back in Rosedale after that, sir?'

181

'Most certainly, Fenwick, but make a thorough job of this one. There could be a lot at stake.'

Jim left the office feeling a little more buoyant; Rosedale was still a prospect. The next three days were hectic for him. He found a carrier willing to transport the men as soon as the weather was open enough and briefed the man he had appointed foreman of the group, with the promise of an extra payment if the full complement of workers arrived in Rosedale. Jim then hired himself a horse with the necessary saddle and panniers, deeming this the best mode of transport for exploring the country-side and finding a possible route for Sir Francis's new venture.

George Jordan watched the *Adventurer* with pride as she sailed up the Tyne to her berth beside The Quay. He had eagerly awaited her arrival from Spain with a shipment of wine, lace and silks for his good friend Theodore who, along with their sons, stood beside him now. Once the gangway was run out they made to go on board but Captain Rockingham was quickly ashore.

'Good day, Captain,' George greeted him cheerily. 'Good voyage?' But already he knew from the Captain's grave expression that something was not quite right.

'Good day, gentlemen. Our voyage was excellent and the cargo is first class,' Captain Rockingham returned politely, but his face still bore a serious expression. 'As you know, we had part of the cargo to deliver in Hull and, as instructed, I enquired of the manager you left in charge there if all was well and picked up a written report from him.' He handed an envelope to George. 'He asked me to tell you these are the bare facts and you should draw your own conclusions.'

'This sounds serious,' said George gravely as he took the envelope. He glanced at Theodore and raised an eyebrow. 'Go on board, Theo. You too Robert ... have a look at the cargo. Mark and I will join you in a few minutes.'

Theo nodded but made no comment. Captain Rockingham called to his First Mate to escort Mr Addison who was coming on board. The Mate signalled his acknowledgement and went to the top of the gangway to await Theo's arrival. The Captain stood to one side while George read the letter from his Hull manager.

When he had finished, his expression was full of misgiving. 'Captain, how soon can you have this ship turned round? I must get back to Hull as soon as possible.'

'I see the stevedores are standing by to unload. There will be victuals to take on board ...' His words came out thoughtfully. 'I'll have her ready to sail on the morning tide.'

'Splendid!'

'What is it, Father?' Mark asked with concern.

'In a moment, Mark. As I might be away from Newcastle for a little while I wonder if you would all like to come with me.' He turned back to Captain Rockingham. 'Can you arrange for that?'

'Of course, sir. It will be easy enough. You won't require overnight accommodation. I'll make my quarters available so that Mrs Jordan and your daughter can have somewhere to rest.'

'Admirable. Mark, we'll have a word with Mr Addison and Robert then get off home to warn your mother and sister of the pending voyage.'

They hurried on board and found Theo and Robert examining the manifest with the First Mate.

'Theo, we've got to hurry off. The information I have received from my manager in Hull requires me to get there as soon as possible.' George's expression and tone left Theo and Robert in no doubt that he had something serious to deal with.

Although George gave no explanation, Theo automatically offered, 'Can I do anything?'

'Not regarding this. I have asked Captain Rockingham to have the *Adventurer* ready to sail as soon as possible. He says we can sail on the morning tide. I'll have to get off home and inform Paula and Adele. I feel sure they'll want to come as I could be away a month or more.'

Theo had noted the Captain having a word with the First Mate and now he was already shouting orders to the men standing by to start the unloading. 'Most of this cargo is mine,' said Theo. 'It will save time if all of it is put into my warehouses. Your orders can be distributed from there. Your manager will have the necessary paperwork.' Theo turned to his son. 'Go and get our men to help, and inform Zac of what is happening.'

'Yes, sir.' Robert hurried away to tell their manager of the new arrangements but his mind was already trying to assimilate the fact that this news was taking Adele back to Hull and nearer to

Redbourne. He had seen her only once since the New Year, four weeks ago. While Emily and Zelda had returned to Elston Hall, he and his father had stayed on in Bell House, convenient for their offices and offering accommodation to George and Mark, too, so they could be near their work while also looking for a town house. One had been acquired two weeks ago and was now being renovated.

'Theo, Mark and I must away. I thank you sincerely for your generosity these last four weeks. It has made things much easier for me.'

'Think nothing of it,' he returned, dismissing the thanks with a wave of his hand. 'I'll keep an eye on your property in town and see that the builders and decorators fulfil their contracts.'

'That's thoughtful of you and it will be a comfort to know that everything is in good hands while I cope with the situation in Hull.' He shook Theo's hand in a firm grip and then, with Mark close on his heels, hurried from the ship.

Once he had informed Zac of the new arrangement Robert returned to his office, wondering if he would get the opportunity to see Adele before she left. The only chance he could think of was when she came to board the *Adventurer* tomorrow morning.

Adele received her father's news with mixed feelings. The only time she had seen Robert in the last four weeks had been in the company of others, which had not been conducive to trying to clear the air between them. Her dreams since the Ball had not helped matters; two men still drifted in and out of them, without either dominating. Now she wondered if fate had played a hand in her destiny. She was going back to Hull. Redbourne was not far across the Humber, though that did not necessarily mean that Philip would become a closer part of her life. Yet ...

But now the imminence of departure made her wonder if Robert would come to see her sail. Was this one of the cards that fate was playing? Would her destiny be decided by whether or not he came to The Quay?

Robert woke with a start, instinctively knowing he had slept in. Cursing the servant who had been instructed to wake him, he swung out of bed, ignoring the chill February morning, completed his ablutions and dressed quickly. He quietly raced down stairs, fearing to wake his father.

'Where the devil is Garth?' he demanded, glaring at Cook. 'He was supposed to wake me!'

'Sir,' exclaimed the woman, shocked at the attitude of this young man whom she had always regarded as good-natured, 'he was taken ill during the night and sent home.'

Robert's lips tightened in exasperation.

'Breakfast, sir?' asked the Cook, polite but cool, trying to ease the situation which she saw had shocked the kitchen maid.

'No time!' snapped Robert, storming from the kitchen. He grabbed his hat and redingote and left by the front door.

Invigorated by the frosty air and thankful that

the January snow had not been supplanted by any in February, he hurried through the almost deserted streets.

A pale light suffused the sky from the east and gave an eerie quality to the mist swirling along the river. Ships, stark black, sailed ghost-like across the water. Others lay at their berths, awaiting orders that could send them across the world.

He reached The Quay and broke into a run but after a few steps pulled up short.

The *Adventurer*'s berth was empty!

The ship, ghostly in the pale morning light, was mid-river, moving through the swirling mist that soon hid her from his sight. A vicious curse exploded from his tight lips then he stood frozen to the spot, gazing at nothing.

The rumble of a cart broke the silence, penetrating his disappointment and seeming to emphasise the hopelessness of his situation. Adele was on that ship; he could do nothing to bring her back. She would not know he was on the quayside, had come here 'specially to say goodbye, to declare his love and see her sail.

He walked dejectedly to the Addison's offices and let himself in. He flopped into the chair behind his desk and stared unseeing at the papers that awaited his attention. His thoughts were all else-where – with a girl who was sailing away from him. He cursed himself for the jealousy he had shown. It might yet force that girl into the arms of another man.

Seeing Robert's door open, Theodore paused in

the corridor and glanced in. He took a step inside the room and saw his son slumped at his desk. 'You're early, son. I wondered where you were when you weren't at breakfast.'

'Came to see the Jordans sail,' replied Robert, his voice expressionless, offering no further explanation.

'And someone in particular, no doubt. I'm sure she'll be back before long.'

Robert made no comment. Resigned to the fact that he had been unable to prevent Adele's departure, he merely shrugged his shoulders.

'I'll be going out shortly,' said Theodore. 'I may not be back before this afternoon.'

Robert nodded and waited for further information but none came. Instead his father hurried to his own office. It was only when his door shut that Robert realised he had not received the explanation that was usually provided when his father was going to absent himself from his office. His mind was instantly alive with all sorts of suppositions. He was still turning them over in his mind when he heard Theodore's door open again. Footsteps were heard in the corridor. He looked in the direction of the open door and saw his father pass by without a glance in his direction.

Robert was quickly out of his chair. He grabbed his hat and shrugged himself into his redingote as he stepped into the corridor. The outside door was just closing. He hurried to it and carefully opened it far enough for him to see out. His father was walking briskly away. Robert stepped outside and followed at a discreet distance, careful not to lose sight of him when they came to more crowded areas.

A quarter of an hour later they reached a quiet street of terraced houses. The front door of every house was reached by climbing five steps, and six steps more led down to a basement area.

Robert hesitated at the corner from where, careful not to be seen if his father looked back, he watched Theodore climb the steps of the fourth house on the right. He knocked and was answered by the same young woman to whom he had handed an envelope at the Ball! She opened the door wider, held out her hand to him. He took it and stepped inside. The door closed behind them.

A chill ran down Robert's spine. What was happening? Why had his father come here? Who was that woman and what was their relationship? He stood frozen to the spot as unanswered questions raced through his mind. He was now in a quandary. What should he do next? He could await his father's return, but after half an hour with still no sign of him, Robert realised that he was attaining nothing.

His steps were heavy as he walked away; his mind troubled. To tackle Theodore would be unthinkable. A son could not question his father about his private life. Besides, what evidence did he have that his father was involved in something unsavoury? Suggesting that he might have a mistress would have a shattering effect on his mother, and Robert could not be party to that. It would also be devastating to Zelda. The scandal was bound to affect her too. Their whole family

could be shunned by former friends. Their association with the Jordans would be destroyed, and
that would include his own with Adele.

It seemed all he could do was to keep quiet; say
nothing. Let life appear to go on as normal. But
that would leave him tormented by this knowledge, a torment he would have to disguise, and he
was not sure he could act a lie. Robert was no saint
but his upbringing and education had taught him
to be open and truthful. Yet his every instinct told
him to forget what he had seen and forget the
conclusions he had drawn. But he knew they
would haunt him and, coupled with his moral
dilemma, prey heavily on his mind. Leading to
what – mental breakdown? Confinement to an
institution? He could not let that happen. He must
find a solution.

Maybe a change of surroundings, another life,
would save him. He could slip quietly away from
home and disappear into another world; absorb
himself in it and leave the lives of those he held
dear untainted. A different life would enable him
to exorcise his troubled mind.

These thoughts occupied him during the next
week during which he and his father moved back
to Elston Hall to join his mother and sister. He was
no nearer deciding what he should do when,
following his father a second time, he saw him in
contact with the mystery woman once more.

Returning to Elston Hall that evening, Robert
packed his knapsack with essential clothes, keeping
them to a minimum. He sorted out his oldest
garments to wear; wrote a brief note and addressed

it to his mother. It was a night with little sleep for Robert who wanted to time his departure for an hour before anyone else was up. He left the note at his mother's place at the dining table and went out into the chill morning air. A thin brushstroke of light on the horizon had not had time to dim the stars.

Halfway down the drive, he stopped and looked back. The house was a black mass against the sky. Home. Robert swallowed hard, counteracting the sentiment he felt rising within him. He swung round sharply and with a brisk, determined step headed for ... he knew not where.

11

Emily and Theo came into the dining room to breakfast together. At the same moment a maid, who had been listening for them coming down the stairs, entered the room.

'Good morning, ma'am. Good morning, sir.'

'Good morning, Phyllis.' Emily smiled at her as she went to her seat.

Theo greeted her too and added, 'I'll have some porridge, Phyllis, please.'

'Yes, sir.' The maid hurried away.

'I've received a letter,' said Emily with curiosity. A touch of alarm came into her voice when, on recognising the handwriting, she added, 'It's from Robert.'

A puzzled Theo said, 'What's he writing to you for? Can't he speak himself? He should be here at breakfast.'

Emily read the note and blanched. 'Oh, no!'

'What is it, Emily?'

She did not reply but held the paper towards her husband. He was quickly out of his seat at the opposite end of the table and took the letter as Emily sank dejectedly back in her chair. He read the contents hurriedly.

'What?' His voice resounded with disbelief.

At that moment Zelda came into the room, but her usual smiling breezy manner evaporated when she saw her parents' troubled expressions. 'What is it, Mama?'

'Robert's left home.' Emily's words were barely above a whisper.

'What?' Zelda stared from one to the other of them in disbelief. 'He can't have.'

Theo held out the note. 'Read this.'

Zelda took it and read:

Dear Mama,

It gives me great pain to write this. When you read it I will be gone. Don't worry. I can look after myself. I will be back sometime but I don't know how long it will take me to collect myself. I need to get away to do that.

Give my love to Father, and to Zelda, and of course it comes to you too.

Your loving son,
Robert

'I don't understand. What's this all about?' gasped Zelda.

Her father had pulled out a chair to sit closer to Emily. Zelda, alarmed by the way the colour had drained from her mother's face, did likewise.

Phyllis came in then with a steaming bowl of porridge, but stopped when she saw the family were not in their usual places and sensed the atmosphere was fraught with tension.

Zelda took the initiative, 'Not now, Phyllis, I'll let you know when.'

The maid left without a word, but they would flow when she reached the kitchen and made the most of having some knowledge, little though it was, that other members of the staff did not. Something was troubling the family. It must concern the letter she had seen in Mrs Addison's place when she had come to lay the table for breakfast.

As the door closed, Theo spoke. 'To answer your questions, Zelda, we don't know. We are mystified. What need has Robert to collect himself? What is troubling him? Can you shed any light on this?'

'I can't, Papa. I don't know. He has never said anything to me.'

'Is he troubled at work, Theo?' Emily asked, her voice firm, desperate to discover an explanation for why her son should leave home.

'He has never come to me and he knew he could. His work is good. He has left no doubt in my mind that, when the time is right, I can hand over to him, leaving the firm in good hands.'

'Then it must be something outside work,' said Emily. 'Has he got into bad company?' She looked at her daughter.

'Not that I know of, Mama.' Zelda gave a little shake of her head. 'No, he wouldn't. Oh, I know some of the young men of his set play hard, but I've never known Robert be drawn in by any of them. He can play as hard as the rest but underneath he's sensible. If he weren't, I'd hear from my friends. Some of them are only too ready to gossip and make tittle-tattle.' She paused a moment then, considering something.

Only a woman would have sensed it but Emily seized on that pause. 'You know something, Zelda!' she pressed her.

'No, I don't, Mama, nothing definite ... but I don't think everything is going well between Robert and Adele.'

'And he thinks a lot of her?'

'You've seen what I have seen.'

'Zelda,' cut in Theo, 'you have been with them more than we have and are therefore able to detect more. As far as I am concerned, I felt they got on very well. In fact, let me be frank ... both George and I saw it as a likely and very suitable marriage.'

'You've discussed it?' said Emily with surprise and just a touch of annoyance that her husband had not mentioned it to her.

'Not discussed. It just came up as a possibility, when we were talking about the way forward for our two firms.'

'You thought of it as a business arrangement!' Emily's lips tightened in disgust.

'No, no.' Theo tried to dispel the idea but she would have none of it.

'If either of them got wind of *that*, it certainly could have thrown doubt into their minds! You must clear that up with George at once and hopefully obtain his assurance ...' Emily's words trailed away. 'We can't. They've gone to Hull.'

'Mama, I don't think it can be that. I think if it had come to their knowledge, Robert would have mentioned it to me. As he didn't, I think it must be something of a more personal nature between him and Adele; something he didn't want to talk about, even with me. I did detect some unease between them at the Ball. Philip Bowen, whom Adele knew before the family came to Cantonville Hall, was paying her a lot of attention ...'

'An old flame that's been fanned again?' snorted Theo.

'And I know, from seeing his reactions that night, that Robert didn't like it. Maybe he and Adele had words.'

'And that is what he means by collecting himself,' snapped her father. 'That girl is to blame for this! I'll get myself off to Hull and sort it out now.' He jumped from his chair as if he was going to leave there and then.

'Sit down, Theo.' During these exchanges Emily had regained much of her composure, though pale and still feeling shocked by the news. The steel within her, which she resolutely kept from showing, now came to the fore. 'If you charge off like that and interfere in their affairs without thinking, you could easily do more damage. You might cause an irretrievable rift between Robert and Adele.'

'But they must be shown that there is no reason for this misunderstanding. There is nothing to prevent them from marrying.'

'Theo,' said Emily firmly, her eyes fixed intently on his, 'I too think a marriage between Robert and Adele would be ideal but, if a situation has arisen that would damage that prospect and cannot be overcome, the marriage should not be forced.'

She saw her husband was about to say something but held up her hand to stop him. 'Let me remind you that society is changing. You and I saw it a few years ago and swore we would allow our children to marry for love, not become embroiled in marriages of convenience. Don't let us do anything to destroy what we hope might be a successful union between Robert and Adele. If something has happened to preclude that, then so be it. It is no good forcing them into unhappiness. Not that I think we would succeed in forcing the issue. Adele, I believe, is too strong-minded to bend to our will or that of her parents. Let things be. Let Robert settle things for himself.'

'But we can't let him disappear from our lives,' protested Theo.

'He says he will be back.'

Theo recognised his wife's determination and respected her for it. 'I'll agree, but on one condition. If we hear nothing within three months we'll instigate a search for him.'

Emily hesitated a moment then conceded.

That same morning, in Hull, Adele sat looking out of the window into the garden at the back of her parents' house. The sun shone and, though there was little heat in it as yet, seemed to promise brighter times ahead. How Adele wished she could see her own life in the same way. Since leaving Newcastle she had been in a melancholy mood. Her mind kept drifting back to those final moments on The Quay when she had looked in vain for Robert, hoping he would come to make his peace with her. But he had not and, as the ship had cast off and manoeuvred into the river, her hopes had been lost in the mist that finally obscured the town from her sight. Tight-lipped, with tears not far from her eyes, she had retired to the Captain's cabin.

Knowing her mother was already there she had taken herself in hand, determined not to show any disappointment, but mothers have a certain intuitive sense, especially when it concerns their only daughter. Paula was sure Adele was hiding feelings that had been hurt by a certain young man in Newcastle, but was wise enough not to interfere at this particular moment. Adele was old enough to tackle her own problems and Paula knew her daughter would seek her advice if necessary.

Wishing that, with the crisis in her father's business solved, they could return to Newcastle, Adele sat lost in thought. Startled by a knock on the door she automatically called, 'Come in.' A maid entered. 'What is it, Eliza?'

'This has just been delivered for you, miss.' She held out an envelope as she crossed the room.

Adele's mind seized on this possibility. A letter from Robert! She glanced at it and her spirits dipped. Her name was printed on it but she did not recognise the penmanship; if it had been copper-plate, maybe she could have identified the sender. 'Who brought it?'

'A stranger, miss. He said he had ridden from Lincolnshire.'

Lincolnshire – that word eradicated thoughts of Robert from her mind. This letter could only be from Philip.

'Is the messenger awaiting an answer, Eliza?'

'He said he was told to do so, miss.'

'Very well. See that he has some refreshments. I will ring when I have my answer ready.'

'Yes, miss.' Eliza left the room.

Adele opened the envelope.

Dear Adele,

I have only just learned, from a business acquaintance, that your father is back in Hull and the family returned with him. If I had known sooner I would have contacted you before now.

I would like to invite you and Mark to a gathering of my friends at Redbourne Manor the weekend after next. I know it is short notice but your return has only just come to my notice. You will know everyone who is coming and I am sure they will all be happy to see you and welcome you back – none more so than I.

I look forward to a favourable answer.

  Your affectionate friend,
   Philip

Adele stared at the words for a moment, not really comprehending what immediate effect they were having on her. Then she read the letter again in a more sober frame of mind. Kind words, thoughtful, anxious to make contact again . . . in fact, Philip had contacted her as soon as he'd heard she was in Hull whereas Robert knew where she was and hadn't bothered to write; hadn't even come to The Quay even though he would have known when she was sailing.

She went to the mahogany secretaire, took out a sheet of paper and a pen from one of the drawers, then began to write. When she had finished she went to the bell-pull.

'Give the messenger this note and ask him to deliver it to Mr Philip Bowen personally,' she instructed the maid.

'Yes, miss.' Eliza hurried from the room, leaving Adele contemplating what she had written and wondering if fate was still taking a hand in her life by delaying her father's decision to return to Newcastle.

After purchasing some food in nearby Hexham, Robert kept to the country roads as he headed south. His first instinct had been to head for Hull and find Adele, but he realised that was not the answer. By contacting her he would be forced to reveal the reason for his leaving home, and that would bring shame on both their families. He would have to forget her and believe she would be happy with someone else ... someone such as Philip Bowen. His priority now was to determine where he should go and how he should live henceforth. He needed to become anonymous in case his father instigated a search, and decided he would call himself Robert Dane. The money he had brought with him would soon be gone; he would have to seek work. But first he must put a good distance between himself and home.

He kept to a brisk pace but after five miles realised he could not continue at this speed. It would be better to keep on steadily and cover the miles over a longer time rather than exhaust himself at the start. He saw few people except in the villages where he ignored the curious looks he was given and greeted the village folk with a cheery 'Good day' until he realised his refined accent made him stand out.

With the sun finally slipping towards the western horizon, a chill came into the air. He realised he must have shelter for the night, but preferably while avoiding human contact for he did not know if his father had taken steps to find him and was not yet far enough away to ignore the Addison sphere of influence.

Shelter was fast becoming a priority when he saw a farmhouse about half a mile off the track he was travelling on. There was a stone-built barn and another outbuilding not far from it.

Robert stood still and surveyed the direction of the barn. He wished it had been further from the house but maybe he could reach it without being seen, be awake early and then away, before anyone from the farmhouse set about their daily tasks.

He turned off the track and headed for the barn, alert to any movement in the open land-scape. He covered half the distance at a brisk walk and then, hunching his shoulders, broke into a steady run, wishing he were not impeded by his long redingote and knapsack, though without them he realised he would have been in for a very unpleasant night. Reaching the barn, he breathed a sigh of relief when he saw that there was no padlock visible. He glanced anxiously in the direction of the house where the only sign of habitation was the yellow light shining out under a curtained window. He pushed the barn door gently open, thankful to the farmer who had kept its hinges well greased.

Inside, the only light came from two small windows set in one of the thick walls. When his eyes adjusted to the gloom he saw that the barn was used as a storage area. The floor was covered with straw that had come from the stack piled in one corner. It was just what he wanted. Robert quickly made himself a bed-nest in the straw and settled down to eat the remains of the food he had bought in Hexham. Then, satisfied, he lay down and fell into the sleep of complete physical and mental exhaustion.

He came sharply awake, body tense, mind trying to shut out the screeching sound that assailed his ears. Light was flooding into the barn. He sat up and saw the figure of a girl silhouetted in the doorway.

'Pa! Pa! Quick!'

Robert started to get up.

'Stay there!' the girl ordered him and stepped forward, menacing him with a pitchfork.

Robert sank back, supporting himself on his elbows so that he could keep his eyes on the weapon in the hands of the girl who now glared at him with open hostility. Her plain brown skirt reached her ankles. A woollen jacket open at the front revealed a dark blue blouse. A shawl had slipped from her hair that now hung loose around her shoulders.

Footsteps came running towards the barn.

'What is it, Sal? What's up?' The man's voice was harsh, thick with a Durham accent.

'Intruder, Pa. Vagrant!'

A tall thick-set man appeared alongside her. He paused, glared at the recumbent figure then stepped forward to tower menacingly over Robert before his eyes took in the situation with unexpected alertness. 'It's all right, Sal,' he said over his shoulder, 'he has no weapon.'

Robert saw the girl visibly relax and, though she still held the pitchfork, she did so with less menace.

'On your feet,' growled the man.

Robert did as he was told. He wanted no trouble.

'Outside, so's I can see you.'

Robert picked up his redingote and knapsack and stepped past the watchful pair. He gave a little shiver when the February cold caught him before he had pulled on his coat.

'Well?' The terseness of the man's query demanded an instant response.

'I needed somewhere to sleep, sir.'

The man let out a loud guffaw. 'Hear that, Sal? I've not been called "sir" before. Note it, my gal. Maybe *you'll* start calling your pa sir!' He laughed even louder.

Sal raised an eyebrow, chuckled and said derisively under her breath, 'That's a likely thing!'

'Hi, Ma, did you hear that?'

Robert saw a buxom woman standing watching them from the doorstep of the farmhouse. 'Get yourselves in, breakfast's waiting. And bring the lad with you!' she called.

The man and his daughter continued to chuckle as they walked back to the house, having indicated to Robert to precede them. He said nothing but stopped before the door.

'You heard her . . . in!' said the man gruffly.

Still Robert hesitated, glancing at the girl as he did so. She read his intention and smiled. 'He's polite too, Pa.' She flounced past Robert, nodding her thanks.

He followed and found himself in a warm, comfortable kitchen. A large pine table with six chairs stood in the centre of the room. A black grate with side oven held a blazing fire above which a kettle hung from a reckon. A pan rested on a trivet hanging from the grate, positioned so that it caught the heat from the fire. The smell of home-made bread made Robert realise how hungry he was. The rest of the room contained chairs placed to each side of the fireplace, a settle and a dresser. This looked to be the home of a hard-working and prosperous farmer.

'You can wash there, lad,' said the woman, indicating the stone sink in the scullery beyond.

'Thank you,' replied Robert and, needing no second bidding, went into the scullery. He ladled some water from a large crock into a bowl in the sink, and in a few minutes returned to the kitchen refreshed.

'Sit thisen down there, lad.' The man indicated a seat at the table opposite him. By the fire the girl was holding a basin of warm milk into which her mother was placing a hunk of salted bread; their usual breakfast. In a few minutes everyone was served.

'Right, lad, what's tha name?' the farmer asked.

'Robert Dane,' he answered firmly.

The man nodded. He spooned some more milky bread into his mouth, a moment his daughter was not slow to seize. 'My pa and ma are Mr and Mrs Swinton and, as you will have heard, I'm Sal.'

'I'm grateful to you, ma'am, and you, sir, for your hospitality.' Robert glanced mischievously at Sally. 'And to you ... for not using that pitchfork.'

'I would have done if you'd tried anything,' she answered seriously. 'And maybe I wouldn't have been as good-hearted as Ma is, feeding you.'

'Now, Sal, you can't begrudge travellers,' her mother intervened.

Mr Swinton grunted. 'Travellers don't doss down in someone else's barn at night.' His penetrating gaze dwelt on Robert a moment. 'And you ain't a vagrant, your clothes are too good for that, and you aren't looking for work.'

'Oh, but I am,' he broke in quickly.

Mr Swinton gave another snort. 'With hands like yours? You ain't done a day's grafting in your life.'

Mrs Swinton saw that the young man was about to protest and said quickly, 'My husband's right, even I noticed your hands, and the cut of your coat tells me you are from a far better off family than ours. So what is it you are running away from?'

Robert was annoyed with himself. He should have thought of these points before setting off. He would have to rectify them immediately he had left the farm. 'Mrs Swinton, I detect concern in your voice. Let me reassure you that nothing bad has precipitated my change of scene. I am not in debt or in trouble, I am simply an independent man needing a change from a life that was stifling me. I felt I must escape for a while in order to sort things out.'

She nodded. 'I accept that, Mr Dane, and ...'

'Robert, please.'

'Very well, Robert. And my husband and daughter will too.'

'All right, son, we accept your explanation,' said the farmer. 'Where are you from?'

'That doesn't matter, sir.'

Mr Swinton shrugged, accepting the slight rebuke.

'Well, where are you going then?'

'Anywhere ... until I decide the time is right to return home. And who knows when that will be?'

'And in the meantime, you will take jobs wherever you are?'

'That's the way I see it, sir.'

'And you'll soil those hands of yours?'

'I may never have done the sort of work to which you are referring but I won't shrink from it. I'll stand alongside any man.'

'Ah, will you now? That's brave talk.'

'Let's try him out, Pa,' put in Sally. 'Since Harry went off to Consett we could do with some help. There's the ditching to finish ...'

'Tha's right, lass,' agreed her father. He looked at Robert. 'I'll give you a week's work. Maybe two. As Sal says, there's ditching to finish.'

'Thanks, sir.' Robert saw this as a good opportunity to harden himself up for what might lie ahead. 'I'll take your kind offer.'

'Kind?' Mr Swinton laughed. 'You may not think so in a day or two! You try to keep up with Sal and you'll realise you have muscles in your body you never knew about. Sal's a stalwart. She insisted from an early age on working on the farm, even though it's not women's work ... well, mostly not. There's only one thing. If Harry returns, as I think he might, I'll have to give him his job back. I promised him I would keep it open for a month.'

'I understand, Mr Swinton.'

'Right, Robert, that seems to be settled,' said Mrs Swinton. 'You'll live in like Harry used to. You can have his old room. That's all part of your wage. Whatever you get paid in cash is up to Mr Swinton.'

'That is most generous of you, Mrs Swinton.'

'I'll pay you what I think you're worth at the end of your employment, seeing it's likely to be short,' grunted the farmer.

'That seems fair to me,' Robert agreed.

'I'll show you round now,' said Sally. She glanced at her father. 'Continue with the ditches after midday meal?'

'Yes, Sal.'

She stood up. 'Come on then,' she urged Robert.

He followed her outside and in the course of the rest of the morning was shown the extent of the farm, which was only small, with its ten medium-sized fields. The stable held a heavy working horse. Ten cows had been let out of their shed and were grazing in one of the fields. Thirty hens kept the family in eggs and fowl with the extras going to market, along with butter produced by Mrs Swinton in a room adjoining the kitchen, and any other produce available on the day. Sally explained she loved those excursions, though it meant her and her mother setting out early to get the most favourable prices and leaving Mr Swinton to do the milking on his own now that Harry had left.

'Why did he leave? Didn't he like farming?' Robert asked as he and Sally leaned on a gate, watching the cows contentedly chewing the cud.

'He was cut out for farming – had been in it since he was a boy and he's twenty-eight now. But he was tempted by the higher wages in Consett at the iron works. Those are what you can see belching out smoke on the horizon.'

'I'd noticed them and wondered what they were.'

'Iron was going to be the great saviour of Consett but things have not gone according to plan. We hear the iron company is in trouble and some parts of it have been closed down. They say it should only be temporary, but that could mean anything. There's a big development taking place along the River Tees at Middlesbrough, though. I hear it will be the Ironopolis of the North. It's attracting hundreds of men seeking work.'

Robert made no comment on this but stored the information away in his mind. It could be useful when he had to move on, as move on he would. His stay on Rush Farm was proving to be very helpful, giving him a good start, but he realised that if his father were making a search for him, he would be more exposed on a farm than among the masses in a town. And a growing town would give him even greater anonymity.

'Your two weeks are up tomorrow, Robert,' said Mr Swinton while they were changing their muddy boots in the scullery at the end of their labours. 'You soon fell into the way of ditching and have done well – Sal has nothing but praise for you. If you want to stay I'll keep you on, unless Harry turns up in the next two weeks.'

'That's very kind of you, Mr Swinton, and I must say I have been happy here, but I think I must move on.'

The farmer did not question him. Though he still knew no more about Robert than he did on the day the young man arrived at Rush Farm, he felt he had no right to pry. 'Very well. The ditching is finished so we'll regard tomorrow as a day worked.'

'That is very generous of you, Mr Swinton. I am grateful.'

'Get plenty into you,' Mrs Swinton said as she put his bowl of salted bread and milk in front of Robert the next morning. 'I've packed you some food to see you through today.'

'Thank you. That is very kind of you.' He relished his humble breakfast, wondering when he would next have such a hearty meal to start the day. 'Are Mr Swinton and Sal seeing to the cows?'

'Aye, they should be in any moment. We've been pleased to have you here, Robert, and I hope you can resolve the trouble that brought you. There's nothing like being with your own family.'

The sincerity of her words brought a lump to his throat, but he made no comment and was pleased when at that moment the door opened and Mr Swinton and Sally came in. When the meal was finished, Robert brought his knapsack and redingote from his room.

'You'll need that on, it's a bit chilly out there,' Mr Swinton commented.

'I'm leaving it here ... do with it what you will. If I take it, it could rouse curiosity about me.'

'Mmm, I see your point, lad,' mused Mr Swinton. 'But you'll need something warm.'

'In the stable there's an old woollen jacket we sometimes use to cover one of the horses,' put in Sally.

'Fetch it in, lass,' said Mrs Swinton. 'I'll see if I can do anything with it.'

The girl hurried from the kitchen.

When she returned, her mother already had a stiff clothes brush ready. 'Ah, that one. I'd forgotten it.' She glanced at her husband. 'It's one your brother left behind.'

'He might want it back,' suggested Robert.

'Good grief, no, that was four years ago. You take it, lad.'

'Thanks, Mr Swinton, but only if you're sure?'

'Here, let me have a go at it.' Mrs Swinton took it outside and gave it a good brushing. Returning to the house, she got out her sewing basket and soon had two patches sewn on. 'There, try it on,

210

but I'm sure it will fit. He weren't the size of his brother – more like you.'

Robert slipped the jacket on.

'Couldn't be much better,' Sally enthused.

'I'll think of you all whenever I put it on, and I'll always keep it – a reminder of you and how you helped me. I'll come back and see you one day.'

'We'd like that,' said Mrs Swinton. 'Take care of yourself. And we hope everything turns out right for you.'

The kindness behind her words stuck in Robert's mind when he headed south once more. He reconsidered the information he had gleaned about Consett and Middlesbrough. The latter was the more likely place in which to lose himself, it seemed, until he decided what to do with his future.

Unbeknown to him, however, that future was already being decided.

12

Mark was coming down the stairs when a maid appeared, heading for the dining room. Seeing him, she stopped. 'Sir, some mail has just been delivered.' She held out a batch of envelopes.

'Thank you. I'll take them in.'

He glanced at them and felt a surge of excitement. One was addressed to him and it was from Zelda. This would brighten his day! But it would be more enjoyable to read it in the privacy of his own room after breakfast, so he slipped it discreetly into his pocket.

His father, mother and Adele were already seated at the table. 'Good morning, everyone,' he greeted them brightly.

Some time later, having curbed his eagerness to read his letter and seeing that everyone else was close to finishing, Mark said, 'May I be excused?'

'Yes. I'll be leaving for the office in a few minutes,' replied his father.

'I'll see you there, if that is agreeable to you?'

George nodded to his son.

Mark took the stairs two at a time, closed the

door to his room behind him and made haste to read his letter.

My Dear Mark,
I send you my earnest felicitations, and as ever I miss your company.

But the real reason for my writing is not so joyous. I have to tell you that Robert has left home. It has been a shock to us all. He left a note on the breakfast table for Mother saying he had things he had to sort out and it was better to do this away from home. He did not say what they were but it seems something has been troubling him. If only he had stayed and spoken of this, we could have helped him. He gave no indication of where he was going or of when he would be back; merely saying he would return in due course. I greatly fear that could turn into never, though I do hope not.

I think Adele ought to know, but I would ask you both not to breathe a word of this to anyone else, not even your parents. I would be in serious trouble if my own parents were to learn I had written to you on this matter.

But, please, if you hear anything of Robert, let me know.

   Your affectionate friend,
   Zelda

Stunned, Mark stared at the letter. This couldn't be true. Robert had always seemed so sensible, so full of the joys of life, enjoying equally his work and his leisure. Mark read the words again and realised he must go and find Adele.

She was sitting at her dressing table, sorting out some trinkets.

'Read this,' he told her, holding out the letter.

The urgency of his voice startled her. She stared curiously at him as she took the paper.

Her face paled when she had read it. 'When did you receive this?'

'It was among the letters I was bringing Father this morning. Seeing Zelda's writing, I kept it to myself.'

Adele raised an eyebrow. 'Just as well or Father would have wanted to know what it contained.'

'So, what do you make of it?'

'I'm shocked,' she replied. Her thoughts, even in these brief moments, had been racing. I hope he hasn't left because of me, she could not help but think, even though in the next moment she told herself she had not caused this.

'I'm astonished. What's got into Robert?' commented her brother.

'How should I know?'

'You've been the closest to him of all of us.'

'Not that close.'

Mark pulled a face.

'Don't look like that, Mark, it's true. If it weren't, Robert would have been on The Quay to see me sail. He wasn't, so what does that tell you about his feelings for me? Why should I care if he's gone or where he is? I hope he turns up, for the sake of his mother and father and Zelda, who must be greatly distressed. Has he thought of that? I see his going off on a whim as a very selfish act.'

Mark was about to protest but, reading his sister's attitude, deemed it wisest to say no more. 'Very well,' he said, 'I will acknowledge this letter, extend our sympathy, and agree to let Zelda know if we hear anything from him.'

Adele nodded but added a little scornfully, 'I don't think that is likely. If Robert wants to disappear he won't contact us.'

Theodore sat in his office, staring morosely at the papers on his desk. These were matters that would normally have been dealt with by Robert and they reminded him of his son. He hadn't realised how much he would miss him, and not only for the work he undertook. The house was not the same without him around. What could have upset him enough to make him leave home? Zelda had hinted that all was not well between him and Adele. She would know that better than he or Emily. But even if she was right, there was nothing Theodore could do about it ... or was there? Emily had urged caution, pointing out that Robert had said he would be back, and Theodore himself had reiterated that he would do nothing for three months. But his lips tightened; his clenched fist thudded against the desk in frustration. He could not wait that long. He needed to know where his son was, make sure he was all right, offer him help.

The obvious course of action would be to see Adele but he did not want to cause friction between the two families, create a situation that could be detrimental to the trading links they had built up; besides, interfering in his affairs of the heart could alienate Robert from his family forever and destroy any chance of a possible reconciliation. Theodore did not want that. What he most wanted now was advice on how to find a missing person.

He pushed himself away from his desk, put on his top coat, automatically set his hat at the angle he always placed it, picked up his cane and left the building. Twenty minutes later he was being shown into the study of ex-Superintendent Bill Jarvis, a tall thin man of fifty-five with thirty-five years of police service behind him. He had only retired when an injury in the line of duty forced him to. He had seen it all, from the early days of haphazard, so-called policing to the much more organised system of today that speedily bore results in the hands of men like Bill Jarvis.

He rose from behind his desk to greet Theodore with a warm handshake. 'It's a while since I've seen you, Theo, and that is my misfortune.'

'Mine too, Bill.'

'Let's take the comfortable chairs,' said the former policeman, indicating two armchairs placed by the fireplace where flames danced cheerily, driving away all thoughts of the drab day outside. 'How's your family?'

'It is because of my son that I'm seeking your advice.'

'Not in trouble with the police, I hope?' asked Bill, his ruddy face taking on a more serious expression.

'No, no,' Theo hastened to say, 'but Robert has left home without a word of explanation as to where he is going.'

'And you want to find him?'

'Yes. I didn't know who to turn to, then I thought that you might be able to advise me.'

Bill nodded. 'I'll do what I can, but first . . . is this because of a family rift?'

'No.'

'Very well. If it had been, I would have told you to go home and sort it out. I won't involve myself in family disputes. So, with that out of the way, let me say that I will need to know all the details. You should hold nothing back or the advice I give you may not be as helpful as it might.' His eyes rested intently on Theo as he spoke.

'Agreed.'

'Good. I assure you that whatever you tell me will not be repeated to anyone unless it is absolutely necessary. And if I direct you to anyone else, it will be to someone I can trust implicitly to keep the information to himself.'

Theo nodded.

'Right, begin at the beginning and leave nothing out.'

Bill listened without interrupting, merely pouring them both a glass of beer to oil the wheels. Then he began firing questions at his visitor. The final one was, 'It seems to me that you believe this girl Adele, of whom you otherwise approve, may be the reason why Robert left. Have you contacted her family? And if not, why not?'

'I have not. There are two reasons. I do not wish to cause a rift in our trading relationship, but more than that – Emily and I do not believe in interfering in affairs of the heart unless absolutely necessary. Let the persons concerned sort matters out for themselves. If they can, most likely they will be united forever. If not, then they are better apart.'

'Very wise. I lost a son through my own inter- ference. Now we don't even see his children ... a great loss.'

'I'm sorry,' sympathised Theo.

Bill brushed aside the display of regret and said, 'So you want my advice on what to do next?'

'Please.'

'There are several courses of action you could take, but what I would advise most strongly is that you come back tomorrow at the same time to meet a young man I think will be able to help you. His name is Bernard Hawkins, but he goes more usually by the name of Barney. He was a young constable on the Newcastle force, injured at the same time as I was. A bright career was spoilt, let me tell you. He's done a bit of private work since.' Bill saw a shadow of doubt creep into Theo's expression so added quickly, 'I'm not making this recommendation from charitable reasons. If I didn't think he could help, I wouldn't suggest him.'

Theo nodded. 'Thanks, Bill. I'll be back tomor- row to meet Barney.'

'Good. Now sit back and relax with a drop more beer and tell me about life along the river. Who's trading with whom? What cargoes are being shipped?'

Theo smiled. 'Still the same old Bill. Curious to hear what's happening ... and subtly diverting my mind from my problem.'

Bill returned his smile. 'I could never fool you.' He raised his glass. 'Here's to our success.'

Theo was on time the following day and found Bernard Hawkins already with Bill Jarvis. No doubt it had been arranged so that Bill could brief him about the man who might be about to employ him.

The younger man was out of his chair as soon as Theo walked in. Without any preamble Bill made the introductions.

'I'm pleased to meet you, sir.' Barney extended his hand and, as Theo took it, each man knew he was coming under scrutiny from the other.

Theo felt the firm grip of a young man who was sure of himself, determined and tenacious. He saw alert eyes that would miss nothing, ready to store away any detail in case it should prove useful. He also saw understanding and consideration behind that steady gaze.

Barney already knew something of Theo's reputation as a man determined to make a name for himself in the mercantile world, though he had not been born to it. His success had been achieved by hard work and good judgement; never once had he ridden roughshod over anyone. There was steel in this man's character, but he could be generous and open-hearted too.

'Sit down.' Bill indicated the chairs that had been drawn up. As they sat down, he said, 'Theo, I have told Barney nothing more than that you wish him to search for your missing son. I thought it best he hear the details from you yourself.'

'Mr Jarvis knows from previous work he has put my way that I prefer it that way. First-hand contact with a possible client enables me to make a better judgement of the various aspects of the case,' said Barney, easing his well-proportioned frame more comfortably into his chair. Intense brown eyes met Theo's. 'I would like you to begin at what you believe to be the beginning ... probably your own suspicions that something was not right in your son's life. Please hold nothing back, even something you might regard as insignificant.'

Theo was surprised; he had expected there would be an interrogation and had been dreading having to reveal private matters, but the gentle modulation of Barney's voice immediately put him at his ease.

'Before you start, sir, let me add one thing. Nothing you tell me will pass beyond these four walls unless it is vital to my finding your son. If you have any questions about me and the way I work, I will gladly answer them.'

'Young man, the recommendation of Mr Jarvis is good enough for me – I trust his judgement – but I will add that what I have seen in these first few moments has impressed me.'

'Thank you, sir. I appreciate that. Now, shall we begin?'

Theo held up his hand for a moment, indicating he had something else to say. 'Before I do, I want you to know that I do not wish my name to be linked with your enquiry.' He saw a flash of doubt in Barney's expression, so quickly added, 'At least, not for the time being.'

'Is there any particular reason for this?' the young man asked.

'I believe if my son hears that I have instigated a search, he may conceal himself. As I will explain, he did say he would return sometime. I have no doubt he would prefer to do so in his own good time.'

Barney nodded thoughtfully for a few moments then said, 'Very well, sir, I'll comply with your wishes. If ever I think it necessary to use your name, I will consult you first.'

'Admirable,' said Theo with relief, a reaction that Barney noted; it made him wonder if there was a deeper reason underlying Mr Addison's request. Theo went on to describe the events leading up to Robert's departure. He left nothing out that he thought might be relevant.

Barney listened without interruption then questioned Theo about Robert's relationship with each member of the family; his attitude to Adele and her family; his opinion of Adele's friendliness with Philip Bowen; his demeanour at work, and if he had had any problems with the people they employed; if there had been any trouble with any of his friends.

'Finally, sir, do you think he might have gone to see Miss Jordan?'

'That possibility crossed our minds and I was prepared to go to Hull to enquire, but my wife persuaded me not to.'

'Why did she do that?'

'She believes that Robert will do as he says in the letter I showed you – he will return of his own accord. But I'm less sanguine. Robert indicates he does not know when that will be – which could imply never. At my wife's prompting I agreed to do nothing for three months, but I find I cannot wait that long.'

'From what you say, and the way you say it, I take it that your wife does not know you are employing me to find Robert?'

'She doesn't.'

'Well, sir, I strongly advise you to tell her so immediately. It may be that at some time in the future I will have to ask her and your daughter some questions.'

'Will that be necessary? I would not wish them to be troubled.'

'It is more than likely that I will need to do so. They may have seen or heard something that you have not; any snippet of information could be vital.'

Theo nodded and said a little reluctantly, 'Very well.'

'Good. Thank you, sir. There is just one more thing ... can you give me the address of the Jordan family in Hull?'

Theodore broached the subject of Robert that evening after he, Emily and Zelda had settled in the privacy of the drawing room.

'There is something I must tell you.' In the slight pause he made, both mother and daughter, recognising the seriousness in his tone, diverted their attention from their books to him. 'It is a confession,' he added, an admission that alerted them

222

even further. 'I have instigated a search for Robert.' He held up his hand in apology. 'I know I said I would wait three months, but I couldn't bear not doing anything.'

The remonstrations he'd expected to come from his wife did not materialise. Instead surprised expressions from both her and Zelda changed to those of relief.

'Thank goodness!' cried Emily.

It was Theo's turn to be surprised. 'I thought you wanted to wait and see if he came home?'

'I've waited long enough. I can't bear not knowing where he is ... how he is.'

'So what have you done, Papa?' put in Zelda, eager to learn if it might lead to their tracing her brother.

Theo told them and explained the initial line of enquiry which Barney Hawkins was going to make in Hull. When he had finished he added, 'I have requested that our name be kept out of the affair, at least until we know it is wise to reveal it. If anyone enquires of us about Robert, we'll say he has gone to visit a relative in Bath. We had all better stick to the same story.'

'Does Mr Hawkins know this?' asked Zelda.

'Yes. And one other thing ... Mr Hawkins may want to talk to both of you.'

Barney spent the next day very discreetly probing the standing of the Addison family but emerged with nothing that might suggest why Robert had left home. Maybe the answer lay with Adele Jordan?

The following day he took the train to York, stayed overnight and then travelled by mail coach to Hull where he was deposited at the Cross Keys in the Market Place. He took a room there. By friendly questioning around the inn he gained some knowledge of the Jordan family and their standing in Hull and obtained directions to their house.

The next day he presented himself at the front door, handed a calling-card to the maid and enquired if Mr Jordan were at home, and if so might he possibly see him.

The girl cast a wary eye over him then said, 'Step inside, sir. I'll see if Mr Jordan is at home.' She crossed the hall to a door on the left. A few moments later she reappeared and said, 'Mr Jordan will see you, sir.' She held the door open.

As Barney entered the room George rose from behind his desk and came round to greet him. He held the card in his left hand and tapped it with his right. 'Newcastle Police, I see. I hope this has nothing to do with my business there?'

Barney felt a wave of satisfaction. One of his old calling-cards had done the trick again. 'No, sir, it hasn't.'

'Thank goodness for that! I've just sorted out some trouble here. When I think things are finally settled, I'll be back to Newcastle – and I hope that will be soon. Now, why are you here, Constable?' George indicated a chair to Barney and, as his visitor sat down, resumed his own seat behind the desk.

'Could you tell me something about a young man named Robert Addison?'

George showed surprise. 'Robert?'

'From your expression, sir, it seems you know him fairly well?'

'I suppose I do. But why come all this way, and why come to me?'

'It is a delicate matter. We wanted to solicit some outside opinions about the young man before approaching the family.'

George nodded and rubbed his chin before regarding Barney with a frown. 'A delicate matter? How delicate?'

'I'm sorry, sir, I'm not at liberty to say.'

George grunted.

'Just give me a character reference first, sir.'

'Well, a fine upright young man, amiable, good company, courteous ... and hard-working, I understand. Your presence here adds a shade of doubt to my assessment but I can't imagine Robert getting on the wrong side of the law. Though, of course, who knows what secrets even our best friends may be hiding?'

'Quite so, sir. Has he visited you here since you returned?'

Barney had shot the question in so quickly that George answered it automatically. 'No, haven't seen him since we left Newcastle.' Barney knew this was the truth but he needed to do a little more probing.

'I understand Mr Robert Addison is very friendly with your daughter.'

'Yes, and I assure you that the relationship is looked upon with favour by both families.'

'Quite so, sir. Would you mind if I had a word with Miss Jordan?'

George frowned thoughtfully. 'Only if I am present.'

'Very well, sir.'

George rose from his chair and started for the door.

'Sir.' The word came so sharply that he stopped in his tracks and swung round to eye Barney. 'Would you mind ringing for the maid and asking her to call your daughter?' Barney put his request with the utmost courtesy. The protest that had sprung to George's lips died before it was uttered.

He gave a half smile. 'You did not want me to brief my daughter before you saw her?'

Barney acknowledged the smile with one of his own. 'Just so, sir.'

George went to the bell-pull and within a few minutes Adele came into the room.

'What is it, Papa? Oh, I'm sorry. The maid did not tell me you had company.' She looked questioningly from her father to Barney who had risen from his chair.

'Adele, this is Mr Hawkins. Mr Hawkins, my daughter.'

Bernard smiled. 'I'm pleased to meet you, Miss Jordan.'

She inclined her head. 'Mr Hawkins.'

'Mr Hawkins is from the Newcastle Police.'

A look of alarm crossed Adele's face but Barney was impressed by how quickly she controlled it.

'Mr Hawkins wants to ask you a few questions about Robert,' explained George.

Once again Barney caught that flicker of alarm and this time it was not brought under control so

226

quickly. 'What do you want to know?' she asked politely.

'When did you last see Robert Addison?'

'A short while before we left Newcastle. I cannot be more specific than that.'

So it had not been a memory to cherish. Had it been she would have come straight out with the date. Was this a sign of trouble between the two young people? His next question might provide the answer.

'Did he not come to see you depart?'

'He did not,' she answered with evident indignation.

Barney ignored this and asked, 'Then, you have not seen him since you arrived here?'

'No. What's this all about, Mr Hawkins?' she asked. In spite of her tone Barney detected concern and judged that this girl still had some feelings for Robert Addison, though they had recently changed. Some trouble had brewed between these two and it was looking increasingly as if that was the most likely cause of Robert's disappearance. The Jordan family knew nothing of that, however, and he was not about to tell them.

'I'm sorry, miss, I am not at liberty to say at this stage of our enquiries. I merely needed some character references from people other than Mr Addison's family before involving them.' He rose from his chair. 'I thank you both for your time and for the information. I would ask one thing more – if Mr Addison does call here please send word to the address on this card.'

★

Thankful that she had not revealed Mark's receipt of Zelda's letter, Adele asked, 'What do you make of that, Papa?' when George returned to his study after seeing Barney Hawkins from the house.

He looked thoughtful as he resumed his seat. 'There is something strange about this enquiry. Coming here looking for references before approaching Robert's family ... that seems to speak of Robert being in trouble with the police.'

'Surely not, Papa,' protested Adele rather quickly. 'Robert wouldn't ...?'

'It makes me wonder, how well do we really know him? After all, it is not a long acquaintance-ship.'

'But he's always been so friendly, so attentive. I like him.'

'No more than that?' George hinted delicately, concerned for her welfare and aware that she had looked kindly on the young man previously.

She hesitated. 'Oh, I don't know, Papa. I have wondered if my feelings were stronger, then Philip reappeared.'

'And you had doubts?'

She nodded.

'Don't rush to any conclusions about Mr Hawkins's visit. Always avoid making snap judge-ments. We don't know if this is a criminal enquiry. His question about Robert visiting us could indicate merely that he has gone missing. If that is the only reason for this enquiry, then the Addisons themselves must have instigated it. Mr Hawkins may well be pretending he has not yet approached them as a cover for the real state of affairs.'

'Whatever it is, I'm sorry if Robert is troubled,' sighed Adele.

That thought haunted her later when she lay down in her soft bed and drew the bedclothes up to her chin, as if to protect herself from the harshness of the world.

Since their visitor's departure the day had proceeded normally enough. George had told Paula and Mark about Mr Hawkins's visit and they had both expressed their concern and hope that it did not signify anything untoward in Robert's life. Since then the matter had not been spoken of again.

But in the quietness of her room, with the curtains drawn back to allow the moonlight in, Adele found she could not help but wonder where Robert was and why the enquiry was being made. What did the police know that they weren't revealing? Could he possibly be a criminal? If he had disappeared because he had done something wrong, then he was piling trouble on trouble. She still could not really believe he had stepped on the wrong side of the law, but as her father had said, how much did she really know of Robert? Her thoughts tumbled over and over, trying to find some reason for the police enquiry.

Finally she pulled herself up sharply and chastised herself for thinking this way. Robert's current situation need not concern her. He had revealed his true feelings for her by not coming to see her leave

Newcastle. His present dilemma need not concern her. There was Philip eagerly awaiting her in Redbourne, and there were his friends. Did she really want any more?

13

The main track from Whitby to Rosedale was open
before the snow had fully disappeared from the
high moors. Betsy and her father took this opportunity to make their first visit of the year to
Rosedale.

With a broad smile and open arms Mrs
Dodsworth greeted Betsy. 'It's good to see you
again, lass.'

'And I'm so pleased to see you, Mrs Dodsworth,'
she said, returning the kiss and hug.

'I hope you've kept well this winter, Sam?'
queried Mrs Dodsworth.

'I have,' he replied. 'Thanks to this lass looking
after me.'

'Come away in. Your rooms have been ready
since the snow started to show signs of going.' She
ushered them into the house.

Betsy could not hold back her query any longer.
'We heard about the disaster on the Ingleby Incline
but no details. Was Jim involved?'

'Aye, lass, he was. Some blame rested on him
but ...'

'Oh, no!' Betsy's face creased with concern.

Her father moved to her side and put a comforting arm around her shoulders.

'. . . fortunately no one was killed,' their hostess continued. 'There was one casualty but he recovered.'

Sam could feel relief surge through his daughter.

'Is Jim in the dale?' she asked.

'No, lass. He was up before the board just after it happened. Because of his quick action and the fact that no one died, he did not lose his job. The board also recognised that in Jim Fenwick they had a valuable man, so Sir Francis sent him on another project. He has not been back in the dale since and, from what I hear, is not likely to be. That could only be rumour, mind you.'

It saddened her to see the hope die in her young visitor's eyes.

In succeeding visits Betsy's first question to Mrs Dodsworth was always, 'Any news of Jim?'

It pained her always to have to say no. Concern that this continual disappointment could have a detrimental effect on Betsy began to gnaw at Mrs Dodsworth until, knowing that the girl lacked a mother's advice, she allowed her own maternal instincts to take over.

'Betsy, I really do think you are going to have to realise Jim Fenwick is not coming back.'

'Don't say that!' she protested, her lips tightening in distress.

'But it looks like being the case and you are going to have to face up to it, sooner or later. Better sooner, then you can take hold of your life

232

again . . . not let it drift on in dreams that don't look like coming true.'

'But I thought Jim . . .'

'He's made no attempt to come back here. Nobody knows where he is or what he's doing. You'd best forget him. There are other fish in the sea.'

With the passing of the months Betsy began to realise that perhaps Mrs Dodsworth was right. She should not let her life drift away.

Dealing with Sir Francis's task was proving more frustrating than Jim had envisaged. Ascertaining who owned the land along the route the railway might take was not always easy, especially when it was found that some people, who greeted the possibility of making a deal with alacrity, had in fact no legal right to do so. Unravelling all this and bringing together a possible route sorely tested Jim's patience. But he needed this work. He revelled in the responsibility, and saw it as a way to regain Sir Francis's confidence in him after the previous setback. The days and weeks slipped by. It was not until halfway through the third month of his absence that he was able to draw his investigation to a conclusion and write up a report for Sir Francis.

Robert left the foundry on the banks of the Tees, near the growing town of Middlesbrough, and joined the crowd of men heading for their favourite pub. Those parched by the heat from the furnaces eagerly anticipated the cooling effect of the beer; others, like Robert, needed to clear their throats of the dust that came with shovelling coal and ore.

'Found any more muscles, Dane?' The question, accompanied by a mocking laugh, came from a burly man, maybe six or seven years older than Robert. There was no amusement in his dark eyes, only contempt and derision for a man he saw as weak and useless.

'Quit riling the lad, Mason.' The passer-by's comment drew support from others around them. 'He's just doing a job of work, same as you.' Art Mason was not liked by most of his fellow workers who knew him to be something of a bully, but a bully who was careful who he picked on.

'Like me? That's a laugh.' He held up broad calloused hands with long, powerful fingers. 'Look at them, then look at his.'

'Aye, look at 'em.' The back-up came from a thin wiry man with a taut muscular build.

'You tell 'em, Luke.' Art egged his sidekick on, knowing Luke's inferior intelligence let him revel in the position of Mason's sidekick. 'I'm Art's mate!' he liked to declare, sticking his chest out and swaggering proudly.

'You seen 'em?' Luke declared now. 'Sissy's hands.'

Realising that they were nearing the Golden Spike and that his audience would be lost in pursuit of the frothing ale there, Art made one last derisive taunt. 'His hands ain't done a day's hard graft in his life! He ain't one of us and you all know it.' Annoyed that Robert was taking no notice of him, he bellowed, 'He's taking up a good man's job.'

'The lad needs a job like anyone else,' someone shouted.

'Leave him alone,' another yelled.

With that they had reached the Golden Spike. In the rush to get inside, someone grabbed Robert's arm and propelled him to one side.

'Could get ugly in there if they keep that up. Let's away to the Anvil.'

Robert saw it was the first man who had stuck up for him and a quick glance behind showed him five other friendly faces. He recognised them as a group who always stuck together. He knew this man was right.

'Thanks,' he said.

The man patted him on the shoulder and held out his hand. 'Dick Bishop.'

Robert shook his hand.

Dick quickly introduced the others then added, as they headed for the Anvil, 'We've seen you around since you were taken on. A loner, aren't you?'

A little embarrassed, Robert said, 'I don't like to stand out.'

'Aye, but that can draw attention to you whether you mean it or not – and that's exactly what has happened. We all know you ain't done work like this before, but we respect you for trying. It's only bullies like Art who'll try to make something of it. A word of warning, though. Watch your back with him.' Without waiting for an answer to that Dick shot him a question and it came so suddenly that Robert answered him automatically.

'Where are you from?'

'Newcastle.'

He silently cursed himself then. He had let his guard slip. So far he had put his origins at much further away.

'Not far from home then?'

'No longer home. Fell out with my father.'

Robert was pleased that at that moment they reached the Anvil and the subject was dropped amidst the men's orders for ale, and talk of getting a football team together, and of a day out by the sea at nearby Redcar organised by a local friendly society. In the men's jovial banter Robert forgot the mockery he'd endured from Art and Luke, but back in the sombre room at his lodgings the incident came back to him, along with Dick's warning.

He had tried to conceal all details of his previous life, but even his time on the farm had not been long enough to disguise his gentleman's origins. He had felt he had been winning after coming to Middlesbrough and getting work in the expanding iron industry there, but after today's incident he realised he had been kept under observation by the likes of Art Mason and Luke Coning who would now be even more eager to trip him up after the support he had received from others more fair-minded.

Robert began to wonder if he had made the right decision in leaving home. Would it have been better if he had just stayed and stifled his suspicions about his father? And what of Adele? Could he have healed the rift that had developed there? Had his own actions pushed her closer towards Philip?

But that would have happened in any case if he had stayed and revealed his misgivings about his father. He must forget all his old worries and think only of the new life he was embracing, he resolved. It did not seem as though his father was trying to trace him.

'Mr Addison, I'm afraid I am making very little progress with my enquiries. I will detail what I have done and where the information has led me so far, but information has been very sparse.'

Barney Hawkins was sitting on the other side of the desk from Theodore. 'Enquiries in Hexham led me to believe your son had been seen there and had then headed south. Naturally I thought he was making for Hull and the Jordans' residence, to contact Miss Jordan. As I reported to you before, however, my visit there proved unsuccessful. I am confident I was told the truth, that your son had not been there, but as a precautionary measure, still believing that the Jordans' house could be his objective, I hired two men to keep an eye on it, day and night. So far there are no reports of any sightings. However, putting myself in your son's shoes and believing that Robert was heading south from Hexham, I realised he must have found shelter somewhere and, in all probability, work.

'That line of enquiry eventually turned up a young man called Robert working on a farm near

Consett. At first the farmer and his family were reluctant to talk to me, which raised my suspicions that this Robert was most probably your son. They were very loyal to the lad and reluctant to speak of him. However, I managed to elicit the information that they thought he might be heading for Middlesbrough after leaving them. Since then I have made further enquiries there but with the population growing so rapidly, because of the expanding iron industry, it is like looking for a needle in a haystack. Men from all over this country and from Ireland are flocking there seeking work.'

He left a slight pause then added, 'So, Mr Addison, at this stage the only course of action I can recommend is that you put out a reward for information leading to the discovery of Robert.'

Theo pulled a face; this was something he had been reluctant to do. As he considered the proposal for a few minutes Barney remained silent. He had learned from experience that, having presented all the facts, it was not wise to interrupt a client busy making up their mind.

'You propose to put up posters?' Theo asked.

'Yes, and pass out handbills.'

'I take it from what you have discovered, even though some of the details remain tenuous, you would concentrate on the Middlesbrough area?'

'Yes, and then widen it out if necessary. You see, the men who head there are all eager to make money. The chance of a good bonus just from spotting a young man in their midst would be attractive to them.'

'Although making such an offer will also attract the cranks and the deceivers, ready to turn an easy penny,' Theodore pointed out astutely.

'True, sir. Any information received will need careful assessment, but it might give us a worthwhile lead.'

Theo nodded then said, 'Very well, but I wish to make some conditions. I do not want people to contact me at home as my family is not to be disturbed. Nor do I want them coming to my office and so our name must not be mentioned in any of this. I am reluctant even to give Robert's own Christian name on the posters since friends have been told he is visiting relatives in Bath, after all.'

'I fully understand, sir, and will keep the description on the posters as general as possible. I am sure that just mentioning a missing young gentleman will bring lots of supposed sightings. It will be my job to sift through these and investigate the ones we think might lead us to your son. I will set up places where information may be given, here in Newcastle and also in Middlesbrough. Everything will be handled with the utmost discretion, I assure you.'

With the procedure agreed, they settled on the amount of the reward to be offered.

After leaving Theodore's office, Barney found a suitable address in Newcastle where information could be left and then journeyed to Middlesbrough to do the same there.

A week later posters and handbills appeared on Tyneside and a day later could be found circulating on Teesside.

★

The bell ringing on the door of the jeweller's shop in Church Street diverted Toby's attention while he was arranging a jet necklace for display on the counter top. 'Mr Thomas!' His eyes brightened. 'Another visit?'

'Aye, Toby, I'm lucky that our Tyne-Thames sailings are continuing and we can call in at Whitby so regularly. Is Father here?'

'He is. Go through, he's in the back. Your sister too.'

A moment later Tom surprised his father and Betsy who were eager to learn how long he might stay this time.

'As soon as our cargo is unloaded, we'll sail again.' He saw disappointment on Betsy's face. 'But I already know we'll be back this day week ... and stay in port possibly a full week after. The *Fair Weather* needs some minor repairs. Captain Payne's away arranging it now. He prefers Whitby's shipwrights.'

'We look forward to entertaining you,' said his father.

Thomas had seen his sister's face brighten at this news but she still seemed a little careworn. 'Still heard nothing from Jim?' he asked.

Betsy shook her head. 'No. I told you what Mrs Dodsworth said and I'm taking her advice.'

'I'm pleased to hear it. You've your whole life before you. I'm sure there's many a good man here in Whitby.'

Betsy smiled. 'Aye, you're right. It's just a matter of finding one to suit me.'

★

Five days later Thomas was aboard the *Fair Weather* in Newcastle after seeing her laden for the return leg to Whitby.

'Useful to have that small cargo to drop off in Middlesbrough,' commented the Captain. 'We'll unload, stay the night and sail on the morning tide for Whitby. Let the men ashore for the night in Middlesbrough ... but make it plain that any absentees will not sail with me again. Make that very clear to them.'

'Aye–aye, sir.'

With the ship safely berthed in Middlesbrough and her cargo unloaded, the crew cast lots for who would mount watch on her and the winners hurriedly departed, eager to make the most of their shore leave. They were soon mingling with men coming off their shift at the iron works. Thomas, knowing the crew might feel uncomfortable if their First Mate accompanied them, slipped away from the men and headed for the Anvil.

'You've seen that poster?' rasped Art, giving Luke a dig in the ribs as they left the works and headed for the Market Place.

'Aye, what of it?' he replied.

'Why don't you learn to read, numb-head? Remember, I read it to you on the way to work,' snapped Art. He pulled it from his pocket. 'There, that one.' He wafted it in front of Luke's eyes.

'Oh, yes.' His eyes widened. 'You took it down!'

'Didn't want anyone else reading it.'

'Why not?'

'You lost your brain? This description's not very clear but I reckon it refers to Dane.'

Luke scratched his head. 'Doesn't give his name.'

'No, but ... oh, what's the use trying to explain? Just take it from me, I reckon it's him and there's a good reward waiting to be claimed.'

The mention of money jolted Luke's memory. 'Aye, you read out the address of where to take the information. Come on, let's get there.'

Art grabbed his arm as his mate started to hurry away. The strength of his grip made Luke wince. 'Don't be stupid. If Dane gets one whiff of that poster he'll be off. We've got to get him now, take him there in person.'

It dawned on Luke what Art was proposing. 'Aye, you're right.' Then doubt came into his voice. 'He may already have seen the poster ...'

'We'll see. I've only noticed that one and it must have gone up late last night or else this morning. I reckon not many will have read it, and if anyone has they're hardly likely to think of Dane unless they're as brainy as us. So if we act now, we'll outsmart anyone else before more notices appear. Come on.' He started to stride away.

Caught unawares, Luke had to run to catch him up. 'Where we going?' he asked as he fell into step.

'The Anvil.'

'Why? We want Dane, not a drink.'

'Numb-head! That's where he drinks.'

'Ah. Good thinking, Art.' Then, with a note of caution in his voice, 'But there'll be Dick and his cronies there too.'

242

'Some of them had to change shifts. And even if the others are there, they don't take Dane home to his lodgings and tuck him in bed.'

Luke chuckled. 'That would be a sight!'

Art punched him in the shoulder. 'Concentrate on what we're going to do.'

'Aye-aye, sir,' said Luke, straightening his shoulders and giving Art a mocking salute.

When they neared the Anvil, Art told him, 'I'll take a look inside, make sure he's there.'

'He'll maybe scarper if he sees you,' Luke pointed out.

'I'm not as dumb as you.'

They stopped before they reached the Anvil.

'Go on then,' prompted Luke. 'What you waiting for?'

'Shut up and wait here,' snapped Art. He hurried into the Anvil by the door to the snug, to reappear in a few moments and rejoin Luke. 'There's only him and Dick. If they come out together, you grab Dane, I'll deal with Dick. There's alleys on both sides of the pub so whichever way they go, we move fast, bundle them into an alley and deal with them there. And don't be too hard on him. Just enough to detain him. We want Dane able to walk.'

'Aye-aye, sir,' said Luke again, his broad grin signalling the pleasure he was going to derive from this and claiming the subsequent reward.

They took up an advantageous position at the end of the alley to the right of the pub door and pretended to be standing in idle conversation.

★

Tom Palmer sat in a corner near the door of the Anvil. He was enjoying his tankard of ale and busily engaging in his other pastime of observing people while basking in the knowledge that he was soon going to have a few days at home in Whitby. The room was not over full and he guessed that this pub was not generally used by the men from the iron works along the Tees.

There were two men standing together at the bar. To Tom's eyes the younger one stood out, though he guessed that to most people he would not; in fact, unless they knew him, few people would take any notice of him. It seemed as if he purposely shrank away, to avoid attracting attention, though few would realise this. He wiped his face with a large handkerchief for the second time since he had settled against the bar. A handkerchief, Thomas noted, whereas most of the men from the iron works would simply produce an old rag to get rid of the dust and grime of their work. That second removal of dirt revealed skin which, though still streaked in parts, seemed smoother than he would have expected from a man working in heavy industry.

Thomas's eyes settled then on the young man's hands as he raised a tankard to his lips. He saw that they bore no calluses, only a few scars and scrapes, but nothing else, leaving him to surmise that this person was out of his true environment. He reckoned a story lay behind this, but it was no concern of his.

Ten minutes later Thomas drained his tankard and rose from his seat. As he moved away from the table he was aware that the young man and his companion had left the bar. The outside door was just swinging shut behind them.

Peering round the corner of the right-hand alley, Art saw Dick and Robert come out of the pub, deep in conversation, and saunter off in the other direction.

'Bundle them into the other alley,' he called in a low voice. 'Now!'

Art had judged their move just right. Dick and Robert were taken so much by surprise that they put up no resistance to the shoulder charge from Luke that sent them staggering down the alley. Art's fierce blow to Dick's head sent him sprawling to the ground in a semi-conscious state, and a kick in the ribs kept him there. Luke locked his arms tight around Robert and pushed him hard up against the wall of the pub.

Thomas stepped outside, paused and looked to left and right. No one visible. He was surprised but shrugged his shoulders and set off to his left. Nearing the entrance to the alley alongside the Anvil, he heard a scuffling sound and a stifled cry of pain. Two quick steps took him to the end of the alley. He saw four figures. Two were locked in combat, and a big burly man was stepping over a prone figure on the ground. He launched himself at the other two, one of whom Thomas recognised as the young man he had studied in the pub. The big burly man threw a punch at the man his companion was restraining. Even though he had his arms

245

pinioned the young man swerved his head, avoiding the full force of the clenched fist, but still was
caught a glancing blow on his cheek.

Thomas didn't approve of this, not at all. He
flung himself at the smaller of the two assailants.
The force with which he connected caused Luke
to release his grip and allowed the young man he'd
imprisoned to drive a blow into Luke's stomach,
causing him to double up. Robert saw his rescuer
fling himself at Art then. The two men crashed
against the wall but Thomas was swifter to react
and drove his fist into Art's eye. He yelled with
pain but Thomas did not let up. Although he took
a couple of blows himself, his fist slammed into Art
time and time again. Luke was regaining his breath
but saw Dick pushing himself to his feet and
realised the odds had now swung against them.

'Get out of here, Art!' he yelled.

At that moment his mate took a vicious blow to
the neck that sent him staggering back, gasping for
air. He shook his head for a moment, calculated
the odds and decided to run for it.

Robert turned to Thomas who was breathing
deeply from his exertions. 'Thanks. If it hadn't
been for you, we could have been in real trouble.'

'What was all that about?' he asked, looking
from one man to the other, but he saw that Dick,
busy feeling the back of his head, was as mystified
as he was.

'They were after me,' said Robert quietly.

'After you?' queried Dick. 'I know they rib you
because they say you're not one of us.' He looked
hard at Robert. 'I knew *that* from the day you

signed on. But, like I say, what you are doing here is your own affair. Would Art and Luke attack us because of that?'

'No, it's because of this,' said Robert. He pulled a poster from his pocket and held it out to Dick. 'I saw it this morning and took it down. I reckon Art and Luke saw one too. They put two and two together and, rightly, made four.'

Dick had been busy scanning the poster as his friend was speaking. He handed it to Thomas and, looking at Robert, asked, 'Is this really about you? There's no picture.'

'Oh, I reckon it's about me. And though it mentions no name, which is Robert Dane,' he added, glancing at Tom, 'I believe my father has offered this reward. So now you both have a chance to turn me in and split the money.'

Dick grinned and glanced at Thomas. 'Now there's an idea.'

Realising Dick had no intention of doing any such thing, he said, 'Aye, it is, so I'd better introduce myself. Thomas Palmer.'

'Dick Bishop.'

They shook hands and Thomas turned back to Robert. 'Now what are we going to do about you? If you stay here, those two will come after you again.'

'Aye, and there might be others when they've seen what the reward is,' Dick pointed out.

Robert looked from one to the other of them. 'You're not going to hand me in then?'

Thomas glanced at Dick. 'Do you reckon he's a criminal?'

'No. Not from what I've seen of him.'

'So this is something personal?' said Thomas, and held up his hand. 'It's none of our affair, of course. If you don't want to tell us, that's your right. We won't hold it against you, will we, Dick?'

'No.'

'Thanks,' said Robert. 'It *is* personal and I don't want to talk about it, I'm afraid.'

'So what are you going to do now?' asked Dick.

'I reckon I'd better get away from here, right away.'

'Anywhere in mind?' asked Thomas.

'No, I'll take things as they come.'

'You'll have to watch those two don't follow you. I reckon they'll be expecting you to return to your lodging house and will be watching it.'

Robert's lips tightened.

'I think I can help out,' Thomas put in.

Both Robert and Dick looked askance at him.

'Do you *have* to return to your lodgings?'

'I have a few things there, but I was travelling light so what's there could be left there.'

'Good,' said Thomas. 'I'm First Mate on the *Fair Weather*. We sail on the morning tide for Whitby. I can get you on board now.'

'A stowaway?' said Robert.

'Aye. You'd have to keep out of sight but I reckon you could do that. It's not a long voyage. Of course, there's tonight to hide as well.'

'I don't want you to get into trouble on my account ...'

'It will be all right. Once we get to Whitby, I'll take you ashore when it's right to do so and we can

248

go to my family. I have a father and sister who live there. They'll let you stay with them until you decide what to do.'

'This is a grand opportunity for you to leave here unseen,' put in Dick.

'It is,' agreed Robert, and stuck out his hand to Thomas. 'Thanks,' he said gratefully. 'Someone was watching over me tonight. They brought you into the Anvil at just the right time.'

'And brought you out at the right time too,' said Dick. 'A minute or so later and it would have been too late.'

'Dick, thanks for being such a friend. I'll not forget you, and when my life is sorted out I'll come and look you up,' Robert told him.

'You do that. No one will know what has happened to you, and Art and Luke won't dare say a word.'

Their handshake was firm, an indication of their mutual trust.

'Thanks for what you did too, Tom. Or I might have had something much worse than the headache and bruised ribs I have right now.' Robert held out his hand to his rescuer.

'You watch out for those two,' Tom warned Dick.

'They won't try anything with me. They know I have too many friends who'd teach them a lesson in return.'

'Good. I'll maybe see you in the Anvil again then.'

'Aye, do that. You can bring me news of Robert.'

'Come on, let's get you aboard. There are only two men on watch at the moment,' Thomas told Robert.

'What about the Captain?'

'He won't be back 'til late. I'll report everyone on board, and then hopefully things will settle down for the night.'

They hurried to the docks with hardly a word passing between them. Once the *Fair Weather* was in sight Thomas slowed his pace. As expected, he saw the two sailors left in charge sitting on a hatch with the top of the gangway kept in their sight. He stopped and turned to Robert. 'Keep back.' He indicated a pile of crates. 'I'll go on board and get rid of those two. When you see me reappear at the top of the gangway, get on board fast.'

Robert nodded and made for cover.

Tom walked briskly over to the *Fair Weather*, swung on to the gangway and strode purposefully aboard. The two watch-keepers got to their feet.

'All ship-shape?' he asked.

'Aye-aye, sir.'

'Good. I'm aboard now and will relieve you. If you fancy a quick gill, be back in two hours.'

'Aye-aye, sir,' they responded brightly, thankful to have a break from the monotony of watch-keeping.

Tom watched them hurry down the gangway and move briskly off down the quay, oblivious to Robert watching them from behind the pile of crates. Once Tom judged them to be in a position from which they could no longer see the ship, he moved quickly over to the gangway and stood still.

Robert glanced along the quay in both directions; the only people he saw were some men engaged in loading a ship further along the quay, far too engrossed in their work to notice him hurrying aboard the *Fair Weather*.

As he stepped on deck, Tom said, 'Follow me,' and led him below, making his way forward through what to Robert seemed like a maze of woodwork. Tom stopped and pushed open a door. 'You aren't going to have a lot of room in here. It's the bow locker, a storeroom for working stores, but we aren't likely to want anything from here on this voyage, it's such a short one.' Tom smiled, looking round the confined area. 'Thank goodness, I expect you're thinking.'

'I don't mind how cramped I am, I'll be all right in here. I'm only too grateful to you for what you are doing,' Robert told him.

'Right, let's go back up for now, but I'm leaving a lantern and means of lighting it. Use it as little as possible and be extremely careful, we don't want a fire.'

'I'll not use it at all.'

'It'll be dark in here.'

'I know, but there's nothing I'll need a light for. And, as you say, it is only a short voyage.'

'But you've got tonight to last through first.'

'I'll be sleeping.'

'Come on then, let's find you some food and drink.' They retraced their steps and Tom led the way into the galley where they selected some food and filled a cask with some water. They returned to the bow locker, safely stored the victuals and then positioned themselves on deck so that they had a view of the quay without being visible themselves.

At this stage neither of them seemed to want to talk. Tom had certain questions but it seemed unfair to put them now. Robert wanted to know more about Tom and why he was risking his position as First Mate to help a stranger, but deemed it wisest to keep those questions until he was ashore in Whitby, undiscovered. Robert took the most of his chance to enjoy the fresh air and light, knowing he would be longing for them when he was confined to the bow locker.

The light was beginning to fade when they heard some out-of-tune singing and raucous banter from along the quay.

'Below now, I'm afraid, Robert,' said Tom, heaving himself off the hatch on which he had been sitting.

Robert pushed himself to his feet and followed him down. Reaching the bow locker, Tom said, 'Whatever you do, don't move from here until I come for you in Whitby.'

14

'Father, Tom should be docking soon, are you coming?'

'You go, lass. I must get this order finished and Toby's too busy with another one to take this over. Go straight home when Tom's ready. I'll see you both there.'

All three of them had been busy at the shop but Betsy's work on the accounts could easily be left. She laid down her pen and rose from the desk where she had been compiling some bills to send to customers. She was pleased to see they reflected an upsurge in trade.

She gave the bodice of her grey dress a little tug to make it more comfortable, tied her small lace-trimmed bonnet under her chin and swung a woollen cape around her shoulders. She was glad of it when she stepped outside; though the day was bright and sunny, the wind had strengthened and was blowing in from the sea. Just the sort of day she liked.

Housewives were busy doing their late shopping before returning home; some idled about, window shopping, while others gossiped. Clerks hurried by about their employers' business, and sailors headed for one of the inns along Church Street, anticipating a night of drinking or else making sure of one last tankard before reporting to their ship.

Betsy passed the end of the street leading to the bridge and continued along Church Street to the quay where she knew the *Fair Weather* would tie up. When she saw the vessel was in the final stages of being manoeuvred into her berth, she quickened her step.

Ropes were being thrown out and wound round the capstans on the quay, enabling the *Fair Weather* to be secured. Betsy felt admiration for her brother when she saw him on deck, overseeing the actions of the crew engaged in docking while Captain Payne supervised everything else from his position close to the wheel.

Betsy wove her way through the crowd gathering to greet husbands, sons, lovers, so that she could be near the gangway to meet her brother.

'It's good to have you back again so soon,' she said, greeting Tom with a hug.

'Father not with you?' he asked, a touch of concern in his voice.

Betsy picked it up. 'He's all right,' she quickly reassured him. 'He has an order to finish and says he will see us at home.'

Tom nodded. 'You'd better not wait, Betsy.' Seeing disappointment on her face, he hastily added, 'I've a job to do before I can get ashore. I'll see you at home.'

'I suppose I shouldn't come between you and your duty.'

''Fraid not. I must go.' He patted her arm and then strode quickly away up the gangway.

Tom set about his usual tasks, taking his time about them. He was beginning to grow anxious about Robert, knowing he must want to escape from the cramped bow locker. If he got impatient and left ... Tom did not dare think of the consequences to his own career. It therefore came as something of a relief when Captain Payne called from the top of the gangway, 'Palmer!'

'Aye-aye, sir.' Tom hurried across the deck.

'Everything is proceeding smoothly. See it finished off and dismiss the crew. I'm going to find out about the repairs – make sure everything is ready for Bosworth and Jackson to start first thing in the morning.'

'Aye-aye, sir.'

Tom watched his Captain leave the ship and head for the bridge across the Esk. The crew did not need much cajoling to get their work finished; they were eager to be ashore for nearly a week. Half an hour later, having seen all the necessary tasks had been done, Tom dismissed the men. They streamed ashore to stay with friends, find lodgings or else a girl who would accommodate them for their leave in Whitby.

Thomas waited until he was sure no one would return for some forgotten item. Then he made his way quickly below decks to the bow locker.

When he opened the door he heard a long sigh of relief from Robert.

'Have you been all right?' asked Tom anxiously.

'Yes. A bit stiff, though.' He stretched to ease his

muscles from the unnatural position they had had to take up during the night.

'That'll soon wear off. Come on.'

They picked up the bowl, plate and mug he had used and returned them to the galley on their way up on deck.

Robert breathed in deeply, enjoying the feel of the sharp salt air driving into his lungs after the fetid damp he had endured in his confined quarters.

Anxious to have him ashore, Tom led the way quickly to the quay, his eyes skinned for anyone who might spot a stranger leaving the *Fair Weather*. He need not have worried; people were too engrossed in their own business or anxious to reach their destination, whatever that might be.

The two men fell into step as Tom guided Robert to the bridge, thankful that the crowds had thinned out. They climbed steep Golden Lion Bank to Flowergate, from where they turned into Skinner Street.

'A thriving place,' Robert commented.

'Aye, it is. Not like Middlesbrough or Newcastle, but the trade here is different. Only a few years ago Whitby prospered on the whaling industry with its ships sailing Arctic waters. It supported a shipbuilding trade that achieved a worldwide reputation because of Captain Cook's voyages. It now has a thriving coastal trade and its ships quarter the globe.'

'Were you brought up here?'

'Aye, it's still my home. Used to live in Church Street near where we docked. Father is a jeweller by trade with a shop there. He's done well. With Whitby expanding on to the West Cliff, where we are now, he decided to move to a nicer house in Well Close Square. We'll be turning into it in a minute.'

'But he still has the shop?'

'Oh, aye, he'd be lost without it. It was a life-saver when Mother died.'

They left Skinner Street and Robert found himself in a quiet square of elegant Georgian houses. When they went through the wrought-iron gate and into a small garden, he felt a surge of nostalgia. The three-storey brick house, with its front door to the left of two tall sash windows, and three matching windows on each of the two floors above, reminded him of the doll's house Zelda had had as a child. He tried not to think of that as Tom opened the front door and invited him to step inside.

It was no good, though. Inside, the reminders grew stronger. This house was cosy, warm, a living home, more than mere bricks and mortar. Robert's thoughts flew to a house in Newcastle and another in the Tyne Valley. Had he spoiled them by his abrupt departure? But he would have done so even more by what he would have been forced to reveal had he stayed ... His troubling thoughts were interrupted then when a door burst open and a young woman rushed into the hall, her face bright with joy.

'Thomas, where have you been? We wondered if ...' The words faded from her lips when she saw a stranger with him. Curiosity and enquiry crossed her face.

'Betsy, I'm sorry if you've been worried. There is an explanation. But first I must introduce Robert Dane. Robert, my sister Betsy.'

Robert met Betsy's candid gaze, bowed and said, 'I am pleased to meet you, Miss Palmer.'

'And I you, Mr Dane.' Her eyes had never left him. She saw a handsome young man whose fine features would make any young lady, and maybe some a bit older, look twice. He had a gentlemanly air about him that contrasted with the working clothes he was wearing.

'Is Father home?' asked Tom. The question broke the spell that seemed to have been cast between the newly acquainted.

'Yes. He'll be down in a minute.' As if on cue, footsteps were heard coming to the top of the stairs. 'Ah, here he is.'

Robert saw a slim-built but upright man approaching them, his face lined by care.

'Tom!' He shook his son's hand heartily enough.

'Father, I want you to meet Robert Dane. Robert, my father.'

Robert took the older man's hand. 'I'm honoured to meet you, sir.'

'And I to meet anyone my son brings home.' Sam's assessment of the stranger would not have differed from his daughter's, had they both voiced them. 'Come in,' he added, making for the drawing room.

'Before anyone says anything, I have some explaining to do,' announced Thomas as he closed the door behind them.

'Very well,' said his father. 'Please do.'

They all sat down except Tom who stood in front of the fireplace.

'To put it simply, I found Robert being set upon by a couple of thugs yesterday in Middlesbrough. A quick explanation revealed they were out for financial gain and that Robert needed to leave Middlesbrough as soon as possible. It seemed to me the best way of doing that and leaving no trace would be to stow him away on the *Fair Weather*, bring him here to Whitby and hope you would help him.'

The silence that followed was charged with consideration.

Then Sam spoke. 'Thugs ... financial reward?' He glanced politely at Robert, obviously wondering what a working man might possess to attract such attention.

Robert fished the poster from his pocket and passed it to Mr Palmer.

Sam read it and nodded. 'No name, but you believe this to refer to yourself?'

'Yes, sir. And I believe it was put out by my father.'

'That sounds as if it is a family matter, but I should ask you ... does anything criminal lie behind this?'

'No, sir, it does not.' Robert's denial was firm enough to convince both Sam and his daughter.

Betsy felt relieved to hear this, though as to why she could not say.

'So this is a personal matter, something you would rather not discuss with us?' her father continued.

'Yes, sir. If you think that wrong of me, I will leave rather than embarrass you with my presence.'

Sam raised his hand. 'No. It is your prerogative to decide what to tell us. I will not press you for information. I detect from your demeanour and speech that certain aspects of your appearance are awry with your true condition. Those, besides the fact that my son has brought you here seeking help, are enough for me. After all, Tom could have jeopardised his own position had you been caught stowing away. He must have decided you were worthy of our assistance.'

'I am most grateful to you all, sir, and you do deserve to know more. I come from a reasonably well-to-do family. My mother and father are forward-looking and kind, but in one respect my father's behaviour has caused me misgivings. I would rather not elaborate on this.'

'As I said, that is your right,' said Sam.

'I felt I needed to get away to think things over and sort them out in my mind. I hope you will accept this explanation, and my reassurance that when I've set my mind at ease I will return home, though at this juncture I do not know when precisely that will be. In the meantime, I will support myself, as I did while I was in Middlesbrough.'

Sam, deep in thought, stared hard at him. 'Very well, young man, I accept what you say. You may stay here until you decide what path you must take to reconcile yourself with your father – a step I most urgently advise you to take. I have detected in what you told us, and the way you expressed your concerns, that this rift between you is alien to your feelings and upbringing. But such rifts have a bad habit of widening.' He stood up. 'Nevertheless, stay here as long as you need. Now, Thomas, you are about the same build as this young man so I suggest you find him a change of clothes, let him refresh himself from the rigours of travelling as a stowaway, and then we shall all sit down to eat. I will inform Cook there will be one more.'

Robert was swiftly on his feet too. 'Sir, I cannot thank you enough for your understanding, your hospitality, and above all your kindness. I promise I will be no trouble.'

When Robert was shown to the bedroom he would occupy, he could do nothing but thank his luck that he had fallen in with Thomas Palmer. What comfort after the lodging house in Middlesbrough! He would never have criticised the farmhouse, which had held all the warmth of the family who loved it. There he had felt shielded from the harshness of his new life, despite the somewhat spartan conditions. But here in Well Close Square a comfortable prosperity was evident, though he judged it was never allowed to become excessive. Less comfortable times were not forgotten. Sam was a man who had not let success go to his head, and that example was reflected in Tom's attitude and manner. Robert judged it would be the same with Betsy, though his acquaintance with her was slight as yet. He thought her a pretty young woman with a gentle manner. Though she had said little, he judged she had a mind of her own and those bright eyes, which sparkled so attract-ively, would miss nothing.

He opened the door to a knock from Tom and was presented with a pile of clothes.

'I think you'll need these. You and I are of a similar build.'

'Thanks,' said Robert. 'You are being too good to me.'

'Not at all! If we can't help someone in need then it's time to give up.' He glanced across at the marble-topped washstand. 'I see there are towels. I think there'll be plenty of water in the ewer.'

'Yes, there is. I've already checked.'

'Come to the drawing room when you are ready.'

As he walked down the stairs Robert felt much better and once again blessed whatever or whoever had brought him to this house.

He counted those blessings again when, after a very satisfying meal and a pleasant evening, he lay down in the comfort of a feather bed. He smiled to himself when he thought of his bed the previous night − ropes and sacking in a dark bow locker! Then his thoughts drifted to Adele. How he wished he had seen her before she sailed. He wondered what she had been doing since reaching Hull? Maybe the family had returned to Cantonville Hall. If so, they would have contacted his family and she would know by now that he had left, unless his parents were trying to keep his absence quiet by offering some other excuse for it.

★

As she lay in bed that night Betsy's thoughts naturally turned to the stranger who had come into her home. Chance? Fate? Why at this precise moment in her life? If Tom had not gone to that particular public house at that time, Robert Dane would not be in Well Close Square now. If Tom had not left the Anvil when he did, Robert could well have been detained by unfriendly hands instead of lying in a comfortable bed as now. And she would never have met him.

He was reasonably good-looking, held himself well, and once he'd realised he was among friends had shed his veneer of caution, showing a certain gentlemanly assurance. She knew he had not told them all; he had kept his reason for leaving home vague, but she found that air of mystery only added to his attraction. Caution overtook her mind then. She should not get carried away with thoughts of Robert. He could move on tomorrow, out of her life, never to be seen again, and soon be only a memory wreathed in unanswered questions.

The following morning her steps had an extra spring in them as she hurried downstairs to the dining room. The three men were already there and her breezy 'Good morning' was returned by them all, with Robert springing to his feet to say, 'Good morning, Miss Palmer.'

Betsy inclined her head in acknowledgement of his formality but said, 'Mr Dane, as we are to live under the same roof, I think Christian names would be in order.' She glanced at her father. 'Wouldn't they, Papa?'

'Of course,' he approved. 'It will make for

greater ease.' As breakfast proceeded Sam said, 'Betsy, I suggest you and I go to the shop and get on with the jobs we didn't finish yesterday. Tom, show Robert something of Whitby, and we'll all meet up at the Angel at half-past twelve for luncheon.'

With no one making any query to this plan, breakfast continued amidst pleasant conversation during which Sam was certain that he had done the right thing in inviting Robert to stay. He liked the ease with which the young man had settled here in this short time, and admired the lively mind that kept him asking questions about Whitby and its role in the maritime world.

Robert's interest continued to be demonstrated during Tom's conducted tour of the town. He felt swept back into history by the sight of the ruined abbey, high on the East Cliff, and its nearby Norman church. The town's maritime history intrigued him, stories of its whalemen held his attention, and he was fascinated to watch the shipbuilders at work. Over luncheon, Robert talked enthusiastically about what he had seen and Betsy was struck by his vitality and expressiveness.

'What are your plans for this afternoon?' Sam asked them. 'Or have you had enough, Robert?'

'No, sir. I find Whitby a most fascinating place. But I'm in Tom's hands.'

'I thought it would be interesting if I took Robert round some of the jet workshops. Want to come, Betsy? It's more up your street.'

'I'd be delighted,' she cried, glancing at her father to seek his approval.

'You go then, Betsy,' he said. 'I'll stay here a while and then wander home.'

Fifteen minutes later the three of them were leaving the Angel and crossing the bridge to the East Side.

'I thought we'd go to Mr Verity's,' said Tom. 'Still the best in town, isn't he, Betsy?'

'Yes,' she replied, and then explained to Robert, 'He's in his late forties, name's Jacob, learned his trade from his father who had a natural talent for carving jet.'

'What is jet? I know it's used to create the black brooches and ornaments I've seen as we've gone around this morning, but that's all I know.'

'It's from a special sort of tree, fossilised long ago by the sea, which is now found in seams along this stretch of the Yorkshire coast,' explained Betsy. 'It has been worked and carved since way back in history. It's known the Romans used it and had jet workshops in York. As far as Whitby is concerned, the discovery of exceptionally good jet along this coast gave rise to an important cottage industry. The first operative was a Captain Tremlett who took the chance to develop it commercially. It received a boost from the Great Exhibition of 1851, thanks to the Queen's interest. Now there are numerous small workshops dotted around the town which add considerably to the town's revenue. The one we are going to visit is at the far end of Church Street, close to the one hundred and ninety-nine steps up to the abbey.'

'Sounds as if I'm going to learn something.' Robert smiled at her.

'Oh, you will.' Betsy smiled back at him.

Jacob Verity gave them a warm welcome. He knew Tom and Betsy and politely greeted Robert who was introduced as a friend visiting for a while. He delighted in explaining the running of his workshop and taking them through every stage of production, from an untouched piece of jet to the final product, whether that be a finely carved locket or a flat presentation piece, beautifully etched.

'I'd love to try that,' Robert whispered close to Betsy's ear. Jacob caught the words.

'Mr Dane, from that I take it you may have some carving or drawing talent?'

'Well, I can't compare myself to your workers on the final stages of these pieces, but I learned drawing at school, and at home I did like to tinker about with wood.'

'I could see how interested you were as we were going through the various stages of production. What about coming back tomorrow and having a go?'

'Mr Verity, you'd allow me to do that?' Robert was taken aback by his suggestion.

'Why not, if it interests you? I'll have some tools ready for you tomorrow. Say ten o'clock in the morning?'

Robert looked at Betsy and Tom. 'Will that upset any ...'

'Not at all,' said Betsy quickly. 'It's a chance for you to try something new.' An amused twinkle came into her eyes as she added, 'And it will be fun to see you try to vie with the experts.'

Jacob laughed. 'Don't be too hasty, young lady. We may be unearthing a hidden talent.'

'Thank you, Mr Verity. This has been most interesting and I look forward to tomorrow,' said Robert.

'Tom, I think you had better find him some old clothes to work in,' Jacob suggested.

'I think I'd better,' Tom agreed.

Robert called a general goodbye to all the men in the workshop with whom he had spoken individually when he was given the conducted tour.

'I think you have made a good impression on them all,' said Tom. 'I'm sure you'll have an enjoyable time tomorrow.'

'Probably make a laughing stock of myself.'

'We'll see.' Betsy's smile revealed her true opinion.

'Are you coming to witness my triumph?'

'I wouldn't miss it for the world!'

'I might ask Mr Verity to ban you.'

'You wouldn't dare!'

Both Robert and Betsy felt comfortable with the banter that was passing between them and each instinctively knew the other wouldn't take offence. Light-heartedness overcame them all. Tom felt very pleased it had worked out this way. Their unexpected visitor certainly seemed to be taking Betsy's mind off her previous disappointment.

Their lively mood continued as they took a brisk walk along the West Pier, enjoying the sea air and the breeze that blew over the foam-flecked waves, beating in towards the twin piers at the harbour mouth and the sands of the coastline beyond.

★

Sitting in the window of the drawing room in Well Close Square, Sam was pleased to see the young people's laughter as they came in at the front door. But even amidst such pleasure he felt a touch of sadness – how he wished his beloved Jenny could see them now.

'Did you have a good time?' he asked.

'Splendid,' Betsy replied, going to give her father a hug. 'And tomorrow Robert becomes a jet worker for a day.'

Sam laughed. 'It will take you a lot longer than that to learn it.'

'He's just going to do some etching or carving; he's done a bit of both when he was younger,' Betsy explained.

'Not jet, sir,' Robert put in quickly. 'Mr Verity heard me whisper to Betsy that I'd like to try it and made the suggestion.'

'Well, best of luck. A fine man is Jacob Verity – you are in good hands.'

'Well, Robert, are you ready for your day as a jet worker?' Sam asked as they settled down to break-fast the following morning.

'Indeed I am, sir. I slept like a log after all that fresh air and feel so relaxed here ... for that I must thank you all.'

Sam brushed away his thanks with a wave of his hand. 'Are you two going with him?' he asked with a glance at Tom and Betsy.

'I think I should have a look at the *Fair Weather*. I'm sure Captain Payne will be there and it's as well for me to keep in his good books. I'll walk with Robert to Mr Verity's and then go on to the ship. What about you, Betsy?'

'I'll come with you and then on to the shop. Is that all right, Papa?'

'Of course.'

'So none of you are going to see my masterpiece develop?' chaffed Robert with a grin.

'We can't give up all our time just to see you making a hash of it,' laughed Betsy.

'You might get a surprise,' quipped Robert, his eyes sparkling at this exchange.

'Whatever you produce, son, it will have pride of place in this house,' Sam said encouragingly.

Tom and Betsy accompanied Robert to Mr Verity's workshop in Church Street where they found his employees already at their places, each engaged in the particular process for which they were responsible. Four carvers were seated at a table in the centre of the room. One place lay vacant.

'That's for you, young man,' said Mr Verity. 'I've selected some tools for you and there are a couple of pieces of jet there – see what you can do. You've got four talented men with you. They'll initiate you into the techniques, and then you're on your own.'

'Thank you, sir,' said Robert, noting that the other man seemed to stiffen with pride on being addressed as 'sir'. 'I appreciate what you are allowing me to do. I was fascinated when I was here yesterday. My fingers have been itching ever since.'

'Then let us see what that itch produces,' said Mr Verity. He turned to Betsy and Tom. 'We'll look after him. By the time you come back, about five o'clock, we might have discovered a new talent.'

'Tom, do you know anything else about Robert?' Betsy put her question tentatively as they walked along Church Street.

He glanced at her and saw the intense curiosity she was struggling to hide. 'No more than you heard him tell Father,' he replied. 'I had little time to elicit more under the circumstances.'

'But you trust him?'

Tom paused a moment. 'Aye. From what little I've seen, I would judge him to be of good stock, of fairly high social standing but with no excessive pride in that. I believe he is genuine in what he has told us, but I think there is more to it because, where family is concerned, people always hold back some of the truth.'

'Which could be out of respect and love,' commented Betsy thoughtfully.

'Aye, you're right, lass.'

Continuing on his way, after leaving Betsy at the shop, Tom's thoughts drifted back to their conversation and he wondered if, even in this short time, his sister was feeling a certain interest in the young man he had brought home. Had fate, that had taken him to the Anvil in Middlesbrough, extended its influence further, acting to clear from her mind any hopes she might still harbour of meeting Jim Fenwick again?

★

270

Betsy's mind kept wavering as she tried to concentrate on making entries in the accounts ledgers. She found herself seriously weighing up what she found attractive about Robert. She couldn't help wondering about his relationship with his family and what might have caused such a rift between them. Maybe after she had got to know him better, if she was careful, she could draw the story from him. Her thoughts took on a lighter aspect then and she smiled when she thought of him applying himself to a piece of jet. It was going to be more difficult than he had imagined and she anticipated there would be considerable teasing and joking when she and Tom and her father saw his final effort.

It was close to five o'clock when Tom appeared in the shop. His father and sister were dressed ready to depart and Toby, though he did his best to hide his feelings, was anxious to be left on his own.

A few minutes later they were entering Mr Verity's workshop. The carvers, also getting ready for home, were arranging their tools, each in their own place, so there was no mixing of implements. Though they were similar, each tool was special to a particular individual, moulded to his grip and preferred over any other.

'Ah, now, you've come to see what Robert has done,' Mr Verity greeted them, beaming broadly.

Robert got up off his stool and turned to face them with his back hiding the work on the table. The other carvers and the rest of the workers stopped what they were doing to see the reaction of the new arrivals. They had all been interested in

Robert's progress throughout the day. Their suspicion of a stranger coming among them, albeit invited by their employer, had soon been dispelled by Robert's friendliness. He gave no trouble, merely seeking advice when he felt he needed it.

'Now, Robert, stand aside. We are all eager to see the reaction of these good people,' said Mr Verity.

Sheepishly he shuffled to his right so that the new arrivals had an uninterrupted view of two pieces of jet that lay on the table. They stepped forward, eyes riveted on Robert's work. A charged silence filled the room.

'You didn't do these?' Betsy's voice was filled with disbelief.

'No one else has touched them,' said Mr Verity firmly.

'I don't believe it,' said Tom, but from his intonation everyone knew he did not doubt Mr Verity.

'Amazing,' gasped Sam.

'We have a talented etcher on our hands,' Mr Verity went on. 'What a discovery!' There was no doubting the enthusiasm in his voice.

His observation brought comments of approval from his employees. Jet working was special to these men and they delighted in seeing any new talent emerge, but they had never seen one make such an immediate impact.

They all agreed with Mr Verity as he went on, 'There is no disguising the fact that Robert needs to work a lot more for his gift to develop fully. His prior training in art is obvious. Working in a new medium presented a challenge, but he rose to it very well. Though there is a certain crudeness to these two etchings ... you must remember he was working with tools he had never used before. Nevertheless, you can see for yourselves there is an underlying talent here and I would like to be the one to develop it. So, Robert, I would like you to come and work for me. I'm sure all my employees will be pleased to welcome you if you'll say yes.'

Robert was touched by the murmurs of approval that ran round the room, but more than anything he was elated by Betsy's warm smile of support. Did he see more in it than that? And did he see it tinged with disappointment when he said, 'Mr Verity, I thank you and your employees for making me so welcome today and initiating me into the methods of etching jet, and I thank you for that wonderful offer, but may I think it over first? My answer is dictated by where I see my future lying.'

'Of course, young man. I did not expect an immediate answer.'

'Thank you, sir. I hope I will be able to give you my answer tomorrow. If not, I promise you it will be soon.'

'That's good enough for me,' replied Mr Verity. 'And I hope it will be yes.' He turned away and started to talk to Sam, extolling the virtues he saw in Robert's work. Betsy and Tom turned to the two pieces of jet while Robert exchanged cheery good nights with the men who were leaving for their homes. He knew he had been accepted by them and would continue to be so if he took up Mr Verity's offer. He left them to get his coat.

'I wouldn't have believed this, Tom,' whispered Betsy. 'Just look at this bird.'

'He certainly has talent and an eye for balance and proportion.'

'Balance and proportion? Who would ever have thought my brother would see those?'

'When you have looked at ships in the way I have done all my life, and with the love I have for them, a sense of balance and proportion comes naturally. Look, you can see it here in this other etching.' He pointed to the way Robert had placed two profiles against an indeterminate background.

Betsy nodded. 'The mistakes and lack of technique in his work don't disguise his innate talent. He'll develop even more when he starts carving. I hope he stays.'

15

'I am satisfied that the difficulties here in Hull are now settled and there should be no developments that my manager can't deal with. It is time I returned to Newcastle. I have written to Mrs Chandler at Cantonville, telling her we will be leaving for Newcastle on the *Northern Belle* a week today. She'll sail at noon.' George Jordan sprang his surprise when he and his family came together in the drawing room after their evening meal.

Paula took the decision calmly. 'If that is your wish, I'll arrange everything with Mrs Symonds here. She'll look after the house while we are away. Do I retain the staff as we usually do?'

George gave a nod of agreement. 'Of course. It is by far the best course. I am sure Mrs Symonds will find plenty for them to do.'

Adele tensed. Her father's decision included the whole family. Even though she knew she should not, she made a protest but disguised it as a request. 'May I stay here, please?' To return to Newcastle would only bring thoughts of Robert to the fore again. They would meet his family, and the visit from the police was bound to be mentioned. Since that visit she had pushed Robert to the back of her mind and allowed Philip to occupy her thoughts more and more. He had visited Hull on a number of occasions and had invited Adele to several gatherings of friends at Redbourne Hall.

Philip could not have been kinder or more attentive. She felt relaxed and secure in his company, and knew his inheritance would provide her with a safe future if ever he proposed marriage, which, as time progressed, she was inclined to think a possibility. Whenever that thought occurred, though, she would remember Robert and time spent in his company and feel once again the excitement of being with him ... albeit only in her memories now.

'No, Adele, it wouldn't be practical to keep this house running for one,' said her mother.

'But the staff will be here,' she pointed out.

'Yes, but the whole house is not used. Most of it is closed except for cleaning.'

'Mark could stay too.'

'But I don't want to,' he protested while shooting an angry glance at his sister.

'We are travelling as a family.' George made his statement so firmly that everyone knew this was an order and he would brook no further protest.

Adele fell silent. Then, piqued at gaining no support from her brother, said, 'May I be excused?'

Paula was quick to speak up. It was as if she had anticipated her daughter's request and did not want any refusal to come from George. 'Of course, my dear.'

'Thank you.' Adele stood up and left the room.

She vented some of her feelings as she stormed up the stairs and flung herself down in a chair in her room. After half an hour she realised there was no way she could overturn her father's decision; they would all return to Newcastle.

Even so, she made one last try. When she heard Mark's door open and close, she rushed to his room. 'Why didn't you support me and say you wanted to stay here? Papa might have allowed two of us to do so,' she complained, anger in every word.

'Because I didn't want to,' he replied testily. 'Why should I oblige you? I suppose you want to moon around Philip Bowen.'

'I *don't* moon around him.'

'You certainly do! You should see yourself when he calls on you. Now, if it had been Robert I could have understood.'

'Don't mention his name!' snapped Adele.

'Why not? Surely you don't believe he's a criminal? Is that all the faith you have in him?'

'Does it not occur to you to wonder why the police are enquiring after him?'

Mark shrugged his shoulders. 'It might be "nowt nor summat" as Yorkshire folk would say.'

Adele frowned in disdain. 'Well, I suppose we'll learn more when we get to Newcastle.'

'And won't it be better to know the full story?'

'Do you think that we'll get that from the Addisons?'

'Friends are friends. Whatever has happened, we should give them our support. And, don't forget, it was Zelda who sent us word of Robert's disappearance.'

'It's all right your saying that, you're just think-ing of her.' Before her brother could say anything she went on, 'Oh, yes, Mark. I realise that she is the reason you want to go to Newcastle.'

'And why not?'

'Do as you wish, but if Robert is sought as a criminal and, because of that, folks shun the Addisons, some of the taint will rub off on Zelda. Be warned. I don't suppose Papa would look too kindly on your association with the sister of a criminal.'

Mark gave a little shake of his head. 'You're taking this far too seriously.' He left a small pause then added, 'Or are you just trying to convince yourself that Philip is the one you really want?'

Adele did not answer but gave him a sharp look as she hurried from the room.

Mark smiled to himself. He knew he had touched a tender spot.

Two days later Adele was sorting out some clothes to take with her to Newcastle when there was a knock on her door and a maid entered the room.

'Mr Philip Bowen is here, miss. He presents his card and hopes he can have a few moments of your time.'

'Show him into the drawing room, Eliza. Tell him I'll be with him in a minute or two.'

'Yes, miss.'

When the door closed behind the maid, Adele dropped the dress she had in her hand on to the bed, went to the mirror and patted her hair into shape. She pinched her cheeks, then turned to view herself in the rectangular cheval glass positioned so as to enhance the light from the tall window. Adele smoothed her hands down the bodice of her blue and white striped dress with its wide skirts gracefully supported by a hooped cage.

Satisfied with her appearance, she left her room and walked slowly down the stairs. She paused at the drawing room door, then swept it open, saying brightly as she walked in, 'Philip, how nice of you to call.'

He turned away sharply from the window, smiling widely as he came over to greet her.

'It is I who should thank you for seeing me.' He took her hand and raised it to his lips as he bowed to her. 'I had to come to Hull so thought I would take the chance to see you. I have some news.'

Adele felt her heart race. She needed a few minutes to gather herself. 'Do sit down, Philip. Will you take a glass of Madeira?'

'Thank you. That would be pleasant.' He remained standing while she poured two glasses, brought one to him and sat down in a chair placed to one side of the fireplace. Only then did he sit down opposite her.

He took a sip of his wine and announced, 'I am likely to be spending more time in Hull and hopefully will be able to see more of you.'

'You're leaving Redbourne?' It seemed the natural thing to say following his statement.

He gave a weak smile. 'Oh, no, that will always be my home. We are increasing our grain production there and rearing more cattle. So I put the proposition to Father that it would be advantageous, because of the increased yield, to ship more of our produce through Hull. It would give us access to more markets. Your father's ships would enable us to do that. So, you see, if this can be arranged, I will be spending more time here. I will need a house, of course, and will start making enquiries when I leave here today. More time spent in Hull holds possibilities for both of us.'

Adele's heart was racing. What else was coming? 'Expanding the business sounds very exciting,' she said lamely. 'It will take a lot of organising.'

'It will, but I'm not going to rush it. That's where some consultations with your father should be invaluable.'

'I wish you well. I am sure with your abilities you will make it work.' She raised her glass. 'To your success.'

He raised his in return and said, 'Thank you for your confidence in me. Now, enough of business! It is not going to get in the way of pleasure, I promise. I have been invited to a very dear friend's at Dunholme, just outside Lincoln. She is organising a weekend gathering in three weeks. With her invitation comes a request that I should bring a friend. I would like you to come with me. If you say yes, I will seek permission from your father.'

'I'm sorry, Philip, I can't accept.' His face clouded over with disappointment and she hastened to explain. 'We are returning to Newcastle next week.'

He frowned to hear it. 'How long for?'

'I don't know. It could be quite a while. Father has not indicated when we will return. He wants to be there to see to the new business.'

'I'll be sorry to see you go. I had hoped you had returned to Hull for good.'

'Newcastle isn't the end of the world, Philip. I'd be pleased to see you there if ever you go north.'

'I'll have a lot to see to here in Hull, to make my plans materialise. But I had hoped you would be here to share some of my leisure hours ... it would have given me something to look forward to when I was busy.'

'I'm sorry, but that's the situation.'

He rose from his chair. Adele did likewise and accompanied him to the front door.

'I might be in Hull again before you leave. If I am, may I call to say goodbye?'

'Of course.'

'In case I can't, I'd better say goodbye now and wish you well for the journey.' He took her hand and raised it to his lips. 'Take care, Adele, I think a lot about you.'

For one moment she thought he was going to say more and found herself tensing with relief as the door closed after him. What would she have done had he expressed his feelings more ardently?

As she crossed the hall slowly, she wondered about her own attitude. Was that moment of doubt she had experienced a pointer to her true feelings for Robert? Was she hoping for an explanation that would show his disappearance to have been inno-cent? If only she knew where he was. She hoped that by the time she reached Newcastle his family would have heard from him.

★

Adele was leaving the house to join her mother and Mark in the carriage taking them to the *Northern Belle* when she saw Philip hurrying towards them.

'Thank goodness I'm in time,' he panted. He swept his hat from his head, looked into the carriage and gave his good wishes to Mrs Jordan and Mark. Then he turned to Adele. 'I came to wish you God speed. I shall be thinking of you as you make your journey.'

'Thank you, Philip, and thank you for coming to see me off.' Already she was comparing his determined action with that of Robert when her family had been leaving for Hull. He had chosen not to come, and now Philip was putting himself out to say goodbye.

'I just had to come. As I said when I last saw you, you mean a lot to me.'

Any further exchange was prevented when Mr Jordan bustled down the path to the carriage. 'Good day, young man.'

'Good day to you, sir. Have a pleasant journey.'

'Thank you.' George climbed into the coach.

'Goodbye, Philip.' He leaned forward to kiss her lightly on the cheek, then helped Adele into the coach and closed the door. She met the look in his eyes as the coach moved away.

Her father, sitting opposite, said, 'Now there's a highly eligible young man.'

Adele knew that remark was meant for her but made no comment.

'Good morning, sir.' Robert entered the dining

282

room with diffidence. Yesterday had been a triumph of quiet acceptance by the Palmers and other Whitby folk. He already felt comfortable here, yet knew it could all be marred if he outstayed his welcome.

'Good day, Robert. Did you sleep well?' Sam eyed him critically, trying to assess if this was the real Robert Dane sitting at his table. He believed what the young man had told him so far but he knew there was more to add to his story.

'I did indeed, sir.'

'Good. There is porridge on the sideboard, help yourself.' Sam indicated the large covered tureen.

'Thank you.'

Sam watched as he ladled the porridge into a bowl. 'Are you going to see Mr Verity today?'

'Most certainly. I do not wish to miss the opportunity he has offered me. To pick up such a skill, even in a small way, is something I never expected when Tom saved me. I'm only sorry I won't have time to develop the same skills as I saw in other men yesterday.'

'I take it from your comment that you will be moving on?'

'Sir, I will have to. I have a problem to solve and it is unfair to presume for too long on your kindness and hospitality.'

The door opened and Betsy and Tom came into the room. They were in high spirits and their greetings lightened the serious atmosphere that had been developing between Sam and Robert. But, once they were all seated with their porridge in front of them, Sam returned to his conversation with Robert, telling them, 'Robert is going to Mr Verity's today and was saying he will have to think about moving on.' His eyes were on his daughter as he made the last statement. He thought he saw a momentary glint of disappointment in her eyes. He looked back at Robert. 'You will not be presuming on our hospitality. You are most welcome to stay here.'

'That is very generous of you, sir. If I may avail myself of your kind offer for a short while more, I will be most grateful.'

'Then so be it.' Sam's final approval relieved Robert, pleased Tom, and set Betsy's heart beating a little faster. 'What do you two propose to do today?' he asked, eyeing his children. 'There's no need for you to come into the shop, Betsy, the accounts can wait another week. Spend some time with Tom.'

'I'm away to the *Fair Weather*. Captain Payne won't be around and has asked me to keep an eye on the work being done,' said Tom. 'Can we meet after lunch, Betsy?'

'Why not? I'll walk with Robert to Mr Verity's, do some shopping and this afternoon, Tom, we could recall times we spent playing around the abbey.'

'And call for Robert on our way back,' finished her brother.

'Very well.' Sam laid down his napkin and stood up. 'I'll be on my way. I'll see you all later.'

As the three of them made their way down Skinner Street to Flowergate and then to the bridge, Tom broke away, saying he had to make a call about the cargo they would be taking on board for the voyage to London.

'Are you looking forward to today?' Betsy asked Robert when they were alone.

'I am,' he said with enthusiasm. 'This is something I never even dreamed of. It is very pleasant to turn my artistic skills, elementary as they are, to a new venture.'

'From what I saw of your first efforts at etching jet, I would say your skills were far from elementary.'

'It is kind of you to say so.'

'I don't make the comment out of kindness but because I see talent.' Before he had time to respond Betsy seized her chance to try to find out more about him. 'Do you have any brothers or sisters with the same inclination?'

Relaxed in her company, Robert laughed. 'I have a sister, Zelda, who is a good embroideress but wouldn't know how to use a pencil.'

'I suppose she inherits her skill from her mother?'

'I should think so. Mother is extremely good.'

'So you must inherit her skill in a different form or else get it from your father?'

'Must be from Mother.' Robert hesitated a moment then added, 'May I trust you, Betsy?'

She nodded. 'Of course.'

'I'm not telling anyone else this, not even your brother, but my father has no aptitude at all for art. His world is his mercantile marine business. That and his family.'

Betsy felt very flattered that he was prepared to

confide this much in her. She was beginning to build up a picture of Robert. Mercantile marine business spoke of a port. Tom had come across Robert in Middlesbrough, but she concluded it was unlikely that he came from there. He would have been known, and others, apart from the two thugs Tom had mentioned, would have recognised him. So he must have come from elsewhere. It could be any port but she now felt sure she could detect a trace of a northern accent in his voice, though it had been almost subsumed in a manner of speech that could only have been acquired thanks to a good education.

'Are you engaged in the business too?'

Robert automatically said, 'Yes.'

'And your troubles stem from that?'

He realised he was saying too much. He stared earnestly into her eyes, seeking the reason behind her curiosity. 'Betsy, I don't wish to go into that. If I did, you would only want me to put things right with my father, and in doing so I would risk hurting other people back home. I know you are too good a person to want that, so please accept me as I am until I can do more to resolve my present difficulties.'

Betsy blushed. Robert had seen through her questioning to the trap she'd been laying beneath. She regretted the fact that their conversation had developed this way. 'I'm sorry, Robert. I did not mean to hurt you. I hoped by talking about it to help you. I will just say one more thing.' She hesitated slightly then added, 'Well, two more things. First, I fully endorse Father's invitation to you.

Second, are you sure the answer to your problem can be found here in Whitby?'

Robert shrugged his shoulders and his lips tightened. 'I don't know,' he confessed.

'If I can ever be of help, don't be afraid to ask.' The sincerity in her voice touched him.

'Thank you. When I left home, confused and desolate, I never expected to find comfort and friendship with the Palmer family in Whitby. Their world was unknown to me. They have changed my life for the better, and I hope that through them my true future will be found.' As he spoke his eyes were fixed on her and she held his gaze. Did he detect more than friendship in this young woman who had come so unexpectedly into his life? Had she secrets of her own too?

Betsy was relieved that he had not been annoyed by her probing. She saw no anger in his eyes, rather an intensification of the friendship they already shared. Or was she letting her imagination run riot now that she had given up any thought of holding Jim Fenwick's interest?

'Sir, I presented a full report on the possibilities for developing your plan for a link between the Yorkshire coalfields and Hull three days ago. You told me to come back today,' said Jim Fenwick, facing Sir Francis Weldon in the latter's office in York.

'I did indeed, Fenwick. Your report is very comprehensive – exactly what I wanted – and it certainly gave me a great deal to think about. You have done a good job.'

'Thank you, sir.' Jim sensed that his error in the Ingleby Incline disaster was forgotten, or at least overlooked since he continued to be of use to the company. 'Do you want me to return to Rosedale now?' he asked, realising his prolonged absence could be causing a wider rift from Betsy and anxious to resolve it.

'All in good time, Fenwick, all in good time.'

Jim's hopes faded. What was coming to prevent him from returning to the dale now?

'I want you to go to Newcastle, study the railway situation there and look at the possibilities of developing lines throughout Northumberland and Durham.'

Jim's heart sank even lower. 'That could take a long time, sir, depending on the area to be covered and how detailed you wish me to be.'

'Initially a broad survey, to see if a further, detailed study is called for. Report to me after you have completed the preliminary investigation. Maybe three months' time.'

Jim breathed a little easier. This would only become a long-term assignment if his initial report merited it; there was a break for him in prospect, and that might offer him the possibility of seeing Betsy again.

With his mood lightened by the knowledge that Sir Francis had rewarded his work in the East and West Ridings with a salary rise, Jim sat in a train steaming north to Newcastle the next day. When his report was ready, he could return to York by way of Whitby, taking ship from Newcastle.

★

The Jordans' coach was waiting for them when they disembarked on The Quay. They drove straight to Cantonville Hall and settled in quickly, Paula learning from her housekeeper that the Addisons were in residence at Elston Hall.

'I think it best to visit them tomorrow and get it over with. Theodore and Emily will hear that we are back ... it will look strange if we don't visit them immediately. I think we should *all* go,' Paula suggested.

'I entirely agree,' said George.

On their arrival at Elston Hall the next day, their card was taken by the maid to the drawing room. It immediately brought Emily and Theodore hurrying into the hall where, believing the Jordans knew nothing about Robert, they greeted the new arrivals with the utmost courtesy. Greetings were cordial, though their usual joviality was tempered somewhat. For their part the Jordans did not disclose their knowledge and kept the conversation light as they all went into the drawing room.

Adele managed to whisper to Zelda, 'Thanks for letting me know about Robert.'

'I thought I should. It was best done through Mark.'

Adele squeezed her hand in appreciation.

'When did you get back?' Theodore asked as he closed the door to the drawing room.

'Yesterday, late afternoon,' replied George.

'Then you may not have heard,' said Emily, deciding it was no good hiding the situation from their immediate neighbours, 'that Robert has left home.'

'Well, as you have told us, there's no sense in beating about the bush,' said George firmly. 'We know because we had a visit from the police.'

'You had what?' gasped Theodore, pretending he had no knowledge of the visit.

'Police came enquiring after your son ... when had he last visited us, what did we know of him. I tell you, it was most embarrassing.'

Theodore realised he must speak out.

'First, let me assure you it was not the police who visited you but a private investigator I myself employed to find Robert. To my knowledge, you are the only people who have been questioned. I would earnestly request you to say nothing to anyone else about this. We have put it out among our other friends that Robert is away visiting acquaintances in Bath. Grace and Morgan are the only ones who know that he has in fact left home.'

George, though, had the bit between his teeth by now.

'If we were the only ones to be questioned, it naturally makes my distaste for this matter all the stronger — especially as the man cross-examined Adele about her association with Robert. That was not a very pleasant experience for a young lady.'

'I'm most sorry for that,' Theodore hastened to assure his friend. 'We were hoping the matter would be speedily resolved and that Robert would return home before this.'

'A visit from that person you identify as an investigator, without any explanation as to why Robert had gone missing, naturally made us assume there was a criminal element to his disappearance,'

George continued, unabashed.

'What?' Theodore instantly jumped to his feet. His face started to turn bright red from the neck upwards. 'You thought my son a criminal? How could you?' He glared witheringly at George.

'But, Theo, what else were we to think? Robert disappears and the police make enquiries?'

'Oh, yes, think the worst of course,' he snapped.

'Can you offer us another explanation?' put in Paula testily.

'I believe I can offer you something else.' Emily's voice cut into the heated exchange. 'First, I should point out what you have all overlooked – especially you, George – an investigation does not imply any element of criminality ...'

'But what else could it imply?' Paula retaliated.

'Have you never considered that Robert's disappearance might have something to do with your daughter?' Emily put her question quietly but her voice was laden with implication.

The silence that suddenly descended over the room was palpable.

'Me?' Adele's protest was heartfelt. It brought her mother rising to her defence immediately.

'You have proof of that, Emily?' Paula's reply was delivered coldly.

'It's obvious, isn't it?' she returned, equally frostily. 'Robert had no trouble at home, or at work, or with any of his friends. I can only conclude therefore that Adele was the cause.' She held up her hand to prevent anyone interrupting her. 'Hear me out,' she insisted. 'After all, we know Robert and Adele had been seeing a lot of each other ... something serious must have occurred between them, to cause him to leave home and disappear.'

'Mrs Addison!' Adele had jumped to her feet. She glared angrily at her accuser. 'You are completely mistaken. Nothing I have done could have caused Robert to leave home, and I will not remain here a moment longer to be so insulted.' She stormed from the room. A moment later Mark followed her. Zelda was next on her feet and went after the pair of them.

She caught them at the front door. As they stepped outside, she said, 'I'm sorry. Please don't think badly of us.'

But she could read no forgiveness for her mother in Adele's eyes. 'You, at least, are not to blame. Please, if you hear anything about Robert, let me know,' she told her friend.

'I know a little ...'

Adele hung on her next words but did not hear them because at that moment the drawing room door was flung open and both sets of parents stormed out, still loudly accusing one another over Robert's disappearance.

'I will send you word,' Zelda managed to whisper.

Words of animosity towards the Addisons filled the coach as the Jordans drove home. The friendship that had grown between the two families appeared to lie in ruins.

Later, a distraught Adele faced her parents. 'Mama, Papa, I want you to know that nothing happened between Robert and me to cause him to leave home.'

'My love, we never doubted you for a moment,' soothed her mother, and George added his own words of support.

The Addisons' accusation had highlighted all Adele's feelings for Robert. Now she experienced a strong desire to find out the reason for his disappearance, for she sensed her own future could be bound up in it.

'I only wish I knew where he was,' she said with a sad shake of her head.

The possibility of finding out arrived two days later in a note from Zelda to Mark which arrived just after his father had left for work. On reading it, he took it straight to his sister.

Dear Mark,
Tell Adele that the investigator traced Robert to a farm near Consett. When he left there, the owners believe he was making for Middlesbrough. The investigator believes strongly that that is the case but a search in Middlesbrough has proved inconclusive. However, he did report a brawl he investigated because, unusually, it occurred in a better part of the town.

It happened outside the Anvil public house but he found no reliable witnesses to it. One curious thing, though: near the scene of the brawl he found a screwed-up poster, one of many that Papa had distributed throughout Newcastle and Middlesbrough, but further enquiries revealed nothing and he concluded there was no connection. Sorry that I know no more.

Zelda

'This is the only clue we have and I'm going to follow it up,' Adele announced after reading the note.

'Father won't allow you to.'

'I'll see Mother first. Come with me, Mark.'

They had no difficulty in finding her; the sound of the piano gave her away. When they entered the music room Paula stopped playing and greeted them with a smile. 'Coming to listen?' she asked with a teasing twinkle in her eyes as she tried to lighten the atmosphere.

'I'd like you to read this, Mama,' said Adele as she crossed the room, leaving Mark to close the door and wait in the background.

Paula took the letter and, after reading it, looked up sharply. 'I'd prefer you not to enter into this sort of correspondence with the Addisons,' she said.

'Mama, I've got to prove to them that it was not because of me that Robert disappeared. There must be another reason, and the only way to find out what it is, is to find Robert himself. This is the best lead we have.'

'But a private investigator has found nothing. What do you expect to do that he has not?'

'The investigator must have missed something. I must go and try, Mama. I have to clear my name.'

'You are asking my permission to go to Middlesbrough?' Paula frowned disapprovingly.

'Mama, I must.'

Paula could understand her daughter's resolve and desire to clear herself of any blame. She also read her determination and knew that if permission were not forthcoming, Adele would take it upon herself to go without her parents' sanction.

'Adele, I fear your father won't agree,' she tried to argue.

'Mama, please let me go?' cried the girl, fearing the negative outcome of asking her father.

'No.' Paula shook her head. 'I sympathise but I cannot go against your father. You must ask him yourself.'

Adele grew even more restless as the time for George's return from work drew near. When she heard him come in she rushed into the hall to meet him, leaving her mother and Mark in the drawing room.

'Papa, come quickly!' She held out her hand to him.

He laughed at what he took to be his daughter's excitement over having something to show him. 'Hold on, let me shed my coat.'

Eagerly she took his hat and cane and laid them to one side as he shrugged his coat from his shoulders. He barely had time to lay it across a chair close to the closet before she took his hand and hurried him towards the drawing room.

'I have something important to ask you, Papa.' Even though Adele's heart was pounding, she gave him one of the pleading looks she had adopted to melt his heart ever since she was a child.

He recognised it and knew he was about to be asked a big favour.

As she hurried him into the room he caught Paula's eye but his querying expression brought no response from her except her usual smile and, 'Welcome home.'

'Now, what's this all about?' he asked as Adele sat him down in his chair. 'You must want something?'

'I do, Papa. I want you to let me go and find Robert so that I can clear my name.'

'What?' The word exploded from George as his face darkened. 'Don't be ridiculous.'

'Papa, I've *got* to go. I must clear my name.'

'No matter, you cannot go.'

'Please. I won't rest until I ...'

'No! It's impossible. You cannot travel alone. Your mother can't accompany you, it would not be fit for two ladies ...'

'Poppycock!' snapped Adele defiantly, and almost regretted her insolence when she saw her father scowl.

'Listen to me, young lady,' he replied sternly. 'Curb your temper. There is an investigator on the job. Leave it to him.'

'But maybe I can look places he can't. Ask questions he may not.'

'She has a point, George,' put in Paula calmly, in a tone she knew always had an effect on her husband. 'For instance, there may be things Zelda knows she will only impart to Adele.'

'Zelda's father should get them from her!'

'If you tell him that, it will only widen the rift

between our two families. But Adele and Zelda together – who knows?'

'Please, Father, please!' Adele pleaded with an anguished expression.

'If I said yes, you'd need a male escort. I can't go. I have important clients to see ... no, it's out of the question.'

'I'll go, Father.' All eyes turned to Mark who had sat quietly assessing the situation as it developed. 'It is important to clear Adele's name. Her reputation and that of our whole family are at stake.'

'There you are, Adele. Mark will do it for you,' said George, with some satisfaction that the situation had been dealt with finally.

'No, Father, I will not be able to do it alone,' said his son firmly. 'Adele will have to accompany me. She is the only person who can get the truth of things out of Robert.'

George hesitated. 'I don't like her going,' he started, but was stopped by Paula.

'Mark is right.'

He knew then he was cornered and would reluctantly have to agree. 'Very well,' he sighed.

'Oh, Papa, thank you.' Adele threw her arms round his neck and hugged him. 'Thank you!'

16

Barney Hawkins, with the collar of his oilskin turned up against the rain, hurried through Newcastle's streets to The Quay. He settled his hat more firmly on his head as he bent against the freshening wind, and was thankful he had chosen to wear leather bootees this morning. He felt sorry for the stevedores in their cloth working jackets and worsted breeches, labouring on in such inclement weather to load the ships in time for an afternoon sailing. He would soon escape into the comfort of Theodore Addison's office, though he was not looking forward to the interview itself. His last report, a week ago, had not pleased Mr Addison and Barney felt sure he would not be better pleased today.

Ten minutes later, his oilskin hanging on a coat-stand in the outer office, he was admitted to Mr Addison's room.

'Good day, Hawkins,' Theo greeted him, leaning back in his chair and frowning at his visitor. 'Well, good is not really the word, is it?'

'No, indeed, sir,' replied Barney, trying to sound undeterred nevertheless.

'So, what have you for me? It's a week since we last met. I presume you have been out of town?'

'I have, sir. Thought I would widen my area of enquiry. We can be almost certain your son was in Middlesbrough but all enquiries there, as you know, drew a blank. It is as if he vanished into thin air. Some people there remember a Robert Dane but no one in any detail. He was working as a labourer and simply disappeared. I have pursued various possibilities around Middlesbrough but nothing came of them. I also considered the possibility that he may have stowed away on a ship but concluded that would be out of character for him. Besides, he'd have run the risk of being caught and the consequences of that could be catastrophic.'

'Quite right, Hawkins.'

'So, sir, I decided he had probably moved inland and this last week have been making enquiries in the West Riding.'

'And?' prompted Theo hopefully.

Barney gave a shake of his head and grimaced. 'I'm sorry, sir, I raised not one likely line of enquiry. Oh, yes, there were cranks to waste my time with ... there always are in cases like this ... but from my experience working under Superintendent Jarvis, I can pick them out.'

'So we are no further forward?'

'I'm sorry to say, sir, we are not. No further than Middlesbrough, though it is my honest opinion he has moved on from there. And, I must say, has covered his tracks well.'

Theo looked very thoughtful. Barney, recognising the man's desire not to have his deliberations interrupted, remained silent. Then, his decision made, Theo sat up and leaned over his desk, eyes intent on the investigator.

'Hawkins, I think we should increase the reward money by fifty per cent.'

Barney could not hide his surprise.

'You think that unwise?' queried Theo.

'Sir, it is your decision. I will implement it and follow up any lead it produces, but I must warn you it will probably bring a lot of time-wasters out of the woodwork. People will say anything in the hope of gaining money. There could be a lot of false leads that will only raise your hopes need-lessly.'

'But there is always the chance of getting the one lead we need.'

'True, sir, but ...'

'Then do it.'

'Listen to me and listen hard.' Art Mason glared at Luke Coning. 'That reward for information leading to the whereabouts of Robert Dane has been increased.'

'What's that to us? He got away,' Luke pointed out.

'We can find him.'

'We don't know where he is.'

Art tapped his forehead. 'It's all up here, never fear.'

Luke gawped at him. 'What you on about?'

'The bigger reward makes doing a spot of think-ing worthwhile.'

'But how's thinking going to find Dane for us?'

'Think back to that night he got away from us.'

'All I got was a black eye, a bloody nose and a sore head.' Luke winced at the memory.

'Well, now's your chance to be rewarded for that.'

'How?'

'Listen,' snapped Art, giving him a rough tap on the chest.

'Hey, cut that out!'

Art ignored this. 'I've been using my nous. Dane disappeared immediately after he escaped from us. No one else saw him. Dick Bishop reckons Dane just walked away without a word, he knows not where, and the stranger with him. I reckon he knows more than he's telling, though.'

'How'd you know that? You ain't tackled him about that night.'

'I got my sources.'

'Not that creep Mousey Flanders?'

'Mousey can be useful sometimes.'

'So how'd he find that out?'

Art shrugged. 'I don't know. You never ask where Mousey's concerned.'

'Well, what good's his information anyway? It tells us nothing.'

'That's where you're wrong, dumb-head. Think about it. Dick Bishop's hiding something, and I reckon that something is how Dane came to disappear so completely.'

'Bishop ain't going to tell you! And if you figure on forcing him to tell, count me out – he'll have his pals on us like a ton of bricks and I don't want to suffer the consequences.'

'There ain't going to be any of that. I ain't even going to try asking Bishop. But the fact that he's keeping quiet tells me something ...'

'What?' derided Luke.

'Something illegal went on.'

'What you getting at?'

'You want to get out of Middlesbrough unseen and disappear, how would you do it?'

Luke shrugged. 'I *don't* want to leave Middlesbrough – how should I know?'

Art looked at him in disgust. 'I know you don't, but what if you were Dane?'

'Oh, I see what you mean, but I still don't ...'

'Stowaway!'

For a moment Luke did not comprehend then it dawned on him what Art was getting at. 'Oh ... yes.' He paused. 'But which ship, and when?'

'He'd want to get away as soon as possible, so it would be the first ship to sail.'

'And you reckon Bishop knows?'

'I reckon he might have put the idea into Dane's head but doesn't necessarily know which ship.'

'So we aren't any further on.'

'But I am,' said Art with a smirk of satisfaction. 'I've made some discreet enquiries.'

'Mousey again?'

'No, I ain't that daft. Mousey could link the two things and try and outdo us. The first ship to leave Newcastle was the *Fair Weather* early the next morning, bound for London.'

'London! If Dane stowed away on that we'll never find him. How d'you even try among all those folk?'

'I wouldn't,' replied Art. 'But the ship was putting in to Whitby first for repairs and I reckon that's where Dane went ashore.'

'So you're proposing we give up our jobs and go to Whitby?'

'Yes. With the increased reward, it's worth our while.'

'And what if we don't find him?'

'We can always get another job – come back here even, if we work our week's notice first and leave proper like. But I have a feeling about this. I reckon we'll find Dane by going to Whitby, even if he's moved on from there.'

'Good day, Mr Verity.' Betsy had just turned into Skinner Street from Well Close Square when she saw the jet workshop owner.

'Good day to you too.' He smiled and raised his black top hat. 'I trust you are well?'

'I am.' She smiled at him.

'You look very smart this afternoon,' he commented, admiring her cloak of dark bottle green moiré worn over a lighter green velvet dress whose skirts widened into a series of flounces until brushing the ground. A small straw bonnet, fitting close to her head, was tied neatly under her chin with a white ribbon.

'That is most kind of you, Mr Verity,' Betsy said demurely. She felt it un-ladylike to comment on his clothes but from the look in her eyes it was obvious she approved of his black frock coat and dark blue waistcoat, its long lapels allowing his white shirt to show. His grey trousers had braided side seams and he carried a cane in his right hand and a pair of leather gloves in his left. 'You have escaped jet for the afternoon, I see?'

He smiled. 'Yes, I am taking tea with a friend in New Buildings.'

'And I am on my way to see Miss Jonty who has not been well, though I am pleased to say she is improving.'

'Ah, visiting the sick, how very commendable. My call is social.'

Betsy made no comment. She knew who his friend was – Mrs Clark, a widow of forty-five – and he a widower of fifty! Though she knew some of the more strait-laced among Whitby society disapproved of the association, she herself privately did not. Why should they not find happiness together? It meant no disrespect or lack of love for the partners they had lost.

'We will be walking in the same direction as far as the end of Skinner Street, may we walk together?' he asked.

'Certainly, Mr Verity. It will be my pleasure.'

He matched his step to hers.

'You may like to know, Miss Palmer, that Robert is showing exceptional talent and has such a quick brain he is adapting rapidly to using the tools of the jet trade.'

'I am pleased to hear that, Mr Verity. I know he appreciates the chance you have given him.'

'Well, I could tell from his questions that first day he visited how interested he was in the whole process. Then his comments on the work, without making any adverse criticism or showing off, confirmed he genuinely had an eye for composition. It made me curious which was why I invited him to try something. As you know, he surprised us all. I can see what an asset he is and could be to my trade. I hope he stays. Do you know his plans, Miss Palmer?'

'I do not, Mr Verity.'

'I hope you don't mind my asking?'

'Of course not.'

'I detect there is more to Robert Dane than we suppose.'

'I think you know as much about him as we do. We know nothing of his background, but Father likes him and has told him he can stay with us as long as he wishes.'

Mr Verity pursed his lips for a moment in thought then said quickly but with conviction, 'If your father accepts him without knowing more, then that is good enough for me. As I say, with a talent like that, I hope he stays.'

They parted at the end of Skinner Street and Betsy walked on to Miss Jonty's, deep in thought and pleased by Mr Verity's comments.

She had a pleasant enough visit with Miss Jonty who, at sixty, had spent the majority of her years mourning the loss of her betrothed in a whaling disaster in the Arctic, but had done so without being a misery to others. Betsy left the house to pass by Mr Verity's jet workshop at the time she knew Robert would be leaving.

She was approaching the shop when she saw him come out along with three other workers. She was pleased to see they were all in a jovial mood. They joined the press of people in Church Street and were almost upon her before they saw her.

'Miss Palmer.' Each of the others touched the peak of his cap in a show of respect and then bade Robert farewell.

He smiled at Betsy and said, 'This is a pleasant surprise.'

'I've been visiting and timed my departure to meet you,' she replied.

'I'm flattered. Can we walk a little? I've been shut in most of the day and you know what a jet workshop can be like.'

'Of course! We have time. How about the West Pier?'

'That will certainly put some fresh air into my lungs.'

They walked along Church Street commenting on what was happening around them, observing Whitby folk going about their usual business late on this bright afternoon. It was only when they were crossing the bridge to the West Side that they became aware of the strength of the wind funnelling between the East and West Cliffs from the sea.

'It will be very windy on the pier,' commented Robert, a cautionary tone in his voice.

'I've known it worse,' countered Betsy.

'There'll be a strong sea running.'

'That's how I like it,' she replied with eager anticipation.

'So do I. Come on!' He held out his hand and she clasped it, an automatic gesture that held no embarrassment for her.

They turned in the direction of the West Pier and Betsy told him of her visit to Miss Jonty and how she had met Mr Verity. She passed on the gossip about Mr Verity and Mrs Clark, not in any critical way but with expressions of delight that those two people should be finding pleasure in each other's company. She was gratified when Robert agreed with her view.

'He was praising you,' she went on.

'What have I done to deserve that?'

'He sees great potential in your work.'

'I think it is fairly crude in execution but could become better as I grow more used to the tools. And, of course, with practice.'

'Well, Mr Verity certainly did not hold back in his praise. He hopes you will stay.'

Robert frowned and glanced away from her. 'I will have to move on some time, Betsy,' he murmured.

They had reached the pier by now and, without the protection of the cliff, felt exhilarated by the wind's wild buffeting. 'Why? If you are finding a new life here, why not stay?' Betsy prompted him.

'The problem at home will hang over me.'

'Solve it and then come back.'

'It isn't that easy.'

'Make it so! Mr Verity wants you to stay, and you know you are perfectly welcome to be with us.'

'I could not put on you indefinitely.'

'You have fitted in very well so far. I know Father likes you and welcomes your being with us, especially since Tom is so frequently absent as he is

307

now. We never know when we will see him again. His present sailing schedule between the Tyne and London does give him some opportunities for calling in at Whitby, but that won't last.'

'I've detected that he is ambitious.'

'He is. Tom wants to become Captain Palmer and sail the world.'

'He'll achieve it.'

'And Father will miss him all the more.' Betsy suddenly realised the implication behind her statement. She stopped to face Robert and, with an apologetic expression, quickly added, 'Oh, Robert, I didn't mean that you were a mere substitute for Tom. I know you are not in Father's eyes ... nor in mine. He admires you for yourself, and draws pleasure from your company.'

Robert's expression softened in response to this. 'I took no offence, Betsy. If I bring comfort to your father, in whatever way, I am grateful to be able to recompense him for all his kindness. You and your father have brought me greater peace of mind than I could ever have expected in my circumstances, but I will never be wholly at peace until I resolve my troubles at home.'

'Then do so!' she cried.

'Do you really want me to do that?' There was an earnestness to his question that she hoped she had not misinterpreted.

'Yes, I do.' Her words, caught by the wind, were torn away and a silence charged with emotion stretched between them.

Robert reached out and touched her cheek. 'You are special to me, Betsy. I owe you a great deal for your sympathy and friendship in my time of trouble. Maybe I've made things more of a problem than they really need be.'

'Will talking about it to me help?'

He gave a wan smile and a little shake of his head. 'No, I don't think so.'

'If ever you think it will, I can be a good listener.'

'Just be there for me – that will help.' He placed his hands on her shoulders and stared earnestly into her eyes. 'You are very dear to me, Betsy. Never forget that, no matter what happens.' He eased her to him, touched her lips with his and held the kiss. She did not draw away.

Sleep did not come easy to Betsy that night. She was puzzled that Robert's kiss had revived memories of Jim. Why should that be? Surely he had gone from her life? There was still no word from him, and no news came out of Rosedale. She had long felt guilty about her high-handed treatment of Jim and still felt an urge to take it back and at least restore a semblance of friendship between them. But she doubted she'd ever get the chance now.

Robert too did not sleep easily. Thoughts of Adele haunted his mind. In a strange way the kiss he had shared with Betsy had left him with the feeling he had betrayed Adele ... but he forced himself to shake off that unease. By leaving Newcastle and assuming a new life, he had put behind him the familiar world where, had he stayed, he could have hurt so many people. Each passing day eased his mind further in that respect. And it could remain that way, for now there was Betsy.

It was early afternoon when Theodore returned to his office from the bank and made two entries in the note-books he kept locked away in his desk drawer. He signed several papers, took them to his clerk and then added, 'I am leaving now and will not be back until tomorrow morning.'

He left the office, keeping up a steady pace away from The Quay. As he turned a corner he bumped into a man coming the other way. The apologies that sprang to both men's lips died without being uttered, to be replaced by dark expressions and curt utterances.

'George.'

'Theodore.'

Theodore moved to step past George who prevented him.

'Seeing that we've met, I'll inform you now that Adele and Mark have gone looking for your son.'

'What?' Theodore was astounded.

'They've gone, and I'll hold you responsible if anything happens to them.'

'Hold on . . . I can't be blamed. Adele must be at the root of this trouble.'

'So you said before and I utterly reject and condemn that accusation,' said George with some force.

'Where have they gone?' demanded Theo.

'Middlesbrough. You know yourself that was the last possible sighting of Robert.'

'But I have engaged a private investigator! If

Adele interferes in his enquiries, she'll be even more responsible for Robert's disappearance.'

'Let me tell you this, Theodore Addison.' George poked a finger into his former friend's chest with every word he spoke. 'Adele would not have gone if you hadn't accused her of being implicated. She wants to prove she had nothing to do with it. So, I repeat, if anything happens to her, *you'll* be to blame and will answer to me.' With that he spun round and strode off with an angry determined step.

Seething, Theodore stared after him for a few moments and then turned and continued on his own way.

He knocked at a familiar door in a quiet street and was soon admitted. Not a word was spoken until the door closed. The sound lifted Theodore out of his memories of the encounter with George, but his sigh, though one of relief, told the lady who had greeted him that something was not quite right.

'You look troubled, Theo,' she commented as she took his redingote and hung it on a stand near the front door.

He pulled a face. 'That needn't concern you, Rose. Our arrangement remains our secret, and will remain so until a solution can be found.'

As they were speaking she had led the way into a drawing room, furnished with comfort in mind without being ostentatious.

'Tea or something stronger?' she asked pleasantly, trying to lighten his mood.

'Tea shared with you will be splendid,' he replied.

'Then make yourself comfortable and relax. It will be good for you.' As she went to the bell-pull, she picked up the envelope he had placed on a table beside the window. She pulled the bell-pull three times, a signal that tea was required, then locked the envelope away in the top drawer of an oak bureau.

As she did so he watched her, admiring the graceful way she moved – something that, along with her striking features, had enchanted him twenty-two years ago. At forty-two she still had the porcelain beauty of her youth.

Two hours later Theo left the house, feeling refreshed and relaxed. Robert would be found, and found soon. And when he came home again they'd let bygones be bygones and everything would be just like it always had been.

Two weeks later when Robert came into the house in Well Close Square, Betsy could see at once that he had something to divulge, but because her father was there she did not press him in case it was something personal. They shared much these days and found pleasure in being together. Though neither of them had voiced their thoughts, each in their own way sensed that this closeness could become something more. It was only when they sat down to their evening meal that Robert imparted his news.

'There were rumours buzzing around the work-shop today, though everyone was being discreet about them and certainly kept quiet when Mr Verity was around.'

Sam and Betsy glanced eagerly at him with growing curiosity. Robert kept them waiting while he toyed with his food.

'Come on, Robert, don't keep us in suspense,' pressed Betsy with a touch of irritation.

'Well ...' He paused teasingly. He saw annoyance flare in her eyes. 'Mr Verity left early today.' He concentrated on his food again.

'That's not it,' she snapped, glaring at him.

Sam gave a little chuckle. 'He'll keep you on tenterhooks all the longer if you take his bait.'

Caught out, Betsy snorted, 'He needn't tell us then.'

Robert laughed. 'I bet you'll be all ears in a moment.'

She narrowed her eyes and gave a sharp shake of her head.

'There's a rumour going around that Mr Verity is thinking of selling the workshop.'

'What?' Betsy and her father gasped together.

'That is what is being said.'

'I don't believe it,' said Sam. 'It's been a family business for years.'

'That'll come to an end if anything happens to Mr Verity,' Betsy pointed out. 'He has no one to pass it on to.'

'It will, but he has many years left in him still.'

'True enough,' agreed Robert, 'but that might be why he's thinking of selling.'

'What do you mean?' asked Betsy, Robert's teasing forgotten, and all her attention focused on what he was telling them.

'Rumour also says he has a lady love.'

313

'Mrs Clark!' gasped Betsy.

'No name was mentioned,' Robert confessed.

'That's who it will be,' Betsy said confidently.

'Well, well,' said Sam thoughtfully. 'If it's true, good luck to them.'

'And if it's true,' added Robert, 'I wonder who'll buy his business? They'll not have the same view of me. Mr Verity has been very kind in allowing me to use his workshop. Maybe it's time I moved on.'

'Oh, no,' gasped Betsy, then pulled herself up sharply, chiding herself for exposing her feelings. 'I mean . . . you can't let your developing talent go to waste.'

'Maybe this is a sign for me to get my life sorted out. Go back home and face what must be faced.'

'Why don't *you* buy the workshop, Papa?' The suggestion, bursting from Betsy's lips so quickly, sounded preposterous.

Sam gave a little laugh. 'Me? I'm no jet worker.'

'No, but you know what sells. If you didn't, you wouldn't have done so well by going to Rosedale.'

'Jet is only a small part of what we sell there.'

'But an important part. And if you had the workshop, you would have no need to buy from others and would make more profit on every piece.'

'You are getting a business head on your shoulders, young lady. What you say is true but . . .' Sam let his doubt hang in the air.

'Why not, sir?' put in Robert. Then he diluted the observations he was about to make by changing them to, 'Of course, I do not know the

314

Rosedale trade so cannot truly comment on the possible effects of the purchase of Mr Verity's workshop.'

'Then come with us when we go next week,' Betsy suggested. 'See for yourself.'

'You cannot throw that responsibility on Robert,' Sam pointed out. 'If he knew something about trading ...'

'But I do, sir, I learned from my father,' Robert cut in quickly. Then, realising he had given away something of himself and his past, clammed up.

Betsy picked up on it. She was about to question him further when a quick glance at her father told her he too had noted the revelation, but the cautious light in his eyes warned her to say nothing.

'In that case, Robert,' said Sam slowly, 'your opinion might be of value to me. I would appreciate it.'

'Very well, sir, I will do what I can. If you have no objection, it might be as well if I were put in possession of the relevant figures for your jet trade in Rosedale. I don't wish to pry into your whole business, sir. I only want the information that will be useful to me in making my assessment of this aspect of it.'

'You can provide him with those, Betsy.'

She nodded, excitement gripping her. Surely something would come of this new development.

'You must keep all this under your hats,' Sam pointed out. 'I will give it some thought and make a decision by morning.'

Both Betsy and Robert wondered what that

decision would be. During the night each of them tried to anticipate the ways a favourable decision might affect their future life.

At breakfast the following morning Samuel announced, 'I think there are real commercial possibilities to my buying the workshop from Mr Verity. I will discreetly enquire of him if there is any truth in the rumour of his departure and, if so, ask him not to make it public for a time as I would like to make him the first offer ... if, after our investigation, I do decide to go ahead.' He sensed the pleasure and excitement he had brought to the two young people and wondered if he was possibly forming a solid base for their lives to come.

That evening he reported on his interview with Mr Verity who had confirmed the rumour while stipulating that he and Mrs Clark wanted to keep it a very close secret for a while. He agreed that his past business relationship with Sam counted for much. Because of that he had promised to give Sam the first chance to buy and would not announce the sale publicly unless Sam decided against a purchase.

The days leading to their departure for Rosedale were busy: Sam completing his usual purchasing of items to sell; Betsy providing Robert with information; and he making a careful study of the figures.

On the day of their departure Betsy was woken by a feeling of excitement. She pulled back the curtains on her bedroom window and saw early-morning brightness lighting the sky from the east. Reading it as a good omen, she smiled and let a pleasurable sigh escape from her lips.

Her spirits were still high when they reached Lealholm where they were greeted effusively by Mrs Dobson and her husband. That was extended to Robert whom Sam introduced as a friend from Whitby who was showing some talent in the jet trade.

Robert was struck by the desolate beauty all around as they climbed out of Lealholm and crossed the high wild moors before descending into Rosedale. He could see evidence of farming, but the signs of mining were everywhere too: scars across the hillsides, rows of houses and cottages for the miners and railway workers, engine sheds, warehouses, coal depots, kilns where the ore was burnt to lighten its weight for transportation ... all seeming alien to this remote moorland dale. Yet here were people who were flush with money and eager to spend it. This was the market that Mr Palmer and his daughter had tapped. Was there greater potential in it? They had brought Robert, seeking his opinion.

Mrs Dodsworth gave them a royal welcome and, once introduced to Robert, said she would soon have another room ready for him. After settling them with tea and cake, she busied herself preparing the room. While doing so she continued her assessment of the young man who had arrived with Mr Palmer and Betsy, and Betsy's attitude towards him. She thought there was something different about Robert and could only, at this juncture, assume he came from a level of society that differed markedly from that of the farm labourers, miners and railway workers around the dale. He was more in keeping with the bosses, as she called anyone above the position of foreman.

With that conclusion reached she found herself comparing Robert with Jim Fenwick who she considered had moved into the bosses' class – if low on the ladder, then at least with the potential to climb it. She was wondering if Robert had taken the place of Jim in Betsy's mind. Was the foreman but a memory to her now? These questions were in her mind when she heard Betsy come upstairs.

The girl came straight to the room Mrs Dodsworth was preparing and tapped on the door.

'Come in, lass,' Mrs Dodsworth said, giving the eiderdown a last tug as she straightened up. 'Are the menfolk all right?'

'Yes, thanks. Enjoying a second cup. I came to thank you for showing such hospitality to Robert.'

'That's no trouble. He seems a pleasant young man.'

'We've found him so since Tom brought him from Middlesbrough.'

'So that's where he's from?' mused Mrs Dodsworth.

Betsy did not enlighten her any further on that point but said, 'He's showing real skill as a jet worker and wanted to see where we sold our jewellery.'

Mrs Dodsworth detected a note of pride in Betsy's voice as she revealed this side of Robert. 'Well, you certainly brought him to the right place. I think he'll get his eyes opened on pay day.'

Betsy laughed. 'I think you're right.' Then she

slipped in, 'Have you had any news of Jim Fenwick?'

'Yes, I have. There's talk among some of the workers that he's been sent to Newcastle to do a survey there for Sir Francis.'

Betsy raised her eyebrows. 'Then the Ingleby disaster had no further repercussions for him?'

'It seems not.'

'I'm pleased about that.'

Mrs Dodsworth nodded. Maybe the trouble between Betsy and Jim had been smoothed over, or the passage of time had tempered her attitude to him, or Robert had given her a new perspective on life.

17

'Adele, I want you to stay in the hotel,' Mark said firmly.

'But I should go with you,' she protested.

'No! It will be far easier if I go alone. Then I won't have the worry of looking after you.'

Adele frowned. 'But I won't be any bother and I do ...'

'Mother made me responsible for you so please do as I say,' he cut in. 'Besides, we don't know what this pub is like. It would be most embarrassing if they turned you away, and then any chance of our gaining information could be lost. Just let me do it my way.'

Reluctantly, Adele agreed. All the way from Newcastle this was what she had been anticipating – Mark digging his heels in and conducting the search just as he wanted. In her heart of hearts she knew he was right, but waiting for her brother's return was not going to be easy.

Their journey had proceeded well, though she had been impatient for the carriage to go faster and only grudgingly agreed to an overnight stop on the way. On arriving in Middlesbrough the following afternoon, they had been directed to a good-class hotel in what they noted was a better part of the town. Here the rows of houses were of superior rank to those they had seen nearer the iron works. Mark had booked two rooms for them and one in quarters set aside for the servants of any travellers, in which their coachman was quartered.

Knowing his sister was anxious for news of Robert, Mark decided to visit the Anvil as soon as they had settled in. He had been preparing to leave on this mission when Adele had expressed a desire to go with him.

'I don't know how long this will take,' he warned her, 'but please don't go outside the hotel. I'll ask Walton to be in his quarters just in case you need anything.'

She nodded miserably.

Once he had seen the coachman Mark set off for the Anvil, following the directions he had been given by the hotel clerk.

He viewed the building with critical eyes as he approached and it made a favourable impression on him. The place looked well cared for: its paintwork was fresh, windows sparkling, and brass doorknobs and knockers highly polished. He judged it to be a place that would not generally be frequented by thirsty workers coming off their shift. They would want somewhere nearer their workplace than the Anvil. He began to think that this would not be the best place to start looking for Robert; he had been labouring at the works and, in Barney Hawkins's judgement, any fracas outside the Anvil would have had nothing to do

321

with the iron workers. But Adele had been adamant that this would be the best place to start and he was here to try.

Mark entered the building and found himself in a small vestibule with doors to right and left. Hearing a murmur of voices coming from the left, he tentatively pushed that door open. He saw a long saloon, one side of it occupied by the bar. The reflection in a long mirror set on the wall behind made the room seem wider than it was.

Mark noted that there were about twenty people drinking around the room. The bar shone with regular polishing, glasses sparkled, and tankards stood in four neat rows on the counter in front of the mirror, but the majority of that space was occupied by rows of bottles containing every kind of liquor and spirits imaginable. Mark realised this was not the usual working men's pub. Once again he had the feeling he would get no news of Robert here.

He approached the bar and a smartly dressed, striking woman of about thirty excused herself from the man to whom she was speaking and came over to Mark. Her smile was warm and friendly.

'Good day, sir.' Her voice was touched with a Teesside accent.

'Good day to you, miss,' replied Mark who had noticed she wore no ring on her left hand. 'I'll take a tankard of your best ale, please,' he added, removing his hat.

'Certainly.' She picked up a tankard and proceeded to draw the ale while eyeing him. 'You're a stranger in these parts?'

'Yes, I am.'

'Then let me say welcome and introduce myself. I'm Veronica – been the barmaid here for five years.'

'May I say, this is a very fine establishment?'

'Thank you.' She placed the tankard in front of him and took his money.

'Are you in Middlesbrough for long?' Her question was friendly, not prying.

'I'm not sure. I have some private matters to see to. If I don't get them cleared up before I have to return to Newcastle, I will be back.'

'And you will be welcome here any time you are in Middlesbrough.'

'Thank you.'

Another customer, obviously a regular, entered the bar then and Veronica moved away to serve him. She was thinking about Mark as she did so. A polite young man, quiet-spoken but with a light in his eye that told her he would be difficult to outwit. His manner of speech betrayed a good education. Interesting, she thought.

At the same time Mark was making his assessment of her. He figured she would be strong-minded, prepared to be forthright, but at the same time cautious about passing on information she had heard over the bar.

He took his time over his drink, studying the customers as he did so. None of them seemed likely to have been involved in a brawl; it seemed Hawkins's judgement was correct there. However, he knew Adele would not let him leave it at that.

Seeing him drain his tankard, Veronica came over to him. 'Another, sir?'

'Not today, thanks. That's good ale, though. I'll be back.'

'That will be a pleasure, Mr ...'

Mark knew she was fishing and said, 'Jordan.'

'I hope we will see you again, Mr Jordan.'

He acknowledged her invitation with a gracious nod.

As he headed for the door it opened and a man strode in. Mark had no opportunity to make such a close assessment of him as he had done of the other customers but he did catch their exchange when Veronica greeted him by saying, 'Hello, Dick, you certainly are becoming a regular. We're very pleased.'

'So am I, Veronica. Good fortune smiled on me that evening ...'

'Well?' asked Adele in a voice that was eager for information and hopeful of what she would hear. She had positioned herself in a seat in the lounge from where she could see anyone entering the hotel. As soon as she saw her brother she'd rushed over to him.

'I have no news of Robert.'

Disappointment clouded her face. 'Did you ask?' she snapped.

'No. I ...'

'Why not?' she cut in harshly, her eyes flashing criticism.

'Just keep quiet while I tell you,' rapped Mark, 'but first let us go to the privacy of my room.' He started for the stairs and, knowing it was no good pressing him now, Adele followed.

Once in his room, Mark discarded his outdoor clothes and then, turning to his sister, indicated a chair and said, 'Sit down and listen.'

He told her about the Anvil and its customers. It was catering for a different class of people from those with whom, it was supposed, Robert had become involved.

'But that is not to say he wasn't there,' she pressed. 'Why didn't you ask?'

'I admit that, though it does seem unlikely. I didn't press the matter because I judged it best to gain the barmaid's confidence first. After all, if there was a disturbance, either inside or outside the Anvil, it is only natural she would want it hushed up rather than sully the reputation of the place. I believe if I had come out with an enquiry she would have clammed up. No, best to gain her trust first. I will go back again tomorrow.'

After Mark had made three more visits to the Anvil without any real progress, Adele pressed the matter over luncheon a few days later.

'We cannot go on like this. If we do not look like getting any information here, we had better return home even though I am reluctant to do so. I so want to find Robert and clear my name.'

'Give me one more day. I'm sure I am gaining Veronica's trust ... maybe I can make my queries more direct. Something has been nagging at my mind ever since my first visit, I just can't decide what it is.' A frown of frustration creased his brow.

Expectation brightened Adele's eyes. 'Think, Mark, think,' she urged.

He gave a little shake of his head. 'It won't come.'

'Go over that visit again,' she pleaded.

'I have, time and again, but whatever set this off can't have been much or it would have lodged more firmly in my mind.'

'When you go to the Anvil this evening – I suppose you are going?'

'Of course.'

'Keep an open mind, but once you walk through the door imagine it was that first night over again.'

When he entered the Anvil later on, Mark tried to project himself back to his first visit. There were a few people in the bar just as there had been then; people who, through Veronica, he had come to know as regulars. Veronica herself was behind the bar and, on seeing him, came over to bid him good evening then asked, 'The usual, Mr Jordan?'

'Please.'

'You are becoming a regular. Your work not finished?'

'No, it's not. I'm a bit puzzled by it. Maybe you can help me?'

'Me?' She raised her eyebrows in surprise. 'I don't know how but I will if I can.'

'I am looking for a young man of about my age, name of Robert Dane.'

Veronica pursed her lips doubtfully and shook her head. 'I don't know anyone of that name, but I don't know everyone who comes in here. Regulars, yes. Casuals, no.'

Undeterred, he went on. 'I appreciate that, Veronica, but I know he was in Middlesbrough working as a labourer in the iron works.'

'We get very few of the workers in here. They use the pubs nearer their work.'

'There is something that might link him with the Anvil.'

Again she raised a questioning eyebrow.

'I was told there was a disturbance here some time back and wondered if it might have involved him?'

'Not in here,' she replied sharply.

Mark felt he had touched a nerve. In spite of her strong character, she had gone on the defensive, especially when she went on, a little too quickly, 'Are you a policeman or something?'

Mark laughed. 'Do I look like one?'

'I must admit you don't but there's no saying, is there? I'd have set you down as an uncomplicated young man and now you're trying to sound me out.'

'Veronica, let me reassure you, I am neither a policeman nor an investigator. Let me also say that Robert Dane is not connected with any crime.'

'So why do you want to find him?' she asked, a trace of suspicion still lingering in her eyes.

'For my sister's sake.' The momentary glimmer of curiosity that crossed her face then brought a quick response from him. 'And it's not what you're thinking.'

She gave a little nod, accepting his statement.

'Robert has disappeared from home. His family have accused my sister of being the reason, and she

327

desperately wants to clear her name. The only way she can do that is to find him.'

'You think he was in here?'

'I don't know if the information is solid, but it was also said that there had been some trouble.'

The door opened and Veronica moved away to serve her new customers. That task over she did not come back to Mark but he saw her standing at the end of the bar, deep in thought. Then she turned, picked up a glass from the counter behind her and started polishing it with a cloth. Mark recognised it as the action of someone who wanted to appear to be doing something while actually engaged in thinking something out. Three minutes later he saw her glance in the direction of the door and then look relieved.

Surreptitiously, Mark took in the new arrival and recognised him. The incident as he was leaving the bar on his first visit, slight though it had been, was now sharp in his mind. This was the man he had almost bumped into; this was the one who had said, 'Good fortune smiled on me that evening.' Why had that observation impinged on Mark's mind without his being able to recall it until now? Was there any significance behind it?

As Mark pondered this Veronica had drawn the newcomer a tankard of ale and was now deep in conversation with him. Taking a swig from his own tankard, Mark saw the barmaid glance in his direction. He wondered if he was a subject of discussion. Something told him to wait patiently. Some more customers arrived. Veronica served them. Mark finished his ale and called for another.

Unusually, she took his tankard without a word. As she placed it in front of him, he was aware of someone coming to stand beside him.

'Sir, you are new to these parts. Let me buy you that as a welcome.'

Mark looked at the man and said, 'That is very civil of you, sir. Thank you.'

'Dick Bishop.' The man held out his hand.

Mark took it and felt a firm grip. 'Mark Jordan,' he introduced himself.

'Shall we sit down?' Dick indicated a position away from everyone else. As they turned away from the bar he glanced at Veronica and said, 'I'll let you know.'

Once they were settled at a table, he began, 'Veronica tells me you were enquiring about a Robert Dane because of your sister?'

Mark nodded and confirmed this. 'Can you help me?' he added. 'Did you know him here?'

'I did.' And Dick went on to tell him of their association through work.

'*That's* how you knew him? It surprises me.'

Dick smiled. 'Because I'm drinking at the Anvil and you have realised it is not the usual haunt of men from the iron works?'

Mark nodded, feeling a little embarrassed.

'I'll tell you how that came about. Oh, we knew of the Anvil, but as you've observed for yourself it is not a place that's usually frequented by foundry workers. But one evening leaving work, I and my close mates were caught up in some exchanges with a couple of men, Art Mason and Luke Coning, who were ribbing Robert. It could have

329

got ugly for him but we stepped in, with the result that we shepherded him away to the Anvil and sent the other two packing.

'I soon realised that Robert was of a different class from any of us so I told him he'd be better coming to the Anvil, and that if he wished I would come with him in future. He was grateful for the company. But Art and Luke weren't finished with him, and the reason was that they had seen a reward poster.'

'I know about it,' Mark said.

'They thought it would be easy money. One evening they must have followed us here and lain in wait outside. One of them all but knocked me out while the other tackled Robert. Thank goodness someone left here just behind us. He waded in and Art and Luke scarpered.'

'Was Robert all right?'

'Yes, just a few cuts and bruises. Our main concern was that it would happen again, especially after he told us he had fallen out with his father, and we knew there was a reward being offered.'

'What happened then?'

'The man who had come to our aid had a solution that seemed watertight; one that we thought would make the trail go cold for Art and Luke. This man introduced himself as Tom Palmer, First Mate on the *Fair Weather*. She was to sail early the next morning. He offered to smuggle Robert aboard.'

'As a stowaway?'

'Aye. Palmer was risking his own position.'

'So Robert could be anywhere by now? The far

corners of the earth even?' Despondency had come into Mark's tone.

'Not likely! The *Fair Weather* was putting into Whitby, where she was built, for repairs. Tom, who hailed from there, said he would get Robert ashore and take him home. Then Robert could decide what he wanted to do next.'

'So he could still be in Whitby?' mused Mark.

'It's possible.'

Mark was effusive in his thanks. 'You don't know what this will mean to my sister, and of course to Robert's family if their reconciliation is achieved. We will be ever in your debt. But why did you decide to tell me this? After all, I am sure you were meant to keep Robert's escape a secret.'

'You are right, and I would have done ... had it not been for Veronica.'

'Veronica?'

'Yes. Of course she knew of the fracas outside the Anvil, but did not want to reveal that to you and possibly get me into trouble for aiding and abetting a stowaway. She decided to wait until she was able to tell me of your enquiry. Fortunately I came in this evening and she did. I asked her opinion of you and it was favourable, no police or investigators involved; she liked the look of you and felt sympathetic towards your sister.'

'But yours was the final decision? You could still have held back?'

'Aye, but I put a lot of faith in Veronica's assessment of folk. After all, she has had a lot of experience behind that bar. She was all for me telling you what I could.'

'Then I'm in debt to you both. You must have another tankard with me.'

'That will be my pleasure.'

Mark picked up the two tankards and went to the bar feeling jubilant. Veronica came over to serve him tentatively, clearly fearing that she might have done something wrong. Mark immediately relieved her mind as, in his euphoria, he impetuously leaned over the bar and kissed her. 'Thanks, Veronica, you're an angel.'

She blushed and took the tankards.

Dick was smiling when Mark rejoined him. 'I've never seen a barmaid blush before.' They raised their tankards to each other. 'A word of warning,' added Dick. 'The reward for finding Robert has been increased and Art and Luke have quit their jobs here.'

'You think ...'

'Doesn't matter what I think. Just be aware that those two might be looking for him again.'

'But surely the stowaway idea was foolproof?'

'It looked that way but there is nearly always a shortcoming to every scheme. Watch out for yourself and your sister. Those two thugs will stop at nothing where money is concerned, and the increase will make them all the more determined.'

18

Adele sensed the excitement within Mark as soon as he walked into the hotel.

'You've some news?' she asked eagerly.

He held out his hand to her. 'Let's find a quiet corner.'

When they were settled he told her: 'I've got a lead. There is strong evidence that Robert went to Whitby from here.'

'How is it that Mr Addison's investigator did not discover this?'

Mark shrugged. 'I don't know. It would seem that he did not give its full significance to an incident that took place outside the Anvil. The contacts I made there were wary until I convinced them I had nothing to do with the police and was not a private investigator. And I'm afraid I referred to you also – as a wronged maid looking to find her love. I reckon matters of the heart nearly always bring a response.'

Adele smiled at her brother's subtlety, something she had never noticed in him before. 'Why were they reluctant to talk at first?'

'This fellow I met, Dick Bishop, told me of

someone called Tom Palmer who had helped Robert stow away on a ship. That could have meant serious trouble for Palmer if they had been caught so the whole affair was kept secret. But let me begin at the beginning.'

Adele listened with rapt attention as Mark told his story. 'Wonderful!' she cried when he had finished. 'So it is to Whitby that we go.' She jumped to her feet as if she was about to leave there and then.

'Hold on, Adele,' laughed Mark. 'We can't go tonight.'

'In the morning then,' she said excitedly.

'Adele, take this calmly,' said Mark, worried that his sister's elation would mar her judgement. 'Mr Addison's increased reward will bring others looking for Robert, and remember Dick Bishop's warning about the two thugs who set about him. We should take care, Adele.'

'Yes, Mark,' she replied, but a feeling of elation stayed with her even when she lay down in bed. It was only a little while later, when sleep had not come, that she was able to analyse her feelings. She had set out on this mission to clear her own name, prove she was not the reason why Robert had left Newcastle without a word. But was this the only reason she wanted to find him? Did the flame of love still burn in her? And what of Philip ... safe, dependable Philip? Should she choose a predictable life with him or excitement with Robert? Even his disappearance had a touch of adventure to it.

'Well, Robert, you've seen the situation here in

Rosedale. What is your opinion about the jet workshop?' Sam put the question while they were tucking in to one of Mrs Dodsworth's steak pies.

'I think there is a lot of potential in Rosedale. You have been quick to tap a good market and have made many friends in the dale. They believe that you give them a good deal and are not trying to overcharge them. That faith in you and Betsy is a great asset. So as long as the mines remain open, you are in a very good position to make a decent return on your expeditions here. Now, the question is, will purchasing Mr Verity's workshop be a viable proposition and a similar asset? As I see it, the plain answer is yes.'

Robert saw Betsy's face broaden into a smile that told him this was what she wanted to hear. He continued, 'It will mean you'll have the responsibility of running the workshop, but they are a good bunch of men and I am sure they will help keep the business thriving in the fashion of Mr Verity.'

'If I purchase it, that is my intention.'

'Good. Workers assured of keeping their jobs after a change of ownership should give you every support. Having your own workshop, turning out pieces for sale in Rosedale without having to buy in finished articles, will mean more profit for you on top of what you already make on sales in Whitby. All in all, it seems a wise move to me.'

Sam nodded. 'As young as you are, I think you have kept your mind open to ideas wherever it was you were working before you came here. And you have a way of summing up situations. I thank you for your opinion.'

'I will have to finish with a word of caution. As you are aware, the Rosedale trade is dependent on the mines here remaining open and productive. If ever they close, or their production is affected, your trade in the dale will dip. But you would still have Whitby's trade, and maybe you could then expand into other coastal towns to replace any loss in Rosedale.'

Once again Sam gave a nod without making any immediate comment.

Betsy, fearing this deliberation spelled doubt, said with enthusiasm, 'You've got to buy, Papa. You've got to!'

He smiled. 'How could I refuse such a command?'

'Does that mean you will?' she cried.

'Yes.'

Betsy let out a cry of delight, leaped from her chair and rushed over to hug him. 'You'll not regret it, Papa.'

Robert was on his feet too and held out his hand to Sam. 'I'm sure it will be a good deal. If I may offer a piece of advice from my own experience at Mr Verity's, short though it is, promote Mr Gatenby to overall foreman. He's popular with all the men so there'll be no envy from them, and he has ideas that I'm sure will get the best out of them, if you give him that authority.'

Sam took Robert's hand and said a heartfelt, 'Thank you.'

Betsy was still bubbling with excitement and could not stop herself from hugging Robert. 'I'm so pleased,' she cried. 'I just know this is going to work.'

His arms had come around her as he said, 'Of course it is.'

'And you will be here to be part of it.'

Robert made no comment. He still had his past to consider ... or should he let it go?

Sam read Robert's silence as doubt about the future. He hoped his daughter was not going to be hurt again.

Art and Luke stood on Whitby's West Cliff and looked across the port, straggling around the river and the harbour mouth and climbing the cliff face opposite them. The jumble of buildings overwhelmed Luke. 'It's a rabbit warren,' he muttered. 'How can we hope to find Dane among that lot?'

'We'll find him, I know it,' replied Art firmly.

It had been a tiring journey from Middlesbrough, mostly on foot with only the occasional ride on a farmer's cart. They had spent one night in the open, the other hidden away in the hay in an isolated barn, being up and on the road before the farmer was awake. Luke's constant moaning about the discomfort of every aspect of their journey had started to grate on Art's nerves, though. Finally he growled, 'If you don't shut your trap, I'll fell thee!' Luke was wise enough to know that Art meant it, so he shut up until his mate got fed up with the silence, too, and broke it with, 'Talk, man, talk. But don't rant on!'

Now, on top of the cliff, he reiterated, 'We'll find him. He's down there somewhere.'

'If you say so,' replied Luke sarcastically.

'I do say so!' boomed Art, giving Luke a sharp

dig in the shoulder. 'Now come on, let's find a lodging house. And keep your eyes and ears open for anything that might lead us to Robert Dane.'

The following morning Sam announced, 'I'll take the trap and leave for Whitby immediately after breakfast. Hopefully I'll conclude the deal with Mr Verity and be able to return quickly. You two stay here, there's more selling to do.'

Half an hour later they watched him drive away, responding to his final wave before he was lost from their sight.

As they turned back to the house Robert saw the bond between father and daughter reflected in the dampness of Betsy's eyes. Rather than have her dwell on the parting, he suggested, 'It is a fine day. Should we take a walk before we set out our wares?'

'I would like that,' she agreed. 'I'll put on something more suitable.'

Ten minutes later she joined him outside the cottage.

'You look thoughtful,' she said.

'And you look very smart,' he returned, with admiration in his eyes.

She had changed into a stylish walking dress. A narrow crinoline supported her green velvet skirt above which she wore a tight-waisted pink bodice and a shoulder cape to match her skirt. The small bonnet was tied under her chin with a pretty pink ribbon.

'Thank you,' she said with a smile. 'Now,' she added as they fell into step, 'those thoughts of yours ... I hope you were not rethinking the advice you gave Father?'

He gave a slight shake of his head. 'No, not directly.'

'Not directly? What do you mean?'

'Good day, Miss Palmer.' A voice from behind them cut into their conversation.

They stopped walking and turned to see who it was.

'Ah, Mr Dodsworth, good day to you too,' said Betsy. 'Robert, this is Mrs Dodsworth's son. Mr Dodsworth, this is Mr Dane who is staying with us in Whitby.'

The two men shook hands.

'Taking the air on this fine morning?' queried Mr Dodsworth.

'Yes,' replied Betsy. 'We thought we'd take the left-hand fork at the end of the village, climb the hill a little so as to get a good view over the village.'

'I've some repairs to do at Glebe Farm. I can walk with you to the end of the village. The farm lies in the opposite direction to that you are taking.'

So Betsy had to curb her curiosity about Robert until they'd parted company from Mrs Dodsworth's son, but realised that maybe it was for the best. Their path now weaved its way through a vast expanse of lonely hillside and she knew they were less likely to be disturbed here.

'Now, explain your comment,' she ordered.

Robert looked serious. 'You were excited when your father announced his decision to buy Mr Verity's workshop.'

'Of course I was, especially as you had advised him so.'

'You used the phrase, "And you will be here to be part of it." But, Betsy, I don't know if I will.'

The shock of his announcement stopped her in her tracks. Disbelief was evident in her face. 'What do you mean? Aren't you happy here?'

He reached out to take her hands in his. Desperate to be understood, he gazed into her eyes. 'I'm very grateful to Tom for bringing me here at a time of such uncertainty for me. And I'm more than grateful for the friendship and trust your father has shown me. That gave me hope for the future, though maybe not in quite the way you expected. It goes without saying that your friendship more than any other sustained me. It also gave me hope for the future . . . of a different kind.' She was about to say something but he put a finger gently to her lips and said, 'Hear me out. Please.' She could not deny the entreaty in his eyes.

As he resumed his hold on her hand, he went on, 'Yes, Betsy, I am sure I could be happy here if circumstances were different. I have grown very fond of you. I feel very close to you. For that reason, I must face my past . . . clear what troubles me from my mind. Only then, knowing that the past could not mar a future between us, could I think of settling in Whitby.'

Her eyes dampened more with every word he spoke. They were like darts to her heart, painful in the hope they awakened and the prospect of despair if that hope was deceived. 'I'm desperately trying to understand, Robert,' she cried, her face creased with anguish. 'If you are happy here why let the past spoil things for you?'

'Because I could never forget it. It would always hang like a cloud over me, and I would always wonder if I had made the right decision in turning away from my former life.'

'I can disperse that cloud. I can make you forget.' To illustrate her meaning she raised herself on her toes, slid her arms round his neck and kissed him, letting her lips linger on his.

The embrace sent his head spinning. His arms came around her waist and he held her tight with a heightening desire surging in him. Kiss met kiss in unbounded passion; two hearts reached out to one another.

'Betsy,' he whispered hoarsely.

She yearned for him to say more ... just three words.

Those words were close to his lips but instead he kissed her again. His world reeled. His mind spun.

He could allow her to do what she said but would he ever accept her solution as final? Would his unresolved past remain to haunt him?

He pulled her close again. 'Betsy, if I commit myself now, you would always wonder what secret I held and that could eventually spoil our happiness. I can't make you a promise I might not be able to keep.'

For a moment she was about to demand an explanation but, seeing his earnest expression, held her words back. She had lost one man through impetuosity; she did not intend to lose another. 'Go home, Robert. Sort out your troubles then come back to me,' she murmured.

'I think it might be best for us to return now,' he said gently.

She made no reply but complied. They had reached the outskirts when she asked, 'When will you go?' She could not hide the pain in her voice.

'I don't know, Betsy. The simple answer is, when I think the time is right. But I don't want to outstay the welcome you and your father have extended to me.'

She placed one hand on his arm. 'You'll never do that, Robert.'

'I wonder if Father will get back today?' said Betsy as she joined Robert for breakfast the next morning.

'He left early enough to make the offer yesterday; depends if Mr Verity was available. If they shook hands on it then your father should be back today. He'll want you to know as soon as possible.'

It was an unsettled day for Betsy and Robert. They still had a few orders to deliver but their minds were preoccupied with thoughts of her father's return. It came as a great relief to them both when they saw Samuel coming down the hill into the village. Without a word they both hurried to meet him.

'Father!' called Betsy.

He read the question in her greeting and straightened up on the seat of the trap. 'It's ours,' he called out, a broad smile lighting up his face.

Betsy looked across at Robert, her eyes shining with delight and her mind willing him to stay and be part of this new enterprise.

'Well done, Mr Palmer! I know you will enjoy making a success of it,' said Robert. Then he turned to Betsy. 'And you will, too, I just know it.'

'We will!'

They fell into step beside the trap and Sam told them of his meeting with Mr Verity. 'We sign the papers in a couple of days. Did you get all the orders delivered?'

'Yes, we did, Mr Palmer,' said Robert, 'and took some new ones to be delivered next visit.'

'Good,' said Sam. 'We can get off home tomorrow.'

'You've had enough travelling these last two days, Papa. Shouldn't you take some time off tomorrow?'

'I can relax at home. And I'll need to be there if anything crops up before the signing.'

Betsy could tell from the mood her father was in it was no good trying to persuade him otherwise.

'Very well, but you will let Robert drive the trap back,' she insisted.

'As you wish,' he conceded.

'I reckon this is going to be another day of getting nowhere,' grumbled Luke as he and Art left their lodging house.

'Moan, moan,' said Art in a voice that mimicked Luke's.

'Well, what are we going to do? We'll soon be out of money.'

'Then we'll get a job while we keep on looking.'

'But we don't know whether he's here or ever has been,' squawked Luke.

'Where else could he have got off that ship?'

'Aye, and now he could be over the hills and far away.' Luke pulled a face and flapped his arms like a bird's wings.

Art jabbed him in the shoulder. 'Stop fooling around and keep those eyes peeled.' He quickened his step and deliberately lengthened his stride so that the shorter-legged Luke had to trot to keep up with him.

They headed into Church Street from the yard where they had found lodgings and turned in the direction of the quays. When they reached the corner of Bridge Street, Art pulled up short.

'Bridge is open, there must be a ship coming in.' He pointed down Bridge Street in the direction of the river.

Luke, who was thankfully regaining his breath after his efforts to keep up with Art, merely grunted.

'Let's see it come in,' said his mate.

'Thought we was looking for Dane,' Luke objected.

'Aw, come on.' Art started down Bridge Street and Luke followed, cursing under his breath. They found places among the folk waiting to cross the swing bridge and watched the ship being manoeuvred carefully through the gap before it proceeded to a berth upriver. Art suddenly spun round, grabbing Luke's arm as he did so. 'Come on!' he snapped, and pushed his way back through the crowd who had gathered behind them, bringing black looks and protests, which he completely ignored. Once clear, he released his hold on Luke's arm.

'Hey, you hurt me,' Luke protested, rubbing his arm vigorously.

'Ninny,' mocked Art as his hanger-on trotted to keep up with him.

'What's got into you? First you want to see the ship then you turn away as if you'd seen the devil.'

'It weren't the devil ... but he could lead us to Dane.'

'What are you spouting about?'

'I told you to keep your eyes open. You'd have seen him if you had.'

'Who? Dane?'

'No, nitwit. How could it have been? I said, he could *lead us* to Dane.'

'Who the heck are you talking about?'

'*He* was on deck – the bloke who let into us in Middlesbrough and saved Dane.'

'So?'

'Christ, but you're stupid! I told you I reckoned the only way Dane could have left Middlesbrough was ...'

'As a stowaway!' exclaimed Luke as it dawned on him. 'And you reckon that fella helped him?'

'Aye, I reckon I'm near the truth there. And, if so, that sailor would also have helped him in Whitby. He could lead us straight to Dane!'

They had been following the progress of the *Fair Weather*, Luke thankful that it was slow. They idled among others on the quay, watching the ship manoeuvre to its berth, while all around them stevedores prepared to unload the vessel.

'What now?' asked Luke.

'We watch and wait for him to leave ship, and then

345

we follow him. Don't let him even catch a glimpse of us, though.' Art had been looking round as he was speaking. 'Over there!' He nodded in the direction of a tower of crates piled high on the quay. They were safely in position behind them by the time ropes had been thrown out and men ashore were looping them around capstans so the *Fair Weather* could be drawn close to the side. The gangway was run out. They kept their attention on Thomas whenever he appeared on deck.

After two hours they saw him in earnest conversation with a man they judged to be the Captain and then he disappeared below deck again. A few minutes later he reappeared in a smarter set of clothes.

Noting this, Art said, 'He's coming ashore.'

'You got sixth sense or summat?'

'He don't go and put his best clothes on if he's staying on board,' rapped Art. 'Don't know where I found you,' he added in disgust.

Tom came down the gangway and set off at a brisk pace, heading for Bridge Street. He crossed the bridge and went up Flowergate, then turned into Skinner Street. Art matched his pace, keeping a reasonable distance behind so that the young sailor stayed unaware that he was being followed. Even so Art nearly lost him among the crowds of shoppers on Skinner Street. When their quarry turned into Well Close Square, Art and Luke were only just in time to see him go up to one of the elegant houses there. By the time they took up a position from which they could see its front door, Tom had disappeared.

'We lost him!' moaned Luke.

'No, he's inside.'

'So?'

'We wait.'

'More waiting?' Luke complained.

'It'll be worthwhile.'

Luke grunted, 'If you say so!'

'Shut up and watch.'

Half an hour later, Tom reappeared. He paused on the step, half turned and spoke to the maid who held the door. 'Don't bother making a bed up for me. I'll sleep on board tonight and be back tomorrow evening.' He left not knowing that this exchange had been overheard.

'Ain't we following him any more?' queried Luke when Tom left Well Close Square.

'No point. We know where he's going to be – on board that ship.'

'So what about Dane? We don't even know if he's been here.'

'We soon will.'

'How come?'

'You'll see, but we wait a bit longer yet. We don't want to appear too soon after yon bloke has left.'

'We going callin'?'

'Aye. Smarten yourself up. Yon's a posh house.'

Luke looked at him askance but started to tug his shirt straight.

'No. Wait!' Art stopped him. 'Better still, you wait here while I go on me own. You'll only raise suspicion if you come with me.' He spent a good five minutes wiping himself down, making his clothes look better, and pushing his hair into place. He was about to ask Luke if he would do, but knowing he would reply with some derogatory, sarcastic remark, held his query back. Instead he said, 'I'm off now. Don't you move from here.'

Art's use of the brass door-knocker in the shape of a whale brought the same maid to the door.

'Good day, sir,' she said politely, though there was a look of curiosity in her eyes.

'Good day,' he said. 'I am a friend of Robert Dane's. I am passing through Whitby and was told I might find him here.'

'I'm sorry, sir. He isn't here. He's in Rosedale.'

Art assumed an expression of disappointment. 'Oh, dear. When is he likely to be back?'

'Some time tomorrow, he said, probably near evening.'

'I'm not sure of my plans. If I'm still in Whitby then, I'll call back. Thank you very much.'

'In case you can't, may I tell him who called?'

'Certainly. Say it was Gordon Williams.' Art started to turn away then stopped. 'You say he's in Rosedale . . . where is that?'

'Over the moors.'

Art nodded. 'Then I might try and go that way. Can you give me directions?'

'The best way is to go to Lealholm and cut across the moors from there.' She continued to explain how to get to Lealholm and when she had finished, said, 'That's the way Mr Palmer and his daughter always take and Mr Dane is with them so it is possible you would meet them.' Art was profuse in his thanks then hurried back to Luke.

'Come on, we're off to Lealholm.'

'Lealholm? Where the heck is that?'

'You'll see. We're going there. You'll always remember it as the place where we took an important step closer to making our fortune.'

'Fortune?' Luke grinned and did a little jig. 'Our fortune!'

Art glared at him and gave him a slap. 'Shut up, you fool. Don't draw attention to us. Come on, we're going to hire a trap.'

Within the hour they had a trap with a manageable horse, as requested, had relinquished their room at the lodging house and were on their way to Lealholm, where Art figured it would be best to spend the night so as to be on the moors early the following morning.

It was late afternoon when Adele and Mark reached Whitby and were directed to the Angel Inn. Two rooms were available so Mark booked them for an unspecified period, as well as arranging accommodation for Walton and stabling for the horse.

Adele was on edge to start their enquiries but Mark delayed until they came down for their evening meal. They approached the landlord then.

'Perhaps you can help us,' Mark began. 'We are looking for a friend whom we believe came to Whitby recently, a Mr Dane. Does the name mean anything to you?'

'Dane?' The landlord looked thoughtful. 'Ah, yes. Mr Palmer, his son Tom and daughter Betsy came in here with a young man on one occasion. I believe he was introduced as a Mr Dane. He'd be about your age, I reckon.'

'That's very likely to be him,' said Mark quickly, in an effort to stem the excitement he could sense rising in his sister. 'Can you tell us where we might find him?'

'I believe he was staying with the Palmers, but that might only have been temporary. You really want to see Mr Palmer. He's a jeweller by trade and he and his daughter move around the district a lot. I think your best bet is to enquire at his shop in Church Street ... have a word with Toby who is manager there. He'll best be able to tell you of Mr Palmer's movements.' The landlord glanced at the wall clock. 'You'll have to be sharp, though, the shop will be closing soon.'

'We've found him!' Adele's words were charged with delight as they left the Angel, following the landlord's directions to the shop on Church Street.

'Not yet,' warned Mark. 'He might have moved on. But hopefully we'll learn that when we get to the shop.

'Good day,' he greeted the man behind the counter when he and Adele entered the premises.

'Good day, sir,' replied Toby. 'Good day, ma'am.'

'We are looking for Mr Palmer,' said Mark. 'The landlord of the Angel told us you might be able to help.'

Toby had already formed his opinion of these two strangers. They were well dressed, the young man was well spoken and they were staying at the Angel. All that was good enough for Toby. 'Mr

Palmer is away. He'll be back some time tomorrow, possibly late afternoon, but it will be no good trying to see him then, nor the next day. He has some important business to attend to.'

Mark nodded; Adele wondered if the man was fobbing them off.

'In actual fact, it was Mr Dane we wanted to see. We thought he might be with Mr Palmer?'

'Oh ... yes, Mr Dane is with Mr Palmer. I don't know what his plans are, though.'

'It is a matter of some urgency. If you can tell us where they are and the route they will take, we could possibly go and meet them and do our talking as we all return to Whitby together,' Adele suggested.

'That might be the best idea, miss.' Toby explained the route Mr Palmer usually took.

Adele felt a surge of excitement. Wherever Mr Palmer was, there Robert would be. Tomorrow she would see him, clear her name ... and maybe more than that!

19

'Why so blooming early?' asked Luke, snorting his disgust as Art guided the hired trap out of Lealholm where they had found lodgings for the night. Luke rubbed his eyes against the bright early-morning sun that was thinning and driving the swirling mist out of the moorland nooks and crannies.

''Cos we don't know when Dane and the others will be leaving Rosedale and we've got to find a good place for an ambush.'

Luke brightened. 'Ambush!' He drove his right fist into the palm of his left hand. 'There'll be no one to help Dane this time!' He chuckled, thinking of the revenge he was going to wreak for their previous failure.

'Well, see you get everything right. You deal with the old man. 'Least, I think he'll be old.'

'Doesn't matter, I'll deal with him.'

'And the girl.'

Luke nodded. 'It'll be a pleasure.'

'No messing about,' warned Art. 'Put 'em out cold for a long time. I'll deal with Dane, and then we'll send their horse running.'

They kept to a walking pace across the wild

moor, along the track that led from Lealholm to Rosedale.

An hour later they came to a point where their track was joined by one coming from the north-west. Shortly afterwards, Art pulled the horse to a halt in a dip. Ahead of them the track rose steeply towards a ridge. He surveyed the terrain around them.

'This will do. That other track we've just passed will take us away from Lealholm, so that's the one we take after we get Dane.' As he spoke he was turning their trap round, positioning it to one side of the track. 'Right, now we'll have a good view of them when they appear over that ridge.'

'Aye, but Dane will see us,' said Luke.

'We'll be out of sight behind this 'ere hummock,' replied Art, making a gesture with his thumb. 'They'll be curious about a trap standing here unattended and are bound to stop to investigate. That's when we jump them.'

Luke chuckled. 'Can't wait.'

Art grinned. 'Aye, but you'll have to. I don't suppose you'll moan about waiting this time. Not with the reward we've got coming.'

They sat down and settled themselves in a position where they would not be noticed but had a view across to the ridge.

'What if someone else comes along first?' said Luke, sitting bolt upright as if calamity were about to strike.

'We'll fob them off with some excuse.'

Half an hour later, Art tensed then pushed himself to his feet. Luke sprang up beside him.

'Listen!' commanded Art.

A moment's silence passed between them then Luke said, 'Someone's coming.'

'Aye, and from over that ridge.'

A few moments later a trap with three people in it appeared on the horizon.

'It's them!' Art's voice quivered with excitement.

After a momentary halt, Robert started the horse cautiously down the incline.

Art and Luke watched his every move. They saw the girl point ahead, drawing her father's and Robert's attention to the trap standing at the bottom of the slope. She looked this way and that as Robert eased the animal to the bottom of the incline but saw no one. Puzzled, the older man shook his head. Robert stopped the trap beside the unattended vehicle, looked around, then, seeing no one, put down the reins and jumped to the ground.

Art, not wanting Luke to make a move too soon, had placed his hand tightly on his mate's arm. Now he relaxed his grip and tapped him on the shoulder. At the same time he broke from cover, Luke close behind him.

With his attention on the empty trap, Robert was taken completely by surprise. He had barely had time to look up when Art's shoulder took him in the chest and a powerful arm clamped around him. They crashed to the ground with Art on top, driving his fist into Robert's jaw with such speed and power that darkness immediately flooded in.

Breathing heavily, Art pushed himself to his feet

then and saw Luke dragging the older man from the trap while trying to shake off the young woman who was pummelling him with her fists. She was screaming in shock and helpless distress. Art leaped at her, grabbed her and flung her aside. She smashed into the side of the trap, frightening the horse which shied and rolled its eyes.

'We have nothing!' Betsy screamed, convinced these men were robbers.

The big brute looming over her put back his head and laughed. 'We've got what we came for!' he jeered. His huge hand seized Betsy's arm and he hurled her away from the trap. The horse set off at a fast trot. She crashed to the ground and hit her head on a heavy stone.

Luke threw Sam to the ground after her and drove a vicious kick into his stomach and another to his head, driving all conscious feeling from him.

'Good,' called Art as he and Luke straightened up, breathing heavily. He saw the bolting horse had been held back by the trap which had fallen into a shallow ditch, breaking a wheel, a shaft and much of the bodywork. 'Free that nag!' he ordered.

Luke needed no second bidding. He quickly had the restless animal released from the shafts and, with a sharp slap, sent it into a frightened gallop away from the scene.

Art, busy examining Sam and Betsy, decided they would be unconscious for a considerable time. He grinned with satisfaction as he dragged them to one side of the track beside the broken trap.

'That'll give the impression of an accident to

355

anyone coming on the scene before these two recover. Now, let's get Dane into our trap and be away.'

Within a few minutes he was driving their horse back to the fork in the trail. When they diverted on to the unfamiliar track, which he knew was heading in roughly the direction they wanted to be, he felt more at ease. They would pick up a track off the moors in the direction of Stokesley and Middlesbrough.

Their whoops of delight were carried across the vast landscape by the gentle breeze that had risen as if to herald their triumph.

'We're rich! Rich!' they cried, and rocked with laughter as Art set the horse into a fast trot.

With two days' shore leave in Whitby, Tom was eager to be home and strode quickly to the house in Well Close Square.

'Good day, Lucy,' he called brightly to the maid.

'Welcome home, sir,' she replied, holding the door open. 'They're all away still, sir. Oh, but your father left you a note in the drawing room. Said I was to see you got it, sir. Should have remembered yesterday, I'm sorry.'

'Thank you, Lucy. I'll go and read it.' He started for the drawing room and called over his shoulder, 'Please tell Cook I'm here.'

'Very good, sir.'

Tom shrugged himself out of his jacket and cap and threw them on to a chair beside the drawing-room door. He picked up the letter.

My dear son,

I am sorry we won't be here when you arrive but we will join you the next day. I have been very busy. I will give you the details when I see you, but basically it concerns the purchase of Mr Verity's jet workshop. The opportunity arose to do this but I wanted to consider the full potential of Rosedale as a market. Robert revealed he had some knowledge of trading and the commercial world so I decided to seek his opinion on the matter. I am glad to say his assessment was favourable so now the Palmers are the proud owners of a jet workshop!

More details later when we see each other.

Your affectionate,

Father

A jet workshop! Excitement ran through Tom. Had this come about because of Robert's interest in jet and the ability he had shown? Did this mean he would be here permanently? Had his father made the purchase with that in mind? Tom had much to ponder while awaiting his family's return.

Jim Fenwick stood on the deck of the *Star of Hope* beating in towards Whitby. Seeking passage in Newcastle, he'd thought the ship's name appropriate; after all, he was heading back for Whitby hoping he could gain Betsy's forgiveness and resume the relationship which had had such a marked effect on him ever since his first sighting of her, helpless on the moors between Whitby and Rosedale. He had cursed himself many times for jeopardising that association which he had thought was becoming more than friendship. Now he hoped that, before long, everything would be put right between them.

He fingered the jet necklace he had carried in his pocket since that fateful day in Rosedale. If its previous associations could be forgotten, it would set the seal on the future relationship between Betsy and himself.

With the ship drawing nearer to the coast with every dip of its bow, Jim could not take his eyes off the ruined abbey set high on the cliffs above the town, a beacon of hope to sailors home from an enticing but sometimes treacherous sea. To Jim it signalled a landfall where his life could change forever.

He was impatient as the *Star of Hope* was manoeuvred to its berth, and ashore the instant the gangway was run out. With eyes for no one else but Betsy, he strode quickly to Well Close Square. His knock was answered by the maid who hid her surprise at seeing him again.

'Remember me, Lucy?'

'Yes, sir.'

'Is Miss Palmer at home?'

'I'm sorry, sir. Miss Palmer is in Rosedale but expected back later today. Mr Tom Palmer is here, if you would like to see him?'

'If I might?' replied Jim. Though disappointed that Betsy was not at home, he would at least draw some satisfaction from gaining news of her.

'Step inside, sir. I'll tell Mr Palmer you are here.'

When Tom appeared there was no warmth in

his expression, no welcome in his eyes, and he ignored his visitor's outstretched hand. Jim's heart sank. Betsy's brother must know of his rift from her. His manner did not augur well.

'Mr Fenwick.' Tom's tone was dismissive.

'You must be Miss Palmer's brother,' said Jim easily, trying to lighten the moment.

Tom nodded. 'I believe the maid told you my sister is in Rosedale?'

Jim noted that Tom did not reveal as much as Lucy, which left him with the feeling that her brother did not wish him to meet Betsy. 'She did. I'm sorry Miss Palmer is not here. I was hoping to patch up our past differences and be on friendly terms with her again.'

'I know nothing of my sister's affairs,' said Tom icily, 'unless she chooses to tell me and maybe seek my opinion. I do know you hurt her, however.'

'I regret that and wish to make amends, but it will have to wait for another time. I need to be in Pickering for the night and York tomorrow for a special meeting with Sir Francis Weldon. Please give your sister my good wishes.' He turned towards the door.

Tom stepped round him and opened it. 'Good day, Mr Fenwick.'

'Good day, Mr Palmer.'

Tom raised an eyebrow as he watched Jim Fenwick go down the street. Sir Francis Weldon! He had certainly moved up in the world since Betsy first knew him as a working foreman, and his clothes spoke of better days, too. Maybe...? But

Robert had become part of the family now and Tom could see a future link being strengthened by Samuel's purchase of the jet business.

Reaching Skinner Street, Jim headed for the White Horse in Church Street and then stopped in his tracks. Why the burning hurry to leave Whitby? He had been ruffled by Tom Palmer's attitude and so his immediate reaction on leaving the house was to leave Whitby too. But he had time on his hands. The mount he had hired at the White Horse, to give him freedom to travel, could be picked up any time. If he stayed, there was still the possibility of contacting Betsy later today. He had come all this way from Newcastle to see her; he couldn't just walk away now. If he did not see her before he left Whitby, he did not know when he would be able to visit again; did not know what Sir Francis might have in mind for him. He would keep a discreet watch on Well Close Square from its only entrance via Skinner Street and only make his presence known when the Palmers' vehicle stopped outside the house. He would wait and hope that they arrived before he must leave for Pickering.

Jim was confident that his prospects would be even better after he had presented his latest report to Sir Francis. A bright future beckoned, and he hoped to share it with Betsy.

'There's still no sign of them,' said Mark, scanning the moor ahead. 'We should have waited at Lealholm.'

'No point just sitting there,' replied Adele, irritated by her brother's caution.

'I reckon we should have seen them by now.'

Adele did not speak. She hid the tension and worry that were beginning to stifle her. It would not do to let Mark know she was beginning to agree with him. Let him see that and she knew he would order Walton to turn back. Do that and she might lose any knowledge of Robert's whereabouts. At the moment they knew he was with Mr Palmer and she had a premonition that they were still somewhere on this moor. They had been told this was the main track to Rosedale. Surely they must meet soon?

The trap rumbled on. Ten minutes later, upon reaching a dip in the track, Walton hauled on the reins.

'What's wrong?' asked Mark.

'There's been an accident!' the coachman called out as he flicked the reins to send their horse on.

Mark and Adele craned to see.

An overturned trap lay beside track, its broken wheel and distorted shafts sending out ominous signals.

Adele's hands tightened into fists. Alarm ran through her. Please don't let it be Robert! 'I don't see anybody ...' she said.

'Over there!' Walton pointed ahead to the right of the track. A figure bent over someone lying on the ground.

Two people. Only two. The number thundered in Adele's mind. There should have been three: Robert, Mr Palmer and his daughter. Her eyes swept over the area around the two figures but she did not see a third. Alarm gripped her. She could see that the prone figure was an older man with someone bending over him. A young woman looked up when she heard the creak of the trap and hooves beating the ground urgently. Walton hauled on the reins to bring the conveyance to a swaying halt. Mark leaped to the ground. Adele was quickly beside him.

Their concern for the young woman, who had scrambled to her feet, heightened when Adele saw the cuts and bruises on her face and the ugly weal on her cheek. Her eyes were red with crying and tears still ran down her cheeks, streaking the dirt on her face. Her bonnet gone, her blood-stained hair had lost all signs of careful grooming and straggled to her shoulders. Her dress and cloak were torn, dishevelled and dirty. It looked as though she had been dragged across the track.

Without a word, Adele took her in her arms. The sobs that shook the girl spoke of terrible shock at what had happened and relief that someone was here to help. Adele shushed her attempt to speak. 'In a moment. Tell us in a moment.'

She glanced around and saw her brother rising to his feet after examining the man on the ground. 'Walton, give me a hand to lift him into our trap. He's still unconscious, appears to have had a severe blow to the head as well as several to the face and who knows what else . . .' As he was speaking Mark was taking in the young woman's visible injuries. 'I don't think this was an accident,' he added in a sombre tone.

362

Adele, who had been reading all the signs of a horse bolting and throwing out the occupants of the trap, was astounded by his statement. 'What, you mean ... deliberate?'

Her words penetrated the young woman's sobbing. She nodded her head violently. 'We were attacked!' She stiffened in Adele's arms and looked at her with alarm in her tear-filled eyes. 'Robert ... Where's Robert? They must have taken him!'

The name penetrated Adele's mind like an arrow. 'Robert?' The name sprang from her unbidden. She knew the answer before it came.

'Yes. He was with us. Robert Dane.'

Adele's chest tightened. Not only was she overwhelmed by her concern for Robert but in this young woman's voice there was more than anxiety evident. Adele's eyes met her brother's. Realising he was about to reveal something she thought better left unsaid for now, she flashed him a glance, warning him to say nothing. Her own confusion would be set aside for now. These two people needed help, and quickly.

'Mark, we'd better get them to Whitby as soon as possible.'

With her arm still around the young woman's shoulders, she led her to the trap. 'I'm Adele Jordan,' she introduced herself.

'Betsy Palmer,' came the reply in a voice filled with distress. 'That's my father, Samuel Palmer. Will he be all right?'

'You get in the trap, Miss Palmer. We'll make your father comfortable and take you both to Whitby.'

Betsy sat shaking while waiting for her father to be lifted into the trap. As they were positioning him so that she could hold his head in her lap, his eyes flickered open and a moan came from deep in his throat.

Reassured by this sign of life, Betsy cried out, 'Oh, Papa! Papa!' Tears started to stream again but this time there was relief in them. Seeing a questioning look come into his eyes she said, 'These people found us and are taking us back to Whitby where we can get Doctor Gaskell to see to you.'

He nodded. 'And Robert?'

Though she did not want to worry him any more, Betsy knew it was best to give him a truthful answer. 'The men who attacked us must have taken him.' She was about to say more but saw her father lose consciousness again. She looked askance at Adele who felt his pulse and reassured Betsy he was breathing.

'Why were you attacked? What did the men want?' she asked.

'I don't know, unless they meant to rob us. My father's a jeweller.'

'You mentioned someone called Robert Dane, where is he?'

Betsy bit her lip and shook her head. 'I don't know,' she wailed. 'They must have taken him.'

'Why should they do that? What would they want with him?'

'I don't know!' In spite of her grief and anxiety the girl hesitated to reveal too much of what she knew about Robert.

Adele was mystified by these answers. Was Betsy

hiding the truth? Was there something she didn't want known? Had this any connection with the reward Mr Addison had placed on his son's head?

'But . . .' she started to protest.

'I really don't!' cut in Betsy.

Adele was startled by the sharp note in her voice. Suspicion that Betsy was covering up something mounted within her, but she quickly dismissed such a thought. The girl's reaction could be due to her traumatic experience. Nevertheless, Adele made one more attempt to elicit some information about Betsy's relationship with Robert.

'Were they seeking revenge for something Mr Dane had done?'

'I don't know!'

'A reward? Was Mr Dane a criminal?'

'Of course he wasn't.'

'How do you know? How long have you known him?'

'Not very long.' The answer had come automatically.

'Then why are you . . .'

'Stop asking questions! Who are you? And why all this interest in Robert?' Hostility lay just below the surface of her response.

Before Adele could say anything, Mark intervened. 'My sister is only trying to help. Finding a reason for his abduction could help us deduce where they might take him. Then we can alert the authorities and trace him before any further harm is done.'

His calm attitude and gentle explanation reassured Betsy. 'I'm sorry, but I'm so anxious for him ... I don't want anything to happen to him.'

Adele's mind lurched. This young woman must think a great deal of Robert. What had happened between them? There were so many questions she wanted to ask but until Betsy was in Whitby and much calmer, Adele thought it wiser to hold them back.

When they started to descend from the heights towards Lealholm, Mark asked, 'Would you like us to get help in the village?'

Betsy glanced at her father who, breathing evenly, had slipped into a peaceful sleep. 'I think it best if we get him home to Whitby. There is a track that will help us avoid the village.'

'Very well. You direct Walton.'

Betsy's instructions were precise and, once clear of Lealholm, they began to make better time.

Jim had begun to wonder if he had stayed on a fool's mission. The Palmers' plans might have changed; the time for leaving Rosedale been altered; the horse might have shed a shoe. He really should be getting on his way to Pickering. He could not leave it too much longer. But that might mean he was riding out of Betsy's life forever – not at all what he'd intended by coming here. He'd wait another twenty minutes but that was the limit, he decided. Five minutes later he heard the rumble of a vehicle. With growing excitement he saw it turn into Skinner Street. It must be them. It had to be!

Though he had no knowledge of his father's

intended time of arrival, Tom was getting anxious; he'd thought they would be back by mid-afternoon. He became restless, started pacing the floor, and every few minutes went to the window. How many times he did that and saw nothing but the quiet square, seemingly cut off from the world beyond it, he never knew.

Then, 'They're here!' Though there was no one else to hear him, the exclamation of relief burst out of Tom.

He raced from the room and down the path to the gate, but before he reached it his broad smile of welcome had been replaced by an expression of shock and horror. His dishevelled sister, her face cut and bruised, was being helped from an unfamiliar trap by a young woman he did not know. Meanwhile his badly injured father, whose expression betrayed pain, was struggling to sit up aided by two strangers. There was no sign of Robert.

'What's happened?' cried Tom with deep concern.

Betsy burst into tears and flung herself into his arms.

'You're home, you're safe,' he soothed her.

Sobs shook her body. 'We ... we were attacked ...'

'Where?'

'On the ... moors ... two men ...' she faltered. 'Thank goodness these people came along.' A quick exchange of names followed and then Tom called for assistance from the servants.

'Where's Robert?' he asked.

The question jolted Betsy. 'Robert!' Her wail

367

rose heavenwards. She stood, staring at her brother. 'They must have taken him!'

'What?' Tom couldn't believe it; how had Robert been traced? He'd thought stowing him away on the *Fair Weather*, creating a disappearing act, had been entirely successful.

Betsy's voice rose wildly. 'They've taken him!' She swayed, but Tom held her up.

'You both need a doctor. I'll send for Gaskell. Let's get you inside,' he urged.

At that moment he was aware of someone approaching them. Jim Fenwick! He'd thought that scoundrel had gone. Fenwick's presence could only make matters here worse. An angry dismissal rose to Tom's lips but it was never uttered. He heard a cry and thought his father was in trouble. Automatically he released his hold on Betsy and turned around.

She took a step forward but her legs gave way beneath her. What little colour remained in her cheeks drained away. For one moment her eyes focused on the man who stood close to her. 'Robert!' she moaned, and then her mind became a blank beneath the mist that overwhelmed it.

Jim caught her as she fell and started towards the front door.

'Upstairs, along the landing, second door on the right,' Tom directed him. A quick assessment told him Mark and Walton had his father firmly in their care. 'Father's room is first door on the left upstairs.'

Jim entered the house and started up the stairs. Adele followed him. Tom dispatched a kitchen maid to fetch Doctor Gaskell, sent Cook and Lucy to Betsy's room and then went to attend to his father.

'How are you feeling?' he asked with concern as he entered the bedroom.

Sam mustered a wan smile. 'I'll be all right. Takes more than a couple of thugs to get rid of Sam Palmer.' Tom was pleased to hear his father's voice strengthened by defiance.

'Into bed, Father,' he ordered.

'But ...'

'No protests,' he cut in. 'I want you in bed when Doctor Gaskell comes.' He turned to Walton then. 'Can you see he gets into bed?'

'Yes, sir.'

Tom spoke to Mark then. 'May I see you and your sister in the drawing room?'

While Mark went downstairs, Tom hurried into Betsy's room.

'How is she?' he asked.

'Still unconscious,' replied Adele. 'The shock and the physical beating have taken their toll but I'm sure she'll be all right.' She felt bound to offer some comfort.

'I've asked your brother to go to the drawing room. Would you join him there, please? I'll be with you in a few minutes.'

Jim had been gazing at Betsy throughout this exchange and his expression of concern was noted by Adele. As she left the room to join her brother she was wondering who this man was and what part he played in the girl's life. Which only helped to make her even more uneasy about Robert and his disappearance.

Jim murmured something to Betsy and, after one last look at her silent form, followed Tom from the room.

'I thought you would have been well on your way to Pickering by now,' said Tom as they started down the stairs together.

'I had time to kill so I waited here on the off-chance of seeing your sister. I had almost given up hope.'

'Thank goodness you hadn't! You were there to catch her when she collapsed outside.' Tom's manner and tone were milder; he felt they had to be. Jim must certainly think a lot about Betsy to have waited so long.

'I don't like leaving under these circumstances,' he said, 'but I'm already late for Pickering ...'

'You can't do anything here. You should be on your way,' Tom agreed.

'She thought I was someone else,' sighed Jim.

'Not unusual, I would think, to suffer delusions after the trauma she has been through. Doctor Gaskell will put her right, I'm sure.'

'I hope so. But, tell me, she mistook me for Robert ... who is he?'

'Robert Dane. Sometime back, my ship put in at Middlesbrough. I went to a pub there and when I came out, some thugs were attacking two men I had seen in the bar. I waded in and the thugs made off. It turned out there was a reward out for Robert, and I reckon that's what the thugs today were after.'

'Reward? Was he a criminal?'

'No, he assured me he was not and I believed

370

him. Apparently the reward had been put up by his father with whom he'd had a dispute, causing him to leave home and disappear. The notice gave two office addresses, one in Newcastle and one in Middlesbrough. Fearing the thugs would get after him again, I suggested he could really disappear if I smuggled him aboard my ship.'

'You were taking a big risk.'

'Aye, but I figured we could get away with it. It would only be a short voyage for him; we were going to put in at Whitby for repairs. I decided to take him home with me so that he could decide his future in safety.'

'So he's been here, staying in this house, for quite a while?'

Tom nodded. 'Yes.' Seeing the suspicion in Jim's eyes and sensing the questions coming to his lips, Tom went on quickly, 'It seems those two thugs managed to trace him somehow. I reckon they'll be well on the way to Middlesbrough now. Robert is going to have to face his father and resolve whatever the trouble is between them.'

While he had been speaking they had reached the hall. There Jim retrieved his black redingote and top hat.

'I left something more suitable for my ride at the inn when I hired the horse,' he explained. Then, making up his mind to voice his concern, he asked, 'Was there a close relationship between Robert and Betsy ... something that made her think I was him?'

Tom hesitated a moment. 'I don't know. I was not here with them for long enough to assess that, and I'm not one to probe into my sister's affairs.'

Jim's lips tightened. 'I hope she will soon recover.' He held out his hand. This time Tom took it.

'Thank you for your help,' he said.

Jim walked out of the house, leaving Tom wondering if he would ever return and if he should mention to his sister that Jim Fenwick had come calling on her at last.

20

Tom walked thoughtfully across the hall but before he reached the drawing room the sound of the bell sent him back to the front door.

'Doctor Gaskell! Come in, come in.'

The bewhiskered doctor, a man in his fifties, held himself as straight as a ramrod, an attitude that made some people wary of him until they saw the kind consideration in his eyes and heard the gentleness in his voice.

'What is it?' he asked as he put his small bag on a table beside the front door and took off his hat and coat. 'Your maid seemed very anxious – muttered something about Miss Betsy.'

'Upstairs, Doctor.' As they hurried to the next floor, Tom acquainted him with the bare facts of what had happened to his sister and father. They neared the door of Betsy's bedroom. 'Cook and Lucy are with her,' Tom explained.

'I know your cook,' replied the doctor. 'A most responsible woman. She can remain while I carry out my examination.'

'I'll go to Father and await you there,' said Tom. When he entered Samuel's room he found him chatting to Walton. 'Now, Father, you shouldn't be exerting yourself,' he chided.

'Stop fussing,' Sam responded.

'Doctor Gaskell is with Betsy. He'll see you shortly.' Tom glanced at Walton. 'I'll wait with my father now. Thank you for all you did.'

'It was a privilege. I hope no one will be the worse for their ordeal, sir,' said Walton. 'I'll see that our horse and trap are all right.' He nodded to Sam. 'Goodbye to you, sir.'

Sam smiled and raised one hand in acknowledgement.

When Tom came into the drawing room half an hour later he was full of apologies for keeping Adele and Mark waiting.

'That is the least of your worries,' replied Mark. 'But tell us, how are your sister and your father?'

'Doctor Gaskell is reasonably satisfied with them both. He has told Father in no uncertain terms that he must stay in bed until tomorrow. Father's protesting, but that's his way as far as doctors are concerned. Doctor Gaskell knows him. He has left a sedative so Father should at least get a good night's sleep.'

'Your sister?' prompted Adele.

'At the moment she is a little confused but Gaskell is certain that will clear, possibly by tomorrow morning. He has given her a sedative, too, so hopefully after a good night's rest she'll feel a lot better. Physically there is nothing that won't heal. The cuts and bruises should mend quickly, there are no broken bones, so that is at least something to be thankful for.'

374

'That man who picked her up certainly had an effect on her,' commented Adele, hoping to discover what part Jim played in Betsy's life.

'I'm not surprised. She hasn't seen him for some time and had lost touch with his whereabouts. Coming on top of today's events ... well, it must have been a shock.'

Adele did not dare probe any further. Considering what she had witnessed – Betsy fainting, the way Jim had caught her up, the tender disquiet in the way he'd looked at her – there had to have been feelings between them, yet there seemed also to be more than concern for Robert in Betsy's reaction to his abduction and the way she had mistaken Jim for him.

'I want to thank you.' Tom paused and then said, 'That sounds so inadequate, but we owe you a debt of deep gratitude for what you did today.'

'Anyone would have done the same,' replied Mark.

'It was fortuitous that you came along. Where were you going?'

'Rosedale,' put in Adele, fearing Mark might say differently.

'Then you forsook your journey to bring my father and sister home? Not many would have done that. You cannot possibly resume now; it would be dark before you even reached the moors.'

'We have rooms at the Angel. Our visit to Rosedale was to be a short one,' explained Mark.

'What of Robert Dane?' Adele asked.

'I can't ignore the matter of his abduction. After

375

all, he was a guest in this house. I shall inform the authorities and hopefully they will catch the two men concerned.'

Adele, realising these words were prompting Mark to enlighten Tom about their relationship with Robert, flashed a quick signal to deter him and, glancing at Tom, said, 'We should leave. You have plenty to see to.'

He was profuse in his thanks as he walked with them from the house to where Walton was waiting with the trap.

'Will you make your visit to Rosedale tomorrow?' he asked.

'Alas, no,' replied Adele. 'It had to be today but it doesn't really matter. We return home tomorrow. If we will not intrude on you, may we call to enquire about your father's and sister's welfare before we leave?'

'Of course. Hopefully they will be up. I am sure they will wish to express their own appreciation of what you have done today.'

As he watched them drive away, Tom realised he knew little about his family's rescuers. Recollecting the way they'd conducted themselves, their cultured speech and easy grace, plus the fact that they had a coachman, he deduced they were of a different social level from his family. Adele had seemed interested in Robert ... could he be from the same background? In fact, could she and Mark have come to Whitby looking for him? If so, how had they known where to come and why were they looking for him? It could not be for the same reason as the two men who had abducted him.

As Tom entered the house, though, he cast these questions aside. The welfare of his father and sister were of prime importance now.

'Hawkins,' said Theo, with a gesture of despair, 'how has my son managed to disappear so completely?'

'It's an easy enough thing to do. The world is wide,' replied the investigator, though he knew this was of no comfort to Mr Addison.

'Increasing the reward has had little effect except to bring in a few more cranks with what you soon recognised as dubious information. You were right to insist the reward would only be paid when Robert was delivered in person. You have the office in Newcastle manned so I think it would be as well if you stayed in Middlesbrough. But I must return to Newcastle tomorrow. There's still a business to run, though I know my staff are capable.'

'Don't give up hope, sir. News of the increase in the reward will take time to reach more distant places.'

Theo gave a wan smile. 'You are just like Superintendent Jarvis ... ever-optimistic.'

'He trained me, sir.'

'And very well, may I say? You have applied yourself to this job admirably. It is no fault of yours that we have not uncovered my son's whereabouts.'

'Thank you, sir. Will you call in ...'

His words were cut short by the crash of the door bursting open and someone being pushed inside so roughly that he stumbled and fell. Two men stepped in behind him and loomed over the fallen figure.

'He fits the description. Name's Robert Dane. We claim the reward!' Art's voice thundered round the room, his stance defying anyone to oppose his claim, while Luke eyed Theo and Barney threateningly.

'Robert!' Surprise, relief and anxiety were all bound up in Theo's exclamation as he dropped on one knee beside his son who was struggling to get up. Barney ignored the other two men and helped to get Robert to his feet and then on to a chair. His clothes were dirty and torn; his face bruised and cut. He showed every sign of having been roughly handled.

The questions he wanted to ask Robert poured into Theo's mind but he pushed them momentarily aside. He straightened up to his full height and eyed the two ruffians with a look that drove the triumphant grins from their faces. 'Who are you?' he boomed.

'Art Mason and Luke Coning,' barked Art. 'We want the reward!'

Theo ignored his demand. 'Where did you find my son?'

'On the moors.'

'How?'

Art grinned. 'Used my nous. Reckoned I knew where he'd be. Now, the money.'

'Father, don't pay them!' Robert summoned the strength to stand up. 'They may have left two people dead on the moors.'

'We didn't!' put in Luke. 'They were alive when we ...'

'Shut up!' snapped Art, and gave him a sharp blow on the shoulder.

'That sounds as if you don't really know,' barked Theo.

'What did you do?' demanded Robert, his voice rising with anxiety as he thought of what might have happened to Betsy.

'They were unconscious when we left.'

'So they might have died since!' agonised Robert.

'See here,' snapped Art, adopting a menacing attitude, 'you pay up – or else.'

'Else what?' Robert glared defiance at him. 'You're just a couple of thugs. Don't pay them, Father.'

Art was raising another protest when Theo stopped him. 'I acknowledge that you have brought me my son, but it seems you may have injured or even killed two other people. I intended no violence to anyone. Maybe I didn't make that clear. So I'll give you a quarter of the reward now.' Seeing protests rising from the two men, he went on quickly, 'We'll investigate this matter. Come back in two days and I'll pay you anything further that I think is due. But I warn you, if we find out that anything has happened to those two people, the police will be waiting here for you.' Art glared at him. 'Take it or leave it,' said Theo with a confidence that would not countenance anything but the conditions he had laid down.

Art grunted his agreement.

'Wait here!' ordered Theo. He went into another room and returned a few moments later. 'There you are.' He handed over a wad of notes and emphasised his terms again, so that Art and

Luke could not misunderstand their position. 'You get the rest when we are satisfied no harm has come to anyone. If it has, the police will be waiting.' They muttered their thanks and shuffled out.

'Father, are you really going to pay those two the rest of the money?' Robert protested.

'They won't come back,' replied Theo.

Robert looked surprised. 'But ...'

'Think about it. I threatened them with the police, depending on what we found on the moor. They will never know what we've found so they'll be very doubtful about returning here and possibly facing an enquiry. For all they know, those two people are dead. They'll be satisfied with what they've got and won't risk returning.'

In spite of the possible scenario, Robert had to admire his father's shrewdness. 'Father, I'm sorry ...'

'Wait,' Theo said gently. 'Time enough for explanations.' He turned to the investigator. 'We won't see those two again. I'll lock up, Hawkins. I'll be here with my son until we get everything settled. You take yourself back to Newcastle tomorrow. Let Mrs Addison and my daughter know that Robert has been found and is in good health.'

'Very well, sir. I'll see that they are informed.' He turned to Robert. 'We are glad to have you back, sir.'

'Thanks.' Robert gave him a smile. 'Father hasn't introduced us, so I don't know who ...'

'Bernard Hawkins, private investigator, sir.'

Robert raised an eyebrow. 'My goodness, people *were* worried.'

'Indeed they were, sir. More than that, in fact.' Hawkins touched his forehead in salute and left the premises.

As the door closed behind him Robert started to forestall the tirade he expected. 'Father, I can explain, but I've got to go back ... Betsy and her father might still be lying out there on the moor.'

'Who are these people?' asked Theo.

'Mr Palmer and his daughter befriended me in Whitby. I've got to go ...'

'Whitby? What on earth were you doing there?'

'I've said I will explain, but I have to go back for them.' Robert's voice rose in agitation.

'Where were you attacked?' his father demanded.

'South of Lealholm, a small village on the way to Rosedale.'

'Right, then we'll both go.' Theo made that point clear. He wasn't going to have his son disappear again. He rose from his chair and Robert was swiftly on his feet, ready to follow his father. 'Come to my hotel and get some clean clothes on the way. I'll hire us some horses. While you bathe and change, you can explain everything to me.'

They hurried to the hotel where Theo left his son briefly while he went to hire two horses. He returned after fifteen minutes to find Robert already dressing in clothes purchased on their way to the hotel.

'The horses will be here in ten minutes.'

Robert was relieved to feel he was doing something about Betsy.

Theo sat down and eyed him as he said, 'Now, tell me what this was all about? Why did you disappear? If it was a tiff with Adele...'

Robert, who was fastening his cravat, swung round from the mirror, his eyes widening with disbelief. 'Adele? Have you been blaming her? This had nothing to do with her!'

Theo stared at him. 'It seemed the obvious reason. We naturally concluded that you two had fallen out and ... oh, my God!'

Robert could see in his father's expression a mixture of horror, doubt and contrition. 'You blamed Adele, accused her and caused a rift between our two families?'

There was no need for Theo to admit it in words; the admission was there to see on his face. 'She protested but we didn't believe her ... Since then I've met her father who told me she had gone looking for you and that he would hold me accountable if anything happened to her or Mark who, thankfully, has accompanied her.'

'Where have they gone?'

'I don't know.'

Robert's lips tightened. If anything happened to any of these people – Betsy, her father, Adele, Mark – it was *he* who would be accountable. If only he hadn't queried his father's affairs, which after all were no concern of his. He had meddled and now must face the consequences.

First Robert felt he had to emphasise again: 'Adele had nothing to do with this.'

'So what was it all about? You must have had some reason to leave home. Someone else had to

382

be involved ... don't tell me there is another woman?'

Robert hesitated.

'Come on, out with it! This matter has to be cleared up.'

Robert swallowed. He realised that there was no way out but to face his father with his discoveries. But all this was taking time. Betsy could be lying on a windswept moor; Adele could be in a perilous position. They should be on their way, but his father was still waiting for an explanation.

'Yes, Father, there *is* another woman ... but I have never met her.'

'Don't talk in riddles, son, there isn't time!' snapped Theo.

'And you are involved.'

'I?' Theo looked aghast.

'Father, I know I shouldn't have done it but I did. I could have left it but I didn't ...'

'More riddles!' Theo's look of exasperation set the words pouring out of Robert. 'You left the office one day and I went into yours for some documents I knew you had left there for me. I found the keys to your desk on the floor. You always kept certain drawers locked and I was curious.' He saw his father's face darken.

'And you found two small ledgers?' said Theo, with a small nod. 'You opened them and saw entries you did not understand, though you drew certain conclusions.'

'At first I thought you were transferring the firm's money, but I found no entries in the main accounts to substantiate this. So I was even more inquisitive, especially when I found out that the withdrawals related to actual cash you were handling. Where that cash was coming from I could not deduce, but working on the theory that you were probably getting it from a bank, I followed you.'

'You did what?' thundered Theodore jumping to his feet. 'You spied on me?'

'Father, I felt I had to find out what was going on. You could have been in some kind of trouble. I wanted to help.'

'So?' prompted Theo when his son hesitated.

'I saw you go to a house in a well-to-do part of Newcastle. The door was opened, not by a maid, but by a very smart and beautiful woman, and you went in.'

'And you thought your father had a mistress?'

A pained expression came over Robert's face. 'What else could I think?'

Theo started to chuckle. 'And *that* is why you left home?'

'I wanted time to think, to decide what to do. I could have said nothing but it would have weighed on my mind forever. I could have confronted you and shown my disgust with what you were doing to Mother. I could have dragged it all out in the open but that would have meant breaking up our family and social disgrace besides. And I feared I would lose Adele; that she would want nothing more to do with me. I had to get away, to sort things out in my mind.'

Expecting a tirade from his father Robert was surprised when Theo replied quite calmy and persuasively.

'First, let me say that I understand the quandary you were in ... I would have felt the same ... but you did bring it upon yourself. Now, you say you did not know the lady I visited. In actual fact, you have met her though you were probably too young at the time to remember it now. She is Miss Rose Brookland. I got to know her through charitable work. She had come unexpectedly into a fortune and decided to use it trying to better the lot of the poor in Newcastle.

'She became engaged but the man she was to marry was killed on the day before their wedding. She took this as a sign that she should not marry, and though she has several male friends and has received other offers of marriage, she remains single. I have always kept in touch with her and your mother knows and approves of this. She herself attends some of Rose's charity occasions, though Rose has always insisted that her work should bring her no personal attention. People respect this.

'Now you are wondering how she fits in with your recent discoveries. She has an exceptional brain for finance. In fact, she came to my aid. You know of your uncle's gambling problems, I take it? I am pleased to say that his present attempt to conquer them is succeeding and I don't think he will slip back as he has done on previous occasions, but he has had large debts to clear. I set up a business in Rose's name to provide funds through which I could gradually clear Morgan's debts. You knew nothing about it because it had nothing to do with our company. It was completely separate.

There is no need to go into all the details of this arrangement, which was put in hand so that the people to whom he owes money could not trace where it was coming from and sue for it directly.

'When you saw me call on Rose I was delivering money to be put into that special account from which, through her personal intervention, your uncle's debts will gradually be paid off. He has no access to the account and knows that, unless he makes an effort, we can close it at any time. This seems to have spurred him on. The two small ledgers you found were my own personal records of the transactions. The scheme is working well, so far. Your uncle and aunt appreciate what I have done. So, you see, your suspicions were ill founded.'

'And they have endangered lives as well as making a lot of trouble for people I hold dear. Father, I deeply regret the anxiety and upset I have caused.'

Theodore gave him a curt nod of acknowledgement. 'We have talked long enough. We should be away over the moors.'

They made good time but eight miles from Lealholm darkness had overtaken them, and rain, driven on a stormy wind, was making the ride very unpleasant.

'We're not going to be able to search the moors tonight,' called out Theo as they neared the tiny village. 'We'd better find shelter for the night and start a search first thing in the morning.'

Though his mind cried out to go on, every nerve in Robert's body told him it would be useless. Reluctantly, he agreed and then added, 'I know a place we might be able to get shelter.'

Theo did not ask how he knew of it; he would get to know what Robert's self-imposed exile had entailed all in good time.

Robert guided them to Mrs Dobson's cottage. He threw his reins to his father who remained seated on his horse. Robert slid to the ground and hurried to the cottage door. His knock brought an instant response of, 'Coming.' He heard bolts being drawn back, and then the door swung open. A lantern held high threw light on to his face.

'Mr Dane!' Mrs Dobson gasped with surprise. 'What on earth are you doing here on a night like this?'

'Mrs Dobson, that's my father out there. Can you give us shelter?'

'Of course we can.' As she was speaking, she peered out into the gloom and saw the shadowy figure seated on a horse. 'Mr Dobson will see to your animals.' She half turned into the house and shouted, 'Bob, get yourself here quick!'

'Father, come away in,' shouted Robert.

'My goodness, Mr Dane,' cried Mr Dobson. 'This is no night to be out.'

'No chattering now, Bob,' said his wife. 'Two horses to see to. Mr Dane's father's here.'

Bob grabbed a stout coat from the peg beside the door and crammed a hat on his head. Robert made brief introductions and then Bob was gone.

'Come away in and get out of those wet things.'

'This is very civil of you, Mrs Dobson,' said Theo.

'Not at all, sir. You don't move another inch tonight. We have two spare beds. When the kettle boils, I'll put hot-water pigs in them. Hang your clothes on yon hooks there; they'll be dry by morning.' While they were doing this Martha took a huge kettle from the hearth, filled it with water and put it on a reckon. 'It'll boil in no time on that fire,' she said as if proud of the blaze. 'Then we'll drive out that chill with some good warming soup, and later we'll all have a slice of home-boiled ham.'

'You make my mouth water already, Mrs Dobson,' said Theo jovially as he sat down in the chair near the fire indicated by their hostess.

'Mrs Dobson, have you seen Miss Palmer and her father today?' Robert couldn't disguise the anxiety in his voice and it brought an enquiring look from her.

'No. The last time I saw them was when you were all on your way to Rosedale.' She hesitated briefly then added, 'I tell a lie. I saw Mr Palmer when he returned alone, and then again on his way back to Rosedale.' She frowned. 'Now you turn up and not with Mr or Miss Palmer but with your father, on a night that's not fit for man nor beast.' She looked askance at Robert. 'Something has happened, hasn't it?'

He started to tell her about how they had been waylaid. She held up her hands to stop him. 'Mr Dobson had better hear this. He'll be back in a few minutes.'

The time spent waiting for his arrival was tense. Robert and his father sensed there was something serious to be learned here but they could not press

388

Mrs Dobson; it appeared her husband had an important role to play. An unnatural silence settled on the room, broken only by Mrs Dobson filling two stone hot-water bottles, disappearing upstairs with them, then returning to hang a large soup pan from the reckon.

The door opened, sending a blast of wind around the room. Bob Dobson shrugged himself out of his coat and hung it up. 'It's nithering out there.'

'Come and get yourself warm,' said Theo, starting to rise from his chair.

'Sit yourself down, sir. I've a stool here.'

'Bob, Mr Dane asked if we had seen Mr Palmer and his daughter today,' said Martha Dobson. 'I told him we hadn't. He started to tell me something, but I told him to wait until you were here.'

Robert told them the outline of what had happened.

'And these two men abducted you?' asked Bob, a little incredulously.

'Yes. If it had been robbery, I wouldn't be here now.'

'But why did they...'

'My son had disappeared. I put out a reward for anyone who located him and brought him to me,' Theo broke in, believing the Dobsons were entitled to some sort of explanation. 'Robert insisted on coming back as soon as possible, to try to find out what had happened to Mr Palmer and his daughter.' He eyed Bob shrewdly. 'Mr Dobson, although you say you haven't seen them, I think you have something to tell us?'

Satisfied, Bob nodded. 'I have, but it does not necessarily concern the Palmers.'

'Bob, what is it?' urged Robert.

'Someone coming from Rosedale reported seeing a broken trap. It looked as though it had been in an accident, probably caused by running away downhill. There was no sign of any occupants or of the horse. However, men from the village decided to make a search. People can easily get lost on these moors, especially if they've suffered an accident and become confused. Ten of us went out and saw the trap – it was in a mess. We scoured the moors for a considerable distance from the site of the accident. We found no one but I got to studying the tracks. Thank goodness the rain hadn't started otherwise all the evidence would have been washed away.'

'What evidence?' pressed Robert.

'I saw a set of tracks that didn't match the broken trap's. A vehicle ... I would say it was another trap, but maybe bigger than the first one ... reached the site, reversed and left. There was evidence of a third vehicle but its tracks did not seem to have any bearing on the others.' He glanced at his wife.

She took up the story. 'A trap driven by someone I would put down as a coachman or a groom appeared in the village. The occupants were a young lady and gentleman.'

'You saw them? Can you describe them to me?' asked Robert.

'Not well. They stopped four cottages away and made some enquiry. I would say to ask directions, the way Lizzie Hardcastle was flinging her arms about and pointing. The couple were young, about your age, well dressed, and from the few words I caught, I'd say they were well spoken. That's really all I can tell you about them. However, linking that with what Bob has said, their trap could be the one he says reversed. This couple and their coachman could have found Mr and Mrs Palmer and taken them to Whitby.'

'But wouldn't they have been seen passing through Lealholm on the way back?'

'There is a side lane that skirts the village. They could have taken that and not been seen.'

Mrs Dobson's theories seemed very plausible to Robert; the couple could be Adele and Mark. That possibility brought Adele vividly to mind, and sent his emotions into turmoil.

21

Robert left his bed and went to the window. Anxious to know if the bad weather had cleared, he parted the curtains to peer out. Relieved to see the sky clear but for a few clouds, and the dawn light beginning to creep into it, he poured some water from the ewer into its matching bowl and began his morning ablutions. As he shaved and washed, his mind dwelt on the events of the previous evening.

Earlier much had remained unsaid, explanations been held back, as they were in the Dobsons' house. After they'd retired, he had gone to his father's room.

'Father, we need to talk.'

'Come in, son. Sit down.' Theodore indicated the only chair but Robert left it for his father and sat on the edge of the bed.

He sensed his father's gratitude that Robert had approached him and not waited for a request to be enlightened about the way he had spent his time while away from home.

Theodore listened intently to his account, without interrupting. When Robert had finished, he said, 'I can see that you have a great respect for Mr Palmer and his daughter, and fully understand why. But, as grateful as you are for their kindness, do not blind yourself to all the advantages of your past life and the prospects it may yet hold for you. Don't let them slip away unless you are absolutely sure of a new and fulfilling life to take their place. You say you seem to have a natural aptitude for working with jet, and that there is great potential in the jewellery trade in Whitby and its offshoot in Rosedale. But, remember, they can be transient occupations, unlike the solid mercantile trading company I have built up. It will be yours one day. Remember that there is a good chance too to form a very close alliance with the Jordans.'

Without its being spelled out, Robert knew exactly what his father was hinting at. Memories of the future he had once envisaged for himself haunted him as he dressed. A few moments later he answered a knock on his door.

'You ready, son?'

'Just about, Father.'

Robert turned back into the room, picked up his jacket and slipped it on as he went to join Theodore. They were greeted by the smell of cooking bacon and warm home-made bread as they reached the kitchen.

'Good morning, Mrs Dobson,' said Theodore, and added appreciatively, 'What an appetising smell. It makes me hungry.'

'Good,' she said with a smile, 'and a good morning to you both. I predict it will be a fine day. The sky looks settled.'

'I take your word on that, Mrs Dobson, I'm no weather prophet.'

'Now, I can see Robert is itching to be off to Whitby, so sit yourselves down in there,' she indicated a small adjoining room, 'and I'll have your breakfast ready in a minute. You can't face the day on an empty stomach.'

Before long they were making their thanks to her, then gathering their belongings to go outside where Mr Dobson had their horses ready and waiting for them.

'You have both been most kind,' said Theo. 'If ever I am this way again, may I call on you?'

'Of course, I hope you would not pass us by,' replied Mrs Dobson, then turned to Robert. 'You too,' she added with feeling. 'May God go with you. And may you find what your heart truly desires.'

'Thank you, Mrs Dobson,' he said. 'I'll try to see that I do.'

As they rode away both men turned back to wave goodbye to their kind hosts. Then, having settled himself comfortably in the saddle, Robert put his horse to a gallop and Theo matched it. The two horses stretched out their necks as if sensing their riders' desire to reach Whitby as soon as possible.

'I know you are anxious to see Robert,' said Mark as he and Adele sat down to breakfast in the Angel.

'I am. I would like to get home as soon as possible, but first I want to know why he left home. The Addisons blame me and I wish to clear my name; I want the truth and only Robert knows that.'

'We won't waste any time,' Mark reassured her, 'but let's enjoy our breakfast, then call on the Palmers to see how they are after their ordeal. There is no need for us to stay long. I don't suppose they'll want us to. Then we can be on our way.'

'Very well,' agreed Adele. 'It is something to know that Robert is safe ... or at least to believe he is.'

'He will be. Those two thugs will have taken him straight to his father, there's nothing more certain. They won't have risked harming him. They want the reward money so will deliver Robert promptly and in person. He'll be home safe, ready to be reunited with you, when we get there.'

'I hope he is.'

The horses' pace slowed when Robert and his father set their mounts to climb the steep moorland track; that only exacerbated Robert's desire to reach Whitby with all possible haste and alleviate his anxiety about Betsy's welfare. Reaching the top of the hill behind the village, the two men put their horses into a gallop down the long descent into Whitby.

Sam Palmer rose from his chair near the window when Adele entered the room, followed by Mark.

'Please don't get up, Mr Palmer,' she reproved him, quickly coming to his side.

'Miss Jordan, I am pleased to say I can still receive a charming young lady in the appropriate manner. No thugs would ever stop me doing that.

It is very kind of you to call.' He turned to Mark. 'And you too, Mr Jordan. Please do sit down. My daughter will be with us in a minute or so. She has gone to her room for the book she was reading last night. I must thank you again for all you did for us yesterday. We could have been on the moor for a long time, with serious consequences, had it not been for your intervention.'

'Then I'm glad we came along when we did.'

The drawing-room door opened and Tom came in, his face lighting up with pleasure. 'Mark, Adele, I'm so pleased you have found the time to call. I trust you were comfortable at the Angel?'

'Indeed we were. And we are so pleased to see your father little troubled by his ordeal of yesterday.'

'It could have been a lot worse, but for your timely arrival. We have much to thank you for. Have you walked from the Angel? I didn't see your trap outside.'

'No, it wasn't ready. Our coachman will bring it along shortly.'

Reaching a wider point in the track, the two riders urged on their horses. The pounding of their hooves momentarily drove out all thoughts of anything but sunlight and speed and the whip of the wind against his face, but then quite suddenly Robert found that his mind was filled with thoughts of Betsy. A new life with her in Whitby had much to offer, but even as the possibilities came to his mind the pounding sound drove them out and replaced them with memories of Adele.

They had been so close. Their estrangement, slight though it had been, had only come about because of his own jealousy of Philip. He must put things right with her.

'Miss Palmer, how are you?' Adele rose and held out her hands when Betsy came into the room.

'Nicely, thank you, Miss Jordan. A few aches and pains still, but nothing untoward,' replied Betsy. 'It is most kind of you to call. Are you staying in Whitby?'

As everyone sat down again, Adele said, 'No, we are on our way home now.'

'And where might that be?'

'Newcastle,' replied Adele, 'though we may stay in Middlesbrough overnight.'

'Middlesbrough!' put in Mark. 'That reminds me.' He turned to Tom. 'You said yesterday that you would be going to the authorities to report the two men who abducted Robert Dane?'

Tom nodded. 'Yes.' He shot a querying look at Mark.

'I think my sister and I may know more about Robert Dane than you do. There will be no need for you to go to the authorities.' No one spoke but he knew he held everyone's attention. 'Robert Dane is not his real name. He is Robert Addison. For some reason that we don't know, he left home abruptly leaving no forwarding address. His father engaged a private investigator and, without mentioning his own name or Robert's real one, offered a reward for anyone bringing Robert back to him. He set up offices in Newcastle and

Middlesbrough to deal with the investigation. Meanwhile, Robert's family decided to blame my sister for his disappearance.'

Betsy stiffened, considering what these words might imply. 'So you were looking for Robert when you found us?' She glanced at Adele as she spoke.

'Yes. But I definitely was not to blame for his leaving home. I wanted to find him in order to clear my name. Mark and I were able to trace him to this area and came in search of a meeting with him.'

'And that is how you came to be on the road to Rosedale?' queried Betsy.

'Yes.'

'You must think a great deal of him. Have you known him some time?'

'Yes.'

Betsy was stunned. She'd had no idea that there had been another young woman in Robert's life. She knew nothing of his past, in fact. What other secrets did it hold? Would he ever have told her?

'Why shouldn't I go to the authorities?' asked Tom.

'Those thugs want the reward. They will have taken Robert to Mr Addison, so he will now be safe. His father will have dealt with his abductors in the way he sees fit.'

'But they should be brought to justice,' Tom protested.

'Believe me, Mr Addison is shrewd enough to see that they do not get away scot-free.'

'I think we can leave it there, Tom,' put in his father, and glanced at Mark. 'How did you trace

Robert to Whitby, by the way?'

Mark explained about their visit to Middlesbrough and its outcome.

'I thought by making him a stowaway nobody would trace him,' said Tom. 'You did, and so did those thugs, but thank goodness the outcome was to reunite Robert with his family.'

Robert felt easier when Whitby came in sight and the descent into the town started. He kept up their pace until they reached the straggle of houses on the West Cliff, before turning into Well Close Square at a walking pace. He was out of the saddle at once and he and his father secured their horses to the railing. He pulled the metal bell-pull beside the front door and impatiently awaited an answer.

The people in the drawing room heard a bell ring in the recesses of the house, followed by footsteps hurrying to the front door. Barely a moment had passed when the drawing-room door opened and Robert hurried in.

'Betsy!' Her name died on his lips. He pulled himself up short. He had not expected to see so many people here. His glance took them all in. 'Adele!' Surprise and bewilderment were reflected in his face then and for a moment he did not know which girl to address first.

'Betsy, how are you? I trust you were not harmed?' he said at length.

'I am well, Robert, thank you.' The stiffness of her expression did not go unnoticed by him.

'Thank goodness!' He half turned to Adele then. 'This is a surprise – what are you doing here?'

'I came looking for you.'

'I know that from Father, but how did you trace me?'

'All in good time, Robert,' she said firmly. 'I think you should introduce your father first.'

Robert did so, and in the next hour many questions were answered and events explained. As the talk progressed Adele wondered how far the relationship between Betsy and Robert had gone. He had been deeply concerned for her welfare and recovery, and Adele sensed that Betsy had strong feelings for him, possibly even of love, but could not detect if this was reciprocated.

Betsy in turn wondered about Robert's relationship with Adele before he had arrived so dramatically in her own life. She examined her feelings for him then and wondered if they had been strengthened by her recent rejection of Jim, something that at one time she had deeply regretted. Maybe she had been keen to drown that regret in new feelings for someone else. Throughout the whole of the ensuing hour she studied him and Adele closely.

When Sam invited everyone to stay for a buffet luncheon, Theodore sought out Adele and Mark for a private word.

'I want to acknowledge that we were wrong to blame you, Adele, for Robert's disappearance. He has explained to me why it came about, and I freely admit it had nothing to do with you. The first thing I shall do on returning to Newcastle is to apologise profusely to your mother and father. I hope you will accept my sincere apology now?'

'Thank you,' she said, speaking for Mark as well. 'We bear you no grudge. The past is the past, and that part of it is erased from our minds. I am sure it will be the same for Mother and Father.'

'Would you go to Robert and tell him what I have said?' Theodore requested.

She looked around. 'I will, but he's just gone outside with Miss Palmer.' She felt a pang of jealousy at that, and with it came confirmation that her old feelings for him had not been altered by recent setbacks.

Theodore detected both disappointment and curiosity in her voice. He leaned close to her. 'He cannot talk to her forever.' He took Mark's arm and led him over to Sam Palmer.

Betsy had grasped this opportunity to talk to Robert alone.

'Robert ...'

'Betsy...'

They stared at each other.

'You first,' he said quickly.

She hesitated, her expression troubled. 'Robert,' she said quietly, 'I don't understand why you had to assume another name ... not unless you had something to hide?'

'Then I'll be frank with you, Betsy, I did have something to hide, not concerning my own affairs but my family's. I did tell you I would have to return home one day to resolve things. I thought I made it clear that my future would be blighted if I did not do so. Don't ask me what troubled me because I won't tell you. It is very private.'

'What faith you have in me! Did you not trust me to keep your secret? Was it to be sealed away forever? What else have you kept hidden?' Her eyes flashed angrily. 'You never mentioned Adele!'

'I . . .'

She interrupted him quickly. 'Don't say things you don't mean. I don't believe you ever really loved me . . . more fool me for thinking you did. Adele was always on your mind. I realise that now. I've seen, today, the special bond that exists between you two. I suppose it's only natural coming as you do from the same social background, one in which I could never be at home.'

'Betsy, it was never like that!'

She pulled a face expressing her doubt. 'Don't make matters worse. You used me to try to escape a world that was proving uncomfortable for you. Used me to try to salve your own shortcomings – to try to escape the mistakes you began to realise you had made. I lived in hope of future happiness with you, but it's not to be.' Tears were streaming down her cheeks by now. 'Go to her, Robert. Go to the girl you really love, and who loves you!'

Betsy ran back into the house and upstairs before anyone could see her. In the privacy of her room she flung herself on the bed and wept the hurt out of herself. Finally, composed once more, she steeled herself to walk downstairs, face people again, act as if her world was safe and secure even when she doubted it would ever be so again.

Feeling shocked and bewildered, Robert stood staring after Betsy. Her words still rang in his mind.

402

How much truth had there been in them? He realised now that he had tried to escape a situation that had been very much of his own making – mistakenly, as he had learned in these last twenty-four hours. In doing so he had hurt people and that had probably marred his own future unless he could rescue it by returning to the world where he truly belonged. Was Betsy right about Adele? Even as that question came into his mind, the door to the house opened and Adele stepped out.

'Ah, there you are. I was looking for you, Robert.' Her voice was soft, with a gentleness that transported him back to the times they had spent happily together on the banks of the Tyne. 'There are things I think we both need to say to each other. May we talk?'

Robert's welcoming smile was her answer. He held out his hand. She saw the gesture as an offer of apology and gladly took it. Her touch eliminated all the doubts Robert had felt about his future. He knew now where he was meant to be.

'Of course. Any time. Now and forever.'

At this everything Adele had it in mind to say was forgotten. Instead she asked softly, 'Forever?'

He nodded. 'If you want it that way?'

She smiled. 'You and I have a lot more talking to do, but that can wait.'

He gave a little shake of his head. 'Not everything.'

She looked surprised. 'What do you mean?'

'You're forgetting Philip.'

'You're still jealous!' she teased, then left a slight pause, leaving him wondering what was coming.

'Well,' she went on coyly, 'I've had a letter from Mother telling me Philip has got engaged to a young lady from Spilsby.'

Robert's eyes lit up, revealing his delight at this news. 'Now that's out of the way, the answer to my question please. Do you want us to be able to talk to each other like this forever?'

She smiled into his eyes. 'Yes, I do.'

Sir Francis Weldon sat back in his chair, smoking a cigar with an air of contentment. Two glasses of whisky were set on his desk.

'Fenwick, you have done well for me. Your surveys and reports have been excellent. They have resulted in increased profits and stopped me making some foolish investments that would never have paid off.' He leaned forward and pushed a glass of whisky over to Jim. 'I think we should drink to what you have achieved.' They raised their glasses. 'I have kept my eye on your work since I brought you into the York office, awaiting the best opportunity upon which to engage your talents. Well, it has come up.' Sir Francis paused to take a sip of his whisky.

Jim's heart sank. Since coming to York he had had no free time, and had looked back on his brief visit to Whitby with despair. No sooner had he seen Betsy than she had fainted, another man's name on her lips. He knew he'd lost her, and it was all his own fault.

'As you know, Fenwick, I am beginning to diversify my commercial interests, looking to counteract any future setbacks in any one area. I recall that in your early days as supervisor in Rosedale, you had connections in the port of Whitby. I want you to go back there to explore the possibilities of developing a maritime trade. If it is a viable enterprise, I would wish you to be in charge of its development so it could mean a long-term commitment to Whitby for you. If you have any objection to being there say so now, and I can make alternative arrangements for you.'

Jim could barely believe what he was hearing. Perhaps, after all, it was not too late. He'd be an idiot if he failed to see Betsy at least one more time. Who knows? Her fancy young gentleman may have turned out to be a flash in the pan. No, Jim Fenwick was not ready to give up just yet.

'Whitby will suit me just fine, sir. Thank you for your trust in me,' he said.

'Good.' Sir Francis raised his glass. 'To a successful future!'

'To a successful future,' Jim repeated, but his thoughts were on a different aspect of it entirely while his fingers caressed the jet necklace he always carried in his pocket.